# LIGHT

## FROM

## OTHER

## STARS

BY THE SAME AUTHOR

*The Book of Speculation*

# LIGHT FROM OTHER STARS

A NOVEL

ERIKA SWYLER

BLOOMSBURY PUBLISHING

NEW YORK · LONDON · OXFORD · NEW DELHI · SYDNEY

BLOOMSBURY PUBLISHING
Bloomsbury Publishing Inc.
1385 Broadway, New York, NY 10018, USA

BLOOMSBURY, BLOOMSBURY PUBLISHING, and the Diana logo
are trademarks of Bloomsbury Publishing Plc

First published in the United States 2019
Copyright © Erika Swyler, 2019

LIBRARY OF CONGRESS CATALOGING-IN-PUBLICATION DATA
Names: Swyler, Erika, author.
Title: Light from Other Stars : a novel / Erika Swyler.
Description: New York : Bloomsbury Publishing, 2019.
Identifiers: LCCN 2018034280 | ISBN 9781635573169 (hardback) |
ISBN 9781635573176 (e-book)
Classification: LCC PS3619.W96 L58 2019 | DDC 813/.6—dc23
LC record available at https://lccn.loc.gov/2018034280

2 4 6 8 10 9 7 5 3 1

Typeset by Westchester Publishing Services
Printed and bound in the U.S.A. by Berryville Graphics Inc., Berryville, Virginia

To find out more about our authors and books visit www.bloomsbury.com and
sign up for our newsletters.

Bloomsbury books may be purchased for business or promotional use.
For information on bulk purchases please contact Macmillan Corporate and
Premium Sales Department at specialmarkets@macmillan.com.

This book is dedicated to the Hubble Space Telescope, which opened the universe to me. It is also dedicated to the teachers who did not believe a fifth-grade girl could speak knowledge-ably about the Hubble Space Telescope. You remain embar-rassingly wrong.

Oh! I have slipped the surly bonds of Earth
And danced the skies on laughter-silvered wings;
Sunward I've climbed, and joined the tumbling mirth
Of sun-split clouds,—and done a hundred things
You have not dreamed of—wheeled and soared and swung
High in the sunlit silence. Hov'ring there,
I've chased the shouting wind along, and flung
My eager craft through footless halls of air . . .

Up, up the long, delirious burning blue
I've topped the wind-swept heights with easy grace
Where never lark, or ever eagle flew—
And, while with silent, lifting mind I've trod
The high untrespassed sanctity of space,
Put out my hand, and touched the face of God.

—JOHN GILLESPIE MAGEE JR., "HIGH FLIGHT"

# LIGHT

## FROM

## OTHER

## STARS

# Aboard *Chawla*

NEDDA PAPAS ROSE to birdsong, the sharp, rasping call of a dusky seaside sparrow against a backdrop of waves—a reminder of home and things she'd never see again. When she was asked what music she preferred to wake to, she could think of nothing. Her selections had to be considerate of her crewmates, a task made difficult by the decades-long void in her music knowledge. Evgeni preferred a Russian pop group, which made Thursday mornings excruciating. Birds were the least offensive thing she could think of. Everywhere had birds. Only she knew that a NASA intern had dug through decaying audio archives from the Florida Museum of Natural History to find the call of a species that had been extinct since 1987. She opened her eyes to a holographic sea rolling against a shore of pixels that stood in for crushed shells and glass.

She rolled over to face the window and the black. In the acclimatizing weeks on the International Space Station, she'd watched Earth and waited for nostalgia to hit. The psychologists insisted it would. Viewing Earth from such a distance produced homesickness that masqueraded as introspection, or dangerous elation that preceded violent drops in mood. It happened to her crewmates. For her, the melancholy had waited until they were aboard the module.

There were numerous papers on homesickness in astronauts that Nedda refused to read; comparing herself to a study was disconcerting. She'd adapted to homesickness before and viewing Earth from above didn't move her. Her home wasn't a distance; it was time and a sparrow.

Space was more welcoming than looking behind. She told Dr. Stein, the crew psychologist, this during mandatory video call sessions. To Nedda, psychology and gynecology were similar in that a doctor saw more of your most intimate parts than you did.

Every week Dr. Stein asked, "What do you see out the window?" Her stylus was never on camera, but Nedda could hear it sliding across a tablet.

It was difficult to explain what she saw, harder still to parse its meaning. Space between stars made for easy misery, contemplating how small you were when faced with the universe. Though he was mission commander, Amit Singh looked out as little as possible, preferring star maps, feeds from the telescopes, and data from the probes and terraformers. He remained intent on viewing himself as a person and not a single cell in an organism the size of the universe. Nedda liked feeling small.

"Endless space is endless potential," she'd told Dr. Stein. It was good to sound hopeful. It was trickier to explain that she was looking for light, picking it apart, trying to sense the different wavelengths, searching for the familiar. There was light in the black, on its way to and from distant planets, light from stars crashing into one another, meeting in the space between. Light carried thoughts and hopes, the essence of what made everyone. She had to limit such thoughts or she'd miss the morning video call, fall behind on her work with the plants, and find the printer in her cabin had spit out an antidepressant. Thinking of antidepressants caused a flurry of psychiatric drug names to roll through her mind, everything Louisa Marcanta, their on-board physician, had easy access to, and the things that weren't prescribed any longer. She dwelled on ketamine's structure, a beautiful molecule that made her think of the male and female symbols holding hands.

"Papas? No sleeping in." Marcanta's voice shook her loose.

The hologram flickered out, *Chawla*'s cold white wall replacing the beach.

Morning call to Mission Control was uneventful. *Chawla*'s crew of four crowded the central living quarters to speak to Houston, negotiating signal delays and bureaucracy. Today Marcanta received a video greeting from her niece, whose birthday it was. The girl grinned around missing teeth and clung to a stuffed octopus her aunt Louisa had sent.

Marcanta had automated deliveries for years. Smart. Singh was mad he hadn't thought of it himself. In these moments, there was little difference between being out of the country and being off world. Eyes down, Nedda sorted her notes. Close as they were all forced to live, it remained uncomfortable to witness someone else's personal message. It was more revealing than being naked; it was below the skin, seeing the people they'd never touch again.

Evgeni made a quick report on the module's systems; then they listened to data from on planet. The rovers and bots were making good progress on the platform and dome builds—on pace for arrival. Un and Trio, two of the rovers, were leveling the ground for a landing pad and digging a trench to help direct the steam *Chawla* would create on landing. Dué's soil composition data was within expected range. Nedda reported on hydroponics—they were beginning the first steps of sustaining themselves. There were useable seeds ready for a new cycle, the building blocks they'd need as colonists.

Evgeni's eyesight had grown worse, but he didn't mention it, nor did Marcanta. Nedda and Singh followed suit. It was progressive astigmatism due to lack of gravity, which led to flattened corneas and pressure on the optic nerve from cerebrospinal fluid. Their brains were drowning their eyes. Gravity would eventually fix it, but there were three years left before arrival. The on-board printer generated corrective lenses, but changes were constant and difficult to keep up with. There came a point when vision was beyond correction. Evgeni was nearing it.

Nedda was beginning to suffer the effects. She'd started sleeping with pressure goggles on, though the effort was likely in vain. Thirty-two percent of Earth's gravity awaited them. Even less than Mars. Some sight would be restored, but likely not the 20/20 they'd all tested at. It was a known risk. Evgeni was just unlucky in the speed at which it progressed. Failing sight was a bad break for a module's engineer.

"We've noticed some energy spikes from Amadeus," Evgeni said to the monitor. The life support system ran on its own power, a radioisotope thermoelectric generator, called Amadeus, that was separate from the engines. Amadeus would continue to run on planet, powering the module when it served as shelter.

"Has it damaged anything?" The question came from one of the young people from NASA's Jet Propulsion Lab. A bright red tattoo decorated the side of her scalp. Kato, Jennifer Kato. The tattoo made her easier to remember among the many faces.

"Trajectory and pace are still fine," Nedda said. "Everything is operational. We're just dumping the radiation into our landing water for now." It was less than ideal. The water designated for the steam jets they'd use to soften *Chawla*'s final descent would be radioactive. They'd be landing hot. "The sooner we can fix it the better. We need to minimize atmospheric impacts."

"I'd like the generator development specifics," Evgeni said. "There's something off."

"Just forward your data to us. We'll analyze it and go from there," Kato said.

"Humor me, please. It helps me to know how it came about," Evgeni said.

"Fine, Mr. Sokolov. It'll be in your reader by end of call. If the water cushion's handling the overload, just leave it until we can pin down a precise cause."

When the call ended, Evgeni pressed his hands to his eyes. Squint lines dug into his face. Stout and pale to begin with, space had further rounded Evgeni, making him appear almost mischievous. When he smiled, he resembled a child with a secret.

They put pressure goggles on. The crew was required wear them for four hours a day, but they found it easier to conduct video calls without them. The goggles felt like yet another layer of distance between the crew and Earth. Marcanta looked effortlessly mysterious in hers, like a European model. Nedda didn't wonder about her own appearance; nothing ever worsened or improved her variety of plain.

"How are your eyes? Better, worse, or the same? I can try you on beta blockers to see if that changes your pressures," Marcanta said.

"The same, but also better," Evgeni said. "The lenses help somewhat. The directors look good, like Monet. Maybe Renoir."

"And here you are bugging them for reading material," Nedda said.

"Like you, I'm a glutton for punishment," he said, poking her in the ribs.

Morning calls were followed by two and a half hours of exercise to combat muscle atrophy. The medical team on the ground had added a half hour to the standard amount due to the length of their journey. Marcanta grumbled about it, but Nedda didn't mind; for her the treadmill was release. Had there been no clocks, she might have run for days. There was a screen for videos to simulate running along beaches or through woods. It was preloaded with a trail through the Enchanted Forest in Titusville, not far from where she'd grown up. Dr. Stein thought she should have a reminder of home. The trail base was lined with coffee plants; their waxy purple berries made her think of Denny, and made her miss him. She ran the trail once before deleting the file. Now she faced the window and ran into the black.

Amit Singh clapped a hand on her shoulder. Nedda liked the shape of his fingernails: perfect pink-brown ovals. As good a reason as any to like a person.

"My turn. You all right?" Singh was blinking, still groggy from his last sleep cycle, his hair sticking out like dandelion fluff. He had moon face from fluids stuck in his tissues. The pressure suits did nothing to help their faces. It made Singh look kind. Nedda knew she looked like a drunk.

"Never better. They're sending Evgeni info on the life support drive. Check in with him later, would you? He's not going to admit it, but he probably needs your eyeballs."

She cleaned up from her run and spent the next hours with plants in the lab, bent over slides, checking cell structures, bombarding them with radiation, logging and sending data back to the Mars station. She'd thought about moving her sleep sack to the hydro lab to escape Evgeni's music. As a child, she'd slept in a lab many times. There was a picture of her as a baby, swaddled and sleeping in a file drawer in her father's desk. But sleeping in the lab would cause the printer to spit out a cycle of antidepressants, trigger more bloodwork, and more sessions with Dr. Stein. So, no sleeping in labs.

At dinner, they ate the first cucumbers from Hydro after Nedda had carefully deseeded them. The lack of gravity had wreaked havoc on their structure, and they looked like small watermelons.

"They're watery," Nedda said. "I can try to tweak that in the next generation."

"Watery is good," Singh said. "Hydration is good, we're all water."

"They're pretty flavorless."

"That's the taste of promise," Evgeni said between crunching mouthfuls.

During evening call, Singh discussed making a short video on relativity for students. Un had been knocked out in a sandstorm. Evgeni sent a message to Fiver to fix it. Fiver was a slow-moving bot, and work would suffer until Un was repaired. Still, they were well within their arrival window.

There was no report on eyesight. Evgeni called the files they'd sent on Amadeus *interesting*. "I was not expecting you to send an entire library," he said. "It's a month of reading at least."

"You requested development specifics, Mr. Sokolov," Kato replied. "The files we sent contain everything JPL has from Amadeus's prototype blueprint to 3D modeling of what you're running. We like to be thorough."

"My fault for asking," he said. "I suppose it's better to have too much information than too little."

At the call's end, Dr. Stein said someone had arranged for a private video call with Nedda.

The crew left during the transmission delay in the call transfer.

The appearance of Betheen's face shocked Nedda. The crepe-paper skin of age had at last taken hold. Her mother's hair was loose and now so blonde it was hard to distinguish where color ended and white began. So different from Nedda's own dishwater blonde. In her youth, Betheen had been painfully beautiful, but decades had softened her to more pearl than diamond. Nedda wished she could see her in her office, at her desk. Betheen looked uncomfortable in the gray call booth.

Nedda held her breath.

"Hi, honey."

Her mother's voice could still make her shiver. A signal wasn't like touching her, and yet it was. The room smelled like home, like oranges, which was impossible, because Nedda hadn't started grafting them; the lab couldn't support tree cultivars yet. Her skin goosebumped. She began to cry—flat waterfalls instead of proper drops.

"Oh, honey, don't cry. You haven't even said hello yet."

"Hi, Mom."

"Hi," Betheen said. And then she cried too, which made them both laugh.

"Not that I'm not happy to see you, Mom, but how'd you get the private line again so soon?"

"Desmond Prater died."

Nedda hadn't heard his name in ages, but it made her stomach clench. "How is Denny taking it?"

"He's selling the grove."

"That's why you're calling."

"I thought you should know."

She remembered: running between rows of orange trees, bare feet against rough soil, the dusky yellow dirt, crabgrass where the trimmers couldn't reach, flies. "You'd think Denny would tell me himself."

"It's not easy to get a slot to talk with you, and there are things he may still have a hard time talking about. You can understand that."

But she couldn't. There were parts of Denny's memory she'd never be privy to. And yet. They were tied by the grove and what had happened, a bond formed as much by trauma as friendship. A frayed rope stretched too taut by time and space. He hadn't spoken to her since she'd left, not even when she was on the ISS, before Mars, when it would have been easy. But she couldn't explain why she'd had to leave any more than he could explain what he remembered. "How are you, Mom?"

"I miss you."

Obvious words, but no less painful for it. "You too."

She wanted to ask about work, about Betheen's promotion at the lab, how she liked leading a study, about weather, about anything to keep her mother talking, just to hear her voice. But the words built up and wouldn't come out. They watched light play across each other's faces.

"You're round," her mother said. "It looks like you're finally eating."

Nedda laughed. "If I couldn't get fat on your food, I won't get fat on the stuff we eat. It's just space. It does this."

"All I meant is that you look good. Beautiful."

"Don't lie, Mom."

Betheen bent close to the camera. The lens distorted her, made her eyes doll-like. "Are you happy?"

"I'm fine."

Years hadn't changed her mother's sigh or the way it could shame her.

"Your father understood, Nedda. You have to know that. We did what we had to do. You're doing what you have to do."

"I know." Silence was different in space, stretched tenuously over distance and time, a pristine thing Nedda hesitated to break. "I love you," she said.

"I love you too."

"Are you seeing people, Mom? Are you getting out?"

"All anyone does is ask about you. I practically have to hide. I kept the lab door locked all last week. It was heaven." A quirk of her lips. That too was beautiful.

When the call ended, Nedda scrubbed her face. Desmond Prater was dead. It had been years coming. And part of her had always wondered if she'd feel relief when he finally passed. But Denny was left with the fallout—the grove and his mother. He'd have to do what Desmond had, keep the grove going. Life had an awful way of turning you into your parents.

The rest of the crew was playing poker in the kitchen before Marcanta hooked in for a two-week sleep cycle. Evgeni won more often than not, and his price was making everyone clean up after him. Nedda used the rungs to pull herself across the module, back to her cabin.

Marcanta asked, "You all right, Papas?"

"Fine. Just a call from home."

"Come, see if you can get Singh to tell us where he hid the chocolate," Evgeni said.

"Sleep it off," Singh said. "A good nap always helps. Or you can help me take a look at the Amadeus stuff Evgeni can't read."

Marcanta smacked Singh's head.

"I'll just do the sleep thing," Nedda said. "You know where to find me if you need a hand." When he needed a hand.

She crawled into her sleep sack, let the hologram run, and tried to pick out shells—an angel wing, a surf clam—but found none. She listened to waves crash until they started to make her crazy; then she listened to the dark, to the module. *Chawla* had a heartbeat, a life support system fueled by Amadeus. She listened for power spikes and tried to stop thinking about home, about Denny, about her parents.

It had been a full lifetime since she'd last seen her father. Her love for him was cleaner for the distance.

He was thought. Light, moving through the universe.

As was she.

# 1986: Seven

ON THE NIGHT of January 27, 1986, Nedda Papas sat with her father on the hood of his gray Chevette, the long barrel of a telescope occupying the space between them. They were pulled off the road by the Merritt Island Causeway bridge, attempting to escape the light. The night was edged with waves and wind cold enough to make her ears hurt from the inside.

"We'd have to go out on the water to get any darker," her father said.

"Why can't we?"

"Because it's a school night, we don't have a boat, and I don't know anybody who'd lend us one." He patted her head, his hand a warm weight. "See anything yet?"

"Nope." Halley's Comet was close. They took turns with the telescope, hoping to see a blot of light, a cotton ball stained faint yellow. Nedda recognized Orion's Belt, the Big Dipper, the Seven Sisters, and could read them like a map; it was harder to look for something that wasn't usually there. "Why do people call space the 'heavens'?"

"Oh, I suppose it's because people like to feel like there's someone running things and Heaven is part of that idea. People think of the sky as where God is, that they see God, and God sees them."

"We don't think that."

"We do and we don't. We don't know. Isn't it more interesting to ask what stars are? What they're made of? That we can answer."

As he positioned himself behind the telescope, his cheek brushed her hand, beard bristles scratching against her fingers. Her father's beard was wiry and soft all at once, black without a hint of godly white, but he, like God, knew everything. He explained things and the world opened. Last Christmas, Aunt June had sent a card with a picture of God reaching His hand to a man who was supposed to be Adam. For Nedda, touching God was the gentle scrape of whiskers on the back of her hand.

Her father pressed the telescope lens up against his glasses, cupping his hand around it, trying to block light. "I can't see much either." He wasn't built for telescopes; wearing his Coke-bottle glasses meant smudged lenses and light bleeding in, and if he went without, adjusting the focus couldn't compensate for his eyes. Without his glasses, Nedda was a softened version of herself, and stars were beyond him.

"I'm setting my alarm for four A.M.," she said. "I want a good spot tomorrow."

"Hm?"

"The shuttle launch. You said you'd take me."

"I did?" He surrendered the telescope, lifted his frames, and squinted before setting them back into well-worn divots.

He'd forgotten, actually *forgotten*. She'd been crossing off the days on her calendar since November, and he'd forgotten. "Yes, you did. You and Mom said Denny and I couldn't see the new Freddy movie and I said it wasn't fair because we already saw the first one. You said it was a trade. You'd take me to this launch, special. You promised."

"I did say that, didn't I? I'm so sorry, but I forgot." He put his arm around her shoulders, squeezing gently. "I can't tomorrow, Nedda. I have to be at school early. Next time though, I promise."

"You always have to go to school early. And you already promised and forgot. How do I know you won't forget next time?"

"I'll write it down."

"You said you wrote it down this time."

"Remind me, then. You can remind me every day."

"I will."

"How about this? If you don't tell your mother, I'll let you watch that movie when it's out on video."

"Fine," she said, just like her mother did, so he'd know that it absolutely wasn't fine. She'd already seen the movie, anyway. Denny's mom had dropped them off at the theater on a Saturday afternoon and gave them money to see whatever they wanted.

"I'm sorry, Nedda." He looked it too: tired, his mouth turned down like a sad dog.

The comet came once every seventy-six years. There were other nights they could view it, but he'd chosen this one. He'd borrowed a telescope from another professor. He'd let her eat two peanut butter sandwiches for dinner instead of the beef stroganoff Betheen had planned on making. He'd cut the crusts off the bread. She'd been allowed to pick the music in the car, and he'd let her listen to Wham!, then Madonna. When they'd gotten gas at the station by Jonny's Jungle World, he'd given her an advance on her allowance to get a baby alligator head. It was stuffed in the pocket of her blue satin jacket. She pressed her fingers to the tiny teeth.

He was trying.

"Okay," she said. She forgave him, but added it to the tally of things her parents needed to make up to her.

Hours passed. Nedda's corduroys gave her little padding against the metal, and her bones started to hurt. *Once in a lifetime* was hard to understand when it was impossible to imagine being old.

Her father rubbed his back like he was stiff.

"It's getting late."

"Just a little longer?" She swung the telescope around, searching for sky she hadn't checked yet.

"I'm sorry, this isn't working out, is it? We could try another night."

She shut her eyes. There probably wouldn't be another night. No launch or comet, just a cold night and sore elbows from leaning on the car hood. "Five minutes, Dad?"

"Five," he said. Softly.

Jupiter, Venus, the Pleiades, everything was where it was supposed to be. Nothing was extra or new. She pressed the eyepiece tight to her skin, lashes bumping against the lens. The words came without thought, like breath.

"I see it!"

Perhaps she did see something, stars or planets, but the sky was mostly clouds and cold. She'd never wanted to see something more. Because her father could not see it, because she would never see it again, because he'd tried and seemed like he did feel bad, and there was a baby alligator head in her pocket and crustless sandwiches in her belly, because they were watching together.

The next morning, sitting in her classroom, ten miles and half a marsh away from Kennedy, Nedda was freezing, despite her heavy sweater. Lacelike frost covered Easter, Florida, killing a quarter of the oranges in Prater Grove. It felt like she'd never warm up. She'd write that down later, scrawling *cold* in a marbled notebook. A list would take shape, cataloging all the things she'd try to remember. She'd fill a notebook with her father, letters, and everything she could recollect, knowing that the thoughts would eventually fade. But, right then, Nedda just noticed it was cold for a shuttle launch and wondered if astronauts wore sweaters under their jumpsuits. She'd read nothing about that in her books.

Mrs. Wheeler crouched at the media cart—a large brown industrial trolley with a television belted to it. As she fiddled with the cord, the screen vacillated between snow, static, and waves that looked like rainbows with stomach flu.

Nedda squirmed. She should be there, at the launch. All morning, letters and numbers beat their wings inside her: Mission STS 51-L. That was OV-99. Orbiter vehicle. Judith Resnik flew OV-99. Nedda would fly it. OV-99, STS 51-L. STS. Space Transportation System. STS. STS.

"Oh my god, are you hissing?" Tonya Meyers whispered.

"No," Nedda said.

Tonya, with the permed bangs. Tonya, who set up rows of Weepuls and dog-shaped erasers on her desk. Nedda at least kept her My Little Pony hidden in her book bag, much as she wanted to keep Cotton Candy in her desk. She knew she was a little old for ponies, but at least she knew it. Cotton Candy had fallen out of her book bag at recess once. Once, and everyone knew. Her face had burned so badly she wanted to cry. Tonya had laughed. Punching people was stupid. Stupid people did it, but she knew that one time, just that once, it would have felt so good.

She'd forgiven her father for not taking her to the launch, but that didn't mean she couldn't still be angry. Lately he was too busy for lots of things—dinner, TV, books. His time went to his classes, his lab, and his project. Nothing made you angry like missing someone. She'd asked her mother to take her, but Betheen was working on a cake, the three-day kind, and wasn't going anywhere until every piped line and icing rose was set and perfect. The house stank—sour with solder from the downstairs lab, thick with vanilla and fat from the kitchen. Vanilla was fine, unless you lived in it all day every day. Nedda's mother took the joy out of cake.

News 14's Tuck Broderick swam into view, his skin tanned to a rich purple.

A blur sailed across the room, striking Nedda's cheek with a sodden sting. Spitball. Jimmy La Morte sat to her left, holding the clear plastic tube of a hollowed-out Bic. Great. Jimmy's family drank slough water. His spit probably had bacteria that could rot her skin through. Full of road runoff and decades of pesticides from defunct orange groves, the sloughs were polluted, and anything that survived in the water was tough by necessity. She wiped the gunk from her cheek with her sleeve.

Tuck Broderick backed out of the shot and the camera panned across the crowd. Thousands of faces. She slid her hand into her jeans pocket and took out a small circle cut from paper. A mission patch, like the ones stitched onto the astronauts' space suits. Later, her dad would take her to get a real embroidered patch from Kennedy, but she loved staying up the night before a launch, sketching the patch from pictures in newspapers. She'd had her pony on her desk with her, in its astronaut suit. Betheen had bought it for her, which was the nicest thing Betheen had ever done. This mission patch was good, but not her best. She hadn't had much time after getting home late. The apple on it didn't look right. Maybe she'd gotten the proportions wrong.

On TV, the shuttle was clumsy, an airplane grown too big on good food and lazy beach days. Nothing like the slender rocket she dreamed of—silver like an Agena, but sleeker, shinier, with a room at the top for books, and a steel lab table with microscopes, beakers, lasers, and specimen slides. She dreamed of a jump chair cradling her when g-forces pressed her insides to her spine. She dreamed of a bay window, Pyrex to withstand heat and cold, and watching the air change color until blue faded to black stippled with distant stars. Her father said watching stars was looking back in time; the light she saw had left some star millennia before. She imagined other planets' dinosaurs, and that on one of those distant lights, another Nedda watched Earth, Florida even, and saw the rubbery snout of an elasmosaurus as it raised its head from a swamp.

The countdown began. She tapped her fingers with it. *Ten.* Mission control sounded like a phone call from 1950, raspy and tinny. The classroom clock hiccuped and lost a second. *Nine.* Clouds billowed beneath the shuttle.

"That's steam," she said. "They use water to dampen the sound." Nobody listened. *Eight.* Everything inside the shuttle would be shaking. She pressed her tennis shoes flat against the floor, hoping to feel the rumble.

Tuck Broderick held the *T* in *T-minus* for two full counts. Mission control was at seven by the time he caught up. *Six.* Nedda ran her fingers over her patch, feeling the marks from her pen. *Five.* Jenny Demarco screamed the numbers, just for the chance to yell. The last seconds were lost to OV-99's engines rumbling. Combustion was the boldest chemical reaction. Nothing else had the same excitement. When her dad let her light flash paper, she felt a burst of adrenaline that matched the flame. Nedda folded down one finger for each second left. *Four.* Pinkie. *Three.* Ring. *Two.* The fuck-you finger. *One.* Pointer.

The floor trembled as if waking to shudder off the desks and students it had accumulated while sleeping. Linoleum rolled under her and she laughed. The ground should shake when someone left it. It was like swimming and flying at the same time, like at any second her desk would fall away and she'd fly on the shuttle's trail of fire and steam. Nedda began counting again as pencils rolled from desks. *Five. Six. Seven.* Mrs. Wheeler braced herself against the television. The classroom smelled like dry-erase markers and sweeping compound, and Nedda wished someone had opened a window. Easter smelled smoky and good after a launch.

The shuttle's black nose was an ink blot against the clouds on television. Later, she'd remember the clouds and write them down. Behind her, Keith Wilmer made a fart noise and someone giggled.

"Shut up," Nedda whispered. *Forty-five. Forty-six.* The first two minutes after takeoff were the most important. After two minutes, anything that could go wrong would have already gone wrong. Anything else would happen in space, where no one could see it, or on reentry.

Another wet splat, this time on her neck, just missing her braid. She spun to face Jimmy, whose too-wide-set eyes were full of venom and stupid. He twirled the Bic in one hand and flashed the middle finger with the other.

Last winter, in a fit of attentive parenting, Betheen had demanded that Nedda clean up her language. To do it properly, Nedda wanted to know every single forbidden word and derivation. The shelf by her bed began accumulating lists of every cuss she encountered, and her mother's reaction to them. Gradually the project became less about documentation and more about the evolution of swearing. When she'd exhausted standard swears and their traditional permutations, she invented new ones, compound swears, swears that were only swears on certain occasions, and swears for things most people didn't understand were awful. A stack of pages grew, list after list of a filthy, silent scream. So when Nedda called Jimmy La Morte a cunt, it was based on long hours of copious research.

All movement stopped. The word hung, solid enough that she almost reached for it. But there was no taking sound back—it fanned out like an earthquake. Jimmy's swamp-puppy face went slack and his spitball shooter fell. The clattering mixed with the shuttle launch and the plosive *T* of *cunt*.

"Nedda Susanne Papas," Mrs. Wheeler shouted. All three parts of her name, which only Betheen had the right to use.

Nedda's face went red, but before she could protest, a loud *pop* came from the television.

Marilyn Ellison screamed.

The picture on the TV was wrong. There should be afterburners, condensation from crossing the sound barrier, the silhouette of the shuttle breaking free from the atmosphere. It didn't make sense.

There were eight smoke plumes; smoke, not condensation.

The camera shifted, tracking one streamer, at the head of which was a burning piece of—she didn't know what. Part of the shuttle. She bit her tongue, chewing it between her molars. Combustion changed the state of things and everything wound up as carbon or gas. What was left wasn't a shuttle. It was gas, carbon, metal, and . . . what?

On TV, Tuck Broderick chanted, "Oh, god. Oh, god. Oh, god. Ladies and gentlemen, something's gone wrong." The picture bounced as the cameraman jockeyed for position.

She rubbed the patch drawing, pushing ink into the ridges of her fingertips. The shuttle was gas, carbon, and warped metal. Judith Resnik's shuttle, and everyone inside it. Judy Resnik. Sweaters didn't matter, she thought, and immediately felt sick.

Stillness stretched the moment into a flat image of a classroom filled with students. No breath. No movement. Then Kim Wallace's Trapper Keeper fell from her desk, and the tiny crash shook life back in.

Nedda didn't know the math of how long it would take soundwaves from the explosion to reach the school, not with the humidity, not with being close to sea level. She rubbed the patch. Her dad would know.

Mrs. Wheeler turned off the television and the knob made the same plastic-sounding *click* it always did. She kept her back to the class. Nedda stared at her blouse, which was champagne pink. She knew the color; her mother had the same one from Dillard's, and she'd been wearing it that morning. Mrs. Wheeler wasn't making noise, but she was crying all the same. Marilyn Ellison was too, and she sounded exactly like a cricket frog. Liza Nuñez hiccupped. Nedda could almost see the soundwaves floating, dizzily knocking into shoulders and backs.

They'd watched seven people die.

The PA cut in. Through cracking and hissing, Principal Lauder announced that all classrooms were to report to the auditorium for an assembly. His voice broke on the word *auditorium*. Maybe his back shook too.

Nedda jostled to the front of the line, next to Mrs. Wheeler. The *C* word incident forgotten, Mrs. Wheeler squeezed every shoulder as she counted down the line, then back up. Her eyes were puffy and the tip of her nose had a faint sheen. Her blouse sleeves caught the light, and Nedda pictured her mother walking up and down the line, clasping shoulders. If she said the *C* word again, Mrs. Wheeler would yell at her. She'd be sent to the office. Principal Lauder would call her father and she'd be sent home. Maybe that would make things feel normal again.

She stayed quiet.

Following the line from Mr. Stanza's room, they shuffled down the hall, passing the fifth-grade corridor. She wrapped the patch drawing around her thumb, then locked it into a fist. If she hit someone with her fist like that, she'd break her thumb. How much would it hurt to break a thumb? Not enough. They rounded the corner by the art room and Mrs. Wheeler started gulping like a fish. The drapey bow on her blouse quivered.

"We didn't see it," Nedda said.

Mrs. Wheeler didn't answer.

"My dad told me how light travels before it gets to your eye. I forget the exact speed it goes at, but I can find it for you later. It's like a boat on the water, because it goes in waves. You know when you see something? It's already done. It already happened, because light had to travel to get to you before you could see it."

"Nedda."

"We didn't really see it. Maybe just, like, an echo of it." *Echo* wasn't right. Echo was sound, not light, but it traveled in waves too. That wasn't it, but defining *it* was impossible. "The light went to a lot of places before it got here."

"Nedda, hush. Please."

As cold as she'd been, Nedda was now hot and sticky, and her stomach churned. The patch was stuck to her. If she took it off there would be a small red ink stain, a mirror of the apple. No one was going to tell her parents about the *C* word.

The auditorium was half-full by the time they arrived. The fourth graders came in last, some crying, some chattering, most quiet. There were empty seats from kids who were out sick, or whose parents had taken them to watch the launch. Her class, the sixth grade, filled the middle section. She sat next to Tricia Villaverde, who immediately moved two seats away. Nedda looked around for Denny Prater, but his class was in the back row. When no one took the empty chair, Mrs. Wheeler sat beside her.

Mrs. Leigh, the school counselor, walked to the center of the stage and asked for silence.

Then there was prayer.

While everyone prayed, Nedda thought about light, about combustion. She thought about sitting on the roof with her dad, watching stars. Not just stars—some dots of light were comets, asteroids, nebulas, and planets. Some planets she and her dad had looked at were already gone. It wasn't sad; it was true. Those things were different.

Principal Lauder said there would be early dismissal, then called for another moment of silence. In the row in front of Nedda, Liza sniffled and picked at the fabric on her chair arm. She caught Nedda staring and whispered something to Keith. Nedda looked at the floor, at the ink on her thumb, at the air between her chair and Liza's.

She must have seen millions of dead things, things that were light years away, eons ago. She chewed a small raw spot on her lip. Her feet tapped against carpet. The thump of it felt wrong somehow. Everything felt wrong. She needed to go home, to her dad's small lab in the basement, to curl up on one of the tables like she used to. It had been a long time since she'd last brought a quilt down and made a nest for herself among the books, tubes, and wires—a million years or however long it took light to travel. She'd rest her cheek on the table and listen to her dad talk about space. She'd been little when he'd told her about the beginning of the universe and how the solar system was born. How the sun was like an island, and the planets were ships sailing around it. He'd said, "Pluto is our far star sailor," the way other people said *Once upon a time.* His words opened a door inside her.

She wished she'd brought her NASA book, with six full pages on the "Thirty-Five New Guys," the Astronaut Class of 1978, NASA's first new group of astronauts since 1969. On Sally Ride, on *Challenger*—which she realized was gone now—on Judy Resnik, mission specialist, the second American woman in space. Who Nedda wanted to be. Who was gone now too. They were gas and carbon—and what else? They had to be something else.

She wanted her stupid little-kid pony, but it was in the classroom. She wanted to go fishing with Denny, even if it was too cold. She wanted to smell her mother's perfume until she was sick from it. She wanted to eat all the icing roses off that stupid cake until Betheen yelled. She should be yelled at. For saying *cunt,* for sitting next to Tricia when Tricia hated her. For losing count before the two-minute mark. She shouldn't have stopped counting.

It was her fault.

She wanted not to think about the fact that even though light was a wave, despite the time and distance it had to travel to get from Launchpad 39B to the Thomas A. Covey School, she'd watched seven people die.

Judy Resnik was gone.

# 1986: Fabrication and Loss

END-STAGE PROTOTYPES HAD personalities, and Crucible was an utter bastard. Its frame expanded and contracted with the slightest temperature shift, which today meant every single nut was loose, three seals had cracked, and Theo Papas was swearing. Metal had life in it, which made fabrication a war between satisfaction and frustration. Frustration was winning.

He winged a wrench against the wall and was instantly sorry he did so. A student's head peered through the lab door's window and he forced a wave. He rubbed his eyes, missing the days of graduate school and amphetamine-fueled energy. He missed the access to materials he'd had at NASA. The partnership. He missed having Avi Liebowitz to bounce ideas off. There'd been cutbacks, Theo had been let go, and eventually he'd found a position at the college. He spent his days teaching intro classes and surveys, bargaining for sabbaticals, and trying to convince Dean Babcock that his work was practical, feasible, and worth investment. The dean humored his project, but didn't see its practical applications the way Liebowitz did. Babcock thought he was hunting cold fusion. Half-life acceleration meant nothing to him. The department's main concerns were that the cesium-137 stayed properly shielded and that any patents would name Haverstone College.

Liebowitz knew what half-life acceleration meant. Getting the most out of a smaller mass. Powering bigger things for practical applications. Half-life acceleration could change space travel. Half-life deceleration? He could make something that would run until the proverbial end of the universe. Yet he was stuck in a painted cinderblock room with rows of white shelving stacked with boxes and crates that overflowed with wires, glass tubes, and circuitry. He was being strung along by the school, and they would wring what working years he had left in him for as little money as they possibly could.

But Nedda was happy here. She was near things she loved. Comet watching was good. She'd have something wonderful to remember, and he'd gotten to see it through her eyes. Which was as good as seeing it himself, maybe better.

Were he at home, Nedda would be sprawled across a table in his basement office, asking questions. Part of him had hoped Betheen would be interested too—that she might have wanted to help. But she had put a limit on what she would allow in the house, and Crucible far exceeded that. Radioactive isotopes in the basement crossed the line.

He appraised the damage to Crucible, ducking beneath one of its limbs. Entropy and time weren't the neatest concepts, and his machine's form embraced that chaos. Crucible was a daddy longlegs—a spherical center of glass, gold, and lead, from which long metal legs extended, raising it from the floor and lending it an arachnid appearance. The legs were dual-purposed, supporting the central drum and cooling it as they glided around a magnetized track. Crucible's center had a door into its deep belly that sealed with a broad flange of rubber and lead. It shielded his cesium samples, contained errant radiation, and kept light from escaping and raising eyebrows.

The machine looked like an enormous fuckup. *Enormous* being the key problem.

It needed too much power. He'd stuck to his notes from NASA, from before his hands had been wrecked by psoriatic arthritis. He'd had funding then' and Liebowitz to talk to. Liebowitz, who could have built it the right size. But layoffs left Theo with a professor's salary and seven scrapped half starts, rather than a finished machine that had the potential to revolutionize space travel, medicine, and the concept of time. The arthritis was his undoing. His hands refused to keep up with his mind. Even corresponding with Liebowitz, who'd landed on his feet at Oak Ridge National Laboratory, was difficult most days. When the plaques were angry, his knuckles heated and swelled, making small work impossible. Often, work wasn't possible at all. When he could work, he had to work large, resulting in this Brobdingnagian contraption that could blow the power grid. His initial plans had called for a door only large enough for small test materials—a minute amount of cesium, sample cells for nonisotope work, a lab rat at most. In its current iteration, a small person could climb inside and pull the door closed behind. But he loved Crucible, even if it was ugly.

Five yellowing notices from the facilities manager—a glorified janitor—were on his desk. Today he'd had to come in early to prove that his work was not a fire hazard, that he had proper ventilation, and that any power shorts in the sciences building were unrelated. Even if they weren't. What was one more facilities note? He should have taken Nedda to the launch.

Raising Nedda was painful in ways he hadn't anticipated, as though a cord connected them, its pull as strong as any chemical bond. One day, it would break and she would leave. Eleven was a spectacular age. Her brain was blooming, her mind ripe for learning. She was building new cells to contain everything she learned, forging new neural pathways, and each day she was different, a little more, a little brighter. All the while, his brain was wearing down; every brain over twenty-five was. Nedda was at the point of infinite potential, the moment where genius was born.

What an incredible thing it would be to hold on to that precise moment.

There was wonder in how she pressed her eye to a telescope, how she'd memorized all the lunar craters. What child didn't deserve a lifetime of infinite discovery? What child deserved it more than Nedda?

*What if?*

He tightened a leg joint, righting Crucible again. The seal on the door flange was cracking; he'd have to see if Pete McIntyre had something in his garage that might do the trick. He shook his hands out. The tingling ran through his knuckles, which would be followed soon by burning, as his body attacked itself. When the attack subsided, days, or even weeks, from now, he'd be left with new lumps on his joints and a hand that functioned a little less. The last attack had deformed his ring finger; the top knuckle was now bent as though clamped in a death grip on some imagined thing. He took two aspirin from his shirt pocket and ground them between his teeth.

At eleven twenty A.M., his hands forced him to abandon the lab and college for his car and the drive home to his basement office and his notebooks, to a house that smelled like sugar not meant for him. The flare-up came on quickly. He was adept at steering with his knees and elbows, but shifting was a stabbing pain. His dreams for Nedda, for all the time she had and all the time he wanted to give her, were balanced by an urgent need—to fix himself, to mend a body designed to break.

Once back home and ensconced in his basement workspace—basements, he was forever confined to basements—Theo flipped through his early notes on Crucible, from before it was Crucible. He and Liebowitz had called it the "entropy machine," and its practical applications had seemed endless: deep space travel, fuel conservation, specimen preservation, orbiter reuse. The human potential of it had drawn him, selfishly. Few innovations ever began in pure altruism.

He could hear Betheen pacing upstairs. There was distance in her steps. They'd reached a point where everything meant something else, each conversation was layered, all of it exhausting. When Nedda grew up, Theo knew, Betheen would likely leave him.

But they'd go down trying. That was the price of keeping secrets, even when you both understood it was for the best.

When the ground shivered and announced the shuttle launch, he paused to listen, and to curse the facilities prick and his idiotic notices.

Part of parenting entailed learning the exact expression your child made when you broke her heart, and knowingly breaking it again and again. Nedda's disappointment manifested as a Mendelian cross of Betheen and himself. She turned splotchy like her mother and gnawed on her lip like him. She'd yet to develop psoriasis; for that he thanked Betheen. The good bits. Your child was supposed to get the best of you.

The tremor rattled his desk and a box of notebooks fell, sending up a cloud of dust and knocking over the high-voltage traveling arc he'd gotten to entertain Nedda on Halloween. There'd be a mess at the college later, cracked glass and piping that would need to be replaced, more facilities notices. Crucible's exhaust—a gaseous form of N-Methyl-2-pyrrolidone, a noxious mouthful—tended to melt rubber tubing. Glass had been his only option, fragile and subject to every seismic hiccup.

"Theo!" Betheen's voice carried down the laundry chute.

He heard the crying before he saw her. She gripped the back of one of the kitchen chairs. Betheen was art, empirically beautiful, engendering awe in its full capacity—wonder and fear. He adhered to their rhythm of wait, approach, and retreat.

"Beth?"

"They're dead. They died." Her body clenched, a stiff extension of the bentwood chairback. Knuckles bloodless. She'd held his hand like that once, squeezing his fingers until the joints popped. Now, that too-tight grasp could break him. They pretended they didn't miss those things.

"What happened?"

"It's gone, the whole shuttle. An explosion." A flicker from the living room showed that the television was on. Smoke against blue sky. "They're supposed to be safe now," she said. "Like school buses."

"There's no such thing as entirely safe," he said. There was chaos on the screen, shots of the crowd, the sky, lingering smoke.

"It's irresponsible," Betheen said.

"Everyone knows the risks. They all made that choice," he said.

She turned to look at him.

"Always. You always have an answer."

"It's always the wrong one, isn't it? I'm sorry."

It might have been the light from the kitchen, that it was warmer than lab fluorescents, but he saw the gentle crenellation of her jaw, the wisps of hair that hadn't made it into her clip, and that no matter how straight she stood, she was bent inside—like him.

"Mostly. You're occasionally right."

"Come here."

He opened his arms, and she quickly brushed her lips against his cheek before stepping away. She began scrubbing the countertop as if to sand it bare. "You know they're watching it at school."

The teacher, right. They were broadcasting it in school because of the teacher astronaut. Nedda would have seen everything. "Hell. I was supposed to take her."

The telephone rang.

"One of us is going to have to talk to her. It's probably better if it's you."

"Sure."

"If you keep it cold and clinical, she'll like that. You're good at that," Betheen said. She picked up the receiver, stretched the cord, and let it snap back against the flowered wallpaper. "Yes, this is she. Hello, Mrs. Ocasio."

*Clinical.* After the first miscarriage, he'd purchased an obstetrics textbook. He'd read the chapters on spontaneous abortion aloud to Betheen while she lay on the couch in the front room, hands tucked between her knees. He'd lingered over words and names only circumstance could have brought them. *Kisspeptin.* It sounded innocent, romantic. She'd listened until she fell asleep. When she woke up crying, he'd start again. He could have tried something else, but science was their language, the vocabulary they'd loved together, and the only way he could understand. It *was* warm. In the litany of Latin and Greek—fluctuation of hormones, low plasma levels, percentages—was science, plainly stating it wasn't their fault. She'd breathed chemistry when they'd met. They could break apart the biology of kisspeptin, find the beauty in the math.

Clinical had been enough at first, pulling them through miscarriages until they had Nedda. Then there was Michael, and the wall of silence that came after him, how it had been easier to not talk about him at all, then too difficult to bring him up.

"I understand," she said. "Yes. It makes sense given the circumstances. Absolutely. I'll start the phone tree. Nedda usually walks home with Denny Prater. It's probably best if they keep to that for some normalcy."

She hung up. He reached for her, his hand and hers, and the touch burned in his bones. She let him hold her. Her thumb stroked the rough patch at the ball of his wrist.

"They're letting them out early?"

"Yes," she said. "The kids saw the whole thing. They're in an assembly now. What good that does, I have no idea. What's a few more hours? What's done is done."

"I'll cancel my late class."

"That's probably a good idea."

He used to imagine the lines on their palms crosshatching, locking in place. They held on too gently now. The second hand on his watch did its usual stutter, ticking backward as it reached fifty-five. The sound stretched between them.

"When is she coming home?"

"They're dismissing in an hour."

An hour was a lifetime.

"Mind helping me with the Physics 102 syllabus? It would pass the time. A fresh eye would be good."

Betheen straightened her skirt. "I need to start the phone tree. Then I have to deliver the cake to the Rotary. Rockets might be falling out of the sky, but God forbid a Rotarian goes without lemon cake."

He'd said something wrong again. He should have offered to help her, but he'd already chewed enough aspirin to down a horse. And the Rotarians looked at him like he was a leper.

"Betheen?"

But she was already on the phone again, looking out the window onto the street. On days his schedule allowed, he stood in that same spot, watching Nedda walking home, curtains pulled almost closed so she wouldn't notice. She would appear as a dot in the distance by the edge of the palmettos, with Denny tagging behind her. Hanging moss played tricks with the light, and he indulged the idea that she'd manifested just because he'd wished it. Children were like that in a way, thoughts you'd willed into being.

He wound his watch and pictured his brilliant daughter, whom only he found beautiful, heading to the house but never arriving. Moving forward in fractions. Like Zeno's Achilles and the Tortoise paradox, always approaching, but never reaching.

The television blinked, the picture snapping out. Betheen jumped.

"The station must have cut the feed," he said. A crisp *pop* from the basement echoed through the laundry chute, followed by a faint smell of electrical burning. Power surge. Common enough around launches. "Probably a blown fuse. I'll look."

He was halfway to the stairs when she said, "Stay a minute? Just until I pack up the cake. I don't want to be alone." She didn't meet his eye, tossing the words to the cabinets as she reached for a cake box. Sunlight and the curtains made her yellow, the same butter color as the kitchen.

He stayed.

"I'm sorry I said that. The clinical thing. It wasn't fair," she said.

"It's true. You didn't mean it in a bad way."

"I don't know what I mean sometimes."

"What are you working on?" he asked when he saw her jot something on an index card.

"I'm figuring out something kind of like a water cake. That's a dessert that's sort of like a jelly but looks like a raindrop," she said. "So, texture, surface tension, and sugar. Oh, and alcohol. It's a wedding cake, so champagne."

"That's what all the agar is for?" There were bags of the stuff stashed in the cabinets.

"Kanten flakes, yes. Gelatin is too stiff and not clear enough. It has to have movement to it."

"So you're making alcoholic Jell-O."

"It's not Jell-O. And don't call it 'aspic' or 'gelée' either. I'm making a wedding cake and I'm going to take it to the Orlando Cake Show, and I'm going to enter it in the concept cake category and I'm going to win, thank you. They're small thinkers over there, and they don't understand what cake can do. Or how boring wedding cakes are. Everyone is used to stiff cakes, bricks with icing on them. They think a concept cake is a cake that looks exactly like someone's new house. They don't know what they want—something soft, delicate, intangible, moving. It should change."

The way marriages did.

The fire started running up his spine, and he had to pull his hand away. Shake it out. "I have to work on lectures. Are you sure you don't want to help?"

"This is something good; maybe I can change the way people think about something. Bring in a little more business. I don't want to do your typing anymore, Theo. I can't."

"That wasn't what I meant." He'd just been thinking of her. Though, perhaps it had been the idea of her clacking away on a typewriter.

"I'm sorry," he said.

She smiled. "Me too."

# Crucible

THE GROUND BENEATH Easter is new, geologically fragile, and destined to sink back into the sea and the water below it. A century before, men drained and tilled it and carved rows for the orange trees that were more at home in Easter than anywhere else in the world. They set buildings on the new land, and with each change, it stretched to learn its new shape. Houses were made from what the surrounding land offered: pine wood, limestone, and coral stone. The cement walls of Theo Papas's lab in the sciences building are local sand and local stone and contain fossilized shadows of shells and coral. The shadows echo ocean currents.

*Challenger*'s brutal ascent births a seismic hum that rattles the foundation of the lab. It moves as though alive and searching for water.

A rumble courses down a ventilator hose, jostling a magnetic track.

A metal strut bows and Theo Papas's giant spider begins to kneel, kowtowing to the stone and its memory of life.

The launch blankets the machine with waves of sound and motion. From inside the cradle of glass and gold comes a tiny snap. A hint of smoke, sooty and ripe. A spark, perhaps a reflection of sparks—and then this aberrant charge that moves like a ripple is gone, running through an electrical line. There is thickness to it, like a smooth drip of corn syrup, and air and light bend around it as it flows along wire and cable, threading through buildings, houses, and eventually the Easter Municipal Pumping Station, where the lights begin to flicker like a slow blink. Jeff Guthrie notices, and moves to replace the bulb above his desk. As he reaches, a small static shock runs through him, a charge built up from his shoes on the carpet. He feels it, but not the movement below.

Below the coral stone and the thin crust of land on which Easter sits is sweet groundwater that gives the soil its flavor and makes the oranges grow. Easter Municipal pumps it away to keep the town from sinking, into lakes and ponds behind houses, into canals that line the roadways, making Easter almost an island unto itself.

Beneath Easter and Jeff Guthrie's feet, in the pumps that keep the land drained and dry, water meets spark. In the dark below the ground, in the water, there is no one to see the rippling or its beautiful glow.

# 1986: Mico Argentatus

THE WORLD SCREAMED by, not the jerky fast-forward from movies, but a slick blur of energy. Nedda touched one shoe to the pavement, testing to see if it was right, and a fourth grader smashed into her. The lot was packed with buses and mom cars—wood-panel station wagons that everybody but Betheen drove. Betheen had an old Cadillac, a boat of a car that stuck out as much as she did. A news van was there, and a shiny-haired reporter talked to Principal Lauder.

"Dork." The word came from a group of girls, loud enough to carry, and was directed at her.

The sky rolled, stretching clouds, spreading the pieces of shuttle, molecules, atoms flying on the wind. They were up there; millions of pieces, scattering across Easter, across Florida, the Atlantic, and falling, tumbling, raining.

A familiar shoulder bumped hers.

"Hey," Denny said. "Wanna go?"

The funny little flutter between her stomach and ribs quieted.

They fell into step, weaving through the bus lines, crossing the field to the palmetto forest that separated the school from the south part of Easter and the old park. Tall grass gave way to larger moss-dusted oaks, then palmettos and a path that snaked through the trees, worn by decades of deer and people taking the same trail she and Denny did. Nedda loved dense woods. Snakes. Bugs. Woods that were loud and quiet.

She hadn't spoken since the assembly, not even when Mrs. Wheeler told her to walk home with Denny, and the words were building up. Her ship was gone. Judy Resnik was gone. There was a hole where there hadn't been one before—inside her and in the world too, though that wasn't how holes were supposed to work. She hurt. Sally Ride must hurt. She'd lost a ship, her ship, and her friends. They had to have been friends. Nedda knew ship facts, statistics, but she didn't know something as simple as whether the astronauts were friends. It hadn't seemed important.

It *was* important.

"Hey, look. Coffee," Denny said, dropping to the ground, folding up like a toad. His shaggy black hair mixed with the shadows as he pulled up handfuls of waxy purple berries. Easy. He was so easy. Normal. "I bet we could probably get a gallon out of all this."

She'd been nine, Denny ten, when she'd read that the shiny plants were wild coffee. She and Denny had planned to collect, dry, and roast the berries to make their own brew. They'd stockpiled berries in his treehouse, but rats and birds made off with most of them before they'd gotten around to drying. Later, she discovered that you couldn't make real coffee from this kind of berry, but she never told Denny. It was fun to stuff their backpacks and fill his tennis shoes with them, and she liked him with berries spilling out of every pocket. Happy. He'd dyed his toes purple once when he'd forgotten to shake out his shoes. Purple-toed Denny was her favorite Denny. She crouched down beside him and shoved a handful of berries in the front pouch of her book bag. The skins were tight and smooth, full to bursting.

"Did you see it?" he asked.

"Yeah." She swallowed around a lump of thoughts. *Bolus*, that was the word. Landing on the right word unleashed the rest. "OV-099. OV is 'orbiter vehicle.' Did you know that's what *Challenger* is called? Orbiting is like a controlled fall. OVs fall around Earth." She squinted her left eye. "NASA used *Challenger* for everything. First untethered space-walk, McCandless and Stewart. First American woman in space, Sally Ride. First African American man in space, Guion Bluford. Tons of firsts." Was. *Challenger* was. She poked her fingernail through a shiny leaf, then tore it from the stem, shredding it. "First mission with two women. First night launch. First night landing. First shuttle to land at Kennedy. Three Spacelab missions. It's the workhorse of the fleet. *Challenger* flies more than *Columbia*." Flew. She thought the word again and again until it was meaningless. Then came the names: Scobee, McNair, Smith, Onizuka, Jarvis, McAuliffe, Resnik. Then their faces. There were news clippings tucked in her desk drawer. The thought bolus contained every spec she'd ever read, all of it waiting to be vomited out. Denny didn't need to hear it. She shredded another leaf. "This mission was going to study Halley's Comet. They had a satellite on board that was going to look at it in ultraviolet light. It's gone now. All of it."

"Do you have the patch?"

She dug through her pocket to hand him the drawing, now soft with worry and sweat.

Gangly described them both, but Denny had the hope of growing out of it. Pop Prater was tall and solid. Denny looked like him, the same hair, the same full-face smile, but Denny's was better. He'd busted a front tooth falling off the monkey bars, and it left him with a jack-o'-lantern grin—the good kind. His clumsiness made him good too. Pop Prater looked like who he was, the man who ran Prater Citrus. Denny looked like a friend and was enough like a brother that she sometimes forgot he wasn't. The patch looked at home in his hand.

"This is a good one, really good," he said. "The colors came out cool. The yellow's awesome." He moved to a sunny spot and held it up for a longer look. "Best one yet."

"Thanks." The too many words went away, leaving quiet, the woods, and the hole that was inside her and out. He handed the patch back. Denny didn't care if she talked too much, or not enough. It would be good to stay right there, collecting coffee berries and letting him bump her shoulder. "I don't feel like going home," she said.

"Me neither. I failed a math test and I have to get it signed. Mr. Tressa knows I forged my mom's signature last time."

They scrambled over a fallen palm, its upended roots like dried noodle cakes. To their left, the shadow of a giant tiki head peered through a break in the trees, the fenced-off entrance to Island Paradise Park and Zoo. Long abandoned, parts of the waterslides had toppled. The tiki-head gate was the last remaining landmark of when Easter had been a destination.

They followed a trail away from the park until the palmettoes thinned out and opened onto Pete McIntyre's backyard, where they spent more afternoons than not. Mr. Pete had done maintenance at NASA during Apollo and just after, and he'd developed a habit of picking up unwanted parts when buildings and launch complexes shuttered. His yard was a garden of scrap metal, junk, machinery, and the closest thing Easter had to a space museum.

Nedda wanted all of it.

Mr. Pete charged tourists two bucks to look through his house and gawk at things like the plastic bags astronauts went to the bathroom in on the lunar missions. Nedda and Denny got to gawk for free. Mr. Pete fixed cars now, which meant his yard was also a repository for auto parts and a fully intact truck he'd pulled up from Fox Lake with a winch. On summer weekends, she and Denny would climb in the truck after fishing, their catch in a paint bucket, and wait for sun to warm the water until the snappers squirmed, flapping their frowning mouths.

Denny said it was a 1948 Ford. He paid attention to things like that. He climbed into the truck and flopped down in the back. "Are you coming up?"

"In a sec."

Next to Mr. Pete's screened-in porch was a beautiful oddity—a launch sequencer. Half asleep and waiting for current, it was infinitely inviting. It was from Launch Complex 36A, Mr. Pete had told her, but she'd already known. Shuttle launches ran by computer now, but missiles and satellites still ran analog. The sequencer looked about seven feet tall, was wide as the freezer case at the diner, and painted dull gray. Each light in the rows of green, white, and red was tied to a specific event, and all those signals connected to a pen-and-needle feed that marked every blip and surge on a roll of paper. The wires at the top were held down on breadboard, the same kind of construction base her dad used when he showed her how to make a circuit. She touched a needle. It slid smoothly to the left, and for some reason that made her want to cry.

"Do you think a missile blew them up?" Denny asked. "How much you want to bet it was Russians? I bet you that's what it looks like when a missile hits something. I bet it was small too. Russians make all kinds of stuff extra tiny."

Her face itched where Jimmy La Morte's spitball had landed. "I don't know. But they would tell us, right? The news would at least."

"I guess. Maybe they don't know yet either."

He popped up, tongue poking through the space left by his broken tooth. "Do you think they exploded? It was super quick. What's that gotta feel like? Do you think it was like the microwave? Probably not, right?"

"It wasn't like the microwave."

They'd put marshmallows in the microwave at Denny's house and watched them swell and pop. Denny's mom caught them half a bag in and screeched about going blind from sitting too close. They'd spent the rest of the day talking about eyeballs exploding and playing *Congo Bongo* on his ColecoVision. Denny had seen a horror movie where a guy's eyes popped like balloons and another guy's head exploded.

"Microwaves heat stuff up by shaking all the molecules inside. That's how they cook things. The screen on the door stops the waves from getting out, so you can't cook your eyeballs, no matter what your mom says." Then, to be clear, she said, "It wasn't like that."

"Okay," he said, and a little later, "Good."

She shinnied into the truck bed and tossed her bag over the side, as Denny had done. There was something in the bed.

It took a minute to place; she'd never seen one outside a zoo. It was like opening the refrigerator to find you'd put the toothpaste in while half asleep.

"Denny! A green monkey." When Island Paradise Park and Zoo had closed, animals had escaped or gone missing, mixing with the local wildlife and boa constrictors who'd slipped their owners' cages. One kind of monkey had been an especially good escape artist—marmosets. They'd gone on to breed in the wild, even thrive. When they'd escaped, they'd been white, but the weather and Easter's trees tinted them green with algae and moss. They'd turned nasty too. She'd heard they ripped the heads off rabbits, and one had scalped a girl. She feared them as much as she wanted to catch one and keep it. Here one was, sitting in a small puddle, wet, with a dark catlike tail, red-brown eyes too large for its face, like the stones in Aunt June's clunky bracelet, and pink hands with black claws at the end. Scalp rippers. Speckled with dirt, the monkey blended in with the truck's rust and mud. "It's one of the park monkeys. A silvery marmoset." *Mico argentatus.* She'd looked it up when she wanted to know why there were green monkeys. It was barely breathing, and didn't startle when Denny scooted next to her. The truck wobbled but the monkey stayed still.

"Grab him," Denny whispered. "My mom's got a parrot cage in the garage we can keep him in."

"Quiet, you'll scare him." She inched forward, hands cupped. "Hey, little guy. Hey, fella." Not even a twitch. "I think it might be dead."

"It doesn't look dead."

He was right; it looked warm and alive. And she wanted it. Badly. She wanted to walk into school with a scalp-ripping monkey perched on her shoulder. She tapped by its tail. *Thp, thp, thp.* Its ears were so thin that light came through, and its face was pink and peach, fine-grained, like baby skin. But its mouth was full of needles, ready to murder rabbits. Why wasn't it running? It should run, lunge, lash out, or at least blink.

"Get a stick. I want to see if it's dead." The image of exploding eyeballs rose again. "I don't see flies. If it's dead there should be flies, right? Maybe it's just sick."

"I don't know. There's flies on poop, but poop's not dead," Denny said.

"But poop was never alive either." Something metal poked her side, leaving a smear of sludge on her jacket. "Hey."

"Does a dipstick work?"

"Sure."

When Nedda prodded at the monkey, it almost pushed back against the dipstick. Weird. Another poke met the same resistance, though the monkey gave no sign of moving, that it had ever moved.

"This is weird."

"I don't think he's dead." There was a heartbeat feel to living things, and the monkey had it.

"Pick him up. There's room in my bag and if he wakes up he can eat the coffee."

She started to say that marmosets don't eat coffee, but she didn't know what they ate besides bunny heads and little girls' hair.

"Hang on. I want to see something." She poked it again. The tip of the dipstick missed the monkey, though her aim had been perfect, dead on for the belly. "Huh."

Mr. Pete's screen door slammed. "Denny Prater, are you skipping school?"

"We got let out early. Me and Nedda are walking home."

"Sure looks like it, you being in the truck and all. You in there, Nedda Sue?"

She stuck a hand up and waved. Denny hopped out and went to talk to Mr. Pete. Denny was easy to talk to and he was Pop Prater's kid so everybody knew him; at some point or other everyone in Easter worked for Prater Citrus. Everyone but her dad.

She jabbed with the dipstick again, but couldn't seem to touch the monkey. And it still hadn't blinked. If it was dead she was about to break a million rules. If it was alive, she was about to get scalped. She set the dipstick down and stretched her index finger, pointed at one of the too-big eyes, and stabbed.

There was a slick sort of tingling, then nothing. Her finger slipped, gliding past the monkey's face without touching it, and the animal remained frozen, as though she hadn't threatened to blind it. A drip of water splashed down from the powerline overhead, it too just missing the monkey. The water seemed funny, thick looking, almost opalescent. She grabbed for the monkey's tail and her fingers slid again, skimming over an invisible surface like soap suds, a slippery bubble. The air around it looked strange too, almost like it was bent. She rubbed her hands together, but they weren't slimy. Normal skin, sweat, and the stain from the apple on her drawing.

"What the heck?" she whispered.

Denny and Mr. Pete talked about the accident. "Blam," Denny said. She couldn't pinpoint the moment she'd heard the explosion, or what it had sounded like. She'd heard herself say the C word, screaming, crying, then silence. It could have been *blam*, but that sounded too small. She kicked the truck, startling herself.

Nedda tried to dig under the monkey with the dipstick—one, two, three—then with her fingers—another four, five, six, for a larger sample size. Better data. There was no getting under it, or even touching the patch of water beneath it. Something around the monkey had a bouncy pushback, like pressing magnets together when the poles weren't aligned: resistance, and *strong*.

"Are you all right in there, Nedda?"

"Fine." She would be fine, if he left her be. Why wouldn't it move?

"You'd best head home." Mr. Pete said. "I'd call your mother and let her know you're here, but my phone's out. I guess the lines must be overloaded, or something shorted out somewhere. It keeps going in and out. The power's on the fritz too. Don't worry your folks. Get home. It's looking like a storm out."

"Okay, thank you," she said, though she didn't know what she was thanking him for.

"Tell that mother of yours I said hello. My birthday's coming up and I'm thinking about a cake this year." Mr. Pete turned red like a strawberry every time Betheen brought the car in for repair.

The long way home brought them past Ginty's Bait & Tackle and the Bird's Eye Diner, where Denny could get them free ice cream sodas because his father had loaned Ellery Rees money when the diner flooded. The parking lot was full and a news van was there.

"Did you get it? Is it in your bag?"

"I couldn't get it," she said. "It's not moving and I can't touch it, but I don't think it's dead."

"How do you know if you can't touch it?" He hopped over a tree trunk Hurricane Bob had knocked down.

"There's kind of a bubble around it, almost oily, but not. I don't know. You know freeze frames in movies? It kind of looks like that to me. I want to check on it tomorrow."

"Betcha a gator eats it."

It was too cold for gators. She knew the monkey was supposed to be dangerous, but it was sweet with those round eyes, like her pony. You were supposed to love stuff like that. Cute was a defense mechanism; it made people more open to loving you. She knew that with the certainty of a girl who had never been and never would be cute.

"My dad got me a baby gator head last night."

"Cool. Can I see it?"

"I'll bring it tomorrow. Wait for me by the fire door after school if you want to check on the monkey."

They walked by the shell of Mauna Kea Motor Inn. A sign on the sagging A-frame showed rates for rooms that hadn't been rented since 1974. The *S* in *rooms* dangled drunkenly from one end.

"Okay. Can I see what your dad's working on?"

"He's not done yet, and he uses radioactive stuff, so it's dangerous." It was what her father said all the time. "It has these giant leg things that move around like the teacups at Disney." She stuck out her arms, swinging them. "It's made of metal, maybe steel, and there's a lot of glass too. You know the mag lev track he built us?"

"Huh?"

"That magnetized rail thing he made for our Matchbox cars? He took it apart and used it for part of the track the machine's legs spin around on."

When her dad had brought her to the college to teach her how to plate the inside of mason jars with silver, he'd shown her the machine and let her push the legs once; they'd floated around the track with barely a touch. "There's a door in the middle, and it's big enough a person could crawl in, but there's nothing in there yet. He wouldn't let me go in it either."

She'd asked her dad what was supposed to go inside, and he'd said, "Any number of things, I hope." Which was annoying. Then he'd shown her how to make Sterno out of the antacids he kept in his desk. The flame was bright and blue and it made her laugh that you could make fire from something that was supposed to stop heartburn.

They stopped at the painted rail fence that marked Haverstone House's yard. Denny lingered, throwing rocks at the Victorian mess. Easter's only landmarked house was red, orange, green, and made her eyes want to puke.

"Hey, does the sky look weird to you?" he asked.

There might be something off about it. Maybe it was a little grayer than usual, a little yellow too, but she didn't want to think about why. It might be remnants of the shuttle, of the astronauts. It was probably a storm like Mr. Pete said. "Nope."

"Huh. Okay. I still don't feel like going home. Last time I failed a test it was no TV for two weeks."

"Why'd you fake your mom's signature, anyway?"

"I don't know. It was dumb, but it seemed easier at the time."

"I could help you if you wanted."

"Wouldn't matter. I still wouldn't get it. I don't mind not getting it, but that's what bugs Pop."

"Yeah." She threw a rock as hard as she could, imagining the side of the house was Tonya's face. It landed loudly, a chip of red paint falling off the shingle, which for some reason cracked Denny up. For a second the hole in her closed and it was almost as good as knocking Tonya's teeth out.

"We should probably go," Denny said when he finally stopped laughing.

"I guess." She'd wanted home right after it happened, but home also meant hundreds of sugar roses, icing stink, sitting in her room, and thinking about smoke trails.

"I want to go to the grove later, if you feel like coming. Maybe you can bring the baby alligator head."

"I'll ask." Betheen wouldn't want her to on a school night. Her dad wouldn't either, because he'd kept her up last night. And something bad had happened, so they'd have to sit and talk, until everybody agreed on the right amount of upset to be.

They walked to the turnoff for their houses. Her insides started humming again and they hummed wrong. She needed to light flash paper on fire, or read something, or throw more rocks. Anything.

"Hey, can I see the patch again?" Denny looked at it for a long time, turning it around and around again before giving it back. "It's awesome. I wish I could draw stuff like that. I bet they would have loved it."

Then he turned and walked to his house.

She wasn't crying, no matter what. Crying would only make the anxious buzz inside her worse.

# Dilation and Paradox

SWEET PALMETTO FRUIT, easy climbing, crunchy-juicy bugs in the moss. Wet hands. Damp claws. Hunger, hunger, hunger. Burning belly pit. Leap to the tree above the sharp grass. Wait. Sit. Run. Dart to the wheel of the hard, cold beast, where the heavy fruit sometimes falls, roll into the shade. Scramble, scramble.

The primate brain doesn't rest, never rests. Its thoughts put bees' wings to shame. Its heart beats as fast, or should beat so. But its pulse is trapped, its thoughts suspended. It moves forward, mid-dart, intent on grabbing a plump grub that squirms and writhes in the wet corner of the truck bed.

The wriggling, twisting grub will fill it up until later, when it can dig its fingers into good, sweet fruit, and lick the juice from its fur. Lick its hands, wet. Wet from the water. Cold and thick and wet, strange water.

The grub is gone. Snatched away hours before by a mockingbird that zipped between stocky palmetto trunks. It doesn't know. It didn't see. In its space, the grub is there, fresh and fat, waiting to be eaten.

It is reaching, stretching, yearning. The sun is different. Light is different. Thick, heavy like water. The grub is gone. Two children have come and gone, poked and prodded at its ears (the softness and size of which it is proud; they are better than its sisters' ears, the best by far), its tail, its eyes—though it did not see. It would have bitten them right smart with its pricker-sharp teeth. Fine teeth.

Ribbons of yellow, brown, and blue course into penny-round eyes; screams of color that mean movement, light. Light and food and smell and sound, all of it. It stares, transfixed. It does not know beauty, but for a second that lasts half the night, the world around it is a flower and rain at once. A flower that is raining. For a second lasting half a night, it watches and forgets that it is hungry, that it has others in the trees waiting (brothers, cousins, the great scarred mother) for palmetto fruit and grubs, for little fingers to pick the nits from soft fur.

The longest time it has forgotten hunger was a stretch of two days when it slipped through a hole in a storehouse. Its claws had been good against bitter rind, its teeth made to pierce. It had chewed, drunk down, and gorged on oranges until its belly rounded and it was too full to run when the box it was in was kicked. Those two days were its most desperate, when hunger was replaced by gluttonous need. Eat everything so no one else could get it. Eat everything in case there would never be food again. Eat everything because there were other mouths, other teeth, other claws, and hunger rendered them savage.

The second turned half a night that it forgets hunger (the world careening all around it in frantic blurs it can't discern) is peaceful. It resumes the search for the long-gone grub, unaware that it is reaching, stretching, yearning, but will never touch.

# 1986: Entropy

NEDDA PRESSED HER face into the crevice where her father's arm met his chest. She was too tall to curl up on him anymore, but she tried to burrow deeper. His graph-paper-checked shirt was better than anything.

"You liked Judy Resnik a lot, didn't you?"

"Yes."

"Do you want to tell me about it?"

Judy Resnik was an engineer. Judy Resnik was shy, but she did what she wanted anyway. She smiled with her teeth in pictures. She was fearless. Or not, maybe not. "No."

"Okay, but you might feel better if you did." His arms tightened around her and she felt him wince. His knuckles were swollen, hands hot, but he patted her back gently. She should let him go or get him aspirin. She wanted to wail, but she saw the lab table underneath his bookshelf, the peg board with all his tools. Crying in a lab didn't feel right. If you broke something or made a mistake, you could get mad, but sad didn't fit. So she talked.

"She had one hundred forty-five hours in orbit and helped design *Discovery*'s arm. She was an electrical engineer." It was like opening a closet door—everything fell out. "Judy Resnik played piano and had a picture of Tom Selleck in her locker." Mr. Pete had a bank of lockers from NASA in his house and she could fit inside them. It was good to be small in an orbiter because there was no extra room in them. Mid-mission, Judy Resnik had held up a sign that said HI DAD. Nedda loved her dad too. She told him about *Challenger*'s insulation, the felt that made it lighter, about how much it could haul, about ceramic tiles. His hand stilled when she stopped talking, like he knew when she was empty.

"That's an awful lot. Do you feel better?"

"I guess." But she didn't. She pulled away and climbed onto the lab table. She wished she'd brought a quilt. "Can't we just blow something up?"

He took down the small metal box filled with flash paper they'd made over the summer. He let her light as many as she wanted, holding each sheet out with a pair of tongs. The flame was bright and felt like everything, like explosions, like Jimmy La Morte, like Tonya's stupid face.

When the room got smoky he tried to open the window, only to pull back in pain.

"You're having a bad hand day."

"More of a bad everything day. It'll pass."

"Are they getting worse?" His silence was answer enough. "Is there anything that makes them better?"

"Not at the moment, but there will be soon. That's not for you to worry about. Dads get old and fall apart. It's what we do."

"I don't want you to fall apart."

"Good news. I don't either, and I don't plan to. But let's talk about something else. What's my Little Twitch been up to?"

The name settled on her like a hug. She was his Little Twitch because she gnawed through pencils, bounced her feet when nervous, and chewed her lip. Because it felt good. Because moving made thoughts work better.

She could tell him about the *C* word, and the weird color of the sky. The monkey. But things happened if you talked to your parents about wild animals that might or might not be dead. Things like animal control and disposal. The monkey was hers and Denny's and it was good that way, something they could keep and figure out, just them. "Nothing."

"Nothing?"

"Does the machine at work have a name yet?"

"It's called Crucible."

She knew the word from *Johnny Tremain*. The machine hadn't seemed like something you'd use to melt metal. She folded her legs on the table and sat on her feet. Staying like that long enough would make them go numb; then they'd flare back to life with buzzing pain. Maybe that's what her dad's hands were like. "Are you going to melt stuff in it?"

"Not precisely. Think of it as a speed machine. I'm speeding up and slowing down entropy. Have we talked about entropy? Heat loss? I'm explaining this badly, aren't I?"

"Yes," she said. Honesty was important in science.

45

He paced the room. She bet he taught classes like this, arms waving as he walked in front of rapt students, stopping when something was important. "Let's say I have a bowl of marbles, half red, half white. Red on one side of the bowl, white on the other. Now, you come along and shake up the bowl. Do those marbles stay divided or do they get mixed up?"

"They mix."

"Right. Entropy is you, shaking up the bowl, that progression of things. Entropy is how things move from order to disorder. It's also one way of thinking about and measuring time."

"Oh."

"Are you with me?"

She tugged at the end of her braid. She didn't want to say no, but she didn't want to lie.

"Try this. Think about how you get hot when you run. No. A better example—stove coils." His arms stayed carefully away from his sides, hands touching only air. "The heat that comes off the coils is energy. It's the same energy that powers the stove. Outlet to plug, through the wires, to the stove circuits, to the coils. The coils heat up, spending the energy. Once it's heat, the energy is big, wide, and disorganized like the marbles you shook up. It's hard, pretty much impossible, to put that energy back how it started. So entropy is moving from that electricity in the system to the heat that's gone out into the air, off the stove coil." He stopped. "Did I make it worse?"

"No?"

"Crucible arranges things. Specifically, it arranges energy. It can disorganize it faster to get a lot of heat from something all at once, instead of a little at a time. It can also organize things. If I can stop something, a system, from getting disorganized, if I can keep it perfect, it's a little like stopping time in the system."

"Why?"

"Okay, back to organization."

"No." She cut him off before he could start in on marbles. "Why would you want to stop time?"

"Ah. Better question." He sat, letting her look down on his hair, the wiry curled mop, thick as his beard and streaked with white. It looked like steel wool. "You're growing up too fast, Little Twitch. Maybe I want to keep you with me longer." He smiled, but it was tight, square. "What if you could stop all the wear on things like bridges? Or make food that lasts twice as long before it goes rotten? A doctor could stop joints from breaking down."

"You want to use it on your hands."

"It might eventually help someone like me. I'm looking for a contained area of effect. And I'm also looking for a patent, so everyone will know you're the smartest daughter of the smartest man in the world." That smile was a good one.

"Have you tried it?"

"The last test shorted out the lab, so it's not quite right yet."

Crucible's door had looked like the hatch on an Apollo capsule, right down to the hinges. She'd wanted to crawl inside. It was stupid to send grown men into space when a girl would be a better fit.

"What happens to them now? The astronauts? Not their bodies, I know that already. I mean who they were."

"I don't know exactly," he said. "No one does. That's part of why people like me and you ask questions and build things. Finding answers to smaller questions gets us closer to answering bigger things."

That didn't help and she told him so.

"I think what's left is our thoughts. They're impulses, signals that bounce back and forth inside our heads, like the energy we talked about earlier. Maybe when we're gone what's left are these signals and impulses, traveling across the universe as heat and light." His shoe tapped out a familiar, comforting rhythm on the floor.

Nedda's foot mimicked his, and this too was a little like a hug. "Do you think they're still out there?"

"They might be."

"Okay." She helped him put away his notebooks, sliding a thin journal onto a shelf.

Betheen's voice echoed down the laundry chute. "Theo? The mixer won't start. Can you flip the breaker?"

Her parents were happiest with stairs and a closed door between them. The laundry chute ran between Theo's lab and the kitchen above, and they used it like a soup-can telephone. Her father yelled up, her mother called down, and Nedda checked the electrical box, running her fingers over fuse labels. If one was blown, he wouldn't be able to replace it today anyway. KIT. OV & OUT. The fuse was fine and the breaker hadn't tripped. She told her father and he shouted up the chute.

"Maybe it's the motor."

"I know what a burned motor smells like, Theo."

Shouting had a way of erasing things, and a way of making things that couldn't be erased want to disappear. Nedda slipped away, balancing on the sides of the stairs to keep the boards from squeaking.

"It's stuck in the outlet you shorted."

"Betheen, it's not a short."

Nedda had to pass through the kitchen to get to her room, which meant back-to-the-wall and edge-of-the-room inching to avoid Betheen's notice. Which she did, until her mother smacked the chute closed.

The fight was done.

Betheen braced a bare foot on the Formica countertop and pulled at the mixer's cord, tugging until her hair shook with the effort, crisp blonde waves vibrating. "He doesn't think about anybody else. He doesn't think. Now the stupid thing is stuck in a dead outlet."

Her mother was fascinating, if a little frightening.

"In here, Nedda," Betheen said. "Hands on the cord." Something fluffy and white was in the mixer, thick and fizzing.

"What was it?"

"Champagne water cake."

"That sounds gross."

"Please, no comments. Just pull."

Nedda groaned anyway. She linked her hands by Betheen's, pinkie touching her mother's thumb. She'd tried champagne on New Year's once; it was bitter and the bubbles hurt your tongue more than soda. Like champagne, her mother's perfume was too much. It was supposed to be magnolias, but mixed with sweat and Aqua-Net, the scent was entirely her own. Nedda had longed for it that morning, but Betheen was someone you missed terribly until she was there.

"On three."

Nedda yanked hard, but the plug didn't budge. She tugged again. No movement.

"Lean into it, for Pete's sake."

"I am," Nedda shouted.

"Don't shout, just lean harder." They tugged and the cord bit their skin. Nedda was sandwiched between Betheen and the counter, her mother's leg wrapped around her, an embrace gone wrong. A laugh bubbled up and she couldn't hold it back.

Then Betheen slipped, kicking Nedda's feet out from under her. For a moment they were flying, rushing to meet the floor, and then they were on top of each other. Nedda sprawled half on the linoleum, half on Betheen, head tucked beneath her mother's chin. The mixer dangled from the counter, suspended by its cord, which was still firmly stuck. That was wrong.

Betheen lay on the floor, looking up at the ceiling. Nedda squirmed, but Betheen grabbed her hand and held it. Her palm was warm and the pulse tickled, softly thrumming the same way the green monkey had. Marmoset. Silver marmoset.

"Wait. Just wait a minute," Betheen said.

"Should I get Dad?"

"What could he do that we haven't tried?"

"Maybe he could flip the breaker, take the outlet from the wall, cut the cord, install a new one." Though not today. Nedda tried to pull her hand away, but her mother squeezed it, skin soft like a quilt and just as stifling. Nedda wanted the heavy gloves her father used when he dealt with electricity. It felt good to hold someone's hand when wearing thick gloves, like they were a mouse and you had to be careful.

"It's fine. I'll mix by hand, or start cookies for the diner instead."

"Okay." Nedda moved to get up, but Betheen tugged her back down.

"Stay? Just for a little while." She squeezed her hand again. "We don't spend enough time on the ground looking up at things."

"Mom, are you okay?"

"Your dad talked to you about what happened?"

Nedda's stomach tightened. "Yes."

"I'm sorry you watched that. There are things people shouldn't see, especially not children."

"I'm not a little kid."

"No, you're not." She squeezed Nedda's hand once more, and then was on her feet, rummaging through cabinets. "It's amazing how quickly time passes. Yesterday you were in baby shoes." She set a stack of bright yellow mixing bowls on the counter. "Let's see what we can make of this mess."

She'd watched the launch too. Betheen had also seen the astronauts die.

Nedda wanted to say something, about light and time, the thing she'd told Mrs. Wheeler. She didn't.

Her mother poured the strange mixture into a new bowl and sprinkled it with powder from a green plastic bag on the counter. The bag had writing all over it in another language. Then whisking, familiar and irritating. *Flittap, flittap, flittap, flittap.* Betheen's forearm was a knot of thin-roped muscle born from bending food to her will.

There was a small skip in the whisking. "Do you want to help me figure this out?"

"What is it?"

"It's water cake, only I'm using champagne, and it's exactly what it sounds like. It looks like a clear bubble but it tastes like whatever you want it to."

"Like Jell-O?"

"No, much better. Champagne and orange extract, maybe Flame Red grapefruit, and it's going to dissolve into nothing. It'll be soft. Imagine setting a stack of raindrops on a table, a table that has slots in it and glasses underneath them, and all the raindrops you don't eat melt into the glasses. Wedding cake you can drink if you want."

It sounded wonderful and impossible. "Cool."

"I think so. I think I can win the Orlando Cake Show with it. Do you want to help? I'll have to do a lot of experimenting."

"Yes," she said.

"Good," Betheen said. Then, softly, "Thank you."

Nedda sensed she was supposed to say something else, but couldn't figure out what.

"I have homework."

"Of course. Go."

Once in her room, she turned out the lights, flopped on the bed, and stared at the sticker stars on the ceiling. They glowed just enough for her to make out the Sea of Tranquility on the puffy moon sticker by her window.

She flipped on her nightstand light and pulled out a notebook, sandwiched between her bed and the wall. Her cursive too messy, she wrote in print.

*Dear Judy,*
*You're gas, carbon, and star parts.*

Her stomach hurt. Gus Grissom had said space was worth it, that the conquest of it was worth your life. And he had died.

Dinner was a quick, uncomfortable silence—thrown-together fried chicken Nedda thought of as "fight cutlets." Pale, dry, and flavorless. Her father argued with absence. Her mother argued with food. Something in the kitchen smelled like seaweed.

Before bed, she turned to a fresh page in her notebook and began a list, titling it *Observations*. It grew from the morning, from the cold, the explosion, the monkey, and the mixer. She underlined the word *monkey* three times. She'd long suspected people had been lying about the monkeys, but she'd seen one, it was real, and she couldn't touch it. She wrote the sky's weird color. She wrote *entropy* with three asterisks next to it and left room for notes. Then *champagne water cake*. She turned the page and wrote the astronauts' names. Seven. Like Friendship 7. Lucky 7. 7UP. 7th Heaven.

She turned back.

*Dear Judy,*
*You're gas, carbon, and star parts. You're light and heat. You're*
*spreading everywhere all at once, like the universe. Nerves aren't*
*as quick as combustion, so I bet it was probably too fast to hurt. If*
*you did hurt, it's okay. Your light will reach the moon. It'll touch*
*the lunar rover and make it less lonely.*
   *Love,*
   *Nedda*

# 1986: The Dogs

THE AIR SMELLED off. Two sniffs told Rebekah La Morte that there was too much dog piss in it. She smelled the dog piss only when it got too hot or the wind really picked up, but it was cold and still. There was something else in the air it too; maybe it was from the space shuttle, but who wanted to think about breathing that in? She hefted a bag of Purina over her shoulder and kicked the screen door open with her flip-flop. The dogs looked off too. Kind of flat. Not that greyhounds ever got a proper flop to them, but a greyhound taking ill was all ribs and bones and looked like a squashed birdcage. Fast dogs, but almost made of glass. One explosion, not even as bad as a thunderstorm, and they were all wrung out. Bad news. That asshole from Sanford was supposed to look at them tomorrow.

"Jimmy, you fed them, right?"

"Yeah, Mom."

"Don't 'Yeah, Mom' me."

"Yes, ma'am. I fed them. Watched them eat too." Her son's voice was high, threatening to crack soon, which made the fact that he was a whiner worse. His dad hadn't seemed the type; he must have gotten it from her side of the family. Her mother could bitch up a storm when needed, but god, did it shame her that her son was a whiner.

"Well, keep an eye out. I've got a buyer coming and the dogs are dragging like they've been through the desert."

The pups were a pile of brindle and brown and they weren't bouncing enough, not like they should be. Rebekah opened up Mama Girl's kennel, a tall chain-link fence box, and watched as the bitch limped out and threw herself on Rebekah's feet.

She'd be tired too if she had six pups. One at a time was more than enough. Rebekah had never been happier than the day Teresa got married and she'd finally gotten her bathroom back. That girl was half mousse and hairspray, and it had been hell on the plumbing. A pipe snake Rebekah made from a coat hanger still hung on a hook in the bathroom. Jimmy didn't care for washing much beyond a washcloth and the kitchen sink, and she wasn't about to push him on it. There weren't enough showers in the world to get rid of the smell of kennel. Especially when some of the kennels weren't cleaned enough. A gargantuan pile of shit sat in the back corner of Mama Girl's kennel, a monument to exactly how Mama Girl felt about her latest litter.

"Jimmy? What did I say about hosing down the kennels?"

Her son didn't answer. There was crashing around in the kitchen, which meant he was fixing himself a sandwich. Well, that was something.

The pups started to yelp, and Rebekah looked up. The sky had a funny yellow color to it, and it smelled like hurricane. That's what it was. Too much water and lightning in the air. It was the wrong time of year for it, but definitely the right sky. If she were running a boat, she'd haul ass back to dry land. No wonder that shuttle blew up. NASA idiots launching the day before a hurricane.

Mama Girl whimpered. Her face had the long hang of a horse.

"All right, then. We're doing this? We're doing this." Rebekah lifted Mama Girl and groaned at the weight.

"Jimmy, get your ass out here and help me bring in the pups. It feels like lightning."

Mama Girl yowled and Rebekah patted her head as she struggled with the door. But the dog kept whining at something in the pond.

The water behind the La Morte house was too small to be called a lake, or even a proper pond. Rebekah liked to think of it as a hole, but the truth was that it wasn't much more than a large puddle from Easter's sewer system. Rather than let its undesirables run into the Indian River, Easter pumped it into the land that butted up against the La Morte backyard. You could call it an *overflow receptacle*, but whatever words you chose didn't make it pretty or smell nice. On most days it buzzed with mosquitos, grasshoppers, and a few dragonflies. As Rebekah looked, she realized what Mama Girl was bothered by. There were clouds rolling off it, and the sawgrass was curling up and rotting. It smelled like boiling weeds. Boiling weeds while it was freezing cold outside. That had governmental bullshit written all over it. Easter Municipal had pumped straight sludge out on the land before, but never anything boiling.

"Jimmy, the phone still out?"

"Yeah."

Time to haul herself down to the mayor's office and raise a little hell. She eyed the sky, that storm-yellow tinge to it. "You're staying home tomorrow."

"I'm gonna need a note, Ma. Mrs. Wheeler says I can't miss any more."

"Fine. I'll talk to her, but you're not going in."

The dog whimpered and she took Mama Girl inside, holding the screen door open as Jimmy stumbled out to the pups.

Her son looked like his father, Eddie Ingram, though no one said it—especially not Eddie, who was married. Eddie still got around with girls from everywhere, even though he was starting to look like salt cod and smell just as bad. But she'd gotten Jimmy out of him at least, and that was the good end of the deal.

Jimmy scooted back in, a puppy snuffling in the crook of his arm. It was one of the runts, the one he called Bats, because the dog's ears stuck out like wings. Kind boys were good with animals. Tough boys could give them away. Kind and tough? That was something. She wished she could let Jimmy keep Bats, but Bats was good money because Mama Girl's blood was strong. That pup would be fast no matter how big he got.

Maybe on Mama's last litter she'd let him keep one and train it, let him raise up a bitch himself, get a little business going on his own. A puppy tried to squirm down her collar, gnawing at the edges with teeth too small to do any more damage to an already-wrecked Van Halen shirt. She shoved two pups in a dog bed below the kitchen sink. Their claws couldn't do much damage to the linoleum, and any pee would wipe right up.

"Ma?"

"What's the matter, Sweet Potato?"

"I think the pond's boiling."

Then, like crying infants, the frogs began to scream, a sound that would stay with Rebekah La Morte until the day she died.

# 1986: Bruise and Tape

THERE WAS A specific scraping that meant Denny was on the trellis. He'd started climbing it the day he'd learned to climb trees. He didn't usually knock, but Nedda had shut the window against the cold. She gaped when she saw him. A mottled bruise stretched from the top of his cheek across the bridge of his nose; his right eye wasn't swollen shut, but it was a near thing.

"Sonofabitch. What happened?"

"Can I come in?"

"Yeah, but be quiet." Downstairs, Betheen rattled pots in the kitchen. They had to be the only family in Easter without a dishwasher. "What happened to your eye?"

"Nothing."

"It doesn't look like nothing." There were darker points at the top by his brow and across his cheek, like the deep mark Betheen's fist left when punching down dough.

"It's no big deal."

"How come you won't say?"

"How come you called Jimmy La Morte a cunt?"

"Fine, don't tell me. I don't care." How had he found out? If she wanted him to, Denny would give Jimmy a black eye as bad as his own. He was allowed to do things she wasn't—punch, kick, make somebody hurt when they deserved it. He would too, if she asked. But suffering Jimmy was easier if she didn't talk about him, didn't think about him.

Denny sat cross-legged on the braided rug, a jumble of bones. "He probably doesn't like you because he got left back and you skipped."

"Yeah, but so did you and you like me."

"Sure. But you're cool, and I know I'm dumb. Jimmy's so dumb he doesn't know he's stupid."

She hated when he said things like that. "You're not dumb."

"Then I'm lazy. Did you ask your dad about the monkey?"

"We talked about other stuff."

"Like what?" He picked at one of the rug loops with fingernails still dirty from the truck.

"What happens after you die."

"Easy," he said. "You go to Heaven or Hell. Unless you're Jewish. Josh Ast said Jews don't believe in Heaven or Hell. I bet they're super surprised when they wind up there. Think how pissed off you'd be, being dead and finding out you're totally wrong."

Judy Resnik was Jewish, and Nedda didn't believe in Heaven or Hell. If her dad was right, people who died were just thoughts traveling like light, continuing. It was sad, but not. Being sure about things, like Denny was, seemed easier. "Do you think there's any juice left in the truck battery at Mr. Pete's? Maybe the monkey got electrocuted."

"I don't know. Car batteries drain if you don't run them and cold isn't good for them either."

The phone had been going in and out all day, so it was startling when the kitchen telephone rang. Sometimes Betheen called Aunt June at night, and they would talk for hours, but no one called after nine. Nedda put her ear to the door. Denny scrambled next to her and bumped his brow on the jamb. Some words were muffled, lost to the stairs.

"No," Betheen said. "You know he's welcome here. Of course. And you told him to? Good. Are you all right?" It wasn't Aunt June. Aunt June had hearing aids the size of conch shells and you could lose your voice talking to her. "No, it's no trouble. Theo won't mind. I'm sure he'll barely notice."

Then the call ended. Denny lay on the floor, pressing his hand to his eye.

"Does it hurt bad?"

"Yeah, but not like getting hit with a hardball." Last spring, he'd been hit in the face with a baseball in gym class. He'd been proud that he could read the ball's stitches across his cheek. This bruise had knuckles.

The worst Nedda had been hurt was a broken pinkie toe when she'd fallen through a rotted board in the treehouse behind Haverstone

House. Denny had helped her limp all the way to his house where his mother had taped her little toe to the others and set her on the couch with a bag of ice. "I'll get ice once Betheen's asleep."

"Maybe we could cut the bruise like they do in *Rocky*. It's supposed to let the blood out and help with swelling."

"My mom would kill me if we got blood on the rug."

"Okay, fine. Hey, can I see your mission patches? You've got pictures too, right?"

"Yeah," she said.

"Our TV's busted and I kind of want to see them again."

"Weird. Our TV is broken too."

"Yeah, and a bunch of our lights won't go on. Pop said NASA must have fried some stuff."

"Maybe." Nedda pulled out her Tupperware of mission patches and spread them out across the rug. Mercury 6's stitched Earth butted up against Gemini 5's Conestoga wagon. Then the Apollos. They traced their fingers over names, through Skylab, Apollo-Suyoz, and the shuttles. Then there were no more patches, just drawings. She touched the apple on 51-L. The stupid apple.

"Do you think it hurt? I bet it was too fast," he said.

It was stupid that anything could explode that quickly. Stupid that a whole ship and everyone inside it could be gone. Boom. "Yeah, it was too fast to hurt."

"Good." He held a patch up to the light. Mercury 6, John Glenn.

The warped board on the second stair creaked. They waited for Betheen to pass, but at the top of the stairs, she slowed.

Nedda shoved him toward the bed. "Hide."

Denny scuttled under and pulled the bedskirt down. Nedda dangled her legs over the mattress.

When Betheen opened the door, there was something tucked under her arm, hidden in shadow. "Nedda, I did the wash this morning. There are fresh towels in the linen closet, sheets too. It's time to change them out."

"Yes, Mom."

Betheen stayed half in, half out of the room.

They'd never been caught. Her father didn't go to bed until the middle of the night, long after Denny was gone. Sometimes she would go down to his office and ask what he was working on and he'd tell her about molecules gliding against one another like dancers, how some dances were close like a waltz, and some were far apart like square dancing.

"All right," Betheen said. She took the package from under her arm and tossed it to Nedda.

Cold burned her fingers. Frozen peas.

"Put it on his eye. It's good for bruises," she said. "Keep it down and don't stay up too late. And don't leave your patches out. You'll lose them. Tomorrow we'll try the champagne water cake, okay?"

Betheen closed the door behind her.

Denny's breath was hot by her heels. "Are we in trouble?"

"No, just put these on your eye." She dropped the bag on the floor and went to grab an armful of sheets and a blanket.

"Bossy," he said, without any bite to it.

She should be in trouble, but Betheen had seemed almost nice. She was weird today. Maybe watching the shuttle had been bad for her too. Nedda gave Denny her second pillow; one always wound up kicked to the floor along with her socks anyway.

"It feels like my eyeball's freezing out of my skull." Denny kept the peas on it.

"Your eye is jelly inside, so it kind of is."

"Cool."

"You can take the bed if you want," she said. "I don't mind the floor. It's better for seeing the ceiling stars."

"Nah. The floor's fine. Wake me up early though, okay? Pop gets pissed if we don't have family breakfast."

"Okay." Desmond Prater had hands as big as baseball mitts and just as tough from years of grove work. The bruise was big enough. "I think they're going to cancel shuttles for a while," she said. "They did after Apollo 1."

"That's lame," Denny said. He tossed the peas at Nedda's arm. "I bet it won't be too long, though. You can't have a space center without space shuttles."

"Right."

"That's the good thing about the grove. It just grows, and people always need oranges."

It was true. Other groves on this part of the Indian River had been bought out by the government when the military and NASA moved in. Prater was the final holdout, surviving three killing frosts and a space boom. Denny was a Prater, leaving no question as to what he'd do. He was lucky that he liked the grove. There was something happy about the way it made your sweat smell like grapefruits.

They poked through the Freddy Krueger issue of *Fangoria*. With glue, paint, and spirit gum she could make the same skin effect, and it would be better than the rubber masks from a store, and next Halloween she and Denny could go as Freddy. This year all the girls in Easter went as cats, cheerleaders, or princesses, and Tricia Villaverde had been a fairy with wings her mother made from plastic wrap. Freddy was better.

"Two Freddys is weird," Denny said.

"So you be Jason." If it was her glue they were going to use, her paint, Nedda figured she could dress however she wanted.

"Jason's dumb."

"Well, it's my glue."

"It's my magazine," he said.

Nedda grinned and whacked his arm with it. "Not while I have it, it's not."

Denny leaned back against the bed. "So what's your dad's machine do? What's it like?"

"It's supposed to speed up or slow down entropy—time, I guess."

He made a noise at the word *entropy*.

"I'll show you. Grab me *E*." The bookcase by her desk was filled with the bright red spines of the encyclopedia Betheen had bought two years earlier. She'd begun to read it when she couldn't sleep, and found that she didn't want to stop. She'd worked backward from *Z* and planned on finishing by the end of the school year.

Denny shoved the volume at Nedda. "You read," he said. "My eye hurts."

And it was easier for her. She sat beside him, book propped on her knees.

The encyclopedia had a version of what her father said, but she had to pause to figure out what to skip and what to explain. She grabbed her notebook and jotted down *thermodynamics,* just in case. At the bottom of the entry was a cross-reference. *See also: Time, Arrow of.* She grabbed *T.*

"It's nice your mom got you an encyclopedia."

"She only got it because I didn't want an Easy-Bake."

"Yeah, but you can get those at the mall. You've got to order an encyclopedia special. I bet it costs more too."

"I guess."

"It's nice she's letting me stay," he said.

*I'm letting you stay,* Nedda thought. She could make him leave. She would never, but she could. She flipped through the volume. It had cost more than an Easy-Bake Oven. The encyclopedia had been too much, an embarrassing present that had the feel of an apology. You were supposed to like your mother. She liked Mrs. Prater. Betheen was just different. She was like a sugar flower, crisp and sweet, but not in a good way.

Her eye landed on a line.

As time progresses, the amount of disorder in a closed system increases, creating imbalance. Study of the imbalance and disorder in a system can be used to distinguish between past and present within that system.

Nedda sucked the end of her braid. Her father had said you'd be unable to tell between past and present in a perfect system.

"Got something?"

"Maybe," she said. "What would you do if you could stop time?"

"That's easy. Go to the fireworks store in Renlo and clean them out without getting caught. By the time anybody figured out it was us, we could have set them all off in the Mauna Kea."

"It'd be cooler if we set them off in the tiki head."

"Yeah, like it was breathing fire. Maybe it'd scare out the rest of the monkeys and they'd start ripping faces off."

"I don't think they do that. That little guy is way too small."

"I guess," Denny said. "But it would be cool if you could rewind time. Anytime you broke something you'd just rewind and it'd be back together again. You could take all sorts of stuff back and nobody would ever know but you, right? *Challenger* could be back together and everybody would be alive again."

What if everything was pieced back together wrong, and people mixed with machine—a twisted mess of flesh, ceramic, and metal? "I don't think it works that way," she said.

"Why not? It could."

"It just doesn't." If you rewound and fast-forwarded a cassette enough the tape got thin or crinkled. A tight hurting spot like a star stuck in her throat, and she wished that Denny hadn't come over at all. Which made her feel bad.

"My eye hurts. I'm gonna close it for a while." He pulled his blanket up over his shoulders, nesting on the floor. "Can you pull your window shade down? It's really bright out."

It *was* bright. More sunset than full night, and the wrong color for January. She shivered and yanked down the shade. Cold came from everywhere; the roof, the windows, even leaking up through the floor, though cold wasn't supposed to work that way. Winter wasn't supposed to be like that here either. You weren't supposed to want to sleep in a sweater, and it was rarely necessary to turn the heat on, but all month, everywhere had smelled like burning dust on radiators.

"My dad says you could use the machine to power deep space probes and stuff, but I'm pretty sure he wants to use it on his hands. He wants to make them better, or at least keep them from getting worse."

"That's cool," Denny said. He'd never been frightened by her father's hands, or the plaques when they were bad. He pressed the good side of his face into the pillow. "If the monkey isn't dead, you can have it. I'll give you the parrot cage."

"Thanks." She slipped the encyclopedias back into their slots.

Some nights she stared at the sagging edge of her sticker moon and wished on it—for bunk beds, for a brother she could share a room with. Maybe wishing on a sticker moon meant your best friend wound up on your floor with a black eye. Maybe it was like losing count before the two-minute mark.

She stared up and tried to pretend her ceiling stars were real, but she kept thinking of a cassette tape, pausing, rewinding, fast-forwarding, the tape stretching and thinning until it broke.

# Aboard *Chawla*

EVGENI USED THE magnetic straps to lock himself to Nedda's cabin wall, which gave him the odd appearance of sitting. The text on his reader was enlarged to the point where people on the ISS could probably read it.

"There is no excuse for the power spikes," he said. "This isn't new technology. An issue like this should have been fixed in prototype decades ago."

"Shoddy craftsmanship, cost cutting. We shouldn't even be on *Chawla*, we should be on a ship that has gravity and can take its sweet time getting there. Things change when you're rushed. Things go wrong," Nedda said. A ship with gravity would have helped their bodies hold up. Would have given them more years to establish crops on board. But the colony mission had a timeline: boots on planet by the end of the decade. Droughts, wildfires, and Manila sinking had served only to increase that pressure. Climate change had at last caught and surpassed the rate of technological advances.

"There. Tell me what that says." Evgeni tapped at a word.

"'Strontium.'"

He said something foul in Russian and smacked his leg. The force popped one strap free from the wall, leaving him struggling like an upended turtle. "It is supposed to be plutonium."

Strontium was cheaper, easily available, but not what Amadeus was calibrated to work with. The radiation output, the heat, would be different. "Do we know how much we're running on?"

"Going by mass, a similar amount. It shouldn't have made a difference in getting there."

"But it will once we're on ground." When *Chawla* would be their home, when the life support systems would be most crucial, when they were building their first colony structures.

"Exactly."

"So what do the power spikes mean?"

"Possibly nothing, possibly that our life support system will shut down in deep space. One or the other."

"Shit." She rubbed her eyes, though it made nothing clearer. It bore the hallmark of a classic American "efficiency" scam, but a strontium swap had a certain Eastern European feel to it. "So was it your government or mine?"

"That doesn't factor now. We don't belong to either of them anymore. We're a government of four people, which makes us effective. This is a mechanical problem. We. Can. *Fix*. Things." He jabbed her shoulder.

"I'll run numbers with Amit and see if we can figure out a model."

Marcanta stuck her head in. "Hey, Papas. Just double-checking. Anything special I should know about Hydro while you're out?"

"It's all in the lab books," she said. "But maybe keep an eye on the oat grass. I tweaked the nitrogen levels two weeks ago." Grasses and grains required land, tolerant soil. Oat grass was a hope crop. Wishful botany.

"You, Vodka Veins, out of here. Time to put the old lady to sleep," Marcanta said.

"You tease because you can't live without me," Evgeni said as he pulled himself into the corridor.

"Only because you keep the ventilation system going."

Nedda strapped into the sleep sack and inflated the inside. "You don't have to tuck me in, you know. But thanks."

"I know. I just wouldn't want him talking my ear off about failing life support systems right before I went to sleep. Singh will crunch numbers, Evgeni will work the logistics of a fix, and I'll make sure we don't die from our own mutated bacteria in the meantime. Oh. And fix our eyes. Easy as pie. Nothing to worry about."

"Your bedside manner is amazing."

"I know; I'm a born healer. Keep your legs straight. We don't want your veins cramping up. There you go."

The sleep sack moved body fluids from the extremities back to the center. At first the pressure was like crawling ants, but gradually the rhythmic pulsing had become as necessary to sleep as darkness. Sadly, it did little for sight. Evgeni's vision loss was ahead of the curve, but Nedda had noticed a significant softening in her own world. The pressure suits, contacts, goggles, and sleep sacks were supposed to help, but the progressive astigmatism continued.

"When I'm up again, test my eyes, okay?"

"Sure thing."

Sleep weeks were to slow vision loss and ease the passage of time, making a five-year trip feel like half that. Crew morale was supposed to benefit from them; less time awake with your crewmates meant less time to learn to dislike them, and less time to look out into the blackness of space, dissociating, dislocating.

"Feel like getting knocked out to anything special?"

Marcanta was good at little mothering touches, the sort of thing Nedda could never get a proper grasp on. "Yeah, actually. Do you think anyone can dig up the Beach Boys?" They were far too old for Marcanta's music stash, far too old even for Nedda, but she wanted them nonetheless.

"I doubt I have it, but I bet I know who does. Evgeni loves weird stuff. I'll be back."

*Weird stuff.* Marcanta's insult didn't wound, perhaps because she smiled and seemed to mean it. Perhaps because she smiled with her teeth.

Marcanta returned a few minutes later and snapped a small black chip into the screen in Nedda's cabin. "You're good to go. Need anything else?"

"You're being too nice to me. Do you need something?"

"You're my backup; I should be nice to you, right? Also, I'm probably going to kill the oat grass."

"It's not that."

"I get how you feel about the sleeping. The control thing. I thought I'd make it easier."

"Thanks. Would you mind porting me in? I always bruise myself."

"You do me next time. You need to learn anyway." Somehow Marcanta's hands hadn't dried out. Her fingers were delicate, light, and Nedda barely felt it when her arm was hooked into the forced IV drip. "Sweet dreams."

"Good night, Louisa." Nedda closed her eyes. "Play *Pet Sounds*."

After an instant of shuffling, the familiar harmony started, humming through each chamber of her heart. *Wouldn't it be nice?*

NASA was aware that she'd prefer not to sleep. She told Dr. Stein that she'd already missed enough time; any more was terrifying. Dr. Stein suggested that knowing a time lapse was coming might lessen the fear.

"I'm missing more of my life," Nedda had told her. There was no way to explain what that loss was, the ache of it, or the anger when someone said they understood, someone who couldn't begin to know. Dr. Stein frustrated her; her voice, her smooth features, that her age was hard to pin down—all of these things made Nedda hate her.

Dr. Stein had said, "Are you missing it or is your life simply not as linear as you expected?"

"Why do you ask questions that answer themselves?"

"Because you refuse to ask them."

"You're paid a lot of money to pick us apart."

"Yes, I am."

"I'll have to do the sleep cycles, won't I?"

"Yes."

She slept when scheduled, but refused to pretend she enjoyed it, that it was helpful, or that it did anything to affect crew relationships or anxiety. Science required her to submit to sleep weeks. She was a sample in a study and conditions must be the same across the study; others slept, so she had to sleep.

A low-dose paralytic. A hypnotic. A tranquilizer. Liquid nutrition.


The speakers in Nedda's cabin hummed with the Beach Boys, while the tranquilizer gently eased her terror of losing time. Time was the reason behind everything, another subject she could not mention to Dr. Stein. Then the hypnotic mixed with the paralytic, leaving her floating, disembodied, and lost.

She dreamed and rebuilt the town she missed, the places she remembered, and what happened in between. As a child, she'd twisted embroidery floss around toothpicks, making something called a God's

Eye. The winding was to keep children quiet and calm. Forced dreams wound like that thread.

From above, she looked on a miniature town consumed by kudzu. Matchstick roads leading to Easter from Mims, from Titusville, vanished into forest. It left her uneasy. She neared the ground, traveling over whispers, bumping against the soundwaves of a trucker telling a friend he'd called into the McIntyre shop in Easter for a tow, but no one answered; voices from inland about dropped orders; from Gainesville about how no one had heard from Great-Aunt Ginny in a while.

"Galaxy cake," said an older voice, thin, dry. "Coconut, marshmallows, and lemon, with silver stars. You could only get it at the Bird's Eye in Easter. Have you been there?"

"Lord, it's been forever."

"Can't remember when I last got down that way."

"Yes, Ginny's not real fond of people. I assume she got a bee in her bonnet about something. She'll call when she's ready."

"I had to switch suppliers. Prater keeps missing shipments and won't pick up the phone."

Her eye descended on a house, a small, garishly colored Victorian, and two children, no bigger than pill bugs, walking by it.

She witnessed the town's concealment from the world, how they'd been swallowed, roads consumed by vines, blacktop buckling, shaken from below by vegetation reclaiming what had once belonged to it. She wanted to smell the oranges, but her dream did not allow it.

She tried to close her eyes against the years of hurricanes and cars finding new ways around her little town. Trucks followed roads, unwinding like string.

It was easy to be forgotten.

# 1986: Dawning

**T**HEO FLICKED ON the Geiger counter and listened to the clicks of background radiation in the room. It was the simplest and easiest safety precaution. The radioactive samples he used in Crucible were stored in a lined canister, which he kept inside a small refrigerator. The refrigerator did nothing to prevent radiation leaks, but it appeased the facilities manager, who'd somehow gotten the idea that isotopes could "go bad." Theo took a few laps around the room, noting readings, then suited up. It was ironic that the medical supply company from which he got the endless skin treatments that were likely poisoning him also provided the lead-lined vest and gloves he wore to keep from poisoning himself. The cesium-137 sample was a single microcurie, diluted in water, easily transported in a perfect little jar the shape of one of Betheen's flour canisters. Sealed. As safe as something radioactive could be.

The Geiger counter cackled and sang like a dolphin when he took a reading from the sample. Again, within normal. The noise excited something inside him, a hum of life. He noted the room readings again once the sample was safe behind the flanged door in the drum at the center of Crucible.

The halls were silent. They should be at six in the morning, but the quiet gave him the feeling of being the sole person alive, that his was the only light on, and he and Crucible were alone. On a practical level, working early meant fewer people using equipment, and less of a chance to short the building. Again.

He ignored the twinge from his hand and flipped the switch.

The wonder of watching his machine come to life was something he'd never been able to explain properly. He'd had a moment or two with Liebowitz, when they'd seen satellites launch, but that hadn't been their work specifically; the thrill was muted.

The legs on the machine began spinning, like a dancer's skirt. Slowly, then gaining speed, pushing air across the lab, through his hair.

A cold breeze. He noted the time, jotted observations. A two-degree drop in temperature. Then there came light.

He thought, at first, that it was leaking through the seal on the door in Crucible's drum, but it grew, coming not from the inside of the drum but the drum itself. The metal radiated light, birthing photons. He wrote as quickly as his hands let him, marking the light's quality— *lemonlike, clear*—distinctly unscientific, but descriptors that might help direct him later. The tick in his heart sped up. Six fifteen A.M. The legs too were glowing. He had the sudden vision of a pumpkin turning into a carriage, dullness becoming light and wonder. Crucible spun and blurred in his vision, a burning beacon.

"I know you think your projects are your children," Betheen once said. But that wasn't it. She should know. He'd walked by her strange experiment this morning, a bowl of what looked like surgical jelly she was determined to make into something. Betheen should understand how he felt, what he felt.

His projects weren't children; they were pieces of his mind made physical. An idea he'd torn at for years was whole, and spinning before him, weaving light.

God, but it was beautiful, and he'd made it.

At six seventeen A.M. he flipped the switch again and watched the legs begin to slow, the light ebb. The frame had withstood the force and hadn't shifted. He hadn't shorted the building.

When the legs slowed to a stop, he opened the drum's door, placed a probe inside, and listened to the Geiger counter. The clicks were a slow, clean rhythm.

He forced himself to focus on the numbers, not what it meant or what it might mean. Data first, study and theory later.

The cesium's rate of decay had slowed. He checked the readings twice, three times. He jotted them down again, rechecked, wrote them down once more—his hand was shaking too badly to write clearly—and whooped.

Theo hadn't whooped before. He'd never had cause to. At his wedding he'd been too concerned about responsibilities; at Nedda's birth he'd been too scared to drop her. He'd never had a moment of joy that had been solely his. He bit back the noise, forcing it inside, until he vibrated with it. He'd tell his department head later. After more tests. A repeat performance. He'd tell Betheen tonight, over dinner. He'd call Liebowitz. Liebowitz would have suggestions for other tests, would hammer the idea into his head that it was a fluke, and if it wasn't a fluke, it would demand thorough testing. It was essential to have people to poke holes in your theories, in your advancements. But oh.

A giggle slipped out. And yes, he was trembling. *Ah, Papas, you bastard, you did something good.*

It worked. He pounded his hands against his thighs, the pain sharp, clear, making it real. Joyfully real.

It was preliminary. He'd have to replicate it with other samples. Test the change in the cesium sample over hours, days. He shuffled around, returning the jar to the lead-lined canister, then the refrigerator. He ran the Geiger counter in and around the machine for trace radiation. None. Perfectly contained.

It worked.

He closed his eyes and let the weight of the lead vest hold him to the chair. Good weight. The shadow of Crucible's bright whirling still burned in his eye. He skipped over imagining trials with other isotopes, repeat trials, different samples, the endless documentation and grant requests to follow, patents. He thought of knees that never wore down, hands that never hurt, minds that did not tie themselves in knots with age. And if those thoughts had a lemon-yellow color to them, a clear light, it was natural.

Theo's heart smacked as if to escape, dancing in a way his body did not let him. Inventions were not like your children. Your children were all your flaws shown to you in a way that made you love them: your worst made good. Inventions were your best attempt at beautiful thought. They were objective; they worked or they did not. They had purpose, whether they achieved it or not. They were yours always, in that they did not leave you, or turn away.

It worked.

Theo's laughter echoed down an empty hallway.

# 1986: Grove and Light

S HE WOKE TO Denny's face inches from hers, light from the window glinting in his good eye.

"Are you up?"

"I am now." Her Dream Machine's blue numbers showed 5:15. Why was it so bright out?

"I need to go to the grove. Do you want to come?"

Her brain was like the inside of a pillow. Hadn't he gone yesterday? His shoes were already on. Maybe he'd fallen asleep without taking them off. "I thought you wanted to be home for breakfast."

"There's a thing I busted and I need to fix it," he said. "Will you come with me?"

"You broke something at the grove?"

"Yeah. I can fix it, though."

At six, Betheen would be awake, cracking and whipping whatever needed to go in the oven today.

"Can we go later? I bet Betheen's going to make cake batter pancakes." Nedda had eaten too many cake batter pancakes to like them anymore, but Denny would love them.

"I really want to fix it. I woke up early and I thought about it and I'm pretty sure I can, but I need help. Please come?" He worried his lip against his broken tooth.

"What'd you break?"

"One of my dad's machines. If I wait until after school, he's not gonna let me in the shed, and he'll have one of the Mikes fix it and—I need to fix it. Don't you want to help me take something apart?"

She knew he would go without her. If she said no, he'd wait until she went to the bathroom, then climb out the window. But he didn't want to be alone and neither did she. Nor did she want to miss seeing the inside of whatever it was.

"What if you break it worse?" She pulled her shoes from under the bed.

"I won't. You'll be there."


She got her bike. Denny's was below her bedroom window, leaning against the trellis, cushioned by climbing bougainvillea. The moon shared the sky with the sun, dipping low—a moon Judy Resnik would have liked, one to navigate by. How fast did thoughts travel? If they moved faster than light, they'd have reached the moon almost as soon as the explosion happened. Maybe they were gliding across craters, sailing over dry seas. It was strange for the sun to rise so early in winter. But maybe that's what explosions did, made the air bend light differently. It hadn't been fully dark at night either.

There were no cars the entire two miles east on Acacia Lane or when they turned onto Orange Way, which led to the grove. She pedaled hard enough to power her small headlight, which lit up Denny's reflectors. His headlight was bulky and ran on batteries. Hers was better; her dad made it and it was brighter than any other generator headlight she'd seen. It almost made up for the banana seat. Her lungs hurt—Denny pedaled fast and never checked to see if she kept up. He knew she was there.

At the grove's gravel entrance, Denny tossed his bike and started climbing the fence.

That's when she saw the glow hanging over the trees. That wasn't the word for it, but she couldn't think of what was. The light looked stuck to the trees, or like it came from them, and it was a sick-looking yellow-green. Above the glow was the haze of sprinklers, rain in slow motion.

"Come on," Denny said.

She wanted to stop, but Denny was over the fence and running. She caught her pants on one of the links, tearing a hole in the back, the kind of hole that mending would make a keloid of stitches.

"This way," he said, and took off for the equipment shed, his shoes kicking up a dust cloud.

It wasn't as much a shed as it was a giant metal barn that could house an airplane, but instead stored the grove's larger machinery—trunk shakers, spraying rigs, and things Nedda didn't know the names of. When she reached him, Denny was pulling at the door, using his full body weight to slide it open across a rail made rough by rust.

"Can you get in? Feel around. There's a light switch on the left side. Maybe if you push from the inside it'll open."

She was thinner than Denny, an accident of frame, something from her mother's side. Betheen was willowy. Polite people called Nedda wiry; to everyone else, she was scrawny. Tiffany and Vicky were already pushing toward the promise of boobs. Nedda had dents—dents were perfect for fitting through cracked-open doors. Hand against metal, she searched for the switch. Space walks must feel like that, reaching into nothing, stretching into dark.

The lights went on in the back of the shed first and rolled forward. Hiccupping electric clicks revealed the silhouettes of tractors, shakers, and large-bladed things.

When the door squealed open another two inches, Denny jammed himself through. He went to a pug-nosed machine, a tractor-like thing with a flat front. Tucked up against its side were four circular saw blades that attached to what looked like a folding arm.

It looked like the cargo arm on *Challenger*. *Canadarm*, because it was made in Canada. *Canadarm*, because it said CANADA across it in huge letters. *Canadarm. Canadarm.* She pinched herself to stop thinking the word.

"That's the thing you broke?"

"I wasn't even doing anything," he said.

"Suuuure you weren't."

He popped the hood open with a hollow *thump*, then stuck his arm deep inside. She would have checked for fan blades, sharp things, but Denny always moved like nothing could possibly hurt him.

"What's it do?"

"It's a pruner. It hacks off the tops of trees to keep them from growing too close. I guess you could make hedges with it too. Maybe you do that with kumquats. Ever see a kumquat tree? Kumquat. *Kumm*-kwatt. Kum-*kwatt*."

She laughed, but couldn't shake her nervousness. "How long do you need?"

"I dunno. A little while, I guess."

"When does your dad come in?"

"It depends," he said. "But he always goes to the office first. We'll hear the truck."

"Okay."

The doorway leaked light from the trees. Yellow like citrus, like limes and oranges, grapefruits. A sour kind of light. She peered through the door at the trees again. They were wrong somehow. Almost moving.

A hissing sound came from near Denny's arm. "Can you come here? I need a hand."

The pruner's insides looked like the workings of any car to her—black and oily with a velvety coat of dirt—nothing like the shiny clean things her father built. She grabbed the network of hoses and lines Denny pointed to. Battery cable, a radiator hose, and the rest she didn't know. "How'd you break it?"

A smear of grease on Denny's cheek blended with the dark edge of the bruise. "I didn't. It stopped when I was on it. I didn't do anything different from normal. I know how to drive it."

She believed him. In the summer, he'd taken her out on a tractor, riding it up and down the narrow rows. Lumbering, bumpy. But she'd felt safe.

"Mom wasn't there when I got home from school yesterday, so I came here. Little Mike taught me how to drive it a while back. He shows me how to run stuff sometimes." Little Mike was one of the grove's workers. He wasn't much taller than Nedda, square, and sun browned. There was a Big Mike too. "The door was open, but nobody was in here. I just wanted to make the arm run, swing around at a few things. It's got a separate gear shifter and there's not a lot of stuff you can run with two shifters at once. I wanted to get the blades going a little, because it sounds good. It makes this *whhrrrrrrr*, and it's like a chainsaw but when it goes through trees it's like a lawn mower. I wasn't going to cut any of the trees, I just wanted to swing it around. I got out to the west gate and I was trying to get the arm going, but the gears are sticky. I rolled into a puddle one of the sprayers left, and the whole thing seized up and wouldn't go anywhere. That's when Pop's truck pulled in."

"What'd he do?"

"He hitched it to the pickup to get it back here."

She wanted to ask, to see if he'd say that Pop hit him. But it was the kind of question you couldn't take back.

"Jimmy La Morte shot spitballs at me during the launch. That's why I called him that."

Denny stopped moving. "I can spit in Jimmy's lunch. It'll look like an accident."

"No, that's okay."

"The pruner cost a lot of money," he said and tossed two bolts onto the seat. "And Pop was already in a bad mood about the frost. If I can fix it, it won't be so bad. I know I can. I'm not sure why it stopped. The oil's okay. It's got gas and the battery's good. I thought it had to be the battery because of the cold, right?"

"Cold is bad on rubber too."

He almost smiled. "Yeah, it could be that. Maybe it's a hose line. There are a bunch of hoses on hooks in the back. Can you grab me some? And a knife. There's one in the middle drawer of the red tool cabinet."

Nedda walked deep into the shed, weaving between machines. How were you supposed to not want to take them out, to make them do whatever you wanted, to feel big? Shadows of the vehicles loomed like dinosaur skeletons in a museum, menacing for what they could have been when they were alive, when they were running. She looked for Pop Prater in all those dark places.

She found the hose coils and hefted them off the hook with both arms. "Hey, Den?"

"Yeah?" He looked up from the pruner.

A sputtering sound like fireworks came from the nearest trees as a line of sprinklers turned on, and with it came a shot of light that fell across Denny, a brilliant green-yellow flooding the open door, heavier, thicker than sprinkler mist. Nedda ducked behind a tractor. Denny turned to look, mouth open. His hair blew back.

It was pretty hair, she thought, and then the light devoured him in a flash, blinding her.

Fierce cold froze the snot in her nose and the words in her mouth. A slick of ice brushed her skin—not wet, not dry—cold and glass-like.

She screamed, but the sound was swallowed by light. Breath, her breath was gone, until it crashed back in, gasping, as though she'd never breathed before.

The cold receded as quickly as it had come, leaving in its place a ringing in her ears, and darkness.

Her vision returned as blinking dots, blue and purple ringed by white. Retinal burn. She knew that eyes could get sunburned—that's what snow blindness was. "Denny?"

He didn't answer.

She inched toward him, using the machines for balance, feeling her way. There was the trunk shaker with its wide catch. The table with a toolbox. She called his name. The closer she got to him, the hotter the shed was. Why wasn't he answering? He wouldn't have run. He'd never left her. Not ever. Not when the wheel had come off her bike on the way to the gator park, not even when she'd gotten sick at the lunch table and thrown up on Melissa Simm's red Esprit sweatshirt. There were moths inside her, under her ribs. Or dragonflies. Somehow dragonflies had gotten inside her.

He was still there, sitting on the pruner, looking back, and yet he wasn't. His hands looked larger, his arms looked stretched—thinner. In front of her he was changing. All she could think of was Plastic Man, and how he stretched, but Plastic Man was silly and awful. Denny just looked wrong. His eyes looked wrong. Blurry.

"Denny?"

His mouth blurred too. Had he said something?

There was a wave of heat. With it, he changed.

Denny's arms moved too quickly to see; he raced and blurred like sped-up film. Dents appeared in the pruner's hood. He was beating and kicking it. The air got hotter and hotter. Denny's hair looked longer, unkempt. It began to cover his face, curling and tangling. Then he was a blur, moving too quickly to see. When he next stilled, he was sitting on the ground, back against the pruner. A bald patch was above one of his ears, pale and red, and a soft-looking curl of hair poked from his fist. There was a spit of cold air, and it seemed to radiate from him.

She shouted his name. The second he looked back, something pulled her, a tight string around her middle, around her heart, the empty place that was inside and out of her. The cold broke into heat, and he was once more a blur.

The pruner never moved, never shifted, but it began to rust. Paint bubbled and peeled in long orange stripes then cracked and flaked to the ground, exposing red-brown metal beneath. Months. It should take months outside for something to rust like that.

When Denny next stilled he was taller, thinner. Denny and not.

She ran for him, but something stopped her. Her hands and feet hit something, not a wall, not as hard, but something warm, with a slick kind of give, slippery as one of Betheen's blouses. Like a jellyfish, she thought. A clear baby jellyfish. She leaned in, only to be pushed back.

A bubble trapped Denny inside, like the one around the monkey. But the monkey had been calm, still enough to be frozen. Denny was not.

"Put your hands against it," she shouted. "Feel around!" People who got trapped under ice had to feel along the underside until they found the hole they'd fallen through, eyes closed so they wouldn't freeze. She felt around, but found a seamless wall.

Denny wasn't searching on his side; he was kicking the pruner. Then heat rose and he blurred again. New dents took shape, more paint fell, and a pile accumulated where he'd stood. When he stilled again she knew what was happening. Too fast. He was moving too fast. And the Denny she was looking at was older than he should be.

There were marks on him, cuts that had healed and scarred. His shoes had holes in the toes. His eyes were hungry and lost. There was something animal about him that made her think of bears in zoos, who paced and licked their fur bald in patches. She didn't know this Denny. This was not Denny in the shed with her. He was gone.

Pop would come by. He'd find them. Did it even matter? She hadn't done this. Denny hadn't done this. Her stomach hiccupped. Fear was vinegar in her mouth, startling, nearly painful.

"I'll help," she said. "I'll get help." Could he even hear?

There was a back door to the shed, and she ran to it. She wasn't leaving him—leaving wasn't leaving as long as you knew you were coming back. She'd come back. What if it happened again? What if the sprinklers went on again and there was another light and she got stuck, like Denny? Like the monkey? Stretching and pulling herself apart.

Nedda ran for her bike. The clacking beads on her spokes were explosions in the damp. She should have stopped him from going. She wanted to see how things worked. She hadn't wanted to be alone.

She rubbed her eyes, and her jacket sleeve came away soaked with tears and snot. No good. She had to see to ride.

She needed her father.

She'd been taught that fear was worry that something bad would happen to you. It wasn't. Fear was something horrible happening to someone you love, someone you need, and you being left alone.

# Aboard *Chawla*

**N**EDDA'S DREAM EYE kept traveling as she slept, searching for all the things she missed: the town, the buildings inside it, the houses, rooms, and people, like dolls, whose hearts she knew. The seismic hiccup of the launch rolled through her. She saw glasses break at the Bird's Eye, and Ellery Rees sweeping up a shattered sundae dish. The gators at Jonny's Jungle World sank into their ponds like beans in soup, hugging the murk at the bottom. Then the surge from Crucible ran through her like an electric shock, hot and cold at once. Strong. It coursed through power lines, the lines to the college, the wires in the walls, through the outlets in the labs. It pulsed across a gold-plated switch, shattering a glass divider beneath it.

Light spilled from Crucible, infrared and ultraviolet, escaping everything meant to contain it. Her father's machine was as much hope and wish as it was metal and glass.

The anomaly moved like a stream of water, almost vitreous in appearance. It was time made liquid, nearly solid. The first gelatinous droplets of it traveled in the power lines, pulled along by electricity, spreading through the sciences building and beyond. Around the lines there was a subtle distortion, warping the world the way water bent light. She followed its progression, watching Easter shift, building by building. The powerline between the telephone pole on Latchee Street and Pete McIntyre's backyard was frayed, the result of his longstanding lax relationship with Florida Power & Light, and time dripped slowly down from the wire into the bed of a truck in his backyard. The drops collected, each a clear, shimmering universe in miniature. Solid raindrops like Betheen's champagne cake.

It reached the pumping station, where it met water, the pipes that ran through Easter, the sprinkler systems, the lakes and canals. Though it was decades before Liberati and Maccione would suggest a liquid spacetime, in Easter, atop an aquifer, surrounded by canals and irrigation, time had found a perfect home.

In the water lines the anomaly expanded, wending through the town, and eventually into the irrigation system that misted Prater Citrus, the last holdout grove.

*Don't look.*

The sprayers in the southeast corner spluttered rainbows over trees. A net of time cobwebbed into a translucent dome. It was beautiful and broke her heart. Droplets clung to one another, to the trees, binding to leaves, caressing Flame Red grapefruits' dappled skins, settling into the pores on the pineapple oranges.

Fruits shriveled and rotted, limbs fell and grew anew. Trees decayed and sprouted as she watched.

*Wake up, Nedda. GET UP.*

A figure moved in the south grove, standing outside. She looked closer. Little Mike Costas, watching fruit on craggy limbs shrink back to blossoms, watching trees grow slimmer, straighter, reverting to graft cultivars and root stock that disappeared into the ground.

His thoughts became hers.

He checked his pulse, convinced he was having a stroke. His mother, Yosie, had suffered one at the age of forty-five. She'd known it was happening only when the porch swing began singing to her in English. A lifetime spent stewing in heat and humidity could boil the water off the blood until it clumped like old honey. Little Mike had been poaching himself in the Prater groves since he was fourteen. After an hour or so, he figured a stroke would have already killed him. Whatever was happening was frightening. He walked to the management office, picked up the phone, and dialed Desmond Prater. A man should know when his grove was dying.

Then he was gone, and Nedda was left watching trees die.

She sang to herself softly, watching vines grow, roads buckle, waiting, waiting for Marcanta to wake her up. *Wouldn't it be nice?*

She wouldn't look at the equipment shed.

*Marcanta, wake me up.*


The headache from a sleep week was of hangover proportions, the kind earned from drinking ten different types of alcohol all poured into a cooler—what people used to call swamp juice. Typically, they gave each other grace periods emerging from sleep. But Singh was there.

"Get Marcanta to pump you full of saline. I'll be in navigation."

Nedda croaked. She stuck her finger in the printer, waited for it to spit out Dramamine. It chirped and crunched before burping out the usual pill plus something else. She checked the readout. *Acetazolamide.* She swiped at the screen until it became clear: The printer had determined she required old-world glaucoma treatment.

Marcanta did her eye test during the saline drip.

"Did you put us all on diuretics now, or am I just lucky because I'm a throwback?"

"What?" Marcanta slipped, nearly tugging the line out of Nedda's port.

"I got new meds this morning."

"Shit," Marcanta said. "It must be all the data piling up from the tests. The printer is running backup. If I miss something in bloodwork, the printer catches it and doses precautionary meds. Keep checking new pills with me, okay? We'll learn that I'm an asshole who misses things, but we'll all be healthier." She tapped at her tablet. "Acetazolamide? That's seriously old-school. I wonder if that's just you or if it's all of us."

"Do you want me to take them?"

"For this cycle, yeah. It's worth a shot. Who knows? We'll watch." She didn't sound optimistic, but that was part of what was good about Louisa. She didn't deal in false hope. She was figuring things out with everyone else.

Nedda found Amit staring at a data panel. Soft green numbers flicked across the glass. He rubbed his eyes. It felt wrong that she couldn't see blindness, that her crewmates would look the same as they changed from the inside out. Amit's eyes were the same brown, almost black, they'd always been, the skin below them soft-looking, delicate.

"Hey. Look at this," he said, pulling up a file. "The spikes are at regular intervals. Here, here, and here. The energy that's generated is—it's like strontium on steroids. I don't have a better way to say it."

She pulled closer, hooking her foot on a rung. At the base of Amit's skull was a dark whorl of hair like a hurricane. "Is there any kind of rebound?"

"No. It goes right back to the half-life we should have been getting with accelerated strontium."

"You've done it already, I take it."

"What do you mean?"

"I know you've done the math."

Singh turned away from the screen. He looked at the tip of her nose, not her eyes.

"Normally, without accelerated burn, we'd get about eighty-eight years of power for life support from plutonium-238 and around twenty-nine years from strontium-90. So an isotope fuel swap shouldn't have been a problem. If Amadeus was working properly, even with strontium, we would have had years on planet with life support in the module before the generator gave out. More than enough time to set up other reserves to take care of ourselves."

"Or already be dead from something else."

Singh didn't acknowledge that. "Amadeus wasn't calibrated for strontium, hence the power spikes. With Amadeus's current malfunction, the half-life decreases significantly. If we do nothing and it sticks to this pattern, we can expect life support systems to give out about six months short of when we reach planet."

"There's no turning back for Mars, or a rendezvous, is there?"

"We're too far out. Even if a rendezvous could be arranged, the prep time for a mission like that, not to mention the travel . . . There's not enough time."

"We'd be stranded and still on the same timeline," Nedda said. It was the worst of all possible outcomes, worse than dying on planet. They'd never get there. "Why do you think they swapped plutonium for strontium?"

"Evgeni thinks it's part of a bidding war for more Euro colonist spots on *Fortitude*. Russia is still the biggest strontium supplier, and he who supplies the fuel has more clout when claiming beds on *Fortitude*. If the Euro government proves it can supply the fuel more cheaply than the Americas, they gain control." *Fortitude* was in a hangar back on the moon. Its living quarters were in a spinning drum that generated low artificial gravity. Gravity that would save skin, organs, sight. The collapse of British Sterling had set its build back another five years. Cities were sinking, and fast. One day, *Fortitude* would bring colonists—but they'd be *Chawla's* replacements. Settlers. It would be foolish to not consider that there would also be a land grab.

"Cheaper fuel makes sense if the money gets used for other upgrades. But as far as I know there haven't been any major changes to *Chawla's* original design."

"My guess is the fuel switch isn't about us. It's about *Fortitude* and after. It may even have been approved by the mission directors and higher-ups. If we die, it's a windfall for one government because it proves the other can't be trusted as a fuel supplier. If we don't die, it's a windfall for the other because we can travel more cheaply and efficiently. Marcanta thinks the Americas are betting on failure. If it goes wrong, they cut out the Euro fuel suppliers, and future colonization will be run by your government."

Nedda squeezed his shoulder. "Doesn't matter for us, does it?"

"No."

"So what are our options?"

"We can try to take life support off Amadeus and run it off the main engines, but that leaves us short on fuel. We could try to split the difference between the engine power and Amadeus to see if we can stretch them both, but I don't know how to do the swap, and there's still a good chance we'll wind up short on fuel and not reach planet. We could try to fix Amadeus itself, which makes the most sense, but also potentially exposes us to lethal radiation— Oh, and none of us have worked on a generator like Amadeus before."

"Give me the specs for it."

He sent the data to her tablet. "Should we ask them how we wound up with the wrong fuel?"

"Would it help us?"

"No."

"Then no. We just fix it," she said. "Like Evgeni says, we're in charge."

# 1986: Firecracker Dance

ANNIE PRATER'S FAVORITE secret was the Mariposa Cinema in Cocoa, a deco-style theater that reminded her of childhood trips to Miami. On weekdays, the Mariposa ran dollar matinees of classic films, and Annie had been going to see them twice a week since Denny had started the first grade. A small popcorn and a children's soda was lunch. With no butter, the popcorn was hardly any calories, meaning the soda counted as lunch. The expense was easily hidden in the grocery budget. Just a small fib to Des about the price of eggs and milk, which he never bothered to keep an eye on. But, oh, how the little lie was worth it for two hours alone, sinking into a velvet seat. It was a long drive, and ate up a whole chunk of the day, time that felt stolen and better for the stealing. This week they were playing *Holiday Inn*, which was her favorite. And today she left early. Not because she was avoiding Des. Maybe. And maybe not all that early. The sun was up, so it must be later than she thought. *Holiday Inn.* Bing Crosby, Fred Astaire, and Marjorie Reynolds—who was no Ginger Rogers, but nobody was. It was her favorite for Astaire's firecracker dance. *Bang! Crack!* Boneless, the man was boneless. Yes, there was blackface for the Presidents' Day number, and yes, she knew that was wrong, but it was just the one number, surely that didn't ruin the thing, especially because that wasn't even the point. She'd watch Fred Astaire throw bang snap firecrackers and pop them with his heels, and Bing would sing "White Christmas," and for a little while she'd be Marjorie Reynolds and everything would be fine.

The Mariposa had beautiful gold ceilings and red carpets like Valentine's Day roses. Everything about the Mariposa felt better than life. It made her feel like *more*.

She'd taken Denny there once to see *Lawrence of Arabia*, but Des hadn't liked that it kept him away the whole day. Des also didn't like

Peter O'Toole, because he seemed "light in the loafers." But Annie liked his eyes. He seemed kind and smart and she'd believe anything he told her, which was the entire point of *How to Steal a Million*. She also liked Omar Sharif. That jaw and those cheekbones could cut glass.

Denny had fallen asleep during *Lawrence*. She should have taken him to *Creature from the Black Lagoon* instead.

She'd meant to pick him up, to bring him with her and have a fun day playing hooky, but she drove by Betheen's without stopping. He was having a sleepover, his first one. A co-ed sleepover too. She would have killed for that at his age. This is what she told herself as she headed out to Cocoa and turned her car radio up. But all that came through was static, no matter which station. She flicked it off. Just as well, there would be news on the radio. Those poor astronauts. Denny had seen that too. He needed a little fun, a little time away.

Denny was fine with Betheen, and Betheen owed her. Annie had spent so much time with Nedda, had showed Theo how to grind baby food, and hadn't ever said a word about baby Michael. They both owed her. One night and a morning wasn't much at all.

Her son, her sweet son, with his goofy Fred Astaire smile. Des had hit him. She was married to a man who hit his child.

She turned right off Acacia Lane and noticed steam rising off the Emersons' pond like fog. Fancy, keeping a koi pond. Ted made good money on the stock market, maybe he had new pumps put in. Though why you'd want a fish pond boiling hot, she'd never know. Did you do that before you put in new fish? It looked like a jacuzzi or a bathtub.

Don't throw the baby out with the bathwater. Yes, Des had hit Denny, but it was once. A quick pop, and that was it. Just this one time. And Denny could have gotten badly hurt on the pruner; the blades on it could have ripped his arm right off. Denny had learned his lesson. Des wouldn't do it again either. He wouldn't have to. She knew he felt bad. She could see it in the way he shook right after. Her father had swatted her good and hard once for taking money from the cookie jar, and she hadn't done it again. It would toughen Denny up.

He'd need to be tough. Soft boys got hurt. Des was tough and she liked him that way. Like Robert Mitchum, who made her shiver. Des had made her shiver too.

It would be fine. Denny would be fine.

She drove toward the interstate, but the uneasy feeling just wouldn't shake. Annie knew Denny had climbed out his bedroom window to go see Nedda before, but this was the first time she'd ever told him to do it. Betheen had been so kind.

*Do you want me to send Theo over? Let me send Theo to talk him down. Does Denny need anything? Do you need to stay? Oh honey, you can stay. We've got more rooms than people and enough sweets to feed an army. It's been a rough day for all of us. Come over. You don't even have to answer if you can't right now. Just show up anytime. Theo hardly sleeps, he'll hear you if I don't.*

Kindness made it worse, didn't it? Kindness made what had happened mean something.

Cars were backed up along Red Bug Road. People must be heading over to Kennedy. It'd been so long since an accident, she couldn't remember the last time. There was never traffic this early. She leaned out the window. All she could see up ahead were cars, and the shadows of trees. It looked a bit overgrown, but then the highway department never paid much attention to Easter. She decided to wait it out. There was still plenty of time to make the movie. More than enough to stop for a coffee, then the drugstore to pick up a new eye pencil.

*Please don't waste a good steak on it, but if you've got frozen peas it'll help with the swelling. It'll make him feel like a big guy.*

Where had she seen someone put a steak on a black eye?

Des wouldn't lay a finger on her. He hadn't and he never would. She was his princess, which was good and bad because she loved that, and hated that she loved it too. He wouldn't dare hit her, but he had hit Denny.

Just the once.

He wasn't tough, her son. He might need to be, but she didn't want that. She wanted him to be smiling and liquid like Gene Kelly, with a kind face like Fred Astaire that could make you believe anything. She wanted him to be soft.

She balanced on the brake pedal and imagined filling her pockets with bang snaps, tossing them on the ground, spinning in their sound and smoke. She imagined lighting a whole crate of firecrackers with a cigarette and disappearing in the flash.

# Protraction

A FLASH HITS—LIGHTNING FROM over the grove, plus water from the sprayers. The ones at the south end always overshoot. He's soaking wet and feels like he's made of worms. Not worms exactly, but he's squirming, antsy, and not right, like after sneaking a full cup of coffee from the pot. He could run a million miles all at once and not be tired. His eyes clear. He wipes his face dry and reaches into the pruner, digging for the spark plug caps. Spark plugs, why didn't he think of that?

He calls for Nedda, but she isn't answering. He yells and waits, but nothing happens. She must hear him. She's in the back of the shed by the hoses and ties. He yells again, but she still doesn't answer. She doesn't move.

He jumps from the pruner and finds himself stopped. Huh. He pushes his hand forward and it hits something, something dry and sleek. Warm. He's warm. Hot, even. But it was freezing when they left and yesterday he'd had to wear a jacket. Half the reason Pop is mad is the freeze. His eye hurts but he tries not to think about it.

He tries to walk but encounters the same weird kind of wall, though he can't see anything different about the air, about the ground, nothing. Nedda still isn't moving. She's paused, like on a VCR, but no wiggly line through her. He shouts her name.

He screams until his throat is raw. She doesn't even flinch.

Two days pass. It has to be two days because he's counting seconds and multiplying them by minutes, then hours. He isn't great with multiplication tables, so he writes in the dirt with his fingers. He's slept twice, curled up in the pruner's seat. He's cried four times—but Nedda is the only one who could have seen, so it doesn't matter. She probably can't tell. She's barely moved, though she is moving. Slow motion, not pause. She's turned her head, and her mouth is open a little. It wasn't before. Sometimes, they are almost moving together. It only happens when he gets cold. Then he starts sweating and she stops. If he squints he can see her tongue in her mouth. He watches, wondering if a fly will land on it.

There is a fly near him. It is still, paused, midair. It's close enough to see the veins on each wing, to count the hairs on its back. Everything is still but him. He's in a bubble. He's the Bubble Boy.

He laughs until it isn't funny anymore; then he cries.

When he's sick of crying, he begins ripping the pruner apart, taking out everything he can with his wrenches and his bare hands. He tries to lift the engine block but cuts himself. He sucks the blood. There has to be something, anything, to start the pruner. He's hungry but not. Thirsty, but not. It's got to have been a week. He's gone a week without eating or drinking. That should kill people. It must kill people. He's seen it on *MacGyver* or *The A-Team*, or something. He can't remember. His feet hurt. His fingers hurt.

He wishes Nedda were stuck with him, then feels bad for wishing it.

At some point there is a rumbling, impossibly low, too low to hear, but it settles in his chest like a second heartbeat. It's Nedda. Nedda shouting.

She's slow. Everything is slow but him.

He's the monkey he told Nedda to poke with a dipstick.

She's smart, he thinks. Really smart. She can get her dad, who's the smartest guy ever, and they can fix it. He's lucky. Really, super lucky. What if he'd been stuck and didn't know her?

He sits on the pruner's hood. He waits.

After what he figures is another week, he's run out of songs he knows. Sick of singing the same ones, he makes up his own. He counts things, the seams in the shed's roof, screws he's taken from the pruner, the hairs on the fly's back.

It's a month or so before her hand touches the bubble. He's stopped counting. The cuticle on her left pinkie finger is torn and there's a stain on her thumb that's red. It's a mirror of the apple on the patch she made.

He runs through every movie he's ever seen and tries to remember the dialogue. *The Goonies* was good, but he can't remember much of it other than Chunk being funny and Sloth looking a little like Eddie at the bait shop. *Indiana Jones and the Temple of Doom* is better than *Goonies.* Way better. He saw it four times in the theater, but can't remember any of the words. He thinks about the part where they have to eat monkey brains, and thinks of the monkey in the truck, its head cut open.

A year in and his shoes are too tight. He's picked holes in his pants and pulled the fine hairs from his lower arms. Sometimes, when he remembers his voice works, he says her name. Her arm is closer now. He knows that much, though trying to figure out how much she moves every day is pointless. Sometimes there is a great leap and she'll move a whole foot, but most of the time there is nothing at all. Those odd minutes when he sees her move are cold and they feel like December. He wants to brush the dirt off her face.

He talks to her, but she never answers.

Sometimes he sleeps for more than a day. Sometimes he tries to sleep for weeks. He bites his fingernails to nothing. He's not hungry anymore, but he eats the chewings rather than look at them. If he doesn't, he'll count the weeks and months in pieces of bitten-off fingernails. His toenails have made holes in his socks.

When he shouts now his voice cracks.

His legs are making him itchy. He needs to run, but he can't run, but he needs to run, but he can't run, but he needs.

She puts her hand up to the bubble, his home, the wall of heat between him and the world. He touches it but can't feel her on the other side. She's gone. He's somewhere else too.

He cries.

He sleeps. He dreams sometimes, dreams they are together, the only people in the world.

A patch of hair above his ear curls the wrong way and drives him crazy. He tugs at it. It comes loose with roots and skin and a little blood attached and it feels good. It settles him. He pulls a little more.

Pop will come. Pop will see him on the pruner and he'll know.

He screams for days until he coughs up bits of blood and snot.

It takes her months to walk away, maybe a year, he doesn't know. He pounds on the edges of the thing that holds him, the film, the glass, the air that keeps him in place. Then her back is to him, and he learns it as well as he ever learned her face—how narrow her shoulders are, that her knees bend slightly inward. Her left ankle rolls out and wears her shoe funny.

Her shadow takes a week to disappear.

He doesn't speak, for a year, two years. He looks for her.

By the fifth or seventh year, he doesn't look anymore. He sleeps on the pruner, which rusts around him. He huddles in the chair. He puts his shoes on the ground because they haven't fit in years.

He waits.

# 1986: The Thread

BETHEEN MEASURED KANTEN flakes with a triple-beam balance, weights clunking solidly into notches. As in chemistry, weight was more accurate than volume. A kitchen scale was easier to use, to store, but she loved the satisfaction of hanging five-hundred-gram masses on it, the *shhck* of weights sliding across the beams. It was a balance she'd once used to measure poisons, caustic things, chemicals that ulcerated skin. The scale was purchased with money set aside for her wedding. If anyone had noticed that the flowers at the chapel were crepe paper, they were polite and never mentioned it.

The lamp above the stove flickered. She ought to change the bulb. She ought to change a lot of things. But long relationships bred an abstract desire for something different. Boredom could be what drove you apart, or what kept you together. Staying was habit, as was thinking of leaving. You stayed because you loved them. Sometimes that love changed from a roaring fire to a sweater, but sweaters were warm and held your shape.

Certain recipes were rote, and she used the scale for the sheer joy of it, the tactile comfort of the weights. Inventing new recipes required her tools and her mind, thinking about alkalinity and acidity, beautiful bonds. Texture. Texture was chemistry. The right balance between chew, crunch, give, smoothness, and graininess—it was all in the structure of the fats, sugars, proteins, and water.

She weighed and thought about agar. It was more flexible than gelatin. A sugar polymer. Sugar, instead of peptides and proteins. A cleaner sweet.

At one of Theo's department mixers, a co-worker had brought jelled coffee. It had a clean dark flavor, smooth texture, soft but solid, the most un-gelatin-like jelly she'd ever eaten. Betheen had cornered his wife, an Asian woman whose desperately bored expression mirrored her own.

"This, this isn't gelatin, is it? This is wonderful."

"Oh, no. It's kanten flakes," the woman said. Betheen remembered her name was Jeannie. "It's a kind of dried seaweed. My mother uses it in all sorts of stuff. She sent me some. You can jell anything with it."

"It's brilliant. Where do you get it?"

"Not around here. You have to order it."

She traded her recipe for grapefruit sugar glass for the name of a Japanese grocery supplier.

She'd laughed when the packages arrived and she'd realized kanten flakes were agar, what biologists used as a growing medium. The things she could make with it—sweets that looked like molded chocolate and had the texture of mousse but tasted like lemon drops, or desserts that tasted like vanilla and anise and looked like berries suspended in ice. Up the agar ratio to combat the acidity, and she could make an entire wedding cake from sugar-dusted champagne cubes, with bubbles trapped inside that fizzed on your tongue.

Fuck stiff wedding cakes. Champagne cake would melt in half an hour. If you didn't eat it in time, you could drink it. Presentation would be difficult—she'd need tiers of slotted trays, held up by champagne glasses. But wasn't that the point of food's gentle bonds? They were delightful in their impermanence, a single perfect instant. A champagne water cake could easily win the concept cake category. Last year's cakes were clichés—sculptures of horses, molded chocolate, everything the consistency of bathroom caulk. A cake that wasn't cake, that changed states, would challenge the entire concept of cake. A win could change things. There was the money, five hundred dollars to spend however she wanted. She'd get free advertising, notice, and maybe a client who didn't want dry, flavorless cake tiers, plastic Grecian columns, fondant, or hundreds of sugar pearls. Nedda would like it too: a not-too-sweet dessert that skirted rules. Did Nedda realize that Betheen was gently wooing her? Imagine tricking your own daughter to admit that you liked the same things. Luring her into letting you love her.

Dessert, the secret love language of chemists.

When customers asked why Betheen's baking was better than anyone else's, she forced herself to blush and say her kitchen was downwind from Prater Grove; everything had a little orange blossom in it.

She did not say, "Because I'm a chemist, asshole," though the words always threatened escape. Women at the Society House wanted folksy comfort. Chemistry—though it kept them alive with their heart pills, made their food sweet, and held their dentures in their mouths—was not desired, not from her. Which made her miss Theo, who didn't blink when she ordered kanten flakes and xanthan gum, who smiled when the house smelled like soured papaya and burned sugar. Which made her stay, even though she missed who he was when they'd met, the way he'd been in awe of her. She missed the head rush of the semester she'd spent working with aromatics, and the wonderful terror of seeing her light blue ballet flats in a room full of awkward men in loafers.

She'd loved it, being the only one.

She hadn't known it would change.

Kanten flakes soaking in water, orange rind soaking in alcohol for extract, all of it needed to sit. She grabbed her keys and coat. January meant delivering cookies in the dark, though it wasn't dark today. There was an unnatural brightness to the sky, likely from NASA. People must be investigating the accident; they'd have all sorts of floodlights, helicopters. NASA could light the sky up if they needed to.

She left three muffins on the table for Nedda and Denny. She should have made pancakes, but the line between just right and too much was difficult to navigate. She was reaching but missing with Nedda. June said it was because she'd started trying too late. But how long was she supposed to atone for grief?

She drove. At least she wasn't Annie, who'd married a man who hit children. Theo could be difficult, but he wasn't unkind. She turned left at the Mauna Kea and had to stop for an armadillo, a dark, lumbering shape. They carried leprosy. She felt like she did as well. Her daughter would rather spend time with anyone else. Her marriage had fallen into a habit of not touching. She did bake sales and PTA meetings and tried to make small talk, but she lacked the rapport other women had with one another, the language of shared experience that came from having grown up together. She'd come to Easter as a scientist's wife, without ties. There were still whispers about how broken she'd been after Michael died. She'd overheard the words *nervous breakdown*.

Annie Prater had never judged her.

The Bird's Eye got three trays of limoncello almond cookies. Ritchie Lester took them at the back door, leaning into the Cadillac's trunk, his shirt riding up and exposing the soft handles of a man who worked by taste. She worked by chemistry until ingredients and methods and temperatures built paths in her brain and the sense of five hundred grams was as ingrained as her name.

Motherhood was supposed to be like that, instinctive, natural feeling. But as much as she tried, she couldn't seem to learn it.

Ritchie bumped her hip when he took the trays, an accidental touch that wasn't accidental. She could have sex with him if she wanted. If she appeared the slightest bit willing, Ritchie would bend her across one of the booths and hammer away. It should be reassuring that men would still screw her even though she was long out of her twenties, even though she'd had two children. It wasn't. Men were all different corners in the same room. She ignored the touch and scheduled the next order.

She kept driving. Nedda and Denny should have time. It was good for them to be unsupervised in little bits. It built character, imagination, helped them form their identities. She wound around town before heading for the interstate. Driving gave her peace to slide formulas and recipes around. Royal icing over a chocolate shell holding a strawberry reduction—a bubble that, once pierced, would release a flood of strawberry flavor to be soaked up by thin layers of caramelized sponge cake. It would smell better than perfume. Or better, a faux orange—a thin paraffin shell piped full of orange curd, coated with layers of orange royal icing and dappled with dots of red and brown food coloring. A small real leaf held on by an icing bead. She drifted back to champagne water cake and the Orlando Cake Show. Her first attempt had made an alcoholic brick. Today she'd use more alcohol, less kanten. More liquid. She wanted teardrops. A cake made from a tower of teardrops that would lose integrity. And wasn't that a marriage? People who were trapped by crumb texture, fondant, and flower sculpting would be scandalized. She'd need a magnum of champagne. While Annalise Stevens hand-painted headlights on whatever ridiculous car cake she made this year, Betheen would uncork a magnum into an enormous stockpot of kanten and water. Sip on the extra while the molds chilled.

Dust crystallized orange rinds—Prater orange rinds—over jelled champagne teardrops. And when it was finished, when the cake melted, like the marriages of anyone who purchased a Ferrari-shaped wedding cake, she'd pass around the glasses of sweet champagne her cake had become. And she'd never divulge how she'd done it. Annalise, Veronica of Veronica's Delights, and the beehived women from Candy's Cakery would have to haul their uneaten cars, houses, and horses back to their bakeries. Betheen would spend the night in a hotel, drinking the leftovers, stretched out on a bed she didn't have to make in the morning. Chemistry.

Dreams of a night in a luxury hotel were interrupted when she was forced to a stop behind a line of cars. Red Bug Road became a service road that fed into the highway, which ran the coast for six hours of mindless driving. Every now and then someone would stall on the on-ramp. She looked ahead for the cause of the jam. Drivers were getting out of their cars, and a man paced around a little sedan, notebook in hand. There was a semi from Prater, then Pete McIntyre in his pickup and Annie Prater's Mercury. Had she gotten Denny already? Pete McIntyre was out of his truck and walking around, hand on the back of his neck.

Betheen leaned out the window for a good look. Beyond the semi, the pavement was covered in thick brush. Trees and growth along the roads always needed cutting back, but this was dense—like the untouched areas in the Everglades. More people got out of their cars. The notebook man yelled at the driver in the semi, arms waving.

She knew the look of space reporters in their wilted shirts and horn-rims, men who still thought it was the '60s. If he was headed for Canaveral, he'd need another way. The road had vanished into vegetation too wild to see through. The vines seemed to writhe, pulling back at intervals, revealing savannah-like grasses, only to be reclaimed again by kudzu and creeping moss.

"Jesus." She got out of her car and shouted, "Anybody know what happened?"

"Nope," Pete McIntyre answered. "I was going over to Mims for some parts, and it's been like this for at least an hour. I dropped by the police station, to see if they could put a call into the highway department, but their phones are down."

Police phones were out? Annie was still in her car, Denny wasn't with her. How long had she been here? "Has anyone tried Satsuma Drive yet?" No one had.

The reporter leaned on his car. "Will that get me to 95 or the turnpike?"

"Both." She went to Annie's car. Annie's grip on the wheel was tight, and she looked through the windshield as if the problem might clear at any second. When Betheen tapped on the window, Annie rolled it down, slowly.

"This is crazy. Are you okay?"

"I'm fine," Annie said. "I can get Denny later today. After school, I promise. I don't like putting you out." There were circles under her eyes, but her hair was perfectly blown out in a dark brown Princess Di. Betheen recognized that exhaustion, when your body didn't want to work and your heart and stomach melded into a single organ that hurt, but you still had to blow your hair out because someone would see you. Annie had seen her like that.

"It's not putting us out, Annie. Nedda and Denny were up late, laughing." Enough to let her know her son was all right, not enough to let anyone within earshot know he might not be.

Annie's voice barely left the car. "Thank you. It's silly. Desmond was just blowing off steam. He feels terrible. Denny doesn't mean to, but he pushes every one of Desmond's buttons."

It was impossible to imagine Denny pushing anyone's buttons. He'd never so much as forgotten to wipe his shoes before coming in.

"There's no rush. Nedda's happier when he's around, and it's good to have a break from kids sometimes." She kept her voice light. "If you need him to stay for a bit, that's fine. It's nice to have a boy around. They're so different from girls."

"I couldn't put you out like that."

"Are you sure you're all right?"

"Fine, fine." Her smile was strained. "Thank you, Betheen. You and Theo both."

Betheen wanted to say that everything would be all right, but wishful thinking didn't make it so.

The trucker leaned out his window. "I can't get around unless somebody backs up." Ray Villaverde. His daughter went to school with Nedda.

Betheen shouted back, "Does anyone want to try Satsuma? If it's no good, then John Lee up to Forty-Seven?"

Annie's car lumbered slowly around and the line began backing up. Betheen maneuvered her car into the thin strip between the road and the canal. They caravanned behind Ray Villaverde, driving into that strangely lit sky, a canopy of twilight.

As they crawled down the roads, Betheen dug her nails into the wheel. When they reached Satsuma, the road was wrong, deeply wrong. The canal on the side was gray-brown slush where it should be warm and teeming with bugs. This kind of cold didn't come down here, yet frost had climbed the embankment, and ice—actual ice—covered the blacktop in a sheet so dark and smooth there was no seeing its beginning or end.

When the semi hit the ice, it appeared to be dancing on air as it jackknifed. Theo would have seen equations, momentum, friction, and velocity. Betheen saw the inevitable.

The reporter slammed on his brakes and the sedan spun.

She pumped her brakes, pulled the wheel. "Turn into it, turn into it, turn into it."

The reporter's eyes met hers.

His nose was short, three lumps like a Cabbage Patch doll. His chin was weak and disappeared into his neck—though perhaps that was because he was screaming. His glasses were dark horn-rims, which flew from his face. He turned and turned the wheel.

She tried to shout "Stop turning," but couldn't.

She steered right, hard right, *pumpedpumpedpumped* the brakes, jerked as the left rear panel of her car hit someone else's, and watched the man scream.

She saw his eyes. There was no way to tell the color from across the hoods of two spinning cars, not when one was a Cadillac, not with the morning sun so low, but she knew they were gray with the certainty she knew she was watching a man die.

Time stopped.

He saw her.

His mouth closed.

He was in his midthirties, possibly younger if he was from here, where sun cooked you like a peanut. He was thin-lipped. Light glinted off his wedding band, a gaudy chunk of yellow gold. Gold, a noble metal, was supposed to mean purity or steadfastness, but nothing showed wear like gold. Her ring had been her grandmother's; Theo had smiled about having given her a ring she already owned. There was a pull, tying her to the man across the road.

A fragile bond, van der Waals forces. Butter, softening, melting.

Time stretched. His mouth formed a word. *Help.*

The moment snapped. His car careened, smashing into the semi.

The flip was fast, ugly, so sharp it pierced her breath. After breaking the guardrail, his car landed on its roof, and tipped into the canal.

Twenty, thirty, forty seconds. Minutes vanished, however long it took for the Cadillac to come to rest, for her to breathe, to unhook the seat belt and fall out the door.

The canal was pulling the sedan into it. Like quicksand but worse. Hands were on her shoulders, dragging her back. She'd climbed the rail.

*Help.*

"There's nothing you can do. Stay back." Grease under the fingernails, freckles and scars up the forearms, a gravel voice. Pete McIntyre. "You're okay, you're okay. Mrs. Papas, don't go down there or you'll go with it."

"Someone has to get him," she said. "He's inside. He's in there."

Pete's fingers dug into the meat of her arm. "Don't. Betheen, don't."

"He'll drown."

"He won't."

"How can you watch someone drown?"

"He can't drown, Mrs. Papas. He's dead." Pete loosened his grip. "Here. Close your eyes until I tell you, okay? Then you take one look, real quick."

99

It was easy to follow such a calm voice. He was musky like exhaust—$N_2$, $O_2$, $CO_2$, $CO$.

"Open your eyes," he said. "Now, look."

The cold coming off the canal numbed her. What remained of the sedan's driver's side window was in front of her. The frame was smashed and resembled a squinting eye. Then she saw him.

The reporter's head was flopped back, though *flop* implied motion and his head would never move again. His nose touched the car's ceiling.

There was blood.

"He's gone, see? He can't drown. It was real quick. Close your eyes again, all right, Mrs. Papas? All right, Betheen?" He walked her back to her car. She let him, it was easy to.

She thought of that yellow gold ring, the man's wife. She stepped over things when Pete told her to, walked around a spray of glass. The Cadillac's side had a long gouge down it, and a crushed quarter panel.

Ray Villaverde was outside his truck, saying, "We need the cops, somebody get the cops."

Annie Prater was out of her car too, hands dug deep into the pockets of a blue denim skirt. Their eyes met. There was no connection, no snapping into place, like she'd had with the man. All she saw from Annie was fear.

That pull, that tug, was for the dying. She'd felt it before. Did the man have children?

*Nedda.* She should get home to Nedda. Let her know she was all right.

Betheen got her purse from the floor of the passenger side and dug through the glove box for her lipstick. Aubergine, a color that sounded like promise and wine. It was mostly carnauba wax—long strings of esters with a high melting point, hard as concrete—and oils added for softness. The wax she put on her lips was the same she'd use to polish the car. *Wax lips*, she thought, and bit into her tongue.

He was dead. That poor man had died. Someone would need to get the police. Someone would need to get the highway patrol. Someone would need to be there when Nedda and Denny got home from school. Someone would need to do *everything*. "I have to go," she said.

"I'll drive you home," Pete said. "I'll come back, tow the car to the shop, and take a look."

Her chest hurt. There was ice on the road. Nobody here knew how to drive on ice. She thought of the reporter's neck, the unnatural angle, like a bent elbow. "No, I need to walk. I need to be alone for a bit. Pull myself together."

"Betheen?" Annie's voice. Thin, high.

"I'm fine, Annie. Just get the police."

When Annie pressed again, Betheen forced down a lump in her throat. "I'm fine. It's not all that far, just a mile or two, and I need a minute to clear my head. You understand."

When she began walking, no one stopped her. Betheen ground the heel of her palm into the rib above her breast—muscle, fat, and bone. She opened her coat, pulled down the neck of her blouse, and saw that the seat belt had left a bruise on her chest. It looked like strawberries and felt like someone was trying to take her heart.

She followed the double yellow line, fitting her shoes between the stripes of paint. She pushed at the bruise, and felt the man again, that instant they'd been connected. He'd known he would die. Did his wife know? Did she feel it?

The walk passed quickly. Distances disappeared when you were being pulled to someone you loved. She dug at the growing welt on her chest, grabbing on to what had always been there, the two threads that spun out into the world. The one to Baby Michael still hurt too much to speak about, though for a different reason than at first. After a certain point too much time had passed to tell your child about a sibling they'd never know. The guilt of such a secret brought its own strangely tender ache. The other thread connected to Nedda. It wasn't like Michael's, or the one that had connected her to the dead man. Her daughter might not feel it, but it was there. It formed when you had children, and would be there until the day you died. A carbon–carbon covalent bond pulled Betheen and Nedda tight.

# 1986: Into the Mouth

H ER MOTHER'S CAR was gone, and her father's wasn't in the driveway either. Her dad had three places: the basement at home, the armchair in the parlor, and the lab at the college. Nedda rode hard, the wind in her ears. Pop Prater would be awake soon. He'd find Denny.

The thing around Denny was like the thing around the monkey: not hard, but not exactly soft either. There was an elastic feel to it that made her think of molded gelatin. She'd pushed against it and it pressed back; then something that felt like a static charge ran through her. The air around it had wavered, almost rippling.

There was a moment when she swore she could have talked to him, when the air had been almost normal, but then it changed. What could you touch but not see? Air, baby jellyfish, water when you were in it. Smells. Atoms. You were always touching atoms, but never seeing them. The monkey never moved, and Denny never stopped moving. Opposites. The trees in the grove didn't stop moving either. But they went forward and back. Denny was aging, was going very, very fast. Everything inside him must be moving fast too, vibrating in place, heating up like a marshmallow in a microwave. *Boom.*

Her dad would fix it.

She squeezed her eyes shut and pedaled, trying to find her insides. Her bike wobbled so she opened her eyes again. It would take too long to get there on the road. She made a hard turn to cut through the remains of Island Paradise. What if Denny grew up before her dad could fix it? She would have to go to school without Denny. He'd have to get a house. A family. She turned toward the park's entrance, and the shadow cast by the giant tiki head. What if Denny died before her dad could fix it?

The fence around Island Paradise had been broken since almost the day it had been put up. For months, the bank had repaired it, installing new chain link, but after a year's worth of break-ins, the fence stayed broken and the differences between park and forest faded. Lengths of fence and razor wire poked through creepers and catbrier. Those same vines climbed around the entrance, giving the angry-eyed tiki god a beard. The eyes were empty sockets bored straight through the concrete. Once, gas lights had lit them at night. Now, eerie yellow sky shone through, revealing a bird's nest housed in the left socket.

She rode through the god's mouth. It was concrete, poured and cast, same as the Pinocchio on the mini golf course. Nedda felt like it was watching her.

Kudzu enveloped whole buildings, cracking and pulling them to the ground like a living anchor. It had consumed the waterslide, leaving a wall of leaves and vines in its place. Anything that stood still too long in Easter was devoured by forest. If the monkey never moved, the kudzu would eventually claim it.

That would happen to Denny.

She passed the pond that had held outrigger canoes you could paddle with your feet like a swan boat. It had surrendered to algae and mosses, the water a solid green mass. It steamed, clouds wisping off it in the cold. How could it be hot when everything else was cold? Denny said Jimmy La Morte probably bathed in the pond. There were thick bubbles, and something that might have been a pontoon stuck up from the far end.

The trees gave way to grass and sand and North Satsuma Drive, which backed onto the college. She'd biked through Island Paradise alone. She'd gone through the mouth by herself. She'd thought something like that would make her feel proud or brave, but it didn't. She was terrified.

At the sight of her dad through the narrow window in the door to the lab, she began crying. He *would* fix it, because he knew everything.

She was panting and sweating, there was grease all over her, her lip had a sore spot where she'd chewed it, and Denny was gone.

"Nedda?"

A tremor started inside her, shaking everything, fast. She couldn't say how Denny kicked the pruner as it rusted beneath him, how he stretched and screamed and sped like a movie. She felt like exploding into light and heat and thoughts and everything in the universe all at once, traveling, traveling, traveling. All she could do was cry.

Her father's arms were around her. "What's wrong? Here." The in and out of his breath was a wave, like a pump, like an accordion, like the sun—rise and fall, rise and fall. Beard bristle against her cheek.

She was angry, for crying, for not being able to talk. She tried to swallow but couldn't, and the sobs kept coming. She choked on a bubble of snot.

"Breathe. Breathe, then talk. In, out. Okay?"

She embraced the weight of his arms. He *would* fix it.

"Something's wrong with Denny. Dad, it's really bad." Then all the words tumbled down. She'd ridden through the mouth of the god in the park and she hadn't been swallowed, she'd come out a scream—all the words that had ever gotten trapped were loosed from her.

She talked and kept talking. She told her father about the bruise on Denny's eye, that Pop had hit him because he'd broken a machine, but he'd broken the machine because he'd failed a test and lied about it. She told him about the monkey and how she couldn't touch it and it seemed alive but also stuck, and about the trees in the grove and how the sky looked sick and was light too early, and that everything in the grove was growing and shrinking and dying and growing again. She told him about the sprinklers going on and the blare of light that swallowed up Denny.

"I couldn't see anything; my eyes went all black and purple and when I could see again he was blurry and moving too fast. I tried to get to him, Daddy. I tried, but I couldn't, and I think he's going to die." She leaned into him and her knees hit the lab floor.

"No one's going to die, Little Twitch."

"How do you know?"

"I need you to be specific. What did you see?"

"I told you. The sprinklers went on, there was a flash of light, it was cold, then hot, and I couldn't get to Denny. He's stuck, like the monkey. You don't understand. We have to do something. Daddy, you have to help."

He wasn't listening. If he was listening he'd understand and be writing or pulling things apart, or asking her things. Why wasn't he listening?

"Nedda, breathe."

She tried to breathe, looked at the shelves in the lab, the boxes with wires for circuitry—the resistors and chokes that looked like little ant bodies with wire legs, and breadboard bases to build things on. One shelf had a stack of straight glass tubes, another a stack of bent tubes. Solder. The room smelled like solder, bitter and sharp, like the good parts of home. Behind her father, Crucible's legs moved slowly, barely perceptible, but the shadows were different.

Crucible was different from when she'd last seen it. Its insides were now beneath panels of metal and glass, all the open wiring gone. Three ventilation hoses snaked from it, shiny aluminum tentacles. The legs on it were different, heavier, smoother. The door was closed tight with a thick seal around the edge. The room was cold to keep Crucible cold. Electronics overheating was bad. Denny was overheating. Maybe he was cooking from the inside out, like the marshmallows in the microwave, after all. Maybe she'd lied.

"The machine's on?"

"No."

"It's moving."

"That's residual motion from a test," he said. "There were grounding problems after the launch, there was a short. I did some work this morning, and ran a test to make sure I'd gotten it fixed."

"You turned it on."

"Of course." There was something different about him, a glint that seemed wrong. Happy. He was actually happy. "It worked. It's preliminary, but it works, Twitch. This is good. It's good for us."

"You don't believe me, do you?"

"I'm sure there's an explanation. Just calm down, breathe, and try again."

There was an explanation. Her dad said Crucible organized things, slowing down the progression of chaos, of decay. That it could speed things up too. *See also: Time, Arrow of.* She hadn't told him about Denny's hair, the patch he'd pulled out. The way he'd screamed. Denny wouldn't want her to tell anyone that.

She grabbed her father's hand and squeezed as hard as she could, knowing it would hurt. She wanted it to hurt as bad as Denny was hurting. When he swore she tugged harder, pulling him to the lab door.

He twisted free, doubled over, and cradled his hand, swearing. His eyes were red and glassy. He glared like he didn't recognize her. "What are you doing? Why would you do that?"

"You have to come with me," she begged. "Please, I'm sorry. I'm so sorry, but you have to believe me. I'll show you. Okay? I'll take you to him. I'll show you. Please, you have to come."

"I'm calling your mother."

She'd never thrown something. People who threw things or shot spitballs were too stupid to know how to express themselves, too dumb to figure out what they wanted, or that there were ways to get what you wanted without having to ask anyone. But the voltmeter felt good in her hand, its big red readout bright, like something from *Back to the Future*. The way it smashed when it hit the wall let her know just how much of it was cheap plastic. Then the needle-nose pliers. Then a pen. A pair of heavy gloves.

He'd done this. "You have to fix it."

He was shouting, but she didn't care. If he didn't listen, why should she? Everything on the lab table flew across the room, at Crucible and its legs, the thing that had done it. She threw hard, fast, but nothing seemed to hit.

"Nedda, stop. Calm down." Then his hands were on her shoulders, shaking her. She knew the instant the pain shot through him—his face whitened with it.

"Fine," she shouted. "I'll fix it."

She ran. He called her name, but she ignored it. He'd made the thing that had hurt Denny. She felt like she was sliding, sliding down the surface of something she couldn't see, disappearing into the dark. She grabbed her bike and rode away—from the machine, the lab, his voice, his happiness—from whatever it was that was about to burst.

Two days before she'd been on the hood of her father's car, lying about a comet she couldn't see, lying to please him. And now he wouldn't help. He didn't believe her.

She biked hard, away from him, toward the palmetto forest. She remembered him sweating in the kitchen, steam rising from pans of salt water boiling on the range, fogging his glasses and suffocating the room. It was last winter when they'd done the salt water experiment.

The project began with a question like an itch. "Dad, how much salt is in the ocean?" Sick in bed with the chicken pox, she talked to him. When she could move again they'd tried to measure how much salt was in the Atlantic, the Indian River, and all the bays and marshes nearby—Salt Lake, Fox Lake, South Lake, St. Johns River—because things near the Atlantic tended toward brackish. Their instruments were simple: a mason jar duct taped to a broomstick, disposable pie tins, the electric stove.

Getting samples meant wading into the water in the middle of winter, seafoam blowing across sand like cotton candy. Her father's blue New Balance sneakers got soaked in the salt water and took on the stench of something rotting. Water splashed her hands, forcing the blood from them, leaving her fingers waxy, white, and trembling. Like now.

Brush scraped her forehead but she kept pedaling, gasping.

They'd driven his Chevette when getting samples. She'd tucked her shadow into his as they'd walked to the water, vanishing into the space he cut from the world.

They'd boiled pie tins on the range until the water evaporated, leaving salt behind, clouding the kitchen with all the bodies of water she'd ever touched. A tin weighed 4.25 grams and held sixteen fluid ounces. They weighed the tins before and after boiling with the balance her mother used for measuring flour and sugar. He'd slid the weights and she'd stared at his fingernails, pitted and chalky, as if made of salt. She'd asked if they hurt.

"Always a little, but not much most days. Some days, an awful lot."

"Can't you do anything for it?"

"There's not much for psoriatic arthritis."

Today she'd hurt him. Squeezed his hands. On purpose.

They'd kept data with blue Erasermate pens, multiplying salt and water out to the gallon. With pint jars he'd taught her to put her arms around oceans.

With one machine, he was killing Denny.

She couldn't go back to the grove until she had a solution. If she went to school she'd have to pretend like nothing had happened. She'd have to forget Denny screaming, his rolling eyes, the sick light. She could go to Mr. Pete's yard—there were things there that might help, things in his house, in his garage, in his space museum. Things even she didn't understand.

How did you make a thing sharp enough to burst a bubble you couldn't touch? If you managed to pop it, would it hurt whatever was inside? *See also: Time, Arrow of.* She needed her encyclopedia. She needed home.

Her legs were numb when she passed Haverstone House, and when she let her bike go, she fell under it, a moment of suspension followed by a hard hit on the pavement, the crush of the bike, then crying soundlessly, ragged, painful. The sky was orange-yellow, hardly moving, the clouds still. Wrong. They were up there, the seven. Light, and heat, and carbon—gas and what?

"Nedda."

She tried to shut the voice out, to make it disappear. She needed to organize, to start. To think of something sharp enough.

"Nedda."

A hand. Held out, fingers curled just so.

"Come on, now. Get up."

She rose and fell into her mother, into her coat and blouse, and all the carefulness slid away. Lips pressed against Nedda's forehead. Her mother was cold. Betheen's magnolia and sugar smell was there, but over it was the pricking bite of hairspray, strong, almost sour. Nedda wished she could disappear into it.

"I went to the grove with Denny," she said. The rest was easier to say than it had been the first time; she'd run through the words, flattening them down like a deer path. "Dad doesn't believe me, but I'm not lying, Mom. Denny's hurting really bad, and I left him."

"You're okay, Nedda," Betheen said once she'd finished.

"I'm not."

"Yes, you are. You're scared, but you're fine, you're going to be fine. But we need to do a few things, okay? We need to think." Betheen moved her to the house, arm around her shoulder. It was strange, leaning on her mother this way, but she couldn't stop herself.

"Mom, where's the car?"

"There was an accident. A man was hurt very badly, and the car has to be towed. But I'm fine, don't worry. Come on, Little Twitch. Let's get inside."

The nickname sounded funny coming from her mother, but that didn't matter. "Someone was hurt?"

"Yes. But I'm fine, and you are too. That's what matters right now. Do you think you can write down what you saw? Everything that happened to you and Denny."

"You believe me?" There were muffins on the kitchen table. Three. Corn muffins—not too sweet, the only kind Nedda liked. The stand mixer was on the counter, its cord cut, ragged as though severed by a knife.

"Of course I believe you."

"Why?"

"Because I know you."

At any other time, Nedda would have disagreed; instead, she picked the paper away from a muffin. It hadn't been cake batter pancakes, but something she'd liked. A thoughtful thing. But Nedda couldn't eat it. "He did it. Dad's machine is doing it."

"We don't know that yet. And even if we did, it's not for you to worry about." She leaned into Nedda as if to hug, instead pressing their arms together. "Can you write it down?"

"Okay."

"Good. I want you to do that. And I need you to stay here for a little while. Someone has to let Denny's mother know. And I need to speak to your father."

Betheen wore the same expression as when she piped Australian lace, hours and hours of sugar lattice. She looked determined. Fierce. Did she even like cakes at all?

"Mom," Nedda said; all other words had gone away.

"We'll figure it out," Betheen said. "We'll find a way and we'll figure it out."

Nedda wanted to cling to her longer. She wanted to run back through the tiki head with her mother, so that it would spit them out backward, taking everything back. "Okay."

"No biking. Stay inside and off the roads. Something's wrong with them. I'll be back soon. I promise."

"Okay."

The door closed behind Betheen. Nedda took out her notebook.

*Hot and cold. Fast then slow. Glass. Light. Bubble. Like a shampoo bubble, soap sliding down the side. Pop. How to pop a bubble. Nails. Needle. Pressure. What happens inside a bubble when you pop it? Sprinklers. Green light. Trees forward and backward. Steaming pond. Cold. Weird cold. Dad made something bad, terrible.*

Her pen stopped. It was too hard to describe the way her skin had felt, how she'd lost her vision when Denny was enveloped by the light, the way the air wriggled around him. The rusting pruner. Denny would be safe if she hadn't let him go. But if she hadn't gone with him, she might not have known for days what had happened. Days from now he'd be dead or an old man and might not remember her.

She picked at a muffin. The inside was still a little warm.

Betheen believed her.

# Aboard *Chawla*

SPINAL TAP," MARCANTA said, floating in through the doorway on her back.

"Good morning to you as well," Evgeni said.

Nedda swallowed down her peanut butter toast. It scratched the film that sleep weeks left behind. "Please tell me you don't dream about spinal procedures."

"Better than dreaming about our life support conking out halfway between star systems. This, I can do something about." Marcanta grabbed a coffee bag from the pantry and jammed a straw in it. "Think. The eye problem. Some of it's cerebrospinal fluid, right? A spinal tap would temporarily decrease CSF volume. We'd have to do weekly taps to keep on top of fluid regeneration, but it makes sense: less volume, less pressure. Bingo—the optic nerve gets a vacation."

"Ah. Good. And we get headaches like nuclear bombs," Evgeni said. He munched on something that smelled suspiciously like rehydrated sardines. Nedda brought the peanut butter to her nose; it did little to help.

"Aw, big tough Russian can't handle a tiny headache?" Marcanta looked like she had too many teeth when she smiled.

More crunching, more fish smell. "There is a headache, then there is you poking holes in my spine because you're bored and can't fix the life support system."

"Do it on me," Nedda said.

"Not a chance. You're precious cargo. Trust me, I see your blood-work every week. Someone at the NIH probably frames the data."

Marcanta knew more about Nedda's health than she did. "What's wrong with getting data on the effect of spinal taps on people like me? I'll do it."

"Not happening, Papas. Also, you aren't—you're not good data for the rest of us."

"Singh, then," Evgeni said. "You like him. You won't dig around so much in his back."

"You know he's a baby. He'll want a week in bed with foot rubs." Marcanta tugged her hair into a knot that floated above her head—round-faced and jumpsuited, she resembled a garden gnome.

Evgeni poked her with his finger. "You're afraid you'll hit something, leave him a vegetable, and then who will do the math to fix the drive?"

"I will," Nedda said. "You could try it on Singh before his next sleep cycle. Having the goggles on might amplify the effect." She drained a coffee packet. It tasted almost like the drink she remembered, but thinner, with a mealy feel. It was harder and harder to remember the real stuff, to remember exactly what the plants looked like.

"It's likely wasted effort. The fluid doesn't take long to regenerate; he'd sleep off most of the benefit before I could test him."

"So do it during a regular sleep night."

"Ask him first," Evgeni said. "You're always lurking with needles."

Marcanta grabbed a block of cheese, flipped Evgeni off, and floated to her lab.

"She just wants to help. She's the only one of us who doesn't know *Chawla*'s systems."

"She's intent on stabbing me," Evgeni said.

"Because she likes you."

Evgeni's expression made her think of a pug, both put-upon and shocked.

"What?" Nedda said. "When I was a kid, people said if a boy pulled your hair or dropped paper clips down the back of your shirt, it meant he liked you."

His laugh was a snort. "Ah, yes. Nedda time, where the future is the present, and any action means its opposite. If Louisa wants to stab me, it's because she wants to stab me."

"Maybe. But when a doctor wants to stab you, it's usually to help." She finished the rest of her toast and vacuumed the crumbs.

"I never pulled a girl's hair," he said.

"I know," she said. Denny had never pulled her hair or thrown spit-balls at her, and he'd liked her just fine. Every boy who'd ever called her *throwback*, made her drop her books, or snapped her bra strap, any boy who'd whispered, "You're sexy for a smart girl," had hated her. Paper clips down the back of her shirt were just that—metal against skin.

Evgeni smiled. "Now I know to ask what your intentions are when you pull my hair."

"I won't," she said.

"Pity for us both."

He squinted and rubbed his eyes. There was something more beautiful about them now that they were becoming purely decorative. "After morning call, we should look at Amadeus, yes? You need a break from hydroponics and I'd like to hide from Marcanta's needles."

"Singh is going to want in on it first," she said.

"And yet we're going to figure it out before he does. 'Thank you, Evgeni. You are excellent,' you should say. 'Thank you for recognizing that I am smarter than a sleeping Singh.'"

"Thank you, Evgeni, for recognizing that you're hopeless without me."

"That as well."

There was data to collect in the hydro lab. Then there was the physical work of maintaining root pressure systems, the water cache, adjusting light for growth. She didn't like to leave it for too long; she didn't like to leave it at all, but none of it would matter without life support. Plants didn't keep the lights on, wouldn't keep them warm or clean, and couldn't recycle enough air to sustain them. The things that would sustain them long term were utterly useless in the short term.

"You should let Marcanta stick you. When we fix the drive, it's going to be a bitch if you're blind and don't see planetfall."

"I will," he said. "But you'll forgive me if I'd like to put off discovering there is no cure."

"It isn't only about you. You have to let her help, Genya." She used the soft diminutive, and the name made his shoulders round. His mother must have called him that. His sisters, maybe Marcanta when they were alone. "She needs to help in whatever way she can."

Nedda stayed beside him when the morning call came in and watched his eyes when he removed the pressure goggles and massaged the deep rings they left. Before the call buzzed in, Nedda wound her fingers in the small knot of hair at the back of Evgeni's head. Light, scratchy—a warm steel-wool pad, but soft. She gave it a gentle tug.

"See? I like you fine."

When Mission Control appeared on-screen, Evgeni was laughing.

They said nothing about blindness. Nothing about energy spikes or which government made the swap from plutonium to strontium. The space between Earth and *Chawla* filled with all the things that could not be said.

They worked in the hydro lab so she could keep an eye on the plants. Evgeni insisted he couldn't think without eating, so he munched on an empty tortilla. Nedda couldn't work without coffee. Marcanta thought they were both too particular and showed up with only a tablet.

"Look here," Evgeni said. "Strontium decays too quickly for Amadeus. The energy output is making it spin too fast. Centrifugal force pulls this rod to the side, like a switch. That's when the power spikes."

"So the rod winds up here." Marcanta pointed at one part of the diagram on the tablet's screen.

"Once it's pulled over, it exceeds the heat threshold for its design." Evgeni made a sound with his teeth. *Ffft.*

"Right. Friction from the scraping produces the heat," Nedda finished. The diagram felt familiar, bringing back hundreds of hours spent studying schematics that would have been wasted if all had gone well. She clicked the tablet and watched a three-dimensional rendering spin. Inexplicably, Amadeus was colored an almost pearly pink. Its external structure reminded her of a container she'd built for an egg-drop project, a central chamber with supports around it, built to withstand impact. She clicked back to the interior view. "Once heat builds up, the metal in that middle section expands, pushes on the rod, and pops it back to its original position. That's when the power spike drops."

"Sounds right." Marcanta hooked herself to the wall by Evgeni, looking at his tablet. Had there been gravity, she would be leaning on him, chin on shoulder, Nedda imagined. Space took away the comfort of a lean. Gravity made touch better. If they reached planet, there would be weeks when their skin burned as it learned how to hold their bodies together again. Small touches would be painful.

"So is this as much fun as jabbing us with needles?" Nedda asked.

"Not even close. I just want to know what's going to kill us. Call it a physician's morbid fascination."

"You look sweet but you're quite ghoulish, aren't you?" Evgeni said, and flicked Marcanta's ear.

"Gravity. They didn't account for the effect strontium would have on artificial gravity and friction," Nedda said. The isotope swap had broken the design.

"People who aren't always thinking about gravity forget to plan for it—or for its absence," Marcanta said. "Blindness and dying generators. Same thing. So what do we do?"

"We could crack it open and replace that piece, but the dose of radiation anyone would get while fixing it would probably be fatal," Evgeni said.

"Sure," Nedda said. "But how soon? Would they die before planet-fall? If we can get there and get at least some of us on ground . . ."

"Fast. Days, not months. That's good in some ways, but they're bad days. Chernobyl, Fukushima bad. Paluel bad," Marcanta said.

Paluel still turned Nedda's stomach. She let go of the wall, spinning around onto her belly, letting herself float, letting the air cradle her. The purple grow lights were peaceful, comforting. The hydro lab looked and smelled alive. "That's assuming the rod needs replacing, but it functions properly before Amadeus overheats."

Evgeni tapped on the screen. "Singh's idea of flooding the chamber may be helping, but if the spikes continue, or accelerate . . ."

The water would heat up and form steam, which, with nowhere to go, could blast a hole in the module. "Have you ever seen an old pressure cooker?" Nedda said.

"What's that?" Evgeni asked.

"It was this pot with a gasket that used steam— Never mind. They used to explode a lot. You know, take boiling water, add a lot of pressure and a faulty gasket. Boom."

"Ah. Boom." Evgeni said.

*Chawla's* hum and Singh's ragged snore filled the silence. Sometimes he hummed in his sleep; Nedda had thought it tuneless until Marcanta recognized one of the songs as the theme from a children's program Nedda had never seen.

The diagram of Amadeus rotated on the tablet between them. Nedda traced its lines, which were precise, clean, and had been run through a thousand computers. The failure was human. Thrift, politics, reliance on a beautiful but unrealistic idea that the world could cooperate.

"You all right, Nedda?"

"Yeah, just homesick, I guess. It hits me at weird times."

"All time is weird here," Evgeni said. "Do you want anything from the printer? I've been tinkering with a program to get it to make quaaludes. You won't feel homesick. You won't feel anything."

"Thanks, but no. I need a little space to think."

"It's time to wake Singh up anyway," Marcanta said.

They left her alone to straighten the long beans on their frames, detangling them from the squash. They looked like sea monsters, wriggling wherever they pleased. The sweet potatoes were getting too much light and sprouting in every direction. The beans seemed happiest. They grew fat rather than long. They curled and twisted, but the seeds were viable.

She was mixing a batch of growing medium when the lab printer beeped. The screen blinked:

PAPAS, NEDDA

PLACE HAND

The screen heated her palm, then the printer whirred and spit a tiny pill—green, and smaller than a pencil eraser—into its tray. She searched for it in her tablet. A stronger derivative of propranolol. She read through the uses. Off-label for glaucoma. Anxiety. Not Evgeni's quaaludes, but aimed at the same thing.

*Chawla* knew their fears.

She swallowed the pill and pulled up the diagram of Amadeus. A slight warmth came from the screen as she rotated the diagram with her finger. A gentle, blanketing heat let her know the pill had begun to kick in. In the cold of space and the module, it was welcome. She closed her eyes, and the artificial warmth felt a little like home.

# 1986: Oscillation

THEO BENT BELOW a vent hose, dodging the gaze of someone in the hallway. The window in the lab's door was small, but any underclassman walking the halls this early had the kind of ambition that bred intrusiveness.

He inched his hands into gloves and waited for the throbbing to subside. Nedda had hurt him. Intentionally, which was shocking, but not as shocking as her observation. She was right. Crucible was moving.

He'd shut it off.

He reached for the power switch with his elbow and was met by an uncanny sliding sensation. But not the switch. He tried with his left hand, the better of the two, and felt nothing at all—no push, no pain, only slipping. Oleaginous, yet not.

Crucible was running and he couldn't touch the switch.

His daughter was many things—prickly, smart, sometimes rude—but she wasn't a liar. Nedda had been terrified. That was why she'd hurt him, the only logical reason. Whatever had happened, whatever she'd seen, she believed. And Crucible was running.

*Shit, Papas.*

A dull ache started in his feet, each bone announcing itself as it ground against the next. He ignored it. Pacing was essential for thought. He combed what he knew of the lab's wiring, the circuits, power supplies, and where the lines ran in the building and out to the street— webs of electricity through the town. He plotted a power surge, a pulse, and conceded; there were, at minimum, five ways a surge could run between the lab, the grove, and Pete McIntyre's yard. He should have had his own power supply. A self-sustaining unit.

*Shit, Papas.*

It was on, running.

One glove still on, Theo stumbled down the hallway, unsure of exactly how he meant to get to the grove and the Prater boy. After the damage Nedda had inflicted on his hand, the stick shift would be impossible. He turned back to his office to call Betheen and a heavy body crashed into him, sending him staggering.

A torn flannel shirt, grease, a thin gray rattail of a braid, a nose that leaned like a drunk. With decades of salvage at his fingertips, Pete McIntyre was helpful with parts when other suppliers were slow or too costly. He also had no reason to be at the college.

"Professor," McIntyre said, once he'd recovered. "I was hoping to catch Mrs. Papas. She wasn't at the house and I figured she might have come by."

"No, she hasn't. Why?"

"She was in an accident—she's fine, but I had to tow the car. The axle's busted. She said she was walking home, but she was pretty shook up. The guy who hit her didn't make it."

"Wait, someone died?"

"Yeah, an out-of-towner. It happened quick, he went right into the canal. And the damn thing's frozen too. I never seen anything like it. The trees by the interstate are nutso too. Everything's grown over the roads. Can't barely get out of town. That's how we all wound up on Satsuma."

"But she's fine? Betheen's all right?"

"She wasn't banged up at all. I was going to take her back to the shop, but she said she was fine and wanted to walk home. And you know that look a woman gets when you shouldn't mess with her. My phone's out, so I went by the house to let her know I have her car. When she wasn't there, I thought I'd look for her here, and at least let you know before I headed back." There was a look people got when looking at Theo's skin, like they'd smelled something sour. McIntyre was as nice as they came, but his eyes still left that trail of unease—curiosity, disgust—small enough no one else would notice. "You okay?"

There was no good way to say it. *There might be a frozen monkey in your yard and I may have done something terrible to Denny Prater* didn't trip off the tongue. Neither did *Thank you for not mentioning that my wife would rather walk home alone than come here for comfort.*

"Yes, yes. Just shocked. You're sure she's all right?"

"She seemed a little shook up, but okay."

"Do you have your truck? Of course you do. Right, that's how you got here. I'm sorry, I didn't get much sleep last night. Would you mind giving me a ride?"

"Yeah," Pete said. "You want me to bring you back home or should I take you over to the garage to have a look at the car?"

"Home," he said. Nedda would go there. Betheen would go there. "But would you mind stopping at Prater first? Nedda was after me about something and I don't want her bothering Betheen with it. Not today."

Fifteen minutes later, Theo was braced against the truck door and vomiting onto the gravel at the exit to Prater Citrus. The nausea was sudden, violent, and left him empty while offering no relief. He spat onto the stones. Pete said something Theo couldn't make out through the ringing in his ears. He pulled in as much air as he could until his vision cleared; then he climbed into the truck. Hollow.

"Take me back to the college. Please."

"What was—" Pete began.

"Please. I have to get to the lab."

Pete shook so badly that it took three tries to get the truck into gear.

Theo dissected what he'd seen. The grove itself was pulsing—expanding and contracting temporally. Trees aged, then grew younger, running through their lifespans. The trees. Focus on the trees and not on Denny. Were they growing the same fruit again and again, or was it different each time? It *should* be the same—if it wasn't, it implied a different form of chaos. Perfectly balanced, they rushed forward, then back through their lives, a closed system.

A perfect system.

But even the trees hadn't prepared Theo to see Denny. Nedda had tried to tell him but he hadn't listened. He'd been too excited about Crucible.

Denny Prater was in the equipment shed. Rather, who or what Denny would be in ten or twelve years was in the equipment shed. Alone. A young man—frightened, half-insane, possibly entirely. Isolation caused depression, paranoia, psychotic breaks. There was no real way to measure Denny's time. His movements were fast, blurred; he jumped like electricity. Watching him was like the disjointed movement of a silent film missing frames. It was worst when Denny had paused, and they'd seen how pitiful he looked. Banging his fists against air. Chewing his hands, which bled and healed in an instant. Theo closed his eyes as Pete drove over a rut. There had been piles of hair on the ground, hair Denny had pulled out—and then the piles disappeared. He'd ripped his own hair out. And then what? Where did it go? Had he eaten it? Scratches appeared on his arms and were scarred over in seconds. How long was it for Denny?

The trees were balanced, moving forward, then backward, through their life cycles. Equal and opposite reactions. It was watching basic Newtonian physics applied to time, to growth. Nedda said the monkey was slowed. Stopped. Denny had sped up.

"What did I just see?" Pete said.

There were no answers. What they'd seen was horrifying. The effect was supposed to be contained. It shouldn't have bled out of the lab. Denny's legs, his feet, were no child's. The boy who'd been Nedda's shadow was now a man, wild and trapped.

Sprinklers. She'd said something about sprinklers.

"Pete, do you have sprinklers in your yard? A drain? Water lines, anything like that?"

"Yeah, I got sprinklers and I'm on town water. Why? Holy hell. Someone's got to tell the Praters," Pete said.

"Tell them what?"

"Shit," Pete said. It sounded like a prayer.

When Denny first climbed their trellis, Theo had been relieved. Nedda had needed a friend, and if that friend would also punch anyone who teased her, more the better. He enjoyed hearing them whispering, dissecting movies, talking about bikes, fireworks, and space. He knew that boys were never simply friends to girls, but he'd had faith their differences would make a budding romance impossible. He had faith Denny wouldn't hold her back. Most men didn't take to women who were smarter; it upset what they saw as the proper order of things. Denny's order had been upset—by Crucible. It could have been Nedda, it nearly was her.

*I've probably killed him.*

He rested his forehead on the passenger window, and pictured Denny's rolling eyes, the patchy beard of a young man. He looked like his father. Theo kept his interactions with Desmond Prater to a minimum. He was the kind of man who hadn't cracked a book since high school, who mistrusted scientists, whose head and neck were the same muscular width.

Denny looked like him, but he looked like Annie too—her sharp cheeks, straight dark eyebrows. Annie, who had looked after Nedda when he and Betheen couldn't. Annie, who never mentioned a word about Baby Michael, not to Nedda, and they'd never had to ask. Annie, who had first taken Betheen's cakes to the Society House.

He'd taken her son away.

The time Denny was in, the temporal anomaly, had tension. It was almost like the window glass his cheek rested on, but it had pushed back. It was bubble-like, as Nedda said. Like the invisible barrier around the machine. That meant layers, three at least: time around the outside, a connecting area, time inside. Slow, optimal speed, fast.

"Copper," Theo said.

"What?"

"Pete, do you have any copper? Wiring, pipe—whatever you have. I need a lot. Anything you can get your hands on. I'll pay you for it, I promise. I can fix this. But please, take me back to the college, then bring me whatever copper you can find."

"Denny, he—"

"Please, just do it."

Pete left him standing on the science building's stoop, inhaling the dust left by the truck tires. Theo breathed it in, particles of everything. The surge from the launch must have caused it. It was the only major variant from every other test.

He took wire from the engineering lab, all the spools he could find, and then chewed more aspirin. It was bitter mixed with a lingering sourness, and threatened to have him retching again. Soon the pain would become too much and he'd crumple, cradling himself from the ache. But now the pain was a needle, pricking him to focus. He pulled a wire from its coil with his teeth.

A soft glow came from behind Crucible's door. Light, an intangible thing that behaved as though it had substance, yet never changed states. Light from the Big Bang still traveled the universe. God's light.

He'd lied to Nedda. For years and about so much. He'd said light continued, that people, thoughts, and energy traveled, but it was a lie. There was no continuance, only absence. He hadn't wanted her to feel that absence, not the way he and Betheen did, as a shadow that walked with you. It had been a good lie, one that protected, but his lie meant she'd never understand what he'd meant to do, all the good it could accomplish. He'd meant to preserve life, not destroy it. To preserve power. Extend healing. Buy time for his hands. For Nedda, if she wanted it.

Nedda would never forgive him for Denny. Unless he fixed it. If he fixed it he could explain.

The power in the building had been compromised. He needed a battery, a current to counter a current. Which of the labs would have one powerful enough? Somers had been working on something—no—he was on sabbatical. The wire unspooled in long, loose curls across his work table. It wasn't enough, not even close. He held down one end of the wire with his shoe. He'd ask Pete for batteries—if Betheen's car was with him, the battery was technically his. The battery from his car as well.

Every bite of metal tasted of life. Blood supposedly had a copper taste to it; Theo found it was the other way around. If Dean Babcock saw him, straightening metal with his teeth, reeking of sweat and vomit, there would be no warning or committee, just an order to clean out his desk—the desk he'd rocked Nedda in, whose contents she'd thrown at him. Crucible would be dismantled, and he'd be fired because he looked like a mad scientist. After he'd finally succeeded. Mad scientist indeed. Iron—it too tasted like blood, and he'd need it to fix Crucible, to help Denny. Iron. There was a coat rack, one of the graduate students in engineering had brought in a coat rack. It was stained, old-looking, and a possibility.

Crucible worked. Denny proved it, the grove proved it—multiple time states existed within an few hundred yards of each other. An echo of delight lingered inside Theo, an ugly, yet welcome little fire.

He needed to call Liebowitz, let him know that the centrifuge model worked, but was prone to cracking. Liebowitz would be jealous as hell, which was its own reward. After. Once he'd fixed it. Once he knew *why* it had done what it had done. Water. It was something about water. Electricity. The sprinklers going on. If Denny sped forward, he could be sped back as well. It was a matter of a few tweaks. There would be pullback, physics demanded it. His sample had slowed, Denny had sped up. If Crucible made perfect systems, for one thing to speed, another must slow. If he sped up the sample, somewhere else there would be a slowing. He just had to get it working again. Excitement and fear dulled the pain in his hands. This could be fixed.

He shouldn't be smiling. It was awful to smile—but he *could* fix it. He could fine-tune. Possibility danced inside him. What if?

He saw Michael—his tiny body, the tearing skin, the nascent idea of who a child was meant to be—what could have been if that born-too-soon child was where Denny was, his lungs growing, his heart like a fist punching life, growing stronger?

What if no one had to lose a child that way?

What if? He could hold on to Nedda at this moment, at this perfect age, for as long as they pleased. If she wanted. She would have infinite time to learn. Infinite time to watch comets and launches. There had been a foolish little part of him who'd imagined unwrapping time for her like a present. *All the time to do whatever you want, for as long as you want, if you want it.* Nedda was made for *What if.*

*What if* had joy at its center that burned like Crucible's heart.

No one would have to lose a child. And there would be no more lies.

He would rewind—like the trees shrinking into themselves—to just before, the moment before things had gone wrong, before Michael died. When Betheen still loved him.

A spark shot from a wall outlet. Had he not been in pain, he would have noticed the temperature drop, the steam rolling off his skin.

To know how much copper and iron he needed, he had to know the area of effect. Where its edges were. There were smaller temporal anomalies he knew of—Denny, the grove, and the monkey. Pete said the canal on Satsuma was frozen. How far did Crucible's reach extend? Water pipes, irrigation systems, sprinklers. Canals. They connected somewhere.

Theo shuffled concepts like cards: entropy, sound, and amplification of waves. Light moved like a wave, like sound, like water; time might do the same. He neared Crucible, and couldn't help but admire the cool yellow light, laced with green. Then Theo did what he expressly told Nedda to never do in a lab. He reached out to feel the nature of the light, of this thing that he'd made.

Frigid, it drew the ache from his joints.

Crucible ruptured with light. The glare blinded Theo, and he fell like the dying, a subtle give that led to total collapse. As that light ran through him, Theo was horror and elation.

*What if.*

His every cell came alive, the awareness of it startling—every thought was a live nerve. Pressed to bursting, he cracked, the membrane that held him together shattering like glass. For twenty-five years, he'd been in some degree of agony. The nanosecond it vanished allowed him clarity.

Discovery could be both wonderful and terrible. He'd made such a discovery.

*What if.*

Then his body was no longer his own; it became all the bodies and shapes it had ever been, pulling backward, receding into what it once was. His thoughts were electricity, which, like water, had a flow, like light, was a wave.

This was time.

Theo Papas fell, a diver into a pool, swallowed by his existence.

# Potential

H IS LIFE ROLLS through him as an assault. Every atom in his being is fierce, vibrating, plaguing him with awareness of each particle that makes him, each particle's location in space and time. He was asleep until the light—wandering, unmindful of the electrons inside him, the tension of chemical bonds that make his body, the quarks and gluons holding him together in crackling accord. How did he walk and talk—live—without awareness?

His scarred skin smooths, each cell righting, healing from oxidation; patches of flaking red become soft, new. His joints ache in reverse, pain signals crawl up and inward, and his nerves gather breath. He sees a formula, agony as a function of release over time. He becomes a great convergence, a monstrous and beautiful flexing of bonds. Electrical pulses rush backward, neurons transmitting signals in reverse. He chokes on a glut of memory.

The transition is not calm.

His thoughts skip and he is thirteen, listening to Glenn Miller's "A String of Pearls" through the hiss of his father's record player.

Then he is twenty and watching his father cough himself to death after a failed lung operation. Globs of mucus, the mustiness of sick. Nasal cells remember scent as much as skin holds on to touch, as much as taste digs a trench in the soul. Fear is there, that he will be alone, alone and burying a man who never loved him.

His body pulls once more with a pain that throbs like a migraine, and he is in a room, damp, cool, surrounded by equipment. School, he remembers school—sleeping after a lecture, up too late the night before, an exam in the afternoon, finals next week, and his father just dead. He needs to tell his professors, but the physics department is not known for its leniency.

He is hot, boiling; the bonds in him shake, searing with extension and contraction.

His father is interred in Mangrove Glades Cemetery, a flat plaque as a grave marker. Stones were $523 more than he had. After the plot and the burial, $523 had been too much.

Theo is thirty-two, opening a checking account. Black ink on a pale-yellow check that smells like his pen drawer. It slides across a brown veneer desk in the lobby of Sun Credit Union. Five hundred and twenty-three dollars. He never withdraws it or deposits more. His father's headstone is preserved in numbers, depreciating in value, inflation both mercurial and constant.

He rockets forward, broken skin erupting. His back shrinks and cracks, contorting with decades of compressed time, his joints swell and crook, and thousands of unremembered things, things which have not yet happened—which may yet or never will—bend his neurons, tying them in knots. Theo thrums like a heartbeat, contracting and expanding with time.

Outside are footsteps, another person in the building. Time warps the sound into earthquakes.

*Theo.* There is a pause, then the name again. *Theo.* Someone called him *Professor* once, he knows this. The voice is as familiar as any of the particles that make him.

*Theo.*

The child sleeping by Crucible doesn't know this name. He is Teddy, who wishes he could always wear gloves or mittens to hide his hands, who can't pronounce his own disease, and wishes no one was afraid they would catch it from him.

Forty heartbeats pass. Fifty, sixty, more. He loses count. The old man who curls around the machine can't remember his name. He remembers a woman, a blonde who smells like lemon soap and sadness. He remembers a little girl, familiar like his hand, his arm, part of a body you don't know to miss until it's gone. He misses her. Why does he miss her?

There are feet nearby. They are women's feet, delicate. He should know them. He is certain he should recognize those shoes, that particular pair of feet.

Seventy heartbeats, eighty. He sleeps, wakes, sleeps. He is young again, eleven, and the older boys at Camp Tamiami are laughing as they piss on him in the shower. Their knees are knotty, their legs hairy like dogs. He doesn't fight back. He says nothing when Sprague and Fitz do it, nothing when his own bunkmate joins in. He smells the stink of urine. He sleeps and cries against the machine.

How can the curve of an ankle be familiar? When has he ever looked at women's legs?

He flickers, older, then younger, older again, rumbling through decades, cells warping. He cries for a little girl he doesn't yet know, or knew already—perhaps he's known and forgotten her. Forgetting and remembering web together.

Something is missing. There is a hole in him, something rends.

Somewhere there is a girl with dishwater hair; he knows this; he sees her. Gap-toothed. Reaching to grab a pencil from a desk. Ice cream all over her face, dimpled chin, fingers small and soft. She's lodged in his memory, carved in places she shouldn't be. He weeps.

He's hurt her. He doesn't know how.

Boys, he knows, are brutal and awful. They beat you with their bodies. He is this thing. Girls, women, are smarter. They break you just by living.

# 1986: Kinetic

**D**ESMOND PRATER WOKE with an aching back, which had as much to do with oranges as it did the thirty-odd pounds he'd put on over the last fifteen years. Boss weight. It was good for a man in a position of power to have a little heft to him. He wore it well enough, but not so much on bad weather days. His father used to go on about how weather settling in a body was as good an indicator of danger to the fruit as anything else. Stiff knees meant you checked for frost, wrapped the trees. Tickle in your throat that won't go away? Water more. What was good for the body was good for the oranges.

Fucking fruit.

Did ranchers feel some kind of woo-woo connection to their cattle? Thank God he wasn't psychically connected to a steer. Des hadn't cared much for his old man, who at the end smelled like vinegar and was just as sour. But the stuff about aching joints and cold was solid. His back had been bugging him for days. The trees could handle a day or two of cold, but without a warm turn, it was time to wrap trees or lose more fruit.

He reached to jostle Annie awake, but his hand met cold sheets. Right.

"If you think I'm going to share a bed with you after what you did, you've got another thing coming," she'd said.

"It was an accident. I barely touched him."

"You knew exactly what you were doing."

"Fine. I'm a monster, all right? Are you happy? I'm the bad guy. But I'm the bad guy who's not sleeping on the couch. Not in a house I paid for."

"Fine."

*Fine* was never fine, but at least it ended shit.

His father had never begged his mother, had never apologized for an errant fist either; he and his brother had taken it like they were supposed to. Chin up, no flinching, and whatever they'd done they didn't do again. There wasn't a damn thing wrong with that.

He pulled himself out of bed, cracked his back, and searched for his pants.

Denny had staggered when he'd hit him, actually staggered, which was ridiculous. He and John could take a punch by that age. It was self-preservation. Other boys hit you less once they figured out they couldn't deck you. Sure, maybe he shouldn't have hit him, but Denny had to learn what not to do somehow, and telling him never worked. It hadn't for John or him either. One good punch did. You'd feel it for a week. Denny would remember it every time he looked at that pruner and know that his ass did not belong on a machine he hadn't bought and paid for. Annie would have to get used to that.

The living room was quiet. "Annie? Annabee?"

Silence. He flicked on the lights.

She wasn't on the couch.

"Ann? Denny?"

Coffee wasn't set up. She might have taken Denny out to breakfast, thinking to avoid him. Denny was a sucker for pancakes, pouring syrup all over like he thought they might float.

He stumbled through two cups of instant coffee that managed to be both tasteless and bitter.

He'd been pissed off, but not Annie-packing-up-and-leaving pissed off. He remembered the feel of brow bone against knuckle. He shouldn't have hit Denny that hard; just a little pop would have been enough to teach him. Still, if his son had the balls to try joyriding on an expensive piece of equipment, he should have the balls to walk around with a black eye.

He rummaged up eggs, managed to crack them into a proper scramble, but couldn't get the stove to work. The pilot clicked but didn't catch. Annie had some trick or other she did with the knobs, three times all the way up to high—but he couldn't remember the rest. After a few unsuccessful attempts at lighting it with a match, he gave up. Fuck it. He'd go to the Bird's Eye. Ellery would give him a donut on the house. Annie and Denny were probably there, anyway. Half the town probably was, all talking about the shuttle. There would be reporters trying to get local flavor or whatever they called rolling into a town and knowing nothing about it. Shit. People died all the time. This was just a car crash with a higher price tag.

He left the egg mess in a bowl and grabbed his keys.

The phone rang.

"Mr. Prater? Boss?" Little Mike Costas sounded dazed. Des didn't care if the guys smoked a joint every now and again—hell, before the trunk shaker, it helped to be a little high to climb up those ladders—but Little Mike had never been one of those guys. Whistle clean. A tough rooster of a guy. If he could hire a million more of him, he would.

"Yeah?"

"Boss, there's something wrong with the trees."

"Damn it. It's the freeze, isn't it? How much do you figure we'll lose?"

"It's not a freeze, Boss. It's— You'd better come look."

Driving along Orange Way, Pete McIntyre's truck blew by him and damn near forced him into a ditch. Maybe Little Mike called him in about a part. He was a fast thinker that way, fixed problems before you knew they were problems. On the cheap too. Someone was in the cab with McIntyre. The sun seemed off, but the sky was bright. And the clouds were that funny color they got right before a storm walloped. Must be why his back was acting up. He squinted at the horizon. Then Desmond saw what Little Mike had been talking about and stomped on the brakes. It sure as hell wasn't a freeze.

It looked like the west part of the grove was doing the wave. One whole corner was scrunching down on itself, while just behind it, new trees were sprouting and stretching up.

"*Shee*-it." Bile threatened to appear at the sight of his grandfather's trees shriveling up and dying. What the hell was it?

Little Mike was standing outside the equipment shed with Marco, Jerry Reeves, and one of their boys—Desmond wasn't sure whose. The shed door was cracked open and everyone stood around it like they were waiting for the messiah to show up. Loafing. His fucking trees were dying and they were loafing.

"What the hell's going on? You should be wrapping trees."

Little Mike picked at the brim of a sun-bleached ballcap. "No can do, Boss. We can't get in. Something's kind of . . . I don't know. There's something in there."

"What the hell do you mean *something*? How come nobody got a tractor out?"

"Boss," Reeves said. The squirrelly shit kept eyeing the shed door.

"What? You hiding something from me? You broke something too? I swear I'm the only one who gives a rat's ass about this place."

Des pulled the shed door wide.

He wasn't sure what he was seeing. His son, but not his son. Quick flurries of movement, followed by stillness. His face was squarer. Different. Older. Then the movement began again, frenzied. He watched his son become a blur. There was color and shape where Denny was, where he'd been.

Denny was on top of that fucking pruner, which was rusting all to hell as he watched. Shit. Was Annie in there too? Had she come here with Denny? She wouldn't want to leave him alone, she lived to coddle him. He shouted her name.

"She ain't here, Boss."

"Shut up, Reeves. I wasn't asking you."

Then, suddenly, Denny stopped moving and Des got a good look at him. He was taller than Des remembered, by a lot. He'd grown inches in few hours.

"I found him like this after I called you." Little Mike's voice was low, calm. "The guys and I were getting ladders to see if we could get the east acres covered, but."

But.

Denny kicked furiously at the air, then fell back on the pruner. His son. A young man. There was no shiner, no bruise to show where his fist had connected with his son's face. Desmond swallowed down a sharp lump and reached out.

"Den?"

For an instant, Denny's eyes were on him, but then he was gone again. A soft shape and not a boy. Desmond's hand touched something smooth that looked like—nothing. Like air. Hard air. How the hell could air be solid?

When Denny slowed down again, there were long scratches on his forearms, forearms that were covered in dark hair.

Desmond closed the shed door behind him. He couldn't bring himself to look at his son, not again. He'd known they looked alike, and it had been a point of pride; the Prater chin was a mark of stubborn men since his grandfather and before. There'd never been any question that Denny was his son. Looking in a mirror that showed himself twenty years younger might have been something he'd wished for, but the reality of it made him break into a cold sweat.

"No one goes in," he said.

"Nobody, Boss. You got it. You want me to call Mrs. Prater?" Little Mike asked.

"No. I'll tell her." If he could figure out where she was. "Get the full team in, everybody you can get hold of."

"Chuck isn't coming in. His pipes burst and he says there's boiling water all over his house. Junior said he's stuck in his driveway 'cause of a hedge. I tried some of the Mims guys, but the calls didn't go through."

"A hedge?"

"That's what he said."

"Try the summer kids, then. Somebody's gotta want to make a buck. Whatever trees you can get to, I want them wrapped. And somebody's gotta stay here and watch, make sure nobody goes in that shed. Okay? I'm coming back. If I come back here and this is fucked up worse, heads are gonna roll."

He didn't know what he was saying, didn't care, but the tone got them running. He could still light a fire under anyone's ass. You couldn't let guys like this know when you'd gone to shit or they'd walk all over you.

He had to tell Annie. He had to find Annie. She'd kill him.

Desmond leaned on the shed, his back toward the men, and swallowed down something like panic, but worse. The metal siding was hot, burning his skin. That air, that hard air that his son was in was hot too. Desmond Prater knew himself to be a coward because he couldn't stay with him. He couldn't force himself to watch.

Denny was on the pruner.

"I swear I'll fix it, Pop. Lemme fix it. I can do it."

"You lost the right to touch that machine the second your ass hit the seat without asking, you little shit."

"Des, stop it."

"I can fix it, Pop."

The last thing he'd called his son was a little shit.

He looked out at the trees and noticed Denny's bike leaning against the fence, baseball cards in the spokes. He was unused to seeing it without Nedda Papas's bike next to it.

He had to find Annie.

In his truck, midway down Satsuma Drive, he ran into a backup. He craned his head out of the window and spotted flashing lights. An accident. The brush was high up on the side of the road without the canal, the trees dense, overgrown. There was no way to jack a U-turn without getting stuck. A hedge. Junior was stuck because of a hedge. He threw the truck in reverse.

This had to be some kind of divine retribution for letting loose on Denny. But Desmond's father had belted him and John a good time or two for far less, and nothing bad had ever happened to him. It wasn't like he'd broken Denny's nose. A good knock every now and again was par for the course. Boys ran wild if you didn't keep them in line. Annie knew that. But she'd left before he was up, and so had Denny.

Denny was hardly ever alone. He was always with Nedda.

And what the hell had Pete McIntyre been doing at the grove, and why was he starting to think that Theo Papas had been in that truck with him?

# 1986: Child and Man

BETHEEN WALKED THROUGH the tiki head, a fake god made by men who fancied themselves cowboys, men who built a monkey jungle without thinking about how to care for the monkeys, the same men who made Polynesian-kitsch buildings and put them beside an Old West saloon and shooting gallery.

As she ducked through the torn-down fence, static moved across her skin, a pricking burn, almost like fire. Once, when she'd been a student, someone had left a burner leaking and a small gas explosion singed the hair from her forearms. Fire left vacuums in its wake, a rush followed by absence. Michael had been a fire, and when he was gone, she was hollow, forced to rebuild herself from a molecular level.

Her car was broken on the roadside, near a dead man.

As with everything, there was nothing to do but move forward.

Betheen picked her way through the remains of the park. She'd charted this path to ensure it was safe—if not perfectly safe, then the right amount of dangerous—before telling Annie that the kids were old enough to play outside on their own. Betheen knew the park would be irresistible, so she'd spent two full days making sure there was nothing awful, no hidden drops, and that the rides and buildings were far too broken to be inviting. She'd become a master at distance mothering, the kind that allowed her daughter to get in trouble, safe trouble. Theo didn't understand. He taught, incessantly lectured, never realizing that Nedda would try to be all the things he wished for. She couldn't be. But she'd try until she hurt herself. It's what women did. Some girls didn't need expectations; they needed an enemy. A person who forbid them from swearing so they'd teach themselves to cuss properly.

Her foot snagged on a root that sent her tumbling. She caught herself on the remains of a poured-concrete floor. This was where the butterfly house had been. She remembered it: wings like flower petals, how they'd rest on your arms like the wind kissing you. She wished for ten thousand butterflies, wings beating, hooked feet digging into her clothing, latching on, and carrying her into the sky.

A whisper inside. *Get up.*

Wrongness washed over her. Other women might call it *mother's intuition*, but Betheen recognized the extra sense as what it was—the tension of a chemical bond made long ago, of oxytocin and dopamine, a heady mix that changed you chemically so you'd know when your child was hurt, when your spouse had died.

Nedda: Safe.

Michael: Dead.

Theo: Unaccounted for.

*BETHEEN. GET UP. MOVE YOUR ASS.*

She dug her feet into the loamy ground, got up, and ran.

He'd been a teaching assistant for Physics 101, which she couldn't test out of; Palm Lake High School had refused to let her take physics, routing her into business classes instead. There was such a thing as too smart. Mr. Papas hadn't seen that. Mr. Papas stammered when he said her name. *Miss Squ-squires.* But he called on her, which was more than her professors and other TAs did. And he made an effort not to stare at her legs, which, in the way of anything a person tried not to do, made the staring more obvious. She fell in love with the way he wrote on the blackboard, how every 5 wore a hat that tipped upward. She fell in love with being called on, and being right, and, better still, being permitted to be wrong. She fell in love with chalk and pens and the particular smell of the lecture hall when he was in it. Smoky.

Chemistry made you fall in love with the shape of a jaw: serotonin, oxytocin. Sex was physics, but love was chemistry. She knew why she loved the scent of dry-erase markers, why black hair had become better than any other color, and why a specific pair of glasses made her see the man behind them. A deluge of chemicals.

He'd never asked why she wasn't a biology major, or how she'd wound up in science. He'd said, as she picked up her books before heading to her next class, "Miss Squires, I have a sneaking suspicion you're smarter than I am."

She smiled, the way her mother said debutantes did, the way women did when they knew that they were *better*. She told him to call her Betheen.

She waited until term's end because it was proper, until her exams were graded and she was top of the class as expected. On the first day after winter break, she left her chemistry notes on his desk before his lecture. She'd asked around, figured out which classes he was assisting. The notebook had her address and the number of the dormitory written inside the cover.

She had the hall mother let him up. After all he was a doctoral student—nearly a professor—what did it matter that he was young? Twenty-five and brilliant.

She answered the door in her underwear and stockings. Light green satin. Seafoam.

He tried to hide his skin. The rough patches were continents, large islands on his body's map. She plotted them, touching her lips to each, intent on learning his composition. Noble, in the moral and elemental sense.

Yet they'd still broken. School, marriage, children. She hadn't known the last one might undo the first two.

The hallway to the lab was narrow. His door was closed, but light came from under it, a soft pulsing that meant something was running. When she opened it, damp and cold washed over her, then a biting odor. At first, she thought it was ozone or Freon, but it was nothing so familiar.

It didn't smell like him. His lab, the house—they always smelled like him. Where was he? And the light—it was sun without heat. Alive somehow, generative like the glow of lava or molten metal.

The machine was enormous. A potbellied beast with jointed arms and ventilation piping that reached across the ceiling. How had he managed the build? He must have had graduate students help, people who needed credit to pass his classes. Envy ran through the part of her that still wished they'd been like the Curies. But children meant certain things, and she'd wanted those things, and Marie Curie had wound up dead.

"Theo?"

The chemical smell grew heavier, tart. An ester—a liqueur but without the pleasure.

"Theo?"

Still no answer. There was a soft hissing in the back of the room, the machine humming. She flicked the switch for the overhead, but it remained stubbornly off.

"Theo?"

There was movement.

A picture of him stood out in her memory, Theo at age six or seven, dressed as a cowboy, sitting on top of a pony. He said a photographer had come through his neighborhood with a costume trunk and a pony that was a thousand years old and sick of children.

The eyes were hard to recognize at first, as she'd rarely seen them without glasses. Even the boy in the picture had thick black frames. But the ears were the same, one that stood out like a jug handle, the other pinned close to the skull. The hair. The little boy's hair was his. As ever, psoriasis marked him, though it hadn't yet ruined his joints. By the time she'd met him, his skin had improved, but she'd seen pictures of before, tucked in a box of his father's things. She'd have never known otherwise how bad it had been, how much of him it had consumed. When she asked, he said, "I made it harder on myself. I couldn't stand pine tar soap."

Until then, she hadn't known what the smoky scent was. She'd fallen in love with his medicine. Aromatic hydrocarbons.

This boy, this impossible six- or seven-year-old child behind the machine, was the boy in that picture.

Two legs, two feet, two eyes, two arms, two hands, his familiar fingernails, all the ingredients of Theo, hiding behind his own improbable water cake.

The room grew warm, suddenly unbearably hot, and the machine threw more light. Then the boy fluctuated, spreading and growing, until before her—eyes wet, mouth gasping soundlessly, shaking as if to rattle himself apart—was the young man she'd marry. Skinny, angular. The flaking redness was gone from his face, but wrapped around his torso.

She remembered the discovery of it, rough but supple, as she'd slipped her hand beneath his shirt while he stood in her open doorway. She'd asked if it hurt. He never told her; she learned his aches later. He said she didn't have to touch him if she found it upsetting. He talked about his body the way her grandmother's friends talked about profane language. It made her want to lick him. In that coarseness was a heart he wore across his stomach.

His eyes, Theo's eyes, met hers. She waited for the recognition, the clicking into place she'd had with him in a lecture hall. Lust rose for a man she hadn't seen in years, for the bump on his wrist, the downy hair on the back of his hands, his eyes. This man who didn't know what would happen. The tightness in her belly made her weep. Did he know? Did he remember?

"Theo?"

His mouth moved. She knew the shape. *Miss Squires.*

If she made a sound, it was lost to the light and convolution manifested by the machine. Crucible. Nedda said he called it Crucible. Theo's body retracted, his arms and legs drawing up. Baby fat bloomed, his eyes rounded, widened. The rash danced all over him, flaring, fading, exploding. He seemed a part of the light, dimming and flashing with each stretch and scream. Betheen watched her husband turn inside out until she had to look away.

And then there was an infant—pink-tipped fingers, bow lips—bobbling and squirming as infants did, blinking and startlingly quiet. She could see Michael in this infant, what he had been, what he might have been. Perfect fat limbs. Young enough to still have the plugs that keep amniotic fluid from the nasal passageway. Soft black hair, the first fuzz of a baby.

She reached for him, almost touched, then her hand slipped against something smooth, something she could almost see, slick. Like agar.

There was a child in Theo's lab. A baby. Perhaps it wouldn't be there in five minutes, ten minutes, but it would be back. Her husband, the infant, shifted and writhed.

*Look. Get up. Think.*

She caught her breath. She could walk away. She could try to contact his friend. Who had he worked with—Avi, Ari . . . Lieber?

A manic person, high-pitched laugh. Liebowitz. A fast thinker. She should call his friend Liebowitz.

*Miss Squires, I have a sneaking suspicion you're smarter than I am.*

She turned back, checked her wristwatch and marked the time. She watched.

*Think. Find the pattern. Fix it.*

# Aboard *Chawla*

SINGH REFUSED TO be a pincushion. "If Papas wants to be the guinea pig, we should let her."

Marcanta swore. "I should have just stuck you while you were out. I can't risk Papas. I can't do anything to a Gapper that's not tested on one of us first. I'll probably have to do a puncture on everyone eventually. What's it matter if you're first?"

"Maybe it benefits us to have someone with functional eyes who knows how to fix the on-board systems? Have you thought of that? Do it to Evgeni first. They're his eyes," Singh said.

Nedda didn't want Evgeni to be the first to learn that it was unfixable. While the rings from the mask were painful, she feared the day he wouldn't have them, when he'd given up. For him, and for the rest of them. "I'm perfectly capable of fixing systems and you know it. Besides, Evgeni's a bad sample," Nedda said. "He's progressing faster than the rest of us. He's atypical. Singh, you and Louisa are the baseline. It has to be you or her. Just admit that you're afraid and do it anyway."

"I can't do my own tap," Marcanta said.

Singh took three hours on the exercise bike. It was childish, but Nedda understood. A fluid draw was small, yes, but it was the first admission that it wasn't just *Chawla* that was failing.

She checked the communications schedule. She wasn't slated to speak with her mother for another month. She hadn't expected the disconnect she'd feel at not being able to pick up a phone anytime she wanted. Of not knowing where or when her mother was. She missed the kitchen telephone cord, the yellow spring of it, letting the receiver dangle to unravel a snarl. What she wouldn't give for a kitchen telephone cord that stretched across the universe, knowing that Betheen was on the other end, leaning against a wall, something slightly dangerous bubbling on a burner. Oh, her mother's lean. The strength of her. Nedda positioned a tray of corn seedlings under the grow lights, then brought up Amadeus's schematic. She chewed her lip. Scared was fine. Lonely was fine. You could be those things, as long as you worked.

They saw Singh at dinner. He rolled up chunks of tofu in a tortilla, folding it precisely into something that looked like a wonton. Meticulous. His fingers always clean.

"I'll do it," he said. "Of course I'll do it."

*Chawla* was cold, and while Evgeni enjoyed it, happily floating shirtless between bathroom and bunk, Singh had long maintained a layered modesty. Shirts under sweaters, under jumpsuits. Nedda hadn't seen his back before. He lay on his side, strapped to the table in medical, curled up like a child. *Vulnerable*, Nedda thought. Each vertebra a gentle hill, a sand dune.

Marcanta took her hand and ran it down Singh's spine. "You're looking for the space between. There's something stupid about the human brain that wants to poke anything that sticks out. Don't be stupid. Feel here."

Peaks and valleys like the moon, like Earth, like all of them.

"Still in the room," Singh said. "Person, not a cadaver."

"We know, Amit. Cadavers are better patients." Marcanta let go of Nedda's hand. "For our purposes, it doesn't matter if we get a little blood in the fluid, but it should still be mostly CSF. And obviously, mind the spinal cord."

"Obviously," Singh said.

"You've got a nice back," Nedda said. "The vertebrae look strong." Comfort wasn't something she excelled at.

"Please, just do it or let me up."

Marcanta sank the needle in and Singh inhaled sharply. "Pull back, just a little—like so—and now we wait. We've got a few minutes, Singh. Entertain us."

"Fuck off," he muttered.

"You can do better than that," Nedda said.

Singh repeated himself.

"You're a scientist. Try harder. At least say 'fuck nugget.' If you're going to swear in English, have the decency to use British or Scottish swears." The words rolled out like a satisfying stretch, the kind Nedda hadn't had since Earth. " 'Cunt,' 'twat,' 'cockwomble,' 'bellend,' 'knobend,' 'piss-flaps,' 'wankstain,' 'gobshite,' 'fuck trumpet,' 'jizz trumpet'— anything you want to add a 'dick' to, go with 'trumpet' or 'bell.' There's a literal musicality to it Americans never bothered with," she said. She spouted the long-ago gorgeous list and wondered if all collected data, every list ever made, was waiting for the moment it found its purpose. " 'Arsemonger,' 'cocksplat,' 'clunge.' " Marcanta's husky chuckle echoed in the lab. Every now and again, Singh would repeat a word, his clipped *T* making it elegant.

"Where the hell did you learn all those?" Marcanta asked.

"Research."

Nedda's curses became a lullaby. Singh asked Nedda to write them down to tell Evgeni. Marcanta kept her eye on the vial connected to the needle in Singh's back. As it filled, Singh clamped his eyes shut. Near the end, he bit into his cheek. A small blood droplet escaped, a single perfect bubble filled with chains of molecules, DNA, a microcosm of Singh. Nedda caught it with a tissue.

Marcanta pulled the needle and cleaned the wound. "Look at that. Totally clear, no blood. In residency, you call a draw like that a 'champagne tap,' and your senior or the attending gives you a glass of champagne. Well, they used to, anyway."

"Nice of you to wait until after to get drunk," Singh said.

"Shut up and put your pressure goggles on, Amit. Then, bed. Tomorrow I want to check your eyes before morning call, got it?"

He asked about the headache.

"Only a small number of people get it. Zero g might eliminate it, since you won't get the fluid shift you normally would when you stand. If you get it, you'll know."

"Fantastic," he said.

Before Nedda left for Hydro, Marcanta took her arm.

"Do you think you can do that to me?"

Could she feel her way down Louisa's back, prick her, and not clip her spinal cord? Singh would need to see it on someone else before trying. There was no one else. "I'd rather not have to," Nedda said.

"That's not what I asked."

"Yes, I can do it."

"Good." Marcanta slipped the vial into a drawer. "Here's hoping you're better at nursing than I am at botany."

Later, as Nedda added nitrogen to nutrient gel for the carrots, she thought of a thousand things she might have said to Marcanta, about fear, about responsibility, and what failure meant, but she'd had no words left. She'd spent them on profanity. She turned on her tablet. Amadeus was familiar now, friend and enemy. Switching the isotope had contributed to the problem, but it was also something as simple and monumental as failing to account for zero gravity. *Chawla* was the first ship to tie life support to an accelerated radioisotope thermoelectric generator. Amadeus meant deep space travel for humans. Colonization and species survival. Time. *Fortitude* was outfitted with the same kind of drive but had artificial gravity, a backup kinetic system. Even if they couldn't fix Amadeus for *Chawla*, they had to try. They had to give *Fortitude*'s colonists a foothold, a real chance at survival on planet. For the greater good.

Singh's moans woke her. He couldn't tolerate the lights in his cabin, so she turned them off.

"Too much noise," he said when she tried to talk to him. A sand-paper whisper. "Can't stand my own voice."

In the end, she held his feet, squeezing them between her palms, rubbing through the sleep sack's quilted layers. Her mother had done this for her. She'd had mononucleosis in her last year of high school. Bedridden and crying, the only thing that had anchored her was Betheen rubbing warmth into her feet. Men's feet were strange things, bonier, lumpier than women's. Singh's reminded her of a giraffe—long and knobby. Here she was, mothering a grown man.

She'd never been maternal. Her single-mindedness had blocked that sentiment, or what had happened to her had replaced that partic-ular tenderness with scar tissue. And yet. *Chawla* thrummed around them, breathing. Comfort had once been her father's cold steel lab table. Now, it was a machine with a heartbeat.

She squeezed Amit's feet again and discovered they were flat.

When she left him to sleep, it was with renewed purpose. After three more hours of studying the schematic, there was a small sting in her chest, like the pull of a string. Were she to trace it with her fingers, it would span the distance to Easter. She dashed off a message to Mission Control.

Dr. Papas requests to immediately schedule a private video call with her mother, Betheen Papas. Please inform Betheen Papas that her daughter can't remember the best way to pop a bubble and requires a refresher.

# 1986: The Dead

MARTY NEUHAUS WAS sweating something awful. It came with the suit, which was required, even for pre-planning consults. People liked to think they'd chosen a high-end establishment for their loved one. A wool suit said quality, but it could make you sweat like you'd run ten miles. Marty had a pre-plan coming in at eleven, the Alfresons, for Deenie, who was fading. A delivery blocked one of the exits, which was illegal, so here he was, lugging embalming fluid and cosmetics through the parking lot door and into the embalming room, sweating in his suit, his shirt rubbing his armpits raw.

That he had customers made it worse. He prided himself on dignity for his clients, peace and quiet after a life which was typically not restful.

He hefted and grunted. "My sincerest apologies, Mr. West. I don't usually subject customers to this sort of display, but my assistant is fond of oversleeping."

Mr. West said nothing, and hadn't for the past two days, not since Mrs. West found him on the kitchen floor, having choked on the last pickle in the jar.

Marty's assistant, Reg Peterson, hadn't overslept but had gotten lost, which was bizarre considering he'd managed to get to work without a hitch for seventeen months. But that morning, when he went to turn off the highway for Easter, the exit wasn't there. He'd done three U-turns but couldn't find it going north or south. He figured he must be sick, so he turned back for home.

At his apartment in Port St. John, Reg called the funeral parlor, but the line rang and rang. He tried three more times that day. On the last try, the line cut out. Reg turned on the news, all of which was focused on the shuttle explosion. It made sense that he couldn't get through. The lines must be overloaded.

On the third day of driving and missing the exit, Reg, who was a quiet man, spoke to a waitress at the Howard Johnson's off the highway. Hands clenching a coffee cup, he read her nametag. *Rowenna.* Pretty name. Rowenna's hands were calloused from bleach and dishwashing, and they didn't match the rest of her, which looked like she should be picking shells off a beach somewhere.

"Rowenna, I have a weird question for you. Has anyone come in here over the past few days asking where exit 43 is? I can't find it for the life of me."

"Not that I know of. We had some reporters on their way to the Cape because of that horrible accident, but they're always lost. Mostly we get truckers and folks on their way down to Ft. Lauderdale. We're just a lunch stop on the way to somewhere else, you know?"

In that moment, as Rowenna refilled his cup, Reg heard something in her words—that she might not mean just the HoJo. That she, from her voice and the slump in her shoulders, might feel like a stop on the way to somewhere else. Reg was that way. Picking up bodies, conveying them from home to table to grave.

"It's strange," he said. "I've taken that exit every day for over a year, then two days ago, it up and disappears."

"Well, they're renumbering exits to match miles. Maybe a sign change has got you mixed up."

"Could be," he said.

"Are you all right?" Her hand touched the table, and he saw her dry, cracked cuticles. Like his.

"You know, I'm not sure."

"Me neither, honey. Me neither."

At the end of the third day of breakfast at the HoJo and heartburn from too much coffee, Reg asked Rowenna, "Would you like to look for the exit with me? Maybe you'll catch something I missed."

She tucked back a wave of permed hair. "I've got a break in fifteen minutes. You can take me to the Orange Julius if you're buying."

After two weeks of lunches with Reg, Rowenna did not return from her break. She rolled down the passenger window in his little white Ford and let her hand ride over the wind. They went down to Ft. Lauderdale. Reg stopped talking about the thing that had made him stop at the HoJo in the first place.

It was too many bodies, he decided.

He took a job selling office supplies and found that he loved it; he had a gift for matching people to serviceable paper products. He used the same calm that he had with the bereaved and sold more folders and paper than anyone else.

Rowenna finally felt like a destination. And if she noticed Reg calling a dead number once in a while, it was a small quirk, and one worth overlooking in a man who had made up the most ridiculous lie just to ask her out.

When their little girl, Veronica, turned sixteen and started dating, Rowenna told her, "Wait for the right one. Wait for someone so in love with you that they don't care that they look like a fool, someone who'll imagine up a whole town just to have something to talk to you about."

Reg never said otherwise. Time painted with watercolors, and after enough years, he believed Rowenna was right.


Marty reached into a cabinet, searching for his wax. Reg had rearranged things, and it was impossible to find anything. What was convenient for Reg, at six foot one, was out of sight for Marty, at five foot seven.

"Sorry, Mrs. Lattimer. Oh, I know. That coroner does a number on people. But I'll have you fresh as a daisy. That shower we gave you did wonders." A sundress would cover the Y-shaped incision, but wax was the only solution for a craniotomy.

He was ill prepared for what he saw when he turned around, wax in hand. Mrs. Lattimer, whose repose looked particularly hard-earned, was moving. More precisely, her *skin* was moving; the edges of the Y incision shortened and the threads he'd sewn popped and pulled from their stitches. There was a grinding clunk, the knock of bone on bone.

A cranium locking into place.

The bruising along her back from the hours she'd been on the bathroom floor, blood pooling below the skin as rigor mortis set in, softened and faded away.

"Miriam?" He was a fool to say her name, but what were you supposed to do when a body started sewing itself up on your table? When a body became less a body and more a Miriam Lattimer?

When her knuckles straightened he ran out the side door onto Latchee Street, right into the middle of the road. Miriam's heart was inside her. Vivisected, yes, but what if it sewed up? Her chest, her skin.

No. That wasn't right. He needed a drink. He needed something. The sky was swimming. People. He needed people, living ones. And a drink.

Marty shuffled down to the Bird's Eye, where there were people, and there was rum. Ellery Rees kept a hidden stash of good Cuban stuff he picked up when he went down to the Keys. It was the town's worst-kept secret, along with Mayor Macon's affairs.

Ellery was working the cash register, his sunburned scalp showing through what most people considered a wiseguy haircut. His Hawaiian shirt had a good amount of someone's coffee on it. As much as Ellery was out for a buck, he genuinely liked Easter and could feel when someone was about to walk in, before the bell on the door jingled, before they passed the window and the chipped red lettering on the glass.

"Marty. It's early for you. God, you look like death warmed over. Pun intended, pal, I assure you. Pun absolutely intended."

"Ellery," Marty said. "I need a *beach vacation.*"

"Bit early for that, don't you think? Feels criminal to pour on a weekday before noon."

"Put it in a coffee mug or do what you've got to do. I'll pay whatever you want."

Marty Neuhaus had done Ellery's dad up right and made sure that nobody could tell that half his nose was gone. Marty hadn't charged extra for Senior's casket, even though he'd gotten too fat for the regular width. Marty just pulled Ellery to the side and asked him to pick out a different model. The charge never showed up on the bill. The Rees family didn't forget things like that. He splashed coffee on a heavy pour of contraband and slid that chipped mug right under Marty Neuhaus's nose.

Marty drained the cup and asked for another.

"Okay, Lurch. I like you and all, but you're not exactly a beach bum. You all right? You get asked to do one of the astronauts or something?"

"I . . . I'm not well, Ellery. Miriam Lattimer just stitched herself up on my table."

"No shit?"

Ellery had seen a good number of people go off the deep end, enough to know that everybody went about it differently. His uncle had climbed up a tree and thrown nuts at people when his wife left. When Ted Buller got the shakes, he would go on about commies in the bushes. Some people didn't say anything at all, which was the only way to spot them. Marty was a shocker. Ellery had figured that after all the stuff he'd seen, he must piss ice. Maybe that's what did it, though. Best to let him ride it out, calm down, and get it out of his system.

Ellery gently topped Marty off, then wiped the counter around him. Marty didn't look at Ellery but appeared to lose himself in the slow circular motions of the rag on the Formica.

"Her skin, where the . . ." He drew a *Y* in the air. "Right on my table, it closed up. I'd washed her off, because the coroner always leaves them such a mess. I was set to start on her, when her chest—all the stitches, they zipped right up. They shouldn't have done that. They didn't do that, did they?"

Ellery couldn't parse the distasteful things Marty said. Marty stared at dead bodies, most of them old, most of them people he knew. Ellery hadn't thought about what that entailed, like Miriam Lattimer's naked old-lady breasts sagging like used pantyhose. Marty had seen Ellery's dad's shriveled old-man dick. A job like that could make someone crack. How could you keep looking at bodies and not see people? Or look at people and not think about them dead on your table?

"Hey," Ellery said. "Don't take this wrong, but when I put in too many hours the forks start talking to me. You had a break in a while? I don't mean anything by that, I'm just saying. Take a few days off and let that kid you got handle stuff."

"Reg isn't in. Do you mind if I sit for a while, Ellery? I can't go back there yet."

"Do you want me to see if I can get a hold of Shelly?"

"Yes. Yes, please. I'd call her myself, but . . ."

"But you're shaking like a cold Chihuahua. Gotcha. She's still working at the bank, yeah?"

"Yes."

Ellery started dialing on the phone by the register, only to realize there was no dial tone. "Sorry, Lurch. Lines are out again. Look, just stay. It's a slow day. My soda guy hasn't showed up, and it looks like a storm anyway. Sit until your head gets together, okay?"

Marty nodded and whispered, "Sure. Yes, all right. You're right."

Eddie Ingram slid onto a stool next to Marty.

"Hey, Ellery, can I get some of that stuff? There was an accident on Satsuma. Some guy got damn near decapitated and his car's stuck in the canal, which is frozen. The roads out of here, I don't know, man. There's no getting out. The highway— It's like the woods just— I don't know what the hell's going on." Ed shuddered.

"Lot of that going around." Ellery slid a cup down the counter. He poured another for himself.

# 1986: Pete McIntyre

PETE WAS SURE about a few things. He knew that if there was a fire or freeze, or if another hurricane flattened Easter, he'd be just fine. He'd find something new, start over. He was sure Rita would never get over him, and that's why she was on husband number three. And he was sure what happened to Denny Prater wasn't natural and no kid, not ever, deserved to die like that.

He liked Denny, which surprised him, because the kid's father was the gapingest asshole in the state. Pete McIntyre knew Desmond Prater when he was just a greasy little sonofabitch whose father had somehow managed not to kill the family business. That didn't seem like it took too much skill; the more difficult thing was starting over, which is what every McIntyre man did at least five times in his life.

Pete's father, Red, had run fan boat tours, wrestled gators, run numbers and done time for it, and driven trucks. His mother, Gina Lee, had been the same way. Pete had picked fruit under Jim Prater, scraped roadkill off highways, put out fires for Brevard County, been a janitor at Covey, done maintenance work at Kennedy, and fixed cars. When his back wasn't killing him, he counted himself one lucky bastard.

It'd been bad enough knowing *Challenger* was gone. All those people dead in a second. Nothing set you up for a shock like that, but that was just the deal; part of what made the sky beautiful was the risk that came with touching it. But that kid— In what had already been a bad week, Denny was the worst thing Pete had ever seen. His chest hurt. His heart took bad news before the rest of him, like it meant to crawl out from under his ribs.

Nothing like that should happen to a kid, not anyone's kid.

He and Rita had had a daughter in their early twenties, when they were working at a bar in Mims. Della was like him, but she had the travel bug. At eighteen she'd left to drive to California, where she waited tables. He guessed tables were better there. That was five years back.

Della called her mom, and Rita called him, so that was all right. But if something happened to her, he'd know. He'd feel it. That shitbag Prater should know about his kid.

Copper. Theo Papas said he needed copper to fix it. Fuck it; he'd get some. He picked through his stuff, homing in on where he might have stashed any copper.

The garage suited him. But he missed touching all those things at NASA. People thought it was trash. Casts of hands, feet, and tire treads; stuff that hadn't gone to space, but was right next to it. He hadn't meant to collect this much, but good stuff kept getting tossed. He couldn't—not if he wanted to think of himself as a man—let a goddamn impressive piece of machinery like a crawler transporter piston rust in a dump.

Space junk wasn't a bad way to make a buck either. People who drove over wanting a break from the Mouse, the "I want to see the *real* Florida" types, were happy to dump two dollars to see food tubes, the locker bank, the rover tires, even busted phones from Mission Control. As far as he saw it, there wasn't much difference between taking space junk and keeping cars running; they were both salvage. Some years were shit for fishing, but there'd always be a need for somebody who understood salvage, someone who could fix things. The Prater kid got it; that was part of why Pete liked him.

By the side of the house was a commercial AC unit he'd scored on the cheap from Ellery at the Bird's Eye. He'd been meaning to fix it up. A crowbar peeled away the back like tinfoil, exposing guts and twisted copper tubing. Shit. He didn't know if it needed to be straightened, bent, or what. The professor hadn't said. What would take the least amount of time? No boy should have to stay like that.

When the kids had first started tooling around Pete's yard, he thought about running them off, until he recognized Denny as Desmond Prater's son. He had the same face as his prick dad, but it had turned out skinny this go. Denny liked to stick his fingers in carburetors and engines, which would have been a problem if he broke them, but he didn't; the kid was fascinated by them, almost worshipful. Pete didn't want to kick him out, especially not when he saw the other kid with him was a girl. He'd never had a girl nosing around the yard, not even his daughter. Della had liked the hi-fi in the den, but that was about it.

The little blonde girl was different. She poked at all his good stuff: a busted solar panel for a satellite, the control table he'd grabbed when cleaning out a media room. It was fried and he'd never get it working, but it was good stuff. History was made on it.

It took a couple of days before he placed her: the Papas girl. The professor was an ex-NASA guy, cut loose when they scaled back. He was all right and good for a few bucks for some salvage every now and again. Her mother was a beautiful woman, but cold. She baked like a goddess, but butter wouldn't melt in her mouth.

Nedda was a talker. He'd heard her yak Denny Prater's ear off about everything from dinosaurs to sunburn. It was rough she didn't get her mother's good looks, but worse that she couldn't seem to shut up. But Pete recognized himself in her, save for the talking. Junk rats recognized junk rats. She was careful with things and looked at stuff with an eye to figuring out how it worked. And Denny Prater looked at her like she hung the moon. Desmond Prater didn't have that kind of look for anybody but himself. Pete might be a sentimental idiot for letting two kids work out that they liked each other, but it made him a better guy than Desmond Prater.

Car in, car out. Take a few bucks out of some tourists around a launch. Wake up when his back yelled, go to bed after three beers. Go to Mims on the weekend, see if Rita had another man yet. Keep an eye on the kids. That was what was supposed to happen. Then he'd seen a guy get his head nearly taken off in a wreck. Betheen Papas should probably be dead too, but she'd walked away like nothing had happened. Wouldn't even take a ride. Then her husband had dragged him out to the grove.

He was supposed to be working on her Cadillac, not pulling copper out of his stuff.

None of what he'd seen in that equipment shed should happen.

Denny was a good kid, even if his dad was a shitstain, and good kids didn't deserve what he'd seen. He spotted a refrigerator he'd forgotten he'd picked up. Crowbar in hand he went for it. Hell. He'd rip every inch of copper out of his house if he had to.

# Aboard *Chawla*

THEY'D SET UP a routine where Marcanta did Nedda's spinal taps while she was under; now headaches plagued Nedda's artificial sleep, but the drugs kept her from waking. She dreamed of Easter, of bodies plumping in their graves. Their cells were her own, half-alive, waiting to wake up.

Marcanta said during sleep cycles she dreamed of athletic sex romps in exotic locations with the pop star Jasper Soo. They'd done it in a floating waterfall over the heads of thousands of his screaming fans. "You know, you can dream a week-long orgasm," Marcanta said.

Nedda couldn't.

Evgeni said he dreamed of expensive cars and being on whaling ships and that he once dreamed he was his own wife, and when he'd woken up the printer had already spit out psych meds.

The dusky seaside sparrow trilled, and Nedda's IV self-ejected, sealing the mark it left with skin glue. Her back was sore at the puncture, but her headache had dulled. She lay strapped in, watching fuzzy-edged pixel waves. The lack of gravity was winning. She'd have to tell Marcanta.

She had to fix Amadeus before she couldn't see it.

Marcanta didn't take the news about Nedda's eyes well. She swore and kicked out at the wall, only to propel herself directly into another.

"You bought us a lot of time, Louisa," Nedda said.

"Patronizing only makes it worse, Papas. We're fucked."

"We're getting close on Amadeus, I promise."

"Has Singh come up with any options that don't involve one of us taking a massive dose of radiation?"

Nedda said nothing.

"See? Fucked."

"But we knew that starting out. None of us planned on dying of old age." The first stab at colonization was a guaranteed death sentence, but a noble one.

"Agreed." There was a flatness to Marcanta's voice that hadn't been there before. "Here's hoping I dream up something better, and that Singh doesn't fry us all."

Nedda checked messages. Nothing from Mission Control. Nothing saying that her mother had gotten anything. Had the message been screened? The printer hummed and plinked five capsules into its tray. Vitamin. Beta blocker. Water pill. Iron. Birth control. The iron pill looked larger than normal. She smacked the printer, which knew more about her than she did.

When she passed by central systems control, Evgeni grinned beneath pressure goggles—a sweaty, friendly toad.

"Good dreams?" he asked, speaking over the computer as it chirped air composition statistics.

"A long vacation in the Maldives, swimming in phosphorescence." She should come up with a different dream to make it sound more real, but she hadn't dreamed of anything but Easter in years.

"Always beaches for you. You don't like the snow?"

"Not warm enough for me." She exaggerated a shiver. "We'll be plenty cold when we get there. I guess my brain doesn't feel the need to rush it. After? Feel free to teach me sledding or skiing."

"There won't be snow or enough water to do much," he said.

The planet's water was largely subterranean. The bots were constructing irrigation systems, reservoirs, piping, and receptacles for the water they'd make themselves, pulling from elements of the planet's atmosphere. "And I doubt anyone programmed the terraformers to make you a sledding hill. Singh could mess with the codes, though."

"Who is to stop us when we get there? We will be our own society. Mountains, beaches, we will make whatever we want. Each our own country." He spoke around a mouthful of protein bar; the berry-colored mush reddened his teeth, making him look cheerfully homicidal.

"Neddaland is going to be a tropical island." A tablet was Velcroed to his console, on it a schematic blown up almost beyond recognition. Amadeus. "What's the latest plan?"

"Jettison the water we're using to cool Amadeus so we have direct access, then we use *Chawla*'s cargo arm. We can use the claw to put pressure on the outside of Amadeus, forcing the rod back into its original position and stopping the power spike."

That would leave them without water to use for a forced-steam-landing cushion. "Just jettison it?"

"It's already radioactive."

"Sure, but the winds on planet will disperse it. You're suggesting hitting planet on our asses without padding."

"I am suggesting we try to land without a dead crew."

"So we squeeze Amadeus until the rod pops back in place? Brute force. Was it your idea or Singh's?"

"Mine."

Something struck her as wrong about it, not just flushing the water. "And you want to do this every time the power spikes? Because *Chawla's* not meant to travel with her cargo arm hanging out. Do we know if the cargo arm can handle that kind of force? Not the weight—the crushing."

"It is Russian."

"No offense meant. But there's got to be a way to do this where we don't end up landing without putting our feet out first."

"I can do this, Nedda. I can fix this."

She was supposed to comfort him, but couldn't. Ego demanded more space and time than *Chawla* had. "Then fix it."

Singh's sister got married. The waking crew watched a video of what looked like an entire town dancing. The groom rode a white horse. Afterward, Singh spent the rest of the day in the control cabin, door closed. Nedda used scissors and a box of nitrile gloves to make a large purple carnation for him, then left it in his toiletry kit.

She was harvesting tomato seeds when he found her.

"Did you do this?" His beard obscured his mouth, making his expression difficult to read.

"My mom taught me how to make them with crepe paper." The flower's pointy rubber petals stuck out like an explosion.

"Isn't your mother a chemist?"

"Yes. And she makes the best crepe paper flowers and perfect cakes too. They're not mutually exclusive. Anyway, we don't have crepe paper, so I improvised."

"Why?"

"I saw all the flowers. Roses and carnations aren't exactly critical plants, but I miss them. Don't you?"

"I do." Singh pulled himself forward, floating on his stomach in the hatch between Hydro and the main corridor. He crumpled the bloom in his palm then released it. The petals straightened, hovering inches from his nose.

She started the centrifuge on her sweet potato samples. Later, she would look for subtle changes in their genetics. "Are you okay, Amit?"

"Evgeni's idea is shit. Amadeus puts out a barrier like a force field. The arm can't crush the barrier. It's even pushing the water away. All that cooling I thought we were getting? It's not happening. The force field is keeping the water from reaching the drive."

"Have you told him it's a bad idea?"

"I'm coddling him."

"Don't. He doesn't need that." None of them did.

Singh rolled the ends of the glove flower between his fingers. "It's just you and your mother, isn't it?"

"Yes. You'd like her, I think. We're a lot alike. I've been trying to set up a call with her. They analyze our emails, don't they?"

"Mission Control? Yes. Have you had any extra psych sessions scheduled? Dr. Stein likes to check in if you want more calls than usual." He shrugged. "Who knows? Sunspots interfere with the message system. Storms. I've stopped trying to keep up on things like that, it's pointless. Try sending your request again."

"It worries me. I always assume the worst."

"That's natural. We've lost people," he said.

"There was so much upheaval, all the constant goodbyes—to everything. Maybe it's not even worry, maybe it's grieving? Does that make sense?"

"Sure. I had lots of goodbyes. My stepfather is Irish and a shameless history buff," he said, as though that clarified everything.

"You lost me."

"He said that during the famines when someone left to go to Canada or America, you threw them a going-away party, but it was also a kind of funeral, because you'd never see them again. That person might as well be dead. My party was supposed to be like that. I think I was drunk for a week."

"Did you want that?"

"Of course not," he said. "I kick myself sometimes and wish I hadn't drunk anything at all. Most of what I remember is just a few flashes of my friends, and most of that is spinning. Sometimes I hate all this and wish I'd gotten married instead. But those are the bad days. We can't have bad days, can we?"

"No, the printer makes sure of it."

He smiled. A dark, soft cloud of beard and man. "Watched. We're always watched."

"I lost my dad," she said. *Lost,* as though her father was misplaced, or he'd taken a wrong turn and wandered off. The enormity of it had never fit into speech—how much she missed him, what she'd had to do. Something about the flowers at the wedding, that Singh was aching for his family, had made her say it. Loss was loneliness's best companion.

Amit rolled over, gazing up at the ceiling. It was strange how many conversations they had without seeing each other's eyes, because of location, lack of gravity. "My father died when I was very young, and it troubled me for years. It still does, from time to time. Was it the anomaly? Forgive me, I don't remember the specifics."

She longed for so loose a grip on memory. She missed the word boluses of childhood and wished she could unwind the painful thread without pausing for breath. She settled for short. "He didn't make it out with us."

Whirring from the centrifuge filled the silence.

"I'm sorry," he said.

"Me too."

"I didn't intend to be maudlin. I didn't think the video would bring up such— Well, I put some new numbers in from Amadeus. I've almost got the pattern, I think. Would you look at them? I'm not sure I trust myself."

"Sure."

"Thank you for the flower, Nedda. Try your mother again. It's bureaucracy or sunspots. They're essentially the same."

Nedda reviewed Singh's data by the common area window. The ship lights were dimmed to preserve what circadian rhythms they had left, and the glow from her screen tired her eyes quickly. She switched back to the schematic. Glass, Amadeus had so much glass.

She closed her eyes and listened to a newscast. How many days old was it? There was a partial collapse at the Eiffel Tower, which overshadowed the North American grain shortage and a resurgence of Pan-Euro flu. The reality was likely worse. Briefings they received were highly filtered, only including major events to keep them tied to a sense of Earth. When Evgeni woke, Singh would update him, and let him know his cargo arm plan had been vetoed. Days were ruled by sleep timers, data on the builds, and sketching out ways to repair Amadeus.

Marcanta came up behind her. "Honest truth time. I just did Genya's tap, but I think it's too late."

It wasn't fair.

"Gravity should fix some of it, won't it?"

Marcanta hummed, neither agreeing nor disagreeing. She'd called him *Genya* again, not *Evgeni*. Marcanta had definitely slept with him. Singh showed no interest in Marcanta's advances and kept mostly to himself. But Evgeni and Marcanta needed touch. Singh and Nedda did not. Two extroverts to balance two introverts. The contact, the care, likely made watching Evgeni's progression more painful. "He's no good on any of the mechanical aspects now, and he'll be useless on the ground for at least a month. If we get there. If he can get any sight back."

"We know how to cover for him," Nedda said. "You'll do some of my seed work, I'll help you make sure we don't drop dead, Amit works as Evgeni's backup, and we all work logistics with Amit as lead. We'll manage."

"You've run three-man scenarios."

Nedda turned off her screen. "It would be stupid not to. Besides, it's weirdly calming."

"You've run one where you're the missing man, haven't you?"

"Yes."

"You want to be the one to look at Amadeus," Marcanta said.

"It'll be better if I do. If Singh got radiation sickness, his whining would drive you crazy. At least I'm a good patient."

Marcanta squeezed her shoulder and Nedda tried to lean into it, to give Marcanta what she needed. "How are your eyes doing with contacts? Is the printer keeping up?"

"Fuzzy at the edges. Not terrible, but not what I used to see either."

"I want you to spend more time in the goggles. At night, and at least every other day when you're not in sleep cycle. In sleep cycle, they're on. That's it. If you're going to fix it, you need eyes. I'll think of something else."

"It's not just the CSF that's doing it, is it?"

"No. It's the vitreous fluid in the eye too. It's flattening your lenses. The pressure is wrong," Marcanta said.

"Ever see that old movie *Scanners*?" At Marcanta's blank look, Nedda said, "Never mind." In that moment, she missed Denny ferociously.

"Evgeni's interested in you, you know."

"What?"

"Yeah. It doesn't bother me, if you're wondering."

"But you've slept with him?"

"Sure, but I'm not territorial. It isn't healthy in our situation. Comfort is as important as everything else we're trying to do, maybe more so." She pulled on the ends of her hair. "He's nice. The sex is weird, not at all like in gravity. But what is? He's considerate." The clips on Marcanta's suit clicked against the door.

"I can't right now," Nedda said.

"If not now, when? Sex is the one thing we don't have to be serious about."

Serious. A thing that as a child she'd known that she was not supposed to be. She was supposed to be smiling, laughing, outgoing but also meek, a supporter of other people, a reader of fluffy things and a baker of sweet things, smart, but not too smart—enough to be witty, enough to be charming. "But I am serious. I like being serious."

"I meant that it's healthy to have a few distractions. You're very focused. That's all. I don't mean it in a bad way."

"I guess. But this is all I ever wanted from the time I was a kid. How old were you when you knew you wanted to be an astronaut?"

"It's different for me. I always wanted to be a doctor. Space didn't come until later, probably after the droughts and the wheat blight." When colonization became a must.

"I wanted to be an astronaut more than I wanted to live. And there were less than a handful of women then, out of the entire United States. I watched one of them die." She let her body relax, closing her eyes against the window's light. "There are only two of us. We need to keep us alive."

"I'm only saying it wouldn't hurt anyone if you took a little comfort."

"I know," she said. Nedda tapped her fingers against the window glass. Thick, it had a satisfying *thump*, and the same feel Pyrex used to. Like the rocket windows she'd once dreamed of.

"Okay." In a softer voice Marcanta added, "You know, Dr. Stein told me to stop looking out the window all the time. It makes you homesick."

"Doesn't apply to me." She didn't miss her house or bed, the grove, or the way the dark came alive with animals. She missed her mother and she was homesick for 1985.


Evgeni stopped wearing the goggles. He navigated *Chawla* by feel and innate spatial awareness. He'd been at home in the swimming pools they'd trained for zero g in. Singh had called him Beluga. Nedda imagined Evgeni using sonar, his little *click*s bouncing off *Chawla*'s walls.

On morning call, he'd looked directly at the video screen and ran through his interpretation of the information from the terraformers and rovers.

"The photovoltaic system on Dué is no longer producing to spec, due to a crack from debris. Un can repair it, I believe, without sacrificing much schedule time. It is preferable to have them both fully functional. Trio and Tessera maintain. Fiver can compensate, if deemed necessary."

"Mr. Sokolov, your medical data shows your eyesight has worsened significantly. Why aren't you wearing your goggles?" This from Landon Chauncey, a public affairs officer, who had no business commenting on anyone's health.

"The strap was itching." Evgeni's voice was light, even cheerful. "Additionally, we discovered that the plutonium in the life support system is not, in fact, plutonium, but strontium. Would Mission Control inform us how to proceed? Or why such a decision was made?"

Then followed a good ten minutes of Chauncey and Evgeni yelling across the time delay, dancing around something no one could answer. Chauncey insisted there was no switch, that strontium had always been the intended isotope. Evgeni brought up the North Americans campaigning for control of *Fortitude*.

"You are lying. All the data says you are. You will blame this mistake on Eurasia to bargain for more colonist slots. You are trying to buy your lives at the cost of ours." Evgeni then switched to Russian and a vein popped out on Chauncey's forehead. Evgeni's fist pounded the wall. "You broke our life support."

Yours and ours. North America and Eurasia, or Earth and *Chawla*? Nedda and her crewmates were extraterrestrial. As time went on and colonies formed, different cultures would arise, different worlds, and ties to Earth would be broken by distance. If they survived.

Chauncey spoke over Evgeni, "Mission Control is unaware of—"

"I put in a request to speak with my mother," Nedda shouted.

"What was that?" Chauncey's eyes snapped in her direction.

"My mother. I've been emailing through the request system, and I've had no response. I need to speak with her. Why hasn't there been any response?"

"Unless there's data in your message, the system sorts it into general request files. There've been staff overhauls, interference with Mars. Any number of things can result in a backlog."

Staff overhauls could be responsible for a change in isotopes, for failing to consider friction. They might be killed by staff overhauls. "Well, can you put it through? I have to talk to my mother."

Chauncey coughed. "I will. But in the future, please send any urgent personal requests to Dr. Stein."

Singh shifted the conversation to weather patterns and a sandstorm on planet that had shifted unexpectedly, indicating a nuance to the seasons initial probes had missed.

Evgeni nudged their legs with his feet. They were on their own.

They were splitting one of the few pouches of soju over dinner when Singh said, "Why would you do that, Evgeni?"

"What? If they want to bother me about my eyes, I am within bounds to ask them about a mistake that will kill four people."

"You shouldn't taunt them. They control our information flow."

"We don't need them," Evgeni said quietly. "We are the information flow. Don't you see? We can cut data feeds anytime we please. If we go silent, they lose all data on the project, and it jeopardizes colonization. Bats are dying off, did you know? It is worse than colony collapse was for bees. They don't have time to lose our data and launch again from scratch. They need us; we do not need them."

Singh looked ready to start ten arguments. Nedda grabbed the pouch from him and took her sip. Sharp, clean.

"It's too late, Amit. He's already picked the fight, and he's right, we're in control. And we shouldn't have to clear phone time through a psychiatrist."

"Why do you need to speak to your mother out of scheduled time?" Singh asked.

"Because I need to." Nedda tapped her fingers, thumb to pinkie, to ring, to middle, to index and back, rounds of one hundred twenty. Each two-minute segment made her feel closer to being all right. "She helps me think better."

Tired had a sound—it was Singh's breath. "Fine, keep trying."


The treadmill hummed beneath Nedda as she ran and mapped out new constellations, naming them. Red Bug. Green Man, Whitefoot, Needle. The sudden sound of Evgeni moving close by startled her. She was used to knowing where he was by the sound of his reader. He used a reader for everything, the bot data, the instrument drawers, the names on the hatches and panels. *Chawla's* voice was square and distinctly inhuman.

"Ah, sorry. I didn't mean to scare you."

"Oh, no. It's fine. I was just thinking. I guess I didn't hear the reader."

"It was getting on my nerves, so I turned it off."

"I can imagine," she said.

"It's not at all what I expected it to be."

"Your eyes? I'm sorry."

"No, the trip," he said. "But thank you for not dancing around it."

"I imagined better spaceships when I was little," she said. "But what's adulthood but managed expectations and disappointment."

His laugh was like a dropped rock.

"It is that. As for the blindness, last year, I began to listen to how voices change when the mouth is different—smile, frown, grimace. Your voice gets bright and wide when you are smiling. I don't miss as much as I thought I might. I've managed my expectations."

"You were training yourself."

"Obviously," he said. "There is a lie in my medical record that is, for lack of a better term, not insignificant. There is glaucoma in my family."

"Why did you do it?"

"I needed to be here enough that blindness was nothing in comparison."

She would ask if it was worth it, but knew the answer. This mission was worth missing everything you ever knew, everything you'd ever loved. "Are you afraid?"

"No. It's a relief in some ways to not be staring at screens. You know the Impressionists? It is like that—no definition at all, but there is color. I see you there, some yellow-brown—your hair, am I right? The blue is your suit. I don't know if you are up or down, but I know where you are. You are there in shape and sound. Only soft."

"Don't make it sound beautiful."

"It is, though."

"I'd hug you, but Louisa would think I want to have sex with you."

"Ah, but you do." He pointed his finger in triumph, then clipped into the bike. "Everyone does. It's difficult being so charming. Amit can't keep his hands off me. I'm too much of a good thing. But you are holding out on me, keeping secrets. You are plotting something. That's why you're calling your mother, yes? I had planned on reading your psych files, but now I can't without *Chawla* tattling on me."

She sped the treadmill up. "I need an outside voice, and she's an honest one. I think I know something about Amadeus, but I'm not sure. I don't want to raise too much hope."

"A noble thought, but difficult to do if there's no hope to raise."

"True. I suppose it's better than preparing to die."

"Oh, but we're always preparing to die, aren't we? That is what religion is for: planning to die from the day you are born. It's nice to think that in the end the good are rewarded and bad men get punished."

"I'm pretty okay with whoever switched out the plutonium burning eternally."

"My favorite fantasy," he said. "Louisa believes. Did you know she has a rosary?"

"What, did you see that while you were having sex?"

"It's in her sleep sack."

"That's . . . disturbing."

"Only if it means something to you. I do and I don't believe. Singh calls himself a godless heathen. And you?"

"Like you, I guess," she said. "My dad said when we die we become carbon and gas. But the thing that makes us *us*, the soul, or whatever you want to call it, is energy, light. He said that when people die, they keep traveling. We're all just light traveling across the universe."

"He wasn't entirely wrong," he said.

"But it sounds like he invented his own faith, doesn't it? And that's how I was raised. I'm worse than a godless heathen."

"You are a madwoman, but not for that. So you are looking for God when you stare out the windows?"

"No."

"Good," he said. "It isn't out there."


In her sleep sack, she clicked on her tablet and enlarged the type. There was a message from Dr. Stein instructing her to scan in on the printer first thing in the morning for a medication check and to have Marcanta send new blood sample data.

Her message had been received.

# 1986: Books

THE FIRST RULE was to never let them see your fear. Parents were supposed to be a beacon in a storm—something to that effect. Every parenting book Betheen had read championed a calm demeanor without mentioning that maintaining a calm demeanor sapped every emotional and intellectual reserve you had, and even then, a hand twitch would escape, or a bitten-back swear. Comforting a child was no comfort to a parent.

Nedda was where she'd left her, at the kitchen table, shredded muffin wrappers and a mountain of crumbs beside her; rather than eat, she'd chosen to break her food down to its smallest state. No one ever mentioned how children thwarted all your efforts to keep them alive. Nedda was working in a notebook, and her resemblance to Theo was frightening. What percentage of mannerisms could be pinned to a gene? Or was it all learned behavior?

Betheen turned her wedding ring inward and pressed the stone into her thumb to stop her hand from shaking.

"Nedda?"

"Yeah?"

*Three. Two. One.* "Your father was in an accident." She squeezed Nedda's shoulder, gently. She wasn't typically allowed to be the comforting parent, and it wore like the wrong skin. Nedda stiffened at the touch. Like coat hangers trying to embrace. She waited for the shudder her daughter was holding back, the inevitable tears. They didn't come.

She saw the notes in Nedda's blocky scrawl and picked out words.

*Bubble. Needle. Pop. Entropy. Pulse. Heat. Cold. Clouds. Rubber. Entropy. Black eye. Soap. Water. Soap. Entropy. Water. Soap. Water. Air. Soap. Entropy.*

Betheen had interrupted her work.

"Not a car accident." Nedda's voice was small.

"No."

"A machine accident."

"Yes."

"What do we do?"

"I don't know."

"No." Nedda's fist hit the table. "That's not good enough. You're supposed to have an answer. You're supposed to say you'll fix it. You're my mother and that's what you're supposed to do. So do it."

A sharp daughter, prickly, maybe even a little mean. Good for her. Betheen wished sometimes she'd been meaner. Niceness made girls bend. "I don't know how yet."

"That isn't good enough. Try again."

"Nedda."

Nedda stamped her foot, bouncing her pen from the table. She'd done that when she was two, standing outside Betheen's bedroom door, pounding her feet on the carpet, demanding attention. She couldn't have helped then any more than she could now, but not for lack of wanting.

"He's stuck like Denny, isn't he?"

What Betheen had seen in the lab was something worse than just moving forward. "Yes," she said.

"You're supposed to say you'll fix it. You're supposed to lie to me and make it feel like you're not lying. And then you're supposed to fix it."

Betheen's knees bowed before the rest of her, and her arms went around Nedda, the chairback caught between their bodies. Theo wasn't Theo. He was gone, and she needed him to explain what he'd done, how to fix it, and how to tell his daughter what had happened to him. His little girl—her little girl—glared back. And she should.

"All right. I'll fix it," Betheen said.

"Denny too. You'll fix it."

"Denny too. I promise."

"You don't mean it. You're just saying it because I told you to."

"I promise I'll try. We're going to try, okay?"

Nedda gave way like a sigh. "Okay."

There was no way to apologize to your child for not being the parent they wanted. Betheen would never be Theo, would never have the rapport or the admiration that existed between Theo and Nedda. But she could never hurt Nedda, not the way Theo had.

"He has a friend who might help." Liebowitz's number had been in Theo's things, a stained card in a broken Rolodex. She'd crumpled it walking back, forcing her fear into the paper. The first call didn't go through, ringing endlessly. On the second try, there was no dial tone. The phone was out entirely. Whatever Theo had done was moving, growing.

Nedda was watching. "I'll keep calling, okay? We'll figure it out."

"He has lab books in the basement. He takes notes on everything, always. I can't read them," Nedda said.

Theo had left her the kitchen; Betheen had let him have the basement. The room resembled how she'd come to view him: dozens of half-finished projects, scraps of metal on the floor, drawers of screws, nails, circuitry, the remains of Nedda's tree-ring science project, a small climbing arc, shelf after shelf of notebooks and textbooks so outdated their only practical use was kindling. Scattered among all this were magazines, journals: *Scientific American, Popular Mechanics, Science.* After they'd lost Michael, she'd been in bed, reading grief books, baby books, cookbooks, anything to get her mind back, and he'd had all of this. It would be easy to be angry with him.

But she'd let him have this. After the NASA layoff he'd been tight, pacing in all the spaces she'd carved for herself. He'd taken to standing in the kitchen doorway, leaning in to sniff whatever curd was bubbling on the stove.

"Here," she'd said, "I'll show you. Whisk from the elbow. Let your forearms do the work, not your wrists. Slow at first, to break it up. Then fast to work in the air."

"Why? Why by hand?"

"You learn by hand to understand the feel and the look. The mixer goes too quickly. If you don't have a sense of what you're doing first, you'll overbeat. Don't worry about your fingers. It's all the elbows. We'll stop if it's too much."

"It's so inefficient. Can't we put a timer on and use the mixer?"

He'd put a kiss on the side of her neck. He did every time he complained about tempering eggs or leveling or crumb coating. Emulsions. She'd had a hard time forgiving him for a quart of curd spilled down a stove burner.

Her efforts ended the day he'd argued in favor of box mix.

"It's the same ingredients, Betheen, the exact same."

That it made no difference to him said much about the time he was amenable to giving her, what he refused to learn, and what she could never teach. She'd offered him the basement.

"Write a book, Theo. Build something. Go down there and do whatever you need to do to keep yourself sane."

He'd done this.

"Which books does he work in?" she asked Nedda.

She ducked under her arm. "All of them, I think."

"Then we'll have to look at them all," Betheen said. "Start with whatever's the least dusty, and bring it up to the kitchen table."

"Can't we stay down here?"

"The light's better upstairs and we can spread out," she said. It would be easier too, to be in her space, not seeing all the ways she might have fit into his.

The notebooks were filled with his narrow scrawl, the triangular shapes that might be Delta but could also be his version of an *S*. It was returning to a language after years away, calling back all the typing she'd done on his dissertation. Because by then his hands were hurting. But also, she'd wanted to read it. Even when his hands didn't hurt, she typed faster, and it was what a good girlfriend would do. What a good wife did. Clacking away on her tan Smith Corona, she'd wanted that then—the notion of goodness. Of being a nice woman and wife.

"I don't understand this," Nedda said, pointing to a rushed looking portion of Theo's notes. "Is it about entropy?"

"You're not supposed to understand it yet. And no." Betheen remembered that too, the burning need to know everything. "Where did you learn about entropy?"

"He told me that's what the machine was for. To control it. To speed it up, or to stop it. It's heat loss, energy loss, but it's time too?"

*Oh.* A machine to stop loss. That Theo had built. A book fell from the table and clapped against the linoleum. She sat in the sound, pins running across her skin.

"Mom?"

Betheen's nails dug deep into the meat of her thumbs. "Get me a pen."

For all of Theo's mannerisms, Nedda was undeniably Betheen's daughter, from her blonde hair to the set of her frame. Theo must have wondered what a son of theirs would be like. If at this age he'd have that same build. He must have thought it.

She placed a fierce kiss on the top of Nedda's head, then found a blank sheet in the back of a notebook and drew a slanted *S*. "If you see an 'S' like this or a triangle in front of a slanted 'S,' in a bunch of equations, show me that right away, okay? The equations will look sort of like this. Go through every page. This is called the Boltzmann constant. If you see this 'S' and equations that look like this, I need to see it." He'd be looking to measure kinetic energy at all levels, wouldn't he? She marveled that she still remembered the Boltzmann constant. But she'd read with him, she'd typed for him. She'd been his shadow. There were moments when she'd reached the same conclusion faster, more neatly, but marriage meant certain things; your sense of self changed, your pride got bound up with your husband's. Your accomplishments were his. His accomplishments were yours, or they were supposed to be. It was supposed to be that way. It wasn't. But she'd never had to prove her intelligence or her worth to him. He knew, and the relief that afforded allowed her, at last, to relax. To breathe. It was like that with Nedda too. Everything your child accomplished was better than anything you'd done. You loved them in a way you couldn't love yourself.

"There will be different numbers here and here, but it'll look a lot like this. This is a constant, okay? I need that."

"That could be anything," Nedda said.

"It's going to keep this shape, though. Look for the 'K.' Look for the slanted 'S' and the triangle. That's Delta. It's Greek."

Betheen scanned the shifts in Theo's handwriting, from frustrated to inspired, bad days, good days.

"How come you know all this?"

"Don't think for one second he's the only reason you're smart." Nedda's shocked expression was both satisfying and sad.

"When do I get to know this stuff?" Nedda asked.

"Whenever you want." Later was for talking about chemistry, math, champagne wedding cake, children, and fathers. Now was for hunting. "Keep looking."

Pages and books flew by: things she'd loved in school, a volume on magnetics, an early draft of his dissertation, each notebook a catalog of his errant thoughts. A thought of life without him took root.

But then she wouldn't have Nedda.

You had to love your children. It was supposed to happen instantaneously, when a nurse put a squirming body to your breast to let her suck. Hormones—adrenaline, dopamine, serotonin, estrogen, progesterone, prolactin. That awful oxytocin. Molecules hit molecules and caused reactions, formed connections; hard and soft sciences mixed and created love. But pregnancy with Nedda had been like carrying a parasite, a tapeworm that drained her. She'd dreamed of botflies, that her stomach housed a brood of thousands, ready to burst through, punching holes like a sieve. When Nedda was placed on her chest she was terrified; here was an entire person her body had made, but she knew nothing at all about her, only that she would suffer. For being a girl. For all the things she'd learn she couldn't do. For all the men she'd ever meet.

She couldn't love Nedda right away, and there was science behind that too. Her adrenal glands were overworked. She was still grieving the miscarriages. The chemicals that carried her through labor ebbed and left her dry. Her insides were like wool. She wouldn't love Nedda for another month, when she'd set her on the floor and Nedda lifted her head, looked up, and showed such wonder. Betheen recognized her then, and loved her like she'd been skinned—it was raw, sudden, an overwhelming ache. Nedda was fierce. Determined. Smart—not brilliant, like Theo thought—but hardnosed. Tough, like she'd once been.

And then, eighteen months later, Michael. Love like a rock through a window.

In front of her were notes on classes, a diagram for a perpetual motion machine. And then a list.

- *Peach puree: Good. Spit up once. Smiled. Asked for more.*
- *Strained peas: A solid no. Tantrum.*
- *Stories: Pat the Bunny x3. Goodnight Moon x1.*
- *PUT FUSES ON HIGH SHELF*

The clench in her gut was immediate. She moved on to another notebook, but dog-eared the page.

Nedda had gone through what must have been twenty notebooks, showing her the occasional *S*, but nothing with promise. They were in a stack on the floor. Betheen had accumulated her own pile, notebooks that weren't useful in the moment, but were important nonetheless. His notes on Nedda and, worse, on her.

*Betheen had a good half-hour. Got mail from box. Didn't plug ears when Nedda cried. Ate toast.*

That time for her was a fog, but he'd watched them both, cared for them.

How did you apologize for something that wasn't your fault, an accident of timing, a betrayal of chemistry?

"Mom?" Nedda held up a beaten-up notebook, black, the edges picked at and torn. Theo couldn't ever let things be.

Ten frantic pages of text. The cramped jottings from a moment when he must have been jittery, enthralled by his own genius. A single equation took up three full pages, at the end of which he'd made a crude drawing of a mushroom cloud, labeled with a childish *BLAMMO*. But that was it, wasn't it? Figuring something out was an explosion that forced you to reframe everything you knew. The seven pages that followed were tight equations, open systems, closed systems, and measurements. A dashed note: *CHECK WITH LIEBOWITZ*. A drawing of a sphere, then a teardrop, then something that looked like her mother's ancient washing mangle.

"Good eye. Very good eye." Betheen resisted the urge to kiss Nedda again; it would be too much if she squirmed away. She needed to talk to

Theo, but he was oscillating through himself—was mostly a person she hadn't known or didn't know yet. Oscillating. That was important.

"Mom, we can fix it, can't we?"

The best she could say was "We're going to try."

A knock at the door brought her to find Annie Prater standing at the screen, rocking from foot to foot. The moment she saw her, Betheen knew she couldn't tell her about Denny. That morning was a different lifetime. Before she'd seen Theo.

"Oh, honey. I'm so glad you weren't hurt. That accident was awful," Annie said.

"Yes, I'm fine. I was just shaken." She kept the screen between them, willing Nedda to stay in the kitchen, not to come to the door. "Thanks for checking on me."

"I wanted to see if Denny got off to school all right," she said. "It occurred to me he didn't have a change of clothes, but he didn't stop by. He and Des have the same kind of temper. You know boys, they're waiting each other out, seeing who can sulk harder."

The lie was easy, a perfectly formed thing better than any truth could be. "He was fine this morning. I watched him eat three muffins. Nedda dragged him to school the same as ever. I'm sure he's all right. Children can bounce back from anything, can't they?"

"And you're sure you're okay?" Annie glanced at the door, anticipating an invitation in.

Betheen should ask her about Desmond, make tea, give her one of the lemon cookies from the jar, and ask what she planned to do.

"I'm still a little off. That man, he was so young—I should lie down," Betheen said.

"If Denny comes here instead of going home, you'll let me know, won't you?"

"The second he gets here." In her head she ran through all the steps in making a napoleon—the rolling, the waiting, the custard—anything to keep calm, to keep the lie going. "Are you sure I can't do anything for you, Annie?"

"No, I just—I heard something strange. I ran into Ed Ingram. He saw Marty Neuhaus at the Bird's Eye and—I wouldn't believe it, but you saw the roads—Marty told Ed that his clients, I mean the bodies, they plumped back up. *Plumped.* I wouldn't be surprised if Marty's lost it; it's bound to happen to someone in that line of work. But he swore to Ed that Ross Lattimer's mother had stitched herself up right on his table. He was serious. He said he had to tell Ross. And I was thinking about the roads because Ross is in Mims and there's no way to get there. I'm sure I tried every road. And everyone keeps saying it looks like a storm, and if it does storm and we can't get out of town . . . I know it's silly—but, if the school calls or Denny comes here, will you send him home right away?"

"I will, Annie. I promise."

Annie put her hand on the screen door, tapping a fingernail on a chip of peeling paint. "If it is true, what Marty said, and I know it's not, but if it is and you needed a shovel, I wouldn't say a thing. Anyone with a heart would understand."

Betheen counted each bone in her spine, pictured the way they stacked from coccyx to sacrum all the way through the cervical bones at the base of the skull, locked in place, straight. Strong.

Michael. Michael was in the garden, beneath a solemn slab of Pennsylvania blue slate.

"I can't talk about that, Annie. I can't think about it. I'm so sorry, but I need to lie down for a while."

She gripped the knob long after closing the door. Counted to twenty. Slowly. Annie didn't know she was losing her son. She'd lied to a woman who'd trusted her with her son, a woman who'd helped raise her daughter when she couldn't. Because of Theo.

Anyone with a heart would understand.

"Nedda? Bring that notebook. We're going to see your father."

# Protraction

**T**HERE IS GREAT pressure and pulling that lasts a thousand years. When he is aware of skin, the separation between him and the tender heat that surrounds him, he feels cold, then a burning that lasts for decades. Language does not exist for him, but sensation does, and the intense screeching and shouting of life. Light comes in, filtering through his skin, where before existed only dark. It is wondrous. Muscles contract, forming a rictus of the spirit—oh, so painful—but new. The rhythm inside him speeds. Running with joy, fear, and thrumming, thumping light.

There are sounds. Roaring, screaming. The thousand years before this moment came were water, a gentle thudding of hearts—his, hers— and calm mumblings that came from outside the water, beyond the dark. Now there is light and sound exploding alongside it, a brash herald of the world. And here, brighter, is a murmur he knows; where it had been muted, it is now keen. Clear! Pricking jabs when it had existed before as a brush of sound and vibration. Had he words he'd know it as a voice—her voice, without barrier between them. Had he language he'd hear the panic and worry for her, for himself.

He revels, unknowing what it is to savor, or how the act of savoring bends time and world. Piercing, light and sound both. *Bright, bright, bright.*

Skin pulls and pinches, every sensation seismic, rattling.

There is softness on his back, though it is rough, scratchy compared to the water of a thousand years. He nuzzles against it to learn the feel, test its give. The lower reach of him, well below the place inside that stutters and hammers, is jabbed. Then, more sound, familiar like the mumbles from the water. A deeper, vibrating sound. In the water, he'd been unable to notice the rhythm of the sounds, the structure.

The skin—his skin—is taut. It strains for years, months, seconds in a violent act of unfolding, which he loves and hates in equal measure.

Each sensitivity he picks apart, analyzes, and burns into himself as a new thing understood about his world.

There is pressure in his center, in the heart of the hammering; it is brutal with its force, almost as strong as when he was pushed and tugged from the water. It runs through the extremities and he studies it, never more aware, never more perfect. For weeks, he listens to jangling, crashes, beeps, and pings, the *whooshwhooshwhoosh* of things that are around him, in him, everywhere. Through it all are the warmer sounds, the twin vibrations, the clarion and the deep. He listens for a millennium, perhaps two. And he loves them, loves them so. Even the pressure, the twisting and yanking, yes, even the pricking and the sting. He loves them.

Joy. Such joy. Perfection when compared with the darkness and the water where he'd been.

"It's an impossible decision, but you're sparing him suffering. I'll leave you with him. Take as much time as you need."

"Oh."

"I love you. I . . ."

"Goodbye, Michael."

The sounds are softer, warmer too. He listens to them, devouring their feel until his skin that barely holds together, cell clinging to cell, isn't enough to contain him. The pressure in his chest is warm and good, and so painfully happy that it stops.

His final thought erupts with elation and light, a burst lasting longer than anything he'd known.

His hour. It had been joy. All of it.

# 1986: Infancy and Age

NOTEBOOK IN HER backpack, Nedda jogged to keep up with her mother. Betheen was in her good wool coat, the long pink one with the wide shoulders that made her look like a stick of bubble gum and somehow made it even more implausible that her mother understood the same math as her father.

"You lied to Mrs. Prater."

Denny's mom made mac and cheese with the crunchy top and cut up hot dogs in it. Mrs. Prater played records and sang all the harmonies and listened when Nedda said that harmonies felt good because the sound waves of each note synched up. Mrs. Prater had given her Peaches 'n Cream Barbie last year. Nedda didn't like Barbie, but it was nice of Mrs. Prater to try.

"What should I have said? There's nothing she can do, and nothing will make this better except for fixing it. That's what you want, right? That's what we're going to do." She slowed and put her hand on Nedda's back. Warm, steady.

"What else were you talking about?"

"She saw the car accident. She just wanted to make sure I was all right." Betheen stepped over a fallen trunk, and extended her hand to help Nedda over.

Nedda glared but took it. Her mother had force, direction, and Nedda wished she could absorb it by osmosis.

"It's like a bubble," Nedda said.

"What?"

"The thing that happened to Denny—it's like a soap bubble. You can slide your hand around it, and there's a wall between inside and outside. If you look at it right you can almost see it."

Betheen's hum could have meant anything.

"Is Dad . . . is it like that?"

"It's like water cake," Betheen said. "He's different. I don't think it's exactly like what you saw."

Nedda hoped it wasn't. "Bubbles have three layers—soap on the inside, water, then soap on the outside. The more glycerin there is in the soap, the stronger the bubble. Is water cake like that?"

"It's agar, so no, not really."

"Dad and I did an experiment to figure out what dish soap makes the best bubbles, and it's the one with the most glycerin to water. But that's the stuff that stays on your dishes longer because the water slides off, so you have to use a scrubber to break up the surface tension." She needed a scrubber.

They'd mixed one part water with one part soap, with each variety of soap, and measured the height of bubbles, timed how long the bubbles lasted before they popped. They measured surface tension, testing how many droplets from an eyedropper made a water bead change from round to flat. They measured the height of water beads with playing cards for consistency. It was good to be next to him, to figure out how he knew the way things worked.

"That was a good experiment. I watched a little, but you both looked so happy I didn't want to interrupt."

Nedda hadn't noticed. How many of their experiments had her mother watched? "If it's cold, bubbles last because the water takes longer to evaporate. When it's cloudy and cold, bubbles last a super long time." It was cold in Easter now, the kind of cold that made bubbles last forever.

In the hallway of the sciences building, the light from the lab looked like the grove—cold, pulsing.

"It's okay to be scared," Betheen said. "If you need to, you can stay outside."

"I'm not scared."

"I am."

Nedda wanted to yell a million things—that she was fine, that she did lots of stuff on her own, that she knew the lab better than Betheen. But she didn't want to open the door.

"He's inside?"

"Yes."

You did science when you were scared because the more you understood something, the less afraid of it you'd be. You did things you were afraid of when it was for a good reason. You opened doors. For the greater good.

"You don't have to look," Betheen said softly.

Nedda looked.

There was a little boy in the lab. He was three, maybe—the age they got annoying, pulled your hair, and hung on your legs. He was sitting on the floor, bathed in Crucible's glow. His hair was thick and black. His mouth was open, like he was screaming. Like Denny.

Her father was supposed to be fixing things. He was—

"There." Betheen pointed to the crying boy, who looked younger than three now, maybe one and a half—whenever it was they learned to make that noise that shattered your ears. There were patches of broken skin on his elbow.

*Oh.*

It wasn't staring into a planet's distant past, it was staring into her father's. She wasn't supposed to see this. Looking back was never meant to be this close.

"Mom?"

Betheen sat in a blue plastic chair by the white board, pulled up another, and patted the seat. "We need to wait a while. In a little bit, you may not want to look and that's okay. You don't have to."

She sounded calm. How could she be so calm?

You weren't supposed to see your parents as children. Most definitely not as babies. For a few minutes there was an infant, frightened, howling, though she couldn't hear it. She buried her face in Betheen's shoulder. Going through the books had felt good, like she was doing something, helping. But waiting was the worst kind of loneliness.

Soon, Betheen looked away. "Just a few minutes now." Her breath was warm in Nedda's hair. "Then we'll talk to him. We'll figure it out."

The cold shifted and pockets of air warmed around them. The change was in the light too. "How do we talk to him? Denny couldn't hear me."

"It's when he slows down. You'll see. Get me his dry-erase markers."

The drawing Betheen made used the heavy black marker, spanned the whole of the white board, and made Nedda think of a road sign. The markers were pungent, like things Betheen used—pistachio extract, anise, and rubbing alcohol. A thick vertical line ran from the top to the bottom of the board. Midway down, a broad horizontal line cut through it. Below that, Betheen wrote in clear block letters ME + NEDDA. Next to the vertical was TIME SPEED/DIRECTION. She drew a curve that arced above, then snaked under the horizontal line, the pattern repeating all the way across the board.

Nedda chewed on her braid, grinding the hair between her molars. She could have written to Denny but instead she'd just run.

"Think he can read that without his glasses?"

"Maybe," Nedda said. If he squinted, if he knew where to look. If he could read at all. She stared at the curves. "What is it?"

"Sine. The ratio between a small angle in a triangle and the long side. The math for it makes a curve like that." The marker squeaked as she wrote, SINE = THEO. "Right now, you and I are moving in one direction in time. We're like the long side of the triangle. This is where your father is in relation to us. Or when. It's when he is. You don't have to understand it yet," she said. "We need him to be able to see this, to understand what's happening to him, even when we're not moving in the same time. But if we wait, we'll sync up. I promise."

But her dad was a baby. He'd been less than a baby; for a while she'd been unable to see him at all, there and not there. He was speeding, like Denny, but backward and forward, like the trees. Rewind, pause, fast forward, pause. If you did that too much the tape broke. No matter how tight she tried to hold her insides in, she couldn't stop shaking. "How do you know?"

"I waited. I've seen him older. I don't know exactly when we'll sync up. But we know what he looks like now, and we'll know when it's him from this week, maybe from this morning. When the sine curve approaches 'X,' that's us. He'll be when we are."

Her mother wasn't sure. It was in her voice and in the way her back was perfectly straight. Betheen's hand slid under Nedda's braid, to lightly scratch her neck. When and where had never felt so separate.

"Mom? I'm scared."

"I know."

Her face was hot and she'd lost count of scratches when Betheen said, "You can look again if you want. He's back now, not so messy."

"No," Nedda said. "It's not him."

"It is."

"How do you know?"

"I can tell you about him."

Stories were her father's realm, but she wanted her mother to keep talking, needed the soft scratches and the tickling smell of hairspray. "Okay."

"Your granddad didn't like your dad very much. He loved him, but that's different. Your granddad was the kind of man who never really left the military. He used to wake up at four thirty every morning. He said it was because in the service they used to wake soldiers up with cannons. Your dad says that's a lie, and your granddad just couldn't stand being asleep when he could be awake and pissing someone off."

The word *pissing* was dirty and intimate. "How come he didn't like Dad?"

"They were different people. Your dad is bookish, your granddad wasn't. Your dad loves taking things apart but wasn't always good at putting them back together. He still isn't."

Nedda peeked. The little boy was back, thrashing like Denny did, stretching like Denny, blurring in high speed. Nedda looked away. "What else?"

"School was hard for him," Betheen said. "He told me about all the books he read, how he'd built his own watch from parts, and that he'd once accidentally blown up his mailbox. But he never talks about friends, and he certainly didn't have anyone like Denny. He went to college early. College was easier, I think. Then NASA. He had a friend he worked with there. Some of the notes in those books are his."

"When did you and Dad meet?"

"College. I was an undergraduate in chemistry. He was in graduate school."

Nedda heard the fondness in Betheen's voice. "You went to school for chemistry?"

"Yes."

"How come you're not a chemist?"

"Oh, because I met your dad, and then I wanted other things too. I was so smart. I thought I'd square away my love life, then get to all the rest." She squeezed Nedda's hand.

"Do you miss it?"

"Yes and no. Baking is mostly chemistry, but it's not quite the same. There's less precision, less math, and it's focused mostly on taste and texture. I'd have to go back to school to do anything more. I'm too old now and I don't know how to be in school without your dad. I'd have to learn all over again, which seems silly. But your dad was wonderful. He kept pens in his shirt pockets, like he does now. Sometimes there was chalk behind his ear and it made his hair dusty. The lecture hall had sliding chalkboards that were impossible to reach the top of. Before class, your dad would climb on a chair and write equations from the top all the way down. I came in early just to watch him. He had a beautiful back. My roommate, Mickie, warned me about Greek boys. She said they had double eyelashes and if you looked at them too long you'd fall in love. Mickie was boy crazy, but she was right about the double eyelashes. Though, what really mattered was that your dad treated me like a person. That might not seem like much to you, but it meant everything to me. I spent a lot of time trying to be seen, trying to be heard. He listened." She tugged Nedda's hair. "God, that machine is ugly, isn't it?"

It looked like the kraken on the cover of Nedda's mythology book. It was worse than ugly—it was cruel.

"Look. See the scar on his leg? He got that when he fell from a tree. He was a little younger than you are now. A neighbor's parakeet escaped and he tried to catch it, but the branch he was on broke."

Time passed with her mother telling a version of her father's life, their life together. The shouting through the laundry chute had hidden it, but they loved each other. Her father must know her mother this well, all the stories of her scars, and the way she'd once held her books. Nedda should have known those things too.

"Right now, he's just about the age he was when you were born."

He was in a rare moment of stillness. "How do you know?"

"He started biting his nails then."

Her father's fingernails were always ragged, sometimes bloody; she'd thought it was because psoriasis warped and pitted them.

He lacked the creases and folds that made him her father. His hair was almost a uniform black, but it was him. Had she made him that old? "His face was so skinny." *Is.* His face *is* skinny, though it *was* too.

Sharply, he grew very, very thin. Pale. Time spit forward, his body curled, heaved, as if it might break. *An American Werewolf in London*, but no werewolf broke free, just her dad—older, sadder, gray-looking. He rolled over, almost vanished into a shadow, and blurred once more.

"What happened to him?"

"It was a bad year."

Betheen's nails dug into Nedda's palm. It stung, but Nedda stayed quiet until, like everything with her mother, it became too much.

"You're hurting me."

Something in the room shifted and Betheen let go. "He's almost here. Back up. Let him see the board."

There was nothing hurried about the man on the floor, her father, as he'd been that morning. He moved slowly, but not too slowly. There was none of the awkward skipping or jerking. He moved like her dad, like a man in pain and used to it. The air around her father had changed too. The odd rippled edge that separated Crucible and her father from the rest of the lab had thinned as though stretched.

"Dad?"

Betheen smacked the whiteboard, hard enough to send something clattering to the floor.

He raised his head.

Her mother yelled, truly yelled, "Theo, this is what's happening. You need to tell us what you were doing when it happened. We need to fix it."

His voice was a million doors opening all at once, none of the hinges oiled.

"Dad?"

He flinched. He heard her. He spoke but wasn't at the right speed. What if he stayed this way? What if she never heard him again?

"Theo," her mother said. "Theo, wait; you need to wait and slow down."

"Beth?"

The change was subtle, like a temperature rise, or the prickle of someone staring. He was in the room, not ahead of it or behind it, but there.

"Dad?"

"You shouldn't be here. It's not safe."

"It isn't safe anywhere. It's better she's with me," Betheen said.

"Oh, Little Twitch." He tried to unfold himself, to stand, but his knees buckled and he fell almost as quickly as he rose. He squinted. "Something's wrong with my eyes. It's a stroke. I'm having a stroke."

"It's the machine, Theo. It's broken and we need to turn it off. Can you see the board?"

Nedda walked to him, hand outstretched. His knuckles were still swollen, and she wanted to feel his burning hands, to grab on for a little bit. But there was the slick wall, and Betheen, pulling her away.

"It doesn't work right yet. I tested it. It . . . There's just so much data."

"We have to turn it off, Theo. Focus."

He wrapped his arms around his knees. Where were his glasses? He needed them. He wasn't him without his glasses.

"Why won't my thoughts line up?" His words slurred as the room grew colder. "Oh, Nedda. I'm sorry."

"Why?" Nedda's stomach dropped.

"I wish you could stay. I wanted you to, just a little, just for a while."

His features began to change, subtly shifting.

"Beth?" Her mother's name, a groan and a whisper.

"Theo, focus." Betheen used the full-three-names voice. It worked on him too. Nedda saw the sound of it run up her father's back the same way it did hers. "We've got your notes. Tell us where to start."

"A bubble." He said something else, but Nedda couldn't hear it. Crucible's arms moved around the track. They should make a breeze, but they didn't. The air around Crucible was too thick, almost solid. "A needle, a pin. Pop a balloon. Oh, you can decrease the pressure and things expand until the wall stretches so thin it pops, or— Oh, a needle, a needle. How do you make a needle to burst a thing that isn't there?" He tugged his hair.

"Mom, what's happening?" Frost began sticking Nedda's eyelashes together. She was crying. When had she started crying?

"There's too much inside—I was fixing it, I was about to. Sinkhole. The whole town, it's like a sinkhole. I was trying, fixing it, I think. I'm going away again. Will you come back? If I come back will you be here?"

"We'll stay," Betheen said, and took a step to the machine. It could swallow her up too. Crucibles were for melting things down, metals, but this one melted everything. Her mother's back was made of shadows. "Tell us where to start and we'll stay."

His voice creaked. "No, get Pete. Go get Pete McIntyre. He was going for copper. We saw Denny. He ... We need a current. If you get enough copper—wire, pipe, all of it ... is the power still running?"

"It cuts in and out," Betheen said.

"Get Pete. We need a stable power source. And iron—a core, something strong. Magnetic current." He gnawed on his lip. "The chemicals I had to use, the gases. They're dangerous, poisonous."

"How dangerous?" Nedda asked.

"They're like ammonia and bleach. You have my notes?" His arm convulsed, nerves and muscles dancing.

"They're in Nedda's bag," Betheen said.

"Don't tell her, Beth. When you read them all, you'll know when you see—please don't tell her. I hadn't settled on what to say. I'll figure it out." Whatever else he said was lost. The lines on his lips deepened and his eyes rolled, then fixed, staring at something only he could see. He moved so quickly the subtlest blinks looked like vibrations, a thousand pictures of her father, layered on top of one another.

"Dad?"

Betheen pulled her back, sat her in the chair. The plastic squeaked against her corduroys. Her mother's hands were on her shoulders; her mother's cheek rested on top of her head, sharp but giving, bone and skin.

"He's gone now. He won't be able to hear us for a while."

"There's poison gas in the machine, Mom. What happens if we break it?"

Betheen was silent.

185

Her father's chest and arms wrinkled, like he was drying out inside and his skin was trying to fall away. Maybe it always had been. His hands and feet swelled, his fingers and toes curled, and she had to look away.

"We have to go."

"He's dying, Mom."

"Now, Nedda."

"Mommy, I can't." She couldn't leave again, not even if she was scared. She couldn't leave because she was scared.

"You don't have a choice. You don't want to see him right now. He wouldn't want you to either." Betheen dragged her from the lab with a strength Nedda hadn't expected.

"I *have* to," she said. "He's my dad and he's alone and he's scared."

"It's hard enough to watch when it's not happening fast."

"I have to stay."

"You don't get to see this. I'm not giving you a choice."

Nedda was empty, paper-bag empty, and let herself be pushed down the hallway. The metal on the door handle was too cold to touch. The hall lights were off and they felt their way down the corridor, guided by light from the exit. Nedda tapped her fingers, counting seconds. Pinkie to thumb. Ring to thumb. Fuck-you finger to thumb. Index to thumb. Repeat. Repeat. Repeat.

When they were outside the building Betheen stopped at his car.

"If you want to know what's happening, I'll tell you. Here's what you would see if you stayed. You'd see a face that you love start to fall apart. His eyes will bother him. They'll get red and teary, then cloudy. His skin will break down. His body will give out and his teeth will go. Once his teeth go, everything else goes too and he'll look like a different person. When that happens to someone you love, even if you've seen them every day, it's hard to recognize them. You'd see him and wonder who is that person, and what happened to my father? You'd look for the dad you knew, and you wouldn't always find him. You'd look for his old hair, his hands when they still looked like hands. You'd see little pieces of who he was peeking through that new body, but you wouldn't find him. It's hard enough to watch slowly, Nedda. Don't watch it happen quickly. He wouldn't want that for you."

Nedda tried not to think of her father's mouth—toothless—his eyes gone, his back bent. "Why would you say that? Why would you say such horrible things?"

"Because I'm your mother. Because I love you very much, and because you have a big heart and you don't know not to hurt it."

The sob came from everywhere all at once, "I hate you."

Betheen kissed her hair. "I know. Hate me all you want, but we have to go now, okay?"

Nedda tugged on her book bag's strap, feeling his notebook inside it, listening to her pony's space helmet tapping against the cover as she climbed into her father's car.

Every morning he had two cups of coffee, one he drank right away, and one he held to warm up. He drank it black, because milk first thing made his stomach sour and sugar would rot your teeth. When he trimmed his beard, he didn't always clean the sink up and there would be little lopped off hairs stuck to the porcelain and the top of the soap. The funny thing about soap was that when bubbles popped they left an outline of where they used to be, rings of beard trimmings.

She closed her eyes and felt the car pull out of the parking lot. "Are we going to Mr. Pete's?"

"Yes."

She tried to see if she could feel each turn in the road, the ruts, and still know where she was. Denny said you could tell a car's make and model by the engine's hum and the sound of the exhaust, and you could figure out what was wrong with it by the smell. He was good at it, but she'd only ever learned three cars—the Chevette, her mother's Cadillac, and Pop Prater's truck. She listened for Pop. If Annie Prater couldn't know she and Denny weren't at school, neither could Pop.

Then they reached where College Drive met Red Bug Road. It was gone, hidden under a wall of trees and brush tall and thick enough to touch the sky. Chunks of broken asphalt mingled with roots and gnarled pricker bushes.

"It's like the grove," Nedda said.

"Your father's genius at work." Betheen's laugh was loud and sharp. She put her hands to her face and ground the palms hard into her eyes. "It's everywhere."

187

Her mother was exhausted. But if they stopped for much longer, they might stay there for hours, not moving. Denny and her dad couldn't stay like that.

"Mom? Mommy, come on. I know another way."

They left the car. Nedda took Betheen's hand and led her to a narrow path in the woods.

# Aboard *Chawla*

MARCANTA HAD OFFERED Nedda a sedative, but she hadn't taken it. She wanted to know what a vitrectomy felt like; she wanted to be aware. The farther they were from Earth, the stronger the need was to understand every bit of her body, as though she herself was *Chawla*.

"You're a masochist," Marcanta told her.

"And you're a sadist. Our governments paired us perfectly."

Strapped into a chair, halo brace around her head, the experience was different from what she'd anticipated. She'd assumed she'd be tied into a sleep sack, needle in her arm, while Louisa floated above her. But that left too many variables when a stray movement could be catastrophic.

"It's going to feel like shit," Singh said.

"So you've had a vitrectomy?" Marcanta asked.

"No."

"Then kindly shut up." To Nedda she said, "I've got drops that will numb you up."

"Do I have to have them?"

"Yes. It's a lost cause if you freak out and flail."

"You're sure you can see well enough to do this?"

"I wouldn't trust me in two months, but right now? Yes." Marcanta pulled on her gloves.

Singh tightened the brace; he'd built it with Nedda's materials from the hydro lab—tubing, foam, clips. They'd considered using the printer for a proper halo brace, but there was no way to make one without Mission Control's knowledge and involvement. Nedda's ears were squeezed flat to her head by thick bumpers that Singh had stripped from the armrests in the control cabin. She lay back and listened for *Chawla*'s sounds to fade away. She'd been tuned to the module's heartbeat for years. Now there was only the rush of her own blood.

Singh floated above, his face upside down. She read his words by the flash of lips beneath his thick mustache. "I've got you."

Marcanta slipped her arm into a brace and buckled into a chair. Evgeni handed Marcanta the syringe-looking thing. *Vitrector. Vitreous, vitrified, vitrification.* It had been ages since they'd all been off sleep cycle together for any length of time. Four people in the room was equal parts comforting and frightening.

"Wait," Nedda yelled. "One second. Just one second."

Marcanta stilled. Singh seemed to understand, because the pressure on her ears let up. Evgeni hooked on to Marcanta's arm brace and pulled himself tight to her.

"Nedda, you'll be honest with me, won't you?" he said.

"Yes."

"Have I gotten fat?"

She laughed. They were rounder, all of them, softer too, and not only because their edges were fading. They'd become their nascent selves, borders still unformed. She knew them by their light, the gentle differences—Amit's warm, yellowish brown; Evgeni, who glowed like a pearl; Louisa, who was brighter than all of them. Nedda would know them anywhere; if she lost their shapes, she'd recognize their light.

They would likely die. It was why they were childless, unwed. Freedom of sacrifice. It was a shame that only three people would ever again be in the same room as Evgeni when he sang. Only three people would know that Singh ate with his pinkie out. That Marcanta pulled hairs from her eyebrows when frustrated. Children would know their names, and drive on roads named Sokolov or Papas. Children would know their ship, *Chawla,* and who she'd hauled. A little girl somewhere would rattle off everything she'd read about them, and with it everything she knew about space and time, about light.

"Okay," she said. "I'm ready now." Singh covered her good eye with a patch.

A speculum pulled back her eyelids and anchored her eye in place. Something that looked like a wire clamp coming directly at her should be disturbing, but it was oddly familiar.

"Ever see an eyelash curler?" she asked.

"A what?" Singh shouted.

"Never mind." No one did that anymore. Her mother used a relic.

A memory drifted in, of Betheen at her vanity, lit by a makeup mirror, clamping down on her lashes. *It makes my eyes look more open. If your eyes are open, it's easier for people to look you in them.*

Singh held her arms. She gritted her teeth. They'd decided to operate on her right eye, her weakest. If the operation failed, she'd still have her best eye.

The vitrector was from the lab. Marcanta used it on frogs to test the effects of radiation on their vitreous fluid. The frogs were their coal mine canaries, for the journey, for animal and human colonization.

Evgeni was near her good eye, and time became the sense of Evgeni's hand, Singh's breath, Marcanta's voice. She felt electricity pass between their skin, air in and out of lungs, vocal chords touching. Their bodies were a great metronome, marking seconds, minutes, hours. A beat that swung back and forth, a wave like a sine curve.

"She's breathing fast."

"I'm almost done."

"How much did you cut?" Singh asked.

"Would it make any sense to you if I told you? No. So don't ask."

"It isn't bad, you know. The blindness. I'm fine. None of you have to do this. Certainly not for me. I can teach you how to move this way."

"Hush or leave."

"Louisa—her breathing," Singh said.

"I know. Don't rush me."

"It's not bad at all."

Nedda was in her sleep sack, eye tightly bandaged, ears full of sparrow tittering and waves from the national seashore. She kept her good eye closed, enjoying light from the hologram filtering through the lid with gentle reds and yellows. She was not alone. She smelled Evgeni's sweetly stale sweat.

"No Louisa?"

"She needed to rest," Evgeni said. "It was upsetting for her to do this, I think."

Nedda liked his sometimes-backward phrasing, how his words piled on each other like acrobats, waiting to be flipped. He was warm enough that she felt his heat without having to touch him. She'd always run cold. Her head felt like her brain was trying to escape her skull, clawing its way out every possible exit.

"Painkiller?" she asked.

"Paracetamol is in your IV. Also an antibiotic. No opioids. The printer has left you a beta blocker. Marcanta says don't take it because it will affect your eye pressures."

She mumbled thanks.

"Sleep," he said. "I will make sure you don't rip your eye out."

"What, are you going to hold me down?"

"Never. I'll embrace you until you love me, or Louisa fights me for you."

His back against her side was like the puff of warm air when opening an oven door, sun on your face, home. She heard him say thank you. She slept. When she woke again he'd been replaced by Marcanta.

"Your eye looks good. Vicious headache, right?"

Nedda groaned, then groaning hurt. "Migraine level. If you need a break from Evgeni's music, do him next."

"Noted. I thought you'd like to know that no one's killed your plants yet. Singh went into a panic about Amadeus, so be warned, he's touchy. The printer gave him benzodiazepines, and I made him take an extra. So if he falls asleep on you that's why. Oh, and we had morning call."

"How was it?"

"They admitted we're supposed to run on plutonium, so that's something. Now they're just lying about whose fault this all is. Eurasia blames North America for miscommunication and shoddy engineering. North America blames Eurasia for the isotope mix-up." Marcanta sounded like she was frowning. "They're holding *Fortitude* for at least an additional year in build."

"Shit."

"Yeah. On the upside, you've got a scheduled call."

"My mom?"

"Like they'd tell us. Anyway, you get one more hour to sleep and then we need to run tests before your call. I can't wait to tell you all about how I'm gonna put a blob of oil in your eye when we get on planet."

She tried to sleep, but couldn't. Half of her was traveling; she was crew and ship and what lay ahead. Half of her was an orange grove and a path in the woods and all the people who had walked it.

Betheen was thinner than when Nedda had last seen her, but the screen might be stretching the image. Or this was just seeing with one eye.

"Oh, Nedda, your eye. What happened?"

"It's nothing, Mom. You look thin. Are you eating?"

"No more or less than usual. Maybe a little less. There's a food drive going on for the Coloradans, and I never feel right about eating so much while others go hungry."

"What happened in Colorado? Our news is always late and pretty filtered."

Betheen glanced away. "If they screen your news, it's probably best to let it go."

"But you're not eating."

"Just a little less."

"Martyr."

"Pot, kettle."

"Did you bring it?"

"Yes. It was in the attic. I forgot I'd put all those things up there after the basement flood. It took a minute to find." The flood had ruined the few things of his that were still left.

Something loosened in Nedda's chest. "Oh, thank God. I thought you wouldn't know what I meant."

"How could I not?"

Mission Control monitored calls in the same way it monitored emails. Under the guise of mental health, under the guise of operation management, under the guise of history and preserving a record for posterity, which was fine, until it wasn't.

"Can you hold it up to the camera?"

And there, in the pages of one of his unfinished notebooks, was Betheen's handwriting and the elegant equation. Betheen's hand was shakier now than it had been when she'd written it.

Nedda wrote quickly, stylus sliding across her tablet.

"Why the sudden interest?"

"There's some spiking energy in one of *Chawla's* drives. We're dumping off excess radiation into our landing-cushion water. Singh says it's fine, but it's better to play it safe." Nedda said that seeing him run the calculations had made her want to revisit all the math she'd forgotten. The lie was thin at best. Her mother had always known when she was hiding things. Their eyes met. Nedda knew, for once, she was deeply understood.

"The energy spikes are cyclical?" Betheen asked. "And you wanted to see our old math."

"Yes. Something just feels familiar."

"Well, you plug in the frequency here, the mass, and the energy output." The notebook wavered. "I used estimates here. Children's math."

"What happened to him wasn't your fault."

The notebook pulled away, and Betheen leaned close to the camera, shadows clinging below her eyes. "I know that, Nedda Sue. I do. It wasn't your fault either."

Betheen raised the notebook again, and Nedda finished copying, stretching the skin across her good eye, bending the light to make the writing clear. The room felt larger, darker, like their kitchen at night filled with notebooks and pens, the smell of corn muffins.

After Nedda finished copying the equation, they sat in silence for a moment. It was a waste of signal, but it was Nedda's last luxury, time with her mother, stretched across the universe.

"Do you think it's the same?" Betheen asked.

"I don't know. Maybe? It's possible he worked with someone along the way, maybe a student. You said he had a friend at NASA. I tried to dig around, trace the patent history, but it wasn't clear. I'm not sure it makes a difference."

"I don't suppose it does, but he'd want to know."

"He wanted to know everything. He sometimes thought he did."

"I could have emailed this to you; it would have gotten to you faster."

"It would have been screened. I might not have gotten it for a year or more, and there are some things I'd prefer other people didn't have their noses in. And I wouldn't have gotten to see you."

Betheen would always be striking, no matter how time changed her. No matter how she'd softened. It was in her smile, which had become warm like brown sugar, and wide like the horizon.

"No one tells you how strange it is to see your child as an adult. My mother never said a thing, not when I left for college, not when I married your dad. I always see baby you, even in your flight suit, even when you're talking to press. I always see you pushing up on your little hands, learning how to crawl. I want to scream 'There's my baby, running around in space doing dangerous things, and doesn't anybody know that a stiff wind could kill her?'"

Nothing had killed Nedda, and the woman talking to her from halfway across the sky was tougher than Nedda had ever been.

"You always look the same to me too," she said, though it wasn't true any longer. But it was difficult to say anything more. She thought of her mother, not bent over a stove or in a lab coat, not tucking her into bed, but backlit by the sky, holding out her hand. Telling Nedda, *Get up.*

"How's Pete?" Nedda asked.

"Claiming I burned all of his nose hair off."

"Did you?"

"He should know that just because it smells like lemon doesn't mean it's lemon. Serves him right." She closed the notebook and tucked it away.

"Are you . . . ?"

"I'm not replacing your dad."

"It's okay if you do."

"Well, it's not like I've been celibate, and it's none of your business."

"So you're sleeping with him."

"Nedda."

"Don't be so old-fashioned, Mom. No one worries about that stuff now. They haven't in fifty years."

"Well, I guess I'm antiquated."

"We both are."

"I wish I could help you more," Betheen said.

"You did. You do. More than anyone." She could not say the words she wanted—they were stuck in equations, in memorizing all the subtle changes in her mother, trapped in a barrage of seeing. Later, when the screen blinked black, they spilled.

*You saved my life.*

Her hair hurt when she let it down from its braid. The release of tension made her scalp scream with a joyful kind of pain. Almost enough to explain watery eyes.

Nedda runged her way around *Chawla*, searching for Singh. She found him in his cabin, tucked in his sleep sack and staring at the ceiling.

"Amit, quit fantasizing about our demise. We can fix it, but we need to triple check all our math. Then we get to rip some stuff apart." She tossed the tablet at him and it spiraled slowly, beautifully. His long arm snaked out from the blue cocoon and caught it.

"What the hell?"

"What did I teach you? 'What the fuck?,' 'What the shit?,' or 'Motherfucker' would be appropriate. We can fix Amadeus." Her hands were trembling. "Wait until the benzos are out of your system. You need to be extra careful with the math. We have to check each other."

He was fully awake now. "Sure, yes, absolutely."

"Careful math, or boom," she said.

"Or boom."

# 1986: Mr. Pete's House

THE CADILLAC SAT in front of Mr. Pete's house, one of three dead cars in the driveway. Tricia Villaverde said that's how you knew someone was trash, if there was a car on blocks in their driveway. Nedda didn't think it counted if the person fixed cars. Mr. Pete kept things from being trash; he rescued them. The Cadillac's side was crumpled, paint gone, metal crunched. There were traces of the other car on it, stripes of white paint, glass stuck in the seam of the bumper. Her mother had been inside, French twist rising high over the headrest, elbows braced against the steering wheel. Betheen pulled the seat up far and Dad always teased her about it. "You try looking over a mile of hood," she'd said.

The other person had died. Her mom could have died.

"What happened to the other car?"

"It slid into the canal," Betheen said.

"You're okay?"

"I'm fine."

For right then, it was enough.

Mr. Pete's garage door was open. Nedda was used to seeing him rummaging inside, tossing things into a pile of cords, wires, and tools. But the garage looked different, felt different. The light inside flickered at irregular intervals, distorting Mr. Pete's shadow, and made all the things in the garage seem bigger than they were, scarier.

Betheen squeezed her hand and said, "We can't tell him what happened to your dad."

"Why not?"

"He might get too scared and we need his help. I need your help. I need you, okay? Come on, let's go in."

"Fine." It wasn't fine.

Mr. Pete's front yard had a palm tree that dropped coconuts every-where, dark shapes on a lawn that was mostly dirt, gravel, and bits and pieces that never made it back into cars. The sky was the same color it had been over the grove, though it had taken them what felt like forever to get through the woods. The sun should be high now, but it hadn't moved.

"Mr. McIntyre? Pete?" her mother called.

The lanky shadow put a hand to its eyes. Denny's dad called people like Mr. Pete rat people. Rat people were families who had moved here before Easter was Easter. Hunters, fishermen, and fruit pickers, they'd come down for cheap land, then stayed on after the money ran out, through frosts and fires. Everyone's family came from somewhere to get to Easter, but the people Pop Prater talked about seemed like they'd always been there. You'd see them at the dog track, or racing hot rods, or fishing all day even during the week. Some had hooked up with bootleggers during prohibition. When Island Paradise had been open, they ran rides. After the moon landing some of them sold fake moon rocks. Pop Prater said the whole town could disappear and they'd still be there because they could live off the trees and the Indian River, like the monkeys that escaped the park. He hadn't meant anything good by it. Mr. Pete was one of those people. McIntyres had always been in Easter. They didn't have money like the Praters, but they weren't in the trailer park either. She knew Mr. Pete had done a bunch of different things, but it was good to do different things, to like lots of things. Coffee berries. Magazines. Mission patches. Space junk.

"Mrs. Papas?" Something clattered as it fell from a table. "Are you all right?"

"Pete, I'm sorry to bother you, but Theo is working on a project and he said you might be able to help with materials."

It was a dumb lie. Nedda knew her dad called Pete anytime he needed anything. She watched to see if he bought it.

"Copper," Pete said. "I saw him earlier." He dug his hands into his pockets, a thumb poking out a hole. He noticed Nedda and flinched. "Nedda Sue."

"Hi, Mr. Pete. My dad's having trouble with the phone today, so we're helping." There, that was better.

"He was—his hands were acting up. He had me drive him to the grove to look at something, then I brought him back to the school," Mr. Pete said.

"You saw Denny, didn't you?"

He was supposed to say something about how it wasn't that bad, even if it was a lie. That was the contract, between adults and kids, and why there were moments of silence, assemblies, and why people said stupid things about everything happening for a reason. Mr. Pete said nothing.

Betheen didn't say anything either, and it made Nedda burn.

"He'll be fine," Nedda said. Somebody had to say it. If nobody said it, then what was the point of trying to do anything at all? "We're going to fix it. It's like a soap bubble and we need to pop it. We need a needle."

The lights flickered. A bulb in the back flared before burning to nothing, leaving the rear of the garage in darkness.

"We need a stable power supply," Betheen said. "I remember you lending Ellery Rees a generator after Hurricane Bob."

"Mmh." Mr. Pete rubbed his neck.

"He needs it for an electromagnet," Betheen said.

Mr. Pete looked at Nedda. "Were you with Denny?"

"I thought it was lightning, but it wasn't," she said. Her shoe bottom rolled over a pebble, and she pressed down on it, hard. She wanted it to hurt, but it didn't. She pushed harder. "He's going to be fine." She knew how to lie. Why to lie.

"Well, come on in. I got a pair of generators."

His garage was packed, a jigsaw puzzle of bits of boats, fans, and pieces of what were probably airplanes. In a corner, something that looked like a propeller leaned against the wall. She trailed her fingers over things. Sometimes rightness was a feeling. Sometimes you didn't know something worked until you touched or smelled it and saw where it fit. Denny was oranges, Ivory soap, and moss. Her dad was a hinge creaking, unbent paper clips, and boiling salt water. A launch was rain, ash, and eggs. Those things weren't supposed to fit together, but they did. The things in Mr. Pete's garage, the tool boxes and empty cans of Crush, belonged here.

She touched the propeller, which was from a fan boat, not an airplane. Mr. Pete leaned back, looking at her, then her mother.

"It'd be easier if the professor gave me specifics."

"Consider me his assistant," Betheen said, sugaring her voice, making a willful decision to use sweetness for a purpose. That was power too.

The door into the house was open, and a hall light shone on a row of lockers. Mr. Pete had *everything*: plaster casts of Neil Armstrong's feet, containers of freeze-dried food, toothpaste tubes of roast beef, tire treads that matched the ones on the lunar rover. There were things her father might have worked on, pieces of him other people never saw.

"We'll need a lot of current."

"I can't say for sure if the generators I've got are enough if I don't know the specs of what he's working on. I can talk it through with the professor. If his hands are the problem, I can help."

Nedda cut him off. "Mr. Pete? I have to use the bathroom."

"Sure, sure," he said.

She ducked inside the house. She'd seen the locker bank before; it was from the maintenance building. Mr. Pete said he'd found John Glenn's hard hat in it, but he must have made that part up, because nobody would leave something like that in a locker. She touched the paint. Maybe John Glenn had touched it. Maybe Neil Armstrong. Maybe Judy Resnik. Mr. Pete's house was winding, one of the older houses in Easter that had been built out, torn down, and added on to, but never quite right. There were telephones everywhere, disconnected. Some of them were probably from Kennedy, maybe from Mission Control. Even if they weren't, Mr. Pete told people they were. A fire axe hung on a wall, beside it a faded black-and-white picture of a group of men in gear. Mr. Pete's face was in the back row. Under the axe was a heavy glove, like the kind her dad kept in his lab.

Her dad needed copper. Betheen said he wanted to make an electromagnet; she'd gotten that from his jumbled words, from copper, magnetic current. There was copper in phones, in phone lines, in everything in houses. She walked. Touched. The kitchen had drawers that didn't close, things hanging out of cabinets, screwdrivers and wrenches on the countertops. There were dishes somewhere, she guessed, but one person didn't need a lot of dishes. She only used a plate and a cereal bowl and if you washed those, you wouldn't need anything else.

Something caught her eye. On his kitchen table, a perfect little thing, neat, as though it had just been set there, as though Mr. Pete had been looking at it this morning. A mission patch with efficient machine embroidery, the black, yellow, and red of the German flag. STS 61-A, *Challenger.* A Spacelab mission. James Buchli, Guion Bluford, Henry Hartsfield, Bonnie Dunbar, Steven Nagel, Reinhard Furrer, Ernst Messerschmid, Wubbo Ockels.

Mr. Pete kept things like she did. Liked things that she did. She was what Pop Prater talked about too, a rat person.

From the window, she saw the flatbed. It was where things had started. She'd been in it with Denny.

Easter might have changed, but the truck was the same dark beast on its way to decay. She touched the front fender and her hand came away red with rust. Inside its bed were her footprints, hers and Denny's. She could step into them, stand on the shadows of where they'd been. She tossed her book bag inside, climbed up, and looked around. In the summer, the truck bed had been hot on their backs, the kind of heat that made you think you'd never be cold again.

Now, the cold in the truck had a source point, the spot in the corner and the creature in it. The monkey was small, manageable, far more than Denny, far more than her father. It hadn't moved.

"How come you got off easy?"

The marmoset was so still, so happy looking; she hated it.

Betheen's and Mr. Pete's voices carried from inside the garage.

She jabbed, stabbed, and punched at the monkey as hard as she could, but wound up smacking the truck and jamming her fingers. What was happening to Denny was stretching and pulling his body way too fast. What was happening to her father was the most awful thing she'd ever seen. Her dad might not be in pain—it was hard to tell—but Denny was. He'd scratched himself and pulled out his hair.

She flopped back, looking up. It wasn't day or night, and there were yellow-green ribbons of light across the clouds. The sky was cut through by power lines from the back of Mr. Pete's house to the pole catty-corner from it. Eventually they fed into the transmission towers that ran along the highways. Miles of wire. How much of it was copper?

Water dripped from one of the lines, falling lazily into the truck bed with a pearly yellow glint. It was weirdly pretty, a shooting star.

She'd lied to her dad about Halley's Comet.

Nedda opened her backpack and ran her thumb over Cotton Candy's plastic space helmet, brushed her tail and mane. Then she took out her father's notebook.

*8/31: Growth at this age unpredictable. Ht. Wt. BMI unreliable. Twitches and squirms too much.*

- *Balances on one foot after repeated attempts.*
- *Can do large plastic zips. Refuses snaps. Cries.*
- *Counts fingers and toes.*
- *Knows colors, shapes.*
- *Vocabulary ~500, relies on favorites. "Mushy," "cooperation," and "apogee" cause laughter.*

*Nedda spending days when I work with neighbors. Their son is one year older.*
*Nedda asked where Betheen's belly went. Betheen told her, "Sometimes mommas get big and sometimes they get small again." Impossible not to imagine what Michael would be like.*

It was about her. He'd taken notes on her like one of his experiments, cataloging everything about her. And her mother. Betheen had gotten big, then small again. Her mother had been pregnant. And that name, Michael. After the mention of Michael was a long list of what looked like medical terms, and then dated theories:

*9/15: The problem is time related. Knowledge acquisition is at war with cell death. Children, with their brain plasticity, don't have these challenges. Nedda is too young to grasp that a week is not interminable, that an hour isn't remotely eternity.*

*Q: <u>Are</u> seconds longer for her? <u>Is</u> perception experience? What does an hour feel like?*

*10/15: The problem with time is breakdown. Memory lapses are symptomatic of wear, cell breakdown, data written over too many times. Does thought create friction across neurons? Even children have wear. Growth is wear.*

*10/22: Nuclear family = child as nucleus. Parent = electron, orbiting, hopping shell, never too far, always pulled. Chest pain = psychosomatic atomic bond.*

Nedda's foot bounced against the truck bed. The hollow tapping was calming, as was the feel of the metal. Solid. Was she just an experiment? A specimen to observe and study, to help him form new projects?

*10/30: Magnets to cut friction. Spoiler to vacuum. Air resistance. Fins. Legs. Arms. Blades. COLD.*

*11/5: Posit: Acceleration of entropy to reduce half-life producing greater short-term energy bursts. Entropy stopped locally creates stasis. Stop wear, not activity.*

A spill across the page smelled like old coffee. He didn't always drink his coffee; sometimes he just held it to help with aches. Hot water would have worked, but it didn't smell the way coffee did. The stain and the words below had turned into a frustrated blot.

*11/9: It isn't fair to her to have two broken parents. I don't remember Michael correctly. He's not here, but he's here. We don't talk about him. Betheen can't take it. I can't either.*

*11/15: Posit: If one could pause a life—wear and aging—a single person could learn infinite things. Life is limited by wear on the brain, wear on the joints, wear on the heart. A child deserves infinite time, a perfect heart, a body and mind that won't break.*

*11/16: Betheen said, "A mother is only as happy as her saddest child." And if that child is dead? Then what?*

A dead child. A sibling. She'd had a brother. Her father had never said a thing. Betheen hadn't either.

Pages of messy equations followed, some scribbled through, some with the slanting *S* her mother told her to look for. He'd written in ballpoint pen. It hadn't smeared like her Erasermate, but it ripped the page the same way as when she pressed too hard—the paper thin, the ink almost angry.

*12/1: I want her not to wear, for her to have all the time she'll ever need. I want her to have lifetimes of hours.*

- *A perfect body is frictionless within itself*
- *A child who never leaves you*

*12/7: Isolated heat loss. Isolated entropy. EACH BODY A CLOSED SYSTEM.*
*12/12: What if it's like water? If there is tension to it? If like water, it needs to spin. Centrifugal force at subatomic lvl.*
*12/25: We could be good parents. I could be a good father. We'd have time. And a daughter who wouldn't leave us. She'd have two lifetimes of hours.*

Her father had built Crucible because of her. He'd built it *for* her, and he'd been thinking about it since she'd been a baby. He wanted to stop her from growing up, and not just for her.

For Michael, who was dead.

She tried to imagine her father in the basement, writing things down anytime she wasn't crying, anytime she wasn't demanding attention. She'd seen all his faces, his young self through who he'd been when he'd looked for the comet with her. The man in the notebook was the gray, sick-faced father she'd seen in the lab. The man who'd written that notebook had held her, and she didn't know him at all.

"Nedda," Betheen called.

The end of her braid crunched between her teeth.

He didn't want her to grow up. He never wanted her to leave. Because of Michael, the brother they'd kept secret.

The monkey remained unblinking beside her. She kicked it, hard as she could, but her foot pounded into the side of the truck.

"Nedda?"

Did he want her paused in time, stopped like the monkey?

Stopped was not being able to kick. Stopped was angry and crying and needing to punch something but knowing you couldn't.

He'd told her Crucible was for his hands, for conserving fuel and making things reusable. He said it was to help people.

They'd lied to her about stupid things. Things she should know about, like Michael, about being sad, about how bad things hurt. But her mom didn't lie when she needed her to. It was the simplest, dumbest, most basic lie and she couldn't do it. Her parents could hide an entire person from her but Betheen couldn't say that things would be all right.

Mr. Pete called her now too. The dirt in the truck bed was ruining her jacket's pale blue satin and the pink piping.

Judy hadn't hidden in a truck bed; she'd gone on the shuttle. Judy got up, even when it was frightening. It was probably always frightening. Things that mattered were. Astronauts went up, knowing that they might not come back. They did science, good science, and asked questions, the right ones.

Astronauts got up.

"Nedda Susanne Papas, get your ass over here right now."

*Ass.* Nedda had almost forgotten about the word because it meant so little—*donkey, bottom, butt. Ass* had made her swear list so early on she'd contemplated crossing it off. Her mother made it sound good and angry and scared, too, all those things that rolled inside her. Betheen stood in the door to the screen porch.

"I'm out here." Nedda's head rushed as she sat up. When her vision cleared, she saw the launch sequencer, pristine under the awning on the back of Mr. Pete's house. The awning would keep it mostly dry, but everything in Easter rusted. Everything in Easter was wet.

What if the bubbles around her father and Denny worked like water? Her dad thought as much. He'd written it down.

The sprinklers had been on when she and Denny were in the grove. On cold mornings, water—condensate—dripped from the powerline above the truck. *Plit, plit, plit.*

She grabbed the notebook and scrambled to the ground.

It was hard to see her mother's face, backlit as she was by the porch light. Mr. Pete was nearby, a mess of wires and cables in his arms.

"Stay where I can see you," Betheen said.

"She can't come to much harm back there," Mr. Pete said.

Secrets were like bubbles too, two layers of lie with the truth in between. And they hurt.

"You're shitty liars. You don't even know how to do it right. You think I can't tell when you're lying? Well, you're wrong. I can."

Betheen reached for her and Nedda pushed her back. "No. The thing the machine is making, it works like water. It's like water and bubbles like I said. It's in Dad's notes. And I know why he built it. I know there was a Michael, and he was my brother and he died when I was little and you never told me. I had a brother. And it's not fair you never told me. If you were going to be shitty parents, I should've at least known why." She stomped hard and it felt good. Nedda looked at Mr. Pete. "My dad isn't okay. He's in his lab and he's really hurt, as bad as Denny, maybe worse. My mom can fix it. She's smart, even though she's the shittiest liar in the entire world. And we need your stuff, so do what she says." She squeezed her hands into fists to stop them from shaking. "Everything is fine. We're going to fix it. We're going to fix my dad's machine and my dad and Denny are going to be okay. Because bad stuff doesn't happen to good people and everything happens for a reason. We're going to fix it. That's how you lie. Like that."

# Aboard *Chawla*

S INGH'S ARM HAIR was fine like summer grass; a gentle breath could set it moving. Nedda had read that losing one of your senses changed how you experienced emotions. She wondered if loving the hair on Amit's arms might mean the last days of sight.

Singh smelled everything. On Earth, it would have been unsettling. Had a man sniffed her like that in Easter, he would have spent ten minutes trying to pick himself off the ground, a mouth full of bloody Chiclets. Amit wouldn't get that phrase at all, none of them would. Even so, they knew her so well, so intimately. Boundaries had disappeared with Evgeni's vision. Sleep sacks abandoned, they bunked in a knot of limbs, drifting across *Chawla*'s main cabin, softly bumping into walls, caroming around as a single, four-hearted organism.

Marcanta was the best to sleep near. Louisa's body was giving, she sweat the least, and if you woke with a start, she'd kiss your forehead. Evgeni had difficulty keeping to the sleep schedule and wedged between Nedda and Singh, using their heartbeats to lull himself to sleep. He called them a UN treaty, a peaceful agreement between nations.

Fear made bodies crave touch.

Nedda was on the outside tonight, Singh and Evgeni in the middle. Her eye itched beneath the bandage, keeping her awake.

Singh's fingers touched where the tape crossed her eyebrow. "An eye for an eye," he said into her hair.

"Eye for all, and all for eye," she whispered back. "Sorry if I woke you. It's driving me crazy." He shuffled behind her, locking a leg between hers and Evgeni's, fidgeting. "You're thinking about something. I can almost hear it."

"I wouldn't have volunteered."

"Yes, you would have. You did volunteer, we all did. We're noble little guinea pigs."

"No," he said. "I'm selfish. But you let Marcanta do that to you, knowing it might blind you faster, knowing it could kill you. You volunteered."

Nedda tucked her chin to his chest. The motion set them drifting to the bookcase wall. His beard brushed the top of her head, and she sniffed him the way he did her. Amit smelled like the module, like the vegetal water of the hydroponics lab, like sponge-bath showers, like the alcohol used to clean everything.

Evgeni kicked out and sent them spinning the rest of the way into the bookcase. The landing was soft, but he swore anyway, and untangled himself from their knot. Marcanta woke at the movement.

"I'll go," Evgeni said. "Time to tire myself out on the bike." He felt his way out of the room, then drifted down the hall.

"The printer upped his psych meds this morning," Singh said. "The hypnic jerks are probably a side effect."

Marcanta yawned. "I should watch him. Should I watch him? Yes, Louisa, you should monitor him for other side effects," she said to herself.

"He'll be fine," Nedda said.

Nedda found it hard to tell that Evgeni had moods at all, let alone ones that needed regulating. He appeared to have three settings: happy, stoic, and amorous. It seemed a good way to be.

"Sure. But now I'm going to worry." Marcanta swore and followed him to the gym.

Singh and Nedda rearranged themselves and drifted by the window. The light was filmy now, not clear and cold like it had been in the early days of their departure. She picked at the tape around her eye. It messed with the seal on the pressure goggles, and was a constant reminder of her body breaking.

"Why'd you tell Louisa about his pills?"

"She wants to worry about something. Worrying about someone else feels more productive than worrying about yourself," Singh said. "If you're concerned about someone else, you do your best to make them comfortable. When you're worried about yourself, you're just worrying."

She knew Singh had helped nurse his grandparents in their last days. His grandmother had surrendered to dementia. With his grandfather, it had been a messy cancer, a wasting awfulness that left a gap no words could explain. He'd worried.

"Stripping down medical is the only way I can think of to get the materials we're going to need to fix Amadeus," she said. The idea had been eating at her since she and Singh had run numbers. Medical had almost everything they needed.

"I came to the same conclusion. There are some things we can get from Hydro if you're up for losing them, but not the essentials. Louisa's going to kill us."

Nedda knew differently. Louisa would rip the med bay apart with her teeth if she thought it would help. "Obviously. You're going to have to let her jab you a few times just for fun," she said.

"I guess that's a fair exchange. If you talk me through it, I'll do the walk to Amadeus when the time comes."

"No, you won't. Marcanta and I already decided. If something goes wrong, we can lose me and still survive. If we lose you, our chances of landing go to zero."

Amit squeezed Nedda a little tighter. She let him.

"It's beautiful math," he said.

"I know. Behind every brilliant woman is her doubly brilliant mother."

"How did she think of it?"

"It was the pressure." The same adrenaline that made it possible for humans to lift cars had jolted Betheen's mind to genius.

They floated in silence, Marcanta's and Evgeni's voices quiet and distant, Chawla's engines churning below. Amit was hard against her back, but not pressing. He nudged once, then let it go. The advance wasn't unwelcome, but it was nothing she acted upon. In the last months, they'd begun to feel less like people and more like a symbiotic part of Chawla. Amit was idealistic in his longing. And what was sex but longing? But he was applying ideals to her, qualities she'd never possessed—that she was noble or sacrificing.

"I'm not good, you know," she said.

"I never said you were."

"You implied it, but it isn't true. I'm making up for things."

"What could you have done that was so awful you'd let Louisa cut into your eye and volunteer yourself to walk into a nuclear reactor?"

"It was more like a poke than a cut," she said.

"That's not any better."

"My father built the machine that created the anomaly, that made all the Gappers." She couldn't say the rest, the uncomfortable familiarity of the Amadeus drive, what she and her mother had done.

"And? My uncle killed two people in a DUI, but that has nothing to do with me."

Amit's beard bristles scraped her ear as he turned. Evgeni's cheek was smoother, Marcanta's the softest, including hers. Nedda was still bony, prickly like she'd always been.

"It's not the same. That's two people. My dad ruined the lives of an entire town." When they'd worked Amit's data into her mother's equations, tracked the timing of the surges, she wondered if he suspected. If he did, he was kind, and said nothing.

"I missed the part where you're responsible for that."

"He built it to stop me from growing up, among other reasons."

*Fuck* was a universally satisfying word. Always cathartic, intonation gave it all the meaning it ever needed. Amit's voice was beautiful and he said the word with compassion, an understated *F*, a lovely *K*. "That's messed-up logic. He told you that?"

"It was in one of his notebooks."

"People write a lot of things they don't mean."

"He built the machine. That's proof enough that he meant it. I'm the daughter of a mad scientist, one who conducted human experiments and everything."

"I still fail to see how it's your fault."

"I benefited from what he did. Had I stayed where I was, *when* I was, I'd still be in Easter. I'd be my mother's age. I'd be who my mother was. I wouldn't be here at all. Back then, not even a tenth of the people who'd been to space were women. I'm a person of consequence now. Do you— You can't understand how rare that was then, can you? I was so mad at my father. It took me ten years to figure out what he'd wanted. And he did give me time, it just wasn't the way he intended, and I didn't have a choice. A whole town suffered for it. Everything I do now is important.

Every thought, every blink is something to be studied and considered seriously. I became someone important in a way I could never have been, because of him. Because I was his daughter, and that's inseparable from all the people he hurt. It's a scale I have to balance. I get to do things now, to be here, to explore. I have to do things now, because of what he did. I might lose my eye for Evgeni. I might die trying to fix Amadeus. I might freeze or starve to death on planet. But I'll be of consequence. I *have* to be, because of what he did. Because it was for me."

Amit let her go and floated back to the window, reaching out to touch the glass. "You were a little kid. Children can't process things like what happened to you. The emotional capacity simply doesn't exist. You were eleven, right? When I was eleven I thought babies came out of belly buttons and that if I concentrated hard enough I could communicate telepathically with my tortoise."

Nedda tried to imagine a little Amit, but couldn't picture his face without a beard. "A tortoise?"

"My mother can't tolerate dogs. They remind her of an auntie she hated."

Marcanta chose that moment to poke her head into the room. "Evgeni wants to go under for a while. Are you both okay if he's out for two weeks?"

Amit fiddled with one of the books in the case. "I suppose it can't make the situation worse."

"I took blood samples, just in case. He doesn't need new meds. It's just fatigue. His days and nights are screwing with him. He can't regulate to the ship's lights."

"We could change them," Nedda said. Their eventual sunrise would be another star. Twenty-four-hour days were a tie to a place they'd never see again. The irregularity of Evgeni's days might be their new rhythm. As with his loss of sight, he might have been faster to adapt than the rest of them.

Amit said nothing, only followed Louisa to Evgeni's cabin.

They crowded around Evgeni's sleep sack, pressing tight to his body. His mad grin was contagious. Lightness in human form. He was smart, resourceful, but he'd been chosen above other candidates because he was buoyant, a bright spirit.

"Not a bad way to fall asleep," he said. "A beautiful woman on each side, and a man who doesn't stink and takes care of his hands. I could not ask for more."

"If you make me laugh I'm going to miss the IV port," Louisa said.

When Evgeni's eyes fluttered, Amit leaned in and whispered, "Every woman you dream about is going to have my face."

People who floated, who rose, took others with them. You held on to people like that. You gave an eye for them.


Nedda retreated to her cabin, alone, listening to waves. Amit needed to think of her as good. If she was good, doing noble things, it helped him feel that he was too. Nobility by association, no matter if it was a lie. She preferred Louisa's view of her: a test subject with an opinion.

She chewed on a piece of one of their few remaining chocolate bars, bittersweet filling her mouth. Betheen said the kindest thing you could do for yourself was to once in a while fall asleep with the taste of chocolate on your tongue. Dark chocolate. Betheen mixed pomegranate juice with it and poured it into molds shaped like shells or butterflies. Tart, bitter, rich, and sweet—layers of flavors, each a chemical compound her mother had balanced. Designed to heal.

Missing her mother was an ever-tender bruise. Betheen understood what it was to wake to a culture shift so radical your life could be rewritten. Her father had given her *everything*. He'd given Betheen chances she'd thought she'd lost. She had degrees on the wall to prove it. A lab, a life. Betheen said living with an obligation could take your soul away, but it gave you purpose.

Amit didn't understand. Louisa tried to make her feel better or unhelpfully suggested talking to Dr. Stein. Evgeni, much as she loved him, was barely the same species. He didn't process guilt the way she did.

She closed her eyes and made lists. Cataloging so she wouldn't forget, though she already had.

Glasses, black frames
Graph-paper shirt with pocket
Pocket: two pens, tire pressure gauge

Black hair, curly, gray shot through
Crumbly fingernails
Dent in chin where his beard bristles grew together

Bobby pins, blonde hair
Lemon dish soap
Aqua Net hairspray
Coral nail polish
Clear safety glasses
Pen marks on fingers
Peach fuzz on her chin that catches light
Pocket: greasy lipstick, tissues, wind-up watch

# 1986: Electromagnet

**P**LEASE EAT SOMETHING," Betheen said.

"I'm not hungry." Nedda's stomach made noises, but not the hungry kind.

"The stove is out. How about cereal? Can you do cereal for dinner?"

Nedda poured a bowl of Lucky Charms, swirled it with her spoon, and watched the milk turn rainbow colors and eventually a muddy tan. She'd had a brother. A brother she didn't know. And her mother and father had kept it a secret. Michael had died and it was so bad that her dad had built something terrible. And now he was stuck in it. Denny was stuck in it.

"I'm still mad," Nedda said.

"I'm aware," Betheen said, which had the immediate effect of making Nedda's anger feel pointless.

"You should have told me."

"I should have."

"Can't you just say you're sorry?"

"I would if it would make you feel better."

"Well, it might."

"I'm sorry. We should have told you. We thought it would be easier for you if we didn't."

It didn't feel better. Nedda kicked the table. "Why didn't we stay at Mr. Pete's?"

"Because we need to think and I can't think in a place that cluttered," she said. "Sinkhole. Your dad said something about a sinkhole. Do you remember?"

"No." Sinkholes swallowed cars and houses. She'd seen a story once about a town falling into one, but it was in one of those tabloids that wrote things about Bigfoot and Bat Boy. There was always a rack of them at Ginty's Bait & Tackle.

Nedda peered out the kitchen window. There were cars in Denny's driveway, and all up the street in front of his house, some of which belonged to parents of kids in her grade. There were lots of people in the house too; as they walked around, lights shifted.

Betheen pulled the curtain closed, cutting off Nedda's view. She chewed on a rice cake, the most miserable food that was ever made.

"I have to help, Mom."

Chair legs scraped across the linoleum as Betheen sat down, boneless and heavy. Her breath sounded just as tired. "We need paper, pens, and a calculator."

*We.*

Nedda moved her dad's books to the floor so Betheen could fit two big graph paper pads on the kitchen table. It was weird to see her using his things, weird to see his things in the kitchen. Betheen wrote like she whisked, fast, vines of muscle in her forearms sliding. It was weird that an arm could look smart, but Betheen's did. Nedda looked for the same muscles in her own arm, but figured she wouldn't get them until she was older.

Equations took shape like sentences, paragraphs, whole books in a language she didn't understand. Rows upon rows of letters and symbols, curves and arcs.

"What is that?"

"Calculus," Betheen said. "Well, bad calculus. I haven't kept it up. Calculus—all math—is a language. If you stop using things, stop speaking a language, you forget."

Nedda had skipped a year in math and was just learning algebra. For the first time, letters were involved. It seemed like the more complicated math got, the more letters and symbols there were, numbers vanishing almost entirely. Nedda slid her chair next to Betheen, dragging it in a way that would normally make Betheen yell. But she didn't.

The pull to her mother was almost too much. On the moon, gravity was next to nothing; a jump could make you fly. In a shuttle, you were weightless, always falling, disoriented and free. On Earth, you were supposed to know where you were, how your feet spread on the ground, the weight of your body. But right now the gravity of Betheen was like Jupiter, enough that all your bones would break. She wanted to crush herself into her mother, to breathe her perfume, the hairspray, the ink and paper and the crumbs of rice cake on her pink collar. But she was still furious.

"What's it for?"

"I timed your father," Betheen said. "It's not as specific as it should be, but it's the best I can do given the circumstances. It was easier to see his end point rather than the beginning—but you get what I mean."

"End point?"

"He's moving forward, then backward in time. So, end to end is one full cycle through. I start counting when he's at his oldest, and end once he's old again. It's like a loop. Divide it by half, and you have the midpoint of the cycle, which is about one lifetime. So, I'm taking that and trying to figure out what kind of spike we'd need, when we'd need it, and how it would work."

"You timed Dad."

"I timed how long it takes him to go through a cycle. It varies some, but there's a pattern."

"How long he's alive."

"Yes."

"So you know exactly how old he'll be on the day he dies."

"It's not quite like that—it's the curve I showed you. The top and the bottom are the start and end; we can approach those and estimate." Betheen bit into another rice cake, chewing it dry.

Her father, old and dying. Nedda didn't want to see him young and scared either. She wanted him sitting with her on the hood of the car, looking for comets. And she never wanted to see him ever again.

"He built it because he didn't want me to grow up."

Betheen's pen stopped moving. "What?"

"It's in his notes, I saw it. I hate him," she said. And it was true. It was wrong that someone could make a decision for you, for your whole life, and never talk to you about it, never ask what you wanted. He'd decided all sorts of things just because he could.

She didn't expect Betheen to smooth her hair, sending warmth up her spine, or the way it made her eyes sting. She didn't want to lean into it or for it to feel good, but she did and it did.

"You don't hate him," Betheen said.

"I do."

Betheen leaned back to look at the pages she'd written. "When Michael died, we were both sad for a long time. You were so young. We didn't know what to do, and there was no one to talk to. We did the best we could, and we weren't always good parents, but we loved you so much. No matter what, he loves you."

"It doesn't matter, does it?" Nedda's foot started bouncing, so she pressed her knees into the underside of the table. There would be red marks on her skin that matched the wood grain.

"It always matters."

Betheen pulled her chair back and stood, allowing Nedda to see the pages. There were crossed-out lines, holes in the paper, and what started out as looped, pretty handwriting had slanted into a scrawl that looked almost like her father's. Maybe being smart demanded handwriting like that, another language only certain people could read. Somewhere in those lines and letters was her father's life from beginning to end.

Betheen dropped something into Nedda's hand. The white kitchen timer her dad had gotten for Betheen for Christmas. You could time three things on it at once, down to the second. "Here," she said. "Put in two hours and seventeen minutes, then press start."

The red buttons made a cheerful beep that was wrong, considering. The numbers ticked silently. Seconds were weird; they always took a little longer to pass than you expected.

"That's how long," Betheen said. "Two hours and seventeen minutes, or about four cakes, in and out. The clock in the lab wasn't working, so I used my wristwatch."

"That's not accurate," Nedda said. Swiss watches were supposed to be good, but Betheen's was a Timex you had to wind and the second hand didn't even tick, just swung around smoothly.

"No, it's not," Betheen said. There was a tilt to her mouth that was almost a smile. "And the start and end points are estimates. So I'll lose at least twenty points for sloppy work."

The triple timer was too quiet. Not like the egg timer or the red hour timer Betheen still sometimes used, which whined with a satisfying tick. You should be able to feel time passing in your skin, in your ears.

"How do you know when he ends?" She didn't want to say *dies*.

"You just do. One minute someone is there; then they're gone. You know it, like how you know someone's turned a light off, even if your eyes are closed. It's a little bit darker. There are bonds connecting people," she said. "If something ever happened to you, I'd know. No matter where you were, I'd feel it." She rolled her lips inward, and her mouth almost disappeared. "He's still—you know your dad, he's never still. And when he's gone, he takes all the light with him and it hurts, just under my ribs, like I'm a little less me."

Betheen slid the notepad across the table and put her arm around Nedda's shoulder. It was loose and awkward and didn't feel right, but it was warm when everything else was cold. "About what you read. He didn't mean what you think. It takes a long time and a lot of growing up before you learn that the things you want most aren't always what's good for you." There was a loneliness in her voice Nedda hadn't noticed before.

"What do you mean?"

The knock at the door came like an explosion. Nedda hopped up to get it, but Betheen pulled her back. "Let it go," she said.

The knocking continued, then the doorbell, then the hard *tap* of the brass knocker.

"THEO GODDAMN PAPAS OPEN YOUR FUCKING DOOR."

It was Denny's father.

"I'm getting it," Nedda said.


Pop Prater's cheeks were purple-red with veins on them that looked like the moss you used for bushes in dioramas. She thought about that instead of how mad he was and how bad she felt. If you made a diorama of Pop's face, you'd carve foam, maybe use plaster, stick those little moss things everywhere.

He'd expected her dad or Betheen to answer, which gave her the advantage. She took a breath.

"Hi, Mr. Prater. Did you see on TV yesterday? It was on. The whole thing, the explosion. We were all watching it in class, on the big TV and everything. I don't think anybody's ever seen anything like that before, not on TV. Seven people, all of them, died at the same time. Mrs. Wheeler—she's my teacher—she had even applied to go up in the shuttle, the teacher in space thing? So she was really upset, crying and everything. I bet she thought about being dead too. It's really hard not to think about being dead when you see people die, isn't it? I must have thought about being dead all day. I bet that's how you wind up a funeral director, thinking about dead people too much." Her words ran to dark places, things too close to Denny. She bounced on a porch board and powered on. "So I guess they're probably going to stop shuttles for a while because you have to do that when people die until you know what's going on. They did that after Gus Grissom and his crew died. Everybody just talks about Gus Grissom because he was one of the Mercury astronauts, but Edward White and Roger Chaffee were in there with him too. And NASA stopped stuff for a while until they figured out the oxygen problem. So I bet this wasn't oxygen because they'd figured that out already. But it was really bad weather for a launch. But I bet a ton of people are going to come down through Easter just to try to figure out what happened and it'll get busy—they'll probably want oranges too—and then it'll get empty for a while when they're figuring out how to fix whatever it was."

There was a look that adults got when Nedda dug into a good chunk of words, when a word bubble rose and burst. There was power in letting loose, a tiny rush that she could say anything she wanted, all at once, and no one could stop her. Like Betheen's sugar voice, it overwhelmed.

Pop Prater's eyes widened, trying to figure out how to deal with a child when what he needed was to scream at that child's father. But Nedda kept talking, loudly, about smoke trails and astronauts. She talked like it didn't hurt, though it did and each word made it real. Each word became a brick between her and Denny's father, a brick between her and Denny, who was in the equipment shed, growing older, growing scared, a brick in the wall between her and the things she couldn't stop.

There were limits to what a wall could do.

"I need to talk to your parents," Pop Prater shouted.

He'd shouted at her, actually shouted at a kid who wasn't his; parents weren't supposed to do that. As long as she stayed behind the screen door and the edge of his brown boot never crossed the metal bar that marked the barrier between step and house, it would be fine. His shoe, his foot, needed to slip away from the house, like a soap bubble.

"Desmond." Betheen's voice came from behind her.

"Where's Theo?"

"He's not here right now." Maybe all the shouting down the laundry chute did it, but Betheen had a way of talking that made her seem bigger. Pop Prater was taller than Betheen by a whole head at least, but it didn't seem that way when she spoke.

"I saw him and Pete McIntyre leaving the grove this morning. You know, don't you? You know what happened."

"I'll let Theo know you came by," she said, like she was telling Nedda to clean the dishes or brush the tangles out of her hair—a scold and an order that would not be questioned.

"I know Denny came here last night. My boy was here."

There was a way of fighting where you didn't raise your voice, but every word was a hammer. Shouting without shouting. Nedda'd heard men yelling at each other, but her mother and Pop Prater were doing the other thing, and it was frightening. Pop Prater might punch a man, but right now he sounded like he'd put a pillow over Betheen's head while she slept. Betheen would poison him.

"He was here. He also had a black eye."

The veins on Pop Prater's cheeks looked ready to rupture, like his whole head might explode. He looked at Nedda. "You were with him, weren't you? He never goes anywhere without you. You left him in that shed, didn't you?"

Betheen yanked Nedda's collar, pulling her back, shoving her into the parlor. She closed the door, leaving Nedda inside while she stood on the front stair with Pop.

"You don't get to speak to my daughter that way." Clear, firm, even through the door.

"She knows what happened, doesn't she? He's my *son*. You know what that is. My wife watched your daughter. She took care of her all that time you couldn't be bothered to get out of bed, and she never said a goddamn word about it."

"Desmond. You need to leave, now."

"You haven't seen Denny, have you? You don't know. Ask your daughter. Ask your husband." He spat the word *husband* like Nedda would a swear. "Ask him why the sun didn't come up right, why my trees are dying. Ask your husband what he did to Denny. If he doesn't fix it, if he doesn't . . ."

True things had a flavor—clean like salt and lemonade. Pop Prater hadn't said the words, but he'd kill her dad. That tasted like truth.

"Go home to your wife," Betheen said.

In the parlor, Betheen held her. Nedda was too tall now to bury her head in her mother's side, too old for things like that. All the things that were supposed to be comforting were for littler children. She'd resisted any small indulgences from her mother. She hadn't wanted them, and now that she needed them, her body didn't fit. Nothing fit. Her mother's ribs moved, in and out, fast like a rabbit. "Mom? Is Dad going to die?"

There were too many seconds before Betheen said, "I don't know. But here's what we do. We cry, but no more than fifteen minutes. Any more than that will wear us out and make thinking too hard. Then we work."

"Okay."

Nedda had seen an electromagnet before, had even built one in her father's office. He'd taken a handful of a spaghetti mess of wires and told her to wrap them around a nail.

"Trust me, it'll be neat," he said. He'd let her use a wire stripper to rip the plastic off, revealing shiny copper. They connected the ends to a nine-volt battery.

Then he'd dumped a box of paper clips on the floor, handed her the nail, and said, "Go fishing."

The nail had grown hot in her hands, the current spiraling, warming the metal. But the paper clips clung to it. She loved it—a machine they'd made from nothing. Then it was too hot to hold, and she'd dropped it.

He'd kissed her fingers better. "Looks like we overdid it, Little Twitch. The more you wrap it, the stronger the magnet, but the more heat it makes."

What Betheen was drawing was big, with yards of wiring.

"It's going to get hot," Nedda said.

"It needs to." Betheen's eyes were still red from crying.

"Why?"

"We need to pull Crucible apart, so it has to be strong. We need heat. We need chaos."

But there was poison inside.

The lights at Denny's house blinked on all at once, then shut off. The sky flashed yellow-green, chewing up clouds, light like at the grove. It was a shock like the one that took Denny. The thing Crucible had made was spreading, leaking everywhere. The roads, the lab, the lights in their houses. "It's the whole town, Mom."

Betheen stilled. "Oh god, that's what he meant."

"What?"

"A sinkhole. Why does a sinkhole happen? What's underneath dissolves or collapses, and the top layer breaks. Easter's on water. All our water's from underground. The boat pond in Island Paradise. The canals, they're drainage water. You said the sprinklers went on at the grove?"

"Right before it happened." It. Denny.

"And they were on over the trees?"

"Yeah." A sky of milky rainbows.

Betheen's pen tapped a furious rhythm on the table. "We're floating on top of it. It must be in the water plant too. He's right. The ice, the boiling, the trees. It's in the water. We're a sinkhole."

A sinkhole meant a break in the crust. If you stepped just wrong, if something fell, a crack could open that would grow and swallow everything you knew.

The clock on the range had stopped working and the sky hadn't shifted in too many hours, trapped halfway between day and dusk. It would almost be pretty if it wasn't so wrong.

"We're stuck, aren't we?"

"I don't know. We have to work fast," Betheen said. "What do you think?"

Nedda thought she was asking about the light and the cold that hung around them, but then her mother pointed to the finished diagram. It was the kind of electromagnet Nedda was familiar with, but there were symbols on it she didn't recognize. Her father's drafts were usually done in thick, squared lines. Betheen's had an elegant lean.

The kitchen timer beeped. Two hours and seventeen minutes. Her father had been born, died, and done it in reverse again.

Betheen restarted the timer.

"It's pretty," Nedda said.

"It will have to do."

Her father had lived and died again when Betheen put her hand gently to Nedda's back. "Upstairs now. To bed."

The sky hadn't changed at all. The astronauts might still be in it. The gas, carbon and light that they'd become might be trapped in the sky. Perhaps they were moving around Easter, stuck.

"I was thinking," Nedda said.

"You can think when you sleep too. Bed. No brushing your teeth, and no showering, just in case. That's a nice change, right?"

"Sure."

Betheen followed her upstairs, closed the bedroom window, and rolled down the shade, but the cold still came through. It came up from the floor, from everywhere. When Betheen got up, Nedda grabbed her hand.

"You're scared, aren't you?"

"I am," Betheen said. "But I need to keep working. I'll be downstairs."

"Can you stay for a little?"

The sheets were still on the floor from where Denny had spent the night. Her mother stepped around them, never letting go of her hand, not even when she climbed into bed, next to Nedda.

She must have been tucked in by her mother before, but she only remembered her father, the occasional brush of the scaly back of his hand.

"Did you ever tuck me in, or did he always do it?"

"Not as much as I should have," Betheen said. "It was mostly your father. By the time I could handle it, you were already so grown up you didn't need tuck-ins."

She'd been used to her father, had wanted his voice. She'd wanted stars on her ceiling exactly like the sky. "I know you couldn't take care of me. Would you tell me about Michael?"

Betheen smoothed the sheets over the bottom of the bed. She squeezed Nedda's toes through them, a touch so light it almost didn't happen.

"I got pregnant so soon after you were born, it was a surprise—the best kind. But your brother came too early. He couldn't survive the way he was, and there was nothing doctors could do for him. He didn't even live a day, just a little more than an hour. When things like that happen . . . well, I was very sad for a long time. I still am, and part of me always will be. Remember what I said about light? He took a little of it with him." Her face did something that wasn't a smile or frown, or anything Nedda had a name for.

"I'm sorry I didn't always take care of you the way I should have. I tried, but I couldn't for a while. We didn't start out trying to keep Michael a secret. We decided you were too young to understand, that it was better not to tell you when it happened. Then too much time passed and it was easier to never talk about him at all. Maybe that was wrong, but we didn't know any better."

Betheen tucked a bit of hair behind her ear, and it looked like the way a movie star would do it, a perfect, painful sad. "I wish," she said, but nothing followed.

Nedda blurred her eyes. It made it easier to see the parts of her mother she'd inherited—her neck, the shape of her wrist bones—though everything that looked right on her mother had come out wrong on her.

"Do you miss him?"

"Yes. All the time."

Her brother had lived a little more than an hour. Her father's entire life could pass in two hours and seventeen minutes. Two and a quarter Michaels. What if you counted your life in other people? How many Michaels old was she? How many Michaels since Michael died? Could you count him in launches? Two-minute marks—was one Michael thirty launches? How many *Challengers* made a Michael?

"It doesn't mean I didn't love you," Betheen said. "I do, and I did."

Nedda stared at her clock. Time passed strangely when you were sad. She wished so many things that a pit formed in her stomach. She wished she could sleep. She wished there was something to say to her mother.

"Mom—"

"I'll wake you when we're ready to go to Mr. McIntyre's." Betheen kissed her forehead.

Nedda tried to imagine her brother, Michael, but could only picture him as Denny. She thought about bubbles and how slippery they were, how they popped in the sun as water evaporated, how cold made them last longer and fly higher. If she could, she'd float up in the sky like a bubble. Maybe she'd touch Judy's light. Maybe she'd touch Michael's.

Betheen unzipped Nedda's book bag, took the pony from it, and placed Cotton Candy on the windowsill. Her tail was knotted and her astronaut helmet was all scratched up. Soft somehow. Old and loved.

After Nedda's eyes closed but before she went to sleep, she heard pages flipping and then her mother was on top of the covers beside her, a furnace in the cold. Nedda leaned in to that heat, wanting to dig her hands in, not caring if she got burned. She would hold on until her hands blistered.

# 1986: The Town

EOFFREY MACON, MAYOR, and the second Macon to be so, made the decision to gather while staring down a piece of galaxy cake at the Bird's Eye Diner, his fork halfway in. He'd just gotten through being yelled at by Desmond Prater, who'd barged into his office like a bat out of hell, going on about how his boy was sick, none of his trucks could get out of town, and he couldn't get a call out to anybody, and maybe that was a mayor's responsibility. Geoffrey decided it was time for a break. He was swallowing down a bite, mulling that over, when Ellery Rees told one of the waitresses—Lynn? Julie?—that Marty from the funeral parlor said a body had sewed itself up on his table, and Ed Ingram said there was a car with a dead guy in it frozen in the canal on Satsuma.

Geoffrey Macon had led Easter through hurricanes that should have wiped them away, personal darkness around labor practices at the sugar factory that had been the source of his family's wealth, and a specific town law regarding alligators and where and when you could or could not walk them. But bodies stayed put, stayed dead and preserved—or not—as their families saw fit. They didn't go sewing themselves up. That was for bigger towns with bigger histories, like New Orleans, where they let that kind of foolishness happen in the streets. Sick kids? That was for Brevard East to handle. Phones and power outages, that was for Bell and Florida Power & Light to manage. He'd put Zinnia, his assistant, on it the night before, and that should've been enough.

The cake, for all the coconut and marshmallow, was wallpaper paste in his mouth. Frozen canals in Florida? Dead bodies sewing themselves up? If that wasn't a bridge too far, he might as well resign.

"Ellery," he yelled, "gimme the check. And tell anybody who comes in here there's a town hall meeting at the elementary school at seven. Mandatory."

"Damn good thing," Ellery said. "Little Mike Costas was in here earlier, saying the grove's eating itself up and the Prater kid got himself stuck in some kind of bubble." He leaned in, gut spilling over the table. Ellery was equal parts ooze and ease. "The sun cooks those guys, you know?"

*Those guys.* Geoffrey's father, Geoffrey Macon, Sr., used to talk that way and it was disconcerting to hear words like that come out of a younger man's mouth. People were people, and damn it, Easter was progress. The Last Place Before Space. "Des Prater said his kid was sick."

Ellery leaned in to whisper, the small-town kind of whisper meant to be a shout: "Little Mike says the kid's aging like crazy. Nobody can touch him or even get near."

"Well, I don't know anything about that. Just tell people we're meeting up at seven at the elementary school. I'd be obliged." *Obliged* was the kind of word that Ellery would appreciate. Geoffrey threw ten dollars on the table, too much by three times over. He needed a walk. His lights and phone had been out since the night before, he'd not gotten the proper amount of coffee in him, and Patty's mother was in town besides. That woman had a way of making his underwear crawl up his ass.

Typically, trucks bounced along Red Bug Road with regularity, going to and from Canaveral and the grove, delivering to the Albertson's, but today there weren't any. Used to their rumble, Geoffrey found the absence startling, and it gave weight to what Desmond Prater said. En route to his car, he passed Anita Marvin.

"Seven o'clock tonight at the Covey School, Mrs. Marvin," he said. "I'm holding a town hall. Tell people and bring people. This is mandatory." He added a wink, so as not to be too harsh. People didn't trust a harsh mayor. He'd learned as much from Macon, Sr.

"All right, I'll be there," she said, looking at him as though he'd also cooked too long in the sun.

Come to think of it, Zinnia had never gotten back to him about the power or phones. He looked across the roof of his Lincoln and saw the glow coming off Prater Citrus, a large halo that thrummed in time with the headache taking shape behind his eyes. Well, that was distinctly not right. He ducked into his car, buckled himself in, and let his belt out a hole, needing room to breathe. It was set to be a lulu of a day.

The phones weren't working, so the townspeople traveled door to door, knocking, seeking. Jim Barr rolled his father's wheelchair down the cracked sidewalk, Patricia Barnesdale and her husband rode their bicycles, and the Sandersons walked, their eldest daughter pushing the twins in their stroller. Treat it like a hurricane, they thought; gather where it's safe, up on high ground, away from trees. Collect one another, move forward. Rusted trucks from the grove, filled with workers and their children, parked in the semicircle drive in front of the school. Police knocked on doors, which meant some people hid. Everett Lawrence had a bench warrant for something he'd done at the dog track while high. He couldn't remember what.

Everyone avoided the Papas house. The lights weren't on—though most people had lost power—and most preferred to avoid Theo Papas. He made them uncomfortable, the way he carried on a conversation while thinking about five or six other things. Always shedding pieces of himself everywhere he went. There was a handing off of responsibility. Surely Annie Prater had told Betheen.

No one told Pete McIntyre either. No one told a McIntyre anything. They lived on the edges of Easter's days, as much a part of it as the asphalt or pavement and were spared as little thought.

People flowed from the auditorium into the hallway. The room was well over capacity, but the fire department was there, which made it as safe as a town hall could be with a town too big to fit properly in a single room.

The Praters walked in and the crowd parted. Desmond demanded space, both by size and disposition. Annie walked in front of him, something she rarely did. She looked frayed at the edges, like she'd been crying. One of the Rodriguez brothers said something awful had happened to the Praters' son, but he wouldn't say what.

Mayor Macon winced when he spoke into the microphone and tried to cover it with a cough. He never managed to pick up a mic without feedback, and never did remember that beforehand. He launched into his prepared remarks about contacting FPL about the lights, even though Zinnia couldn't reach them, and getting police and firemen on the roads. *Aggressive flora* was one of his better turns of phrase.

"The sun isn't setting," called a voice from the back of the auditorium. High and nasal, but not someone Geoffrey could immediately place. As though he could personally do anything about when the sun rose and set on Easter. Though it wasn't doing either.

"The priorities are lights and roads. Anybody who is without heat and has difficulty with cold, partner up with somebody who has heat. We're lucky to be a town full of good, kind people. Get to know one another. Love thy neighbor," Geoffrey said.

"My pool's half froze and the half that's not is boiling."

"I tried to wash dishes and there's no water coming out the pipes."

Complaints gathered in a low roll of discontent, which amassed, forming a wave. As a Macon, Geoffrey recognized it for what it was: civic dissatisfaction that would culminate in mob rule.

"Follow hurricane protocol," he said over the chatter. "Make sure you've got flashlights. If you've got running water, bottle it up. If you're on well water—that's you folks on Verdigris Circle—fill the tub now so you can flush the toilet. Use common sense."

"Well water's what busted the pipes."

Mayor Macon coughed, then started in on food safety.

"How do we get food if the trucks can't get in? I'm supposed to get a delivery that hasn't come and the store's almost out of bread."

"The mail hasn't come in or gone out. How am I supposed to pay my bills?"

"Should we board windows?"

"There's no clear roads out."

"My water won't shut off."

"I can't get out of my driveway."

"I can't reach my aunt and she lives by herself."

"My car froze in a goddamn puddle because you never fixed the drainage system."

"Where the hell is the Papas family?" Desmond Prater was a foghorn in the noise. Heads turned at the shout that came from somewhere deep in his gut. They gaped at his red face, the twisted brow.

"Anybody seen the professor since this started? His daughter was out with my son." His fist clenched, the knuckles remembering the feel of smashing his son's eye. "You heard something happened. I know you all did. She was with him. Then Theo Papas was in my grove with Pete McIntyre. And where the hell is he? Where are any of them?"

Susan Lowery had seen Betheen earlier, but not Theo, and she said as much to Barbara Friel, who hadn't thought about checking on the Papas house at all.

"He ought to be here," Desmond Prater said. "I should be able to ask the man a few questions."

Though the crowd of bodies should have made the auditorium stifling, it grew colder. Children shuffled into their parents' legs, and teenagers leaned against walls, casual and broken in their perfect angst. Inside the walls, running along the water pipes and electrical wires, time dribbled, a thick and viscous charge that crept and cringed. Electrons jumped and froze. The clock on the back wall stopped.

"What's Theo Papas got to do with the sun not setting?" Tall, broad, wild, and dirty, Rebekah La Morte was an easy kind of loud. Her son, Jimmy, hid behind her. "You think one man is responsible for that? Show me a man who can keep the damn sun from setting." There was no Mr. La Morte. Rebekah was enough for two. She bred greyhounds and ran charter boats by herself. She'd taken tours out when she was nine months pregnant with that rat of a boy. "Show me, Prater. If he can keep the sun from going down, he's been holding out on us."

Nervous laughter like a layer of smoke.

"I'm saying he knows something, and he's not here to answer for himself," Desmond said.

"The pond out my way is fucking boiling. You ever heard a frog scream? It's like somebody's stabbing a baby. That's some county bullshit. But you go on thinking Theo Papas keeps the sun from setting and boils frogs alive. See if that fixes this government shit. I'll wait."

Mayor Macon cleared his throat, throwing his belly into it. "That's enough now. Everybody watch your language. Keep things neighborly." The microphone sparked. He dropped it, and the spark hung in midair, a ragged line of blue-white light. Geoffrey stared at the spark, moved around it slowly, the light burning his eyes. Pain buzzed in his hand, searing, jarring, making him more alive than he'd been before.

"I think," he said when he regained his voice. "I think we might benefit from talking to the man. I'm sure he'd have some insights. But no one's done anything to be upset about, not as far as any of us know. Let's not go starting a lynch mob."

Some in the auditorium knew enough to cringe, the ones who remembered that Island Paradise Park and Zoo had boasted a photo spot called the "Hanging Tree," and that the old hunting club had once had loose rules and members from the police department, as well as a judge. They were good people, though. And times had changed. Good people didn't form lynch mobs.

When the question arose as to who would look for Theo Papas, Annie Prater began crying. She took Desmond's hand and squeezed it as hard as she could, pushing her nails into his calloused palms.

"Des, I can't take it. I have to go, I need to go to his room. I'll feel better if I can smell his pillow. I need to hold it for a while," she said. "It smells like him, like his hair, like his cheeks."

"Go then," he said. "I'll figure it out."

It wasn't hard for Annie to slip away. Her size and quiet nature made her a ghost in the hallway, a fast-moving shadow.

The front door to the school didn't want to open. As Annie pushed with her shoulder, she noticed a water fountain running though no one drank from it. The stream was flowing, yet not. Stopped, while her son sped ahead. Pain had flowered in her chest when she'd come home to find Des waiting, when he'd taken her to the grove and she saw Denny in that shed. It shifted, settling under her ribs. High, like the way she'd carried him.

Her car sputtered in the strange night—perpetual dusk the color of bile. She turned left instead of right. Betheen Papas had taken Denny in when she'd asked, and Annie had watched Nedda from the time she was small. She'd seen Nedda be kind to her son, never acknowledging that he wasn't as smart as her, never saying he'd done anything stupid, even when he had. Nedda was a little strange, but she was Denny's too. If Denny didn't live, if the son who was everything to her died in that equipment shed, Nedda Papas might be the only other person who remembered him, saw him, loved him even close to as much as she did.

Betheen's car was at Pete McIntyre's. Desmond didn't know that, but Annie did. She'd seen it being towed. She'd seen Betheen crack and pull herself back together. When Betheen walked away from the accident—an accident in which someone had died—it looked the same as Betheen's normal walk. Annie knew then that the wound from Michael had never healed. That would be her life without Denny, if there was life at all. Stiff-backed walking. Gritted teeth.

Annie drove. There were three places Betheen and Nedda might be. The house, the college, or Pete McIntyre's garage. Desmond had been by the house, so they likely weren't there any longer. She'd find them. Then she'd drive to the grove and sit with her son. She'd be with him when he was old and changing. She'd see all the things she wasn't meant to, the painful parts that parents missed when God's order was preserved—the illness, the breaking down of bones and body. For as long as it took, she would stay. No one should be alone.

# 1986: Sequence

Y OU MUST HAVE something," Betheen said. Pete's garage, his yard, his entire home was a storehouse of machine parts, mechanical devices, building blocks for everything. Betheen snapped the gold expansion band on her wristwatch, pinching her skin between the segments. The pinch was all that kept her from shouting. *Can't* wasn't an option.

"I don't see what," he said. He stared at the notebook, scratching the gray stubble on his neck. "I'm working on the copper and I've got enough rebar. Batteries, generators. Power supply and current's not a problem, but getting it to pulse like that? No can do."

Nedda was in his yard, picking through his collection with rodent-like diligence and determination. Every now and again Betheen caught sight of Nedda's braid and fought to keep from calling her inside. Her daughter was a junk rat. That made Betheen smile, inappropriate as it was. She and Theo had done something right.

"I thought maybe an alternator, but I don't know." Pete shoved a cup of coffee at her, sliding it across the kitchen table's peeling shellac. "Sorry if this is no good. You're probably used to better, but it's usually just me and I guess I never cared much." The coffee was mostly grounds, brewed in a dented pot on a chipped gas stove.

"It's fine," she said. There was something subtle and blushing about the way he moved. He looked close to fifty, sagging, but not badly. He was lean, unlike most men his age.

"If you want to keep thinking, go for it. I'll get on the rebar and the coiling. It's going to take me a good while."

She followed, observing a stiffness creep into his walk, a conscious-ness that she was there, a woman in his space. The halls of his house reminded her of Theo in that they teemed with things she'd seen before, familiar phone banks, pictures from office walls. Pete was a space scavenger. Like Nedda. He opened the screen door with a hand on his back, which drew attention to her own aches and pains brought on by lack of sleep—the lurking migraine.

"Did you check on Denny before you came by?"

"No."

"I guess it'd be hard to see him with Nedda."

It was that, yes, but more. Potential loss was terrifying, realized loss was devastating, and the transition between the two was sudden and inexplicable. She should have been awake. She should have stopped them from leaving the house. She should have watched Denny with the care that Annie had watched Nedda.

*Should*, a short word for *Never would be*.

"Mom!" Nedda stood in the back of the truck, something dangling from her hand, a shadow against the sick sky. Betheen ran to her. "Mom, it doesn't work. It's not going to work."

In her daughter's fingers was a small magnet—nail, wires, a D-cell battery. She clung to the battery, their machine in miniature.

"You made this?"

"Dad taught me how. You were working and I didn't want to bother you, so I went downstairs and did it. I thought I could test it on something small. So we could get more information, more data, maybe build it better. But I tried and it doesn't work. It's not going to work."

At first glance Betheen mistook the animal in the truck bed for a baby possum, but then the eyes and ears took shape, its face like a person's. A monkey.

"There's a current. I tested it with paper clips," Nedda said. "I did it right. I know I did it right. I thought maybe because there's metal in the truck and I had the biggest battery we had . . ." She stopped, swallowed as if gulping air.

"Here, let me see." Betheen gently unwrapped Nedda's fingers from the magnet. Wire was coiled tightly around a screw, almost as if a machine had done it, free of wiggles and unnecessary kinks—flawlessly smooth, like a fine icing bead. A D-cell battery, screw threads as guides for the wires, the ends taped carefully to the battery. The screw was hot in her hand, almost burning, as power drained from the battery. A simple but perfect machine. "Go on, what were you thinking?"

"I thought that bending the metal under or around the monkey, even just a little, would change the shape of the bubble, maybe stretch it, and maybe it would break."

"It's perfectly built. Your dad couldn't have done it better."

"It doesn't work. It's too small. What if what we're making is too small?"

"You didn't know the exact size of the truck or that bubble when you built it, did you?"

"No."

"Right." Betheen turned the magnet around in her hand. "Well, we know the size of the machine from your dad's notes. That's why we're making our electromagnet so big. All you had to work with was a D-cell battery."

"That's what was in the basement."

"That's not a lot of power, is it? We're going to be using two generators. One of them kept the whole Bird's Eye running." Betheen wasn't sure if it had been one or two, but she needed to stretch that truth, and not only for Nedda.

"How do you know it's going to be enough?"

"I did the math."

Nedda chewed her lip, mulling the way Theo did.

Beside the monkey in the truck bed was a pool of water, a murk of rust and mud. Above it, something dripped from the power lines. Water-like, but almost pearly, heavy looking. The power lines, the water pipes, all of it was connected. Marvels of engineering pumped Easter dry, moved the water, lit the town, and formed a lattice that both connected and isolated them from surrounding towns and the rest of the county. Theo's machine was in that lattice. Water below, power lines above, the town trapped between. Three layers, like a bubble.

Like Nedda had said.

She swallowed, forced her voice calm. "Nedda, get down from the truck, please."

"But—"

"Now."

Pete leaned against the side of his porch, carefully not looking at them. "C'mon back," he said. "I've got hot chocolate or something around here."

Pete held the door open as her daughter walked inside, like the house was somehow hers. He kept holding the door for her, and Betheen didn't feel eyes on her skin, on her back, anywhere at all.

The absence felt like kindness.

They stripped and twisted wire and cable from everything inside Pete's garage and house, everything except the truck. Betheen's nails split, grease getting under them for the first time in years, and her hands looked younger for having a layer of grime. Nedda twisted wires together into thicker cables. The weight of her daughter beside her was raw and tender.

Nedda whispered and rocked as she worked.

"STS-6: Weitz, Bobko, Musgrave, Peterson. STS-7: Crippen, Hauck, Fabian, Ride, Thagard. STS-8: Truly, Brandenstein, Bluford, Garner, Thornton."

The magnet would rip Theo's machine apart and fill the lab with poisonous gases. Flammable gases. She'd read his notes, seen some of the chemicals that he'd used. He was right; combined they'd be as bad as chloramine. There would be acetylene in the air. A single spark and the room would burn like a blow torch. Theo knew this. He was using a radioactive isotope too, though she didn't know what amount. What would happen if they did nothing at all? She could leave him cycling through his life infinitely. Visit him for the few moments each day when he seemed himself. Every two hours and seventeen minutes she'd feel the snap as their bond broke. Eventually that loss would become like Michael, ever present. And there was Nedda, who would lose her father again and again, without knowing what loss was supposed to feel like.

There was also Denny. Denny, who wasn't near anything dangerous. Denny, who should have an entire lifetime ahead of him.

Pete welded lengths of rebar with a torch. The smell carried the same acrid bite as anise with a touch of benzene to it but came with a fall of sparks both blinding and beautiful. Once, Betheen had looked through the lens of a welder's mask. It made things simple; everything vanished but metal and spark. Now, Betheen's world had narrowed to Nedda, her litany of names and numbers, and loops of two hours and seventeen minutes.

"You know everything Mr. McIntyre has in here, don't you?"

"Yes," Nedda said. "I think he's forgotten about a lot of stuff. He's got a better patch collection than me, but he doesn't look after it." She wiped her cheek, leaving a splotch of grease.

"Do you know what any of it does? How it works?"

"Some. There's no manual for the control table and a lot of his stuff doesn't work. He has it because it's broken."

A whoop came from the side of the house, followed by a thud. "Got to let it cool a minute," Pete yelled.

Nedda sucked a bead of blood from the edge of her thumb. "He likes that I like his NASA stuff, and he knows I won't break it any worse than it already is. He's nice."

"He is," Betheen said. It was important to say that, just as it was important to add, "I'm not."

Nedda's mouth twitched. "Me neither."

When they checked on Pete, he was shoving his hand back into a thick glove, but appeared unscathed. Betheen closed the screen door and something caught her eye, a gray monolith of metal, resting under an awning. It had the look of NASA or military to it. The inside would doubtless be full of copper wiring, but Pete hadn't mentioned it as something they could strip.

"Nedda, what's that?"

"A sequencer from Launch Complex 36A. It ran cues for missile and satellite launches, plus timer checks, system checks."

"So is it like a remote switch, or a trigger?"

Nedda stuck her finger through a hole in the screen, wiggling it, widening the opening. "Yeah, kinda, but you can run a whole series of things off it. Each button is for a different operation and those needles at the top run a giant graph so you can get data on the entire launch and see what happened when, what went wrong. It's cool."

The obsessions, the single-mindedness, the twitches—there was so much of Theo in Nedda. But her daughter's wrists matched her own, as did the shape of her face, her curiosity, and her temper—parts of herself she'd learned to restrain.

"Do you think it still works?"

"I don't know, maybe," Nedda said.

"Let's make it work."

# 1986: Assemble

**N**EDDA HAD STARED at it for months, trying to figure out where each lead used to go. It was a big series of switches and a timer that flicked on and off at intervals. She'd looked in the library to see if she could find everything it had ever launched, but the library didn't have things like that, or NASA or the military kept it secret. But it would have been good to know. There were a million parts to a launch, the mechanical system checks, auxiliary power checks, checks for the main engines, turning the power on to the fuel cells—so many things happened way before liftoff.

"I bet we only need one feed," she said. Something to tell the generator when to power on. Simple. "Mr. Pete?"

He dropped something on the ground, scratched his arm with a wrench, and grunted.

"Mr. Pete, does the sequencer still work?"

"Mitzi? I don't see why she wouldn't. She was working fine when I took her out. They were upgrading systems, moving analog to digital. Mitzi doesn't do digital."

Mitzi. Nedda liked that. The sequencer looked like a Mitzi, and almost had a face where the readout would be: The needles were eyelashes; the buttons were teeth in Mitzi's smile. It was sad that things like Mitzi weren't used anymore. At the space center, unused rockets stood like high rises in the rocket garden, pointing into a sky they'd never get to. They didn't fly. They didn't grow like a garden. They stood and waited to rust.

"If my mom gave you an equation, a time that Mitzi was supposed to turn something on and off, could you make it do that?"

Mr. Pete was quiet. The kitchen timer went off in her mother's coat pocket. Another two hours and seventeen minutes. One father. Two and a quarter brothers.

"I could," Mr. Pete said. "I took some sequencers apart and put them back together a few times when there was a short or when a mouse gnawed on something, but it's been a couple years."

"But they're all the same, right?"

"Mostly."

"We need one of the generators to run the sequencer, then have the sequencer run the other generator to the magnet," Betheen said. "Can you do that?"

He nodded.

"Good. Do it."

She'd get to see a launch sequencer work. It would run and actually do something. She twisted lengths of copper around and around the rebar core, crawling under where Mr. Pete had propped it against the house's siding. Would it be enough? It looked like her magnet, which had done nothing. But she'd guessed, stupidly guessed, which wasn't good practice. Her mom had done math and made a better estimate, even if it wasn't exact. Her mom was always precise—triple-beam-balance-out-to-a-tenth-of-a-gram precise.

Headlights rolled across Mr. Pete's driveway, as familiar as her parents' cars—Denny's mom. Nedda ducked beneath the rebar and hid. She could run home, lock the door, crawl in bed, and never look at Mrs. Prater's face again. She'd never have to look at her, knowing that Denny's mom knew she'd left him. But she stayed, back flat against the side of the house.

"Betheen? I know you're here."

Her mother set down a copper loop she'd been winding. Her hands were chapped and bloody in the V between pointer and thumb. "Nedda, stay here. Keep working, okay? No matter what." Betheen walked to the driveway, dragging her hand along the house's peeling white paint, stepping over the mess and scrap where Mr. Pete had been welding.

Nedda kept wrapping wire, stealing a look. Denny's mother was bent-looking, like she might crack in two.

"Betheen," she said. "The mayor called a town hall meeting at the school. Everyone is there."

"The whole town?" Mr. Pete rose from where he'd been working on one of the generators—an orange-and-black machine that looked like an air conditioner and a tractor had a baby. "What's the occasion?"

Nedda inched forward until she stood right behind her mother. She knew when Denny's mom caught sight of her. She wanted to say how sorry she was, how she should have tried harder to stop him from going, how she shouldn't have left him there. She wanted to say they were trying, but she also wanted to scream at Mrs. Prater. Denny's dad had hit him.

"Desmond thinks that Theo—he's sure he did something. He saw Theo and Pete leaving the grove, right before he found Denny. He wants people out looking for him. He wants to hurt him, Betheen."

The laugh that came from her mother was fierce and loud. "Hurt him? Good luck with that." Betheen's arms went around Denny's mom with a loose softness that looked all wrong on her mother's body.

"He wanted to fix the pruner," Nedda said.

Mrs. Prater stared at her. "He what?"

"Denny was trying to fix it. He thought his dad wouldn't be mad if he could fix it. I told him to wait, but . . ." The words skipped on each other and tied up at the ends. There was no space between them, not enough to say how scared she'd been, that she'd run to her dad, what her dad had done, and how he was stuck now. Part of her was peeling away, leaving only the clump of words. She couldn't look at Denny's mom, or Betheen, or even Mr. Pete, who loved Denny too. Mrs. Prater had helped take care of her. She closed her eyes.

"Oh, honey," Denny's mom said.

"Why are you here, Annie?"

"You helped me."

Those words worked like permission.

"There's something wrong with Theo," Betheen said.

"He's stuck," Nedda said. "He's stuck like Denny, but not the same. I tried to get him to fix the machine and he didn't do it right." She should have known he couldn't fix it. His hands had been bad the past few days.

"Okay," Denny's mom said. "Let me help."

"Why?" Nedda asked. Mrs. Prater had every reason to hate them.

"I don't know what else to do."

Denny looked like his dad, mostly. His hair, his coloring, the way he walked sometimes—kind of bowlegged, but the good kind. The first day of first grade he'd sat next to her in the cafeteria, bit into a carrot, and spit half of it clear across the room. Denny's mom had that mouth.

The electromagnet they'd made, the needle that would pop the bubble, wasn't so much a needle as a bulky tree branch of iron and copper. Four pairs of hands hefted it. She'd never seen Betheen move anything heavier than a wedding cake or the stand mixer, but her mother bent low, taking the weight with her legs, as though practiced. The needle scraped along the bottom of Mr. Pete's truck, a deep screeching that rang her ears. Moving Mitzi was harder. The sequencer was unevenly balanced; Nedda and Denny's mom were much shorter than Mr. Pete, and Betheen bridged the distance between their heights. They tottered forward, wobbling with the awkward bulk, a coffin without handles.

What would happen after? If Crucible stopped, if their plan worked, what would happen? The machine would pull apart. It would leak gasses. Poison. Mitzi was a remote trigger. But her dad wouldn't be able to leave the room. What was there just before gas, carbon, and light? There was a body. When it wasn't ash, wasn't carbon, there was a body. She didn't want to name the body that took shape in her mind. She didn't define it or give it glasses and flaking skin. Specificity gave sadness mass.

Mitzi's sides bit into her fingers. He'd wanted to keep her young. What would it be like to stay this size forever? To be these cells and molecules always? What if she was like the monkey? Who would touch her? Who would check to see if she was still alive? Who would wait for her, watching, looking?

"Lift up, Nedda," Betheen said.

"I'll keep people away from Theo as long as I can," Denny's mom said.

"It's not just for him, Annie. It's safer for everyone, I promise."

Mrs. Prater hugged Betheen again. "I could take Nedda with me, if you want. I'll be sitting with Denny. We'll be far from the lab."

"No." Nedda realized she'd shouted when Denny's mom backed away. She couldn't go back to the shed. Not with her dad the way he was. "I need to help."

Betheen didn't try to calm her down, comfort her, or pawn her off on Denny's mom, and Nedda loved her more for that than she ever had in her life.

"Take a blanket, Annie," Mr. Pete said. "It's likely to get cold in that shed."

"There's coffee berries in Denny's backpack," Nedda said. "They're purple. Some of them are probably squished because he forgets them, but could you take some? Can you show them to him? He'll know what they are."

"Okay, honey."

Then her mom hugged Mrs. Prater.

"I was in Cocoa watching movies when they sent them home from school. If I'd been home, he would never have broken the pruner in the first place. He'd be fine," Mrs. Prater said.

Betheen said, "We're going to fix it, Annie."

It sounded like a lie.

Mr. Pete opened the truck door and Nedda climbed in, slid across the vinyl, and strapped herself in to the middle seat. A jump chair in a shuttle. Any minute the floor would rumble with fire and steam; flame channels would fill, and she would rise, stop asteroids from hitting Earth, find new life, find another world to live on. Save this one.

Betheen sat beside her and held her hand, squeezing the bones so hard it had to be love.

They rolled down Mr. Pete's driveway. She closed her eyes. *One Mississippi. Two Mississippi.* Things slipped between Mississippis. Her dad could die. There was an entire room in the house that belonged to him. You couldn't have a room for someone without that person. There wouldn't be anymore looking at stars. No comets. He'd never know she'd lied to him. She'd never get to tell him why. She dug her fingernails into the seat, peeling up the vinyl.

Forced to turn whenever roads became impassible, they took a circuitous route through Easter that brought them by the abandoned park.

"Oh," Betheen said. "Look."

Over her mother's shoulder, the eyes of the tiki head were alive, bright with gas flames flickering against the twilight. "How?"

"The time anomaly—it must have gotten into the gas lines," her mother said. "The utility grids are connected. It's in the water under and around town. It's above us too, in the power lines."

There was something off about the power lines, a thickness to the air around them, as though it had become liquid. It looked runny like dish soap. The road narrowed; brush and brambles had creeped in from the shoulder to cover the asphalt, parts of which had buckled. Frost heave. Eventually the road was lost between thick forest and palmetto scrub.

It was everywhere.

"Shit." Mr. Pete turned the truck onto a bumpy trail that went under the powerlines themselves, a utility road that ran clear to the shore. He rolled through radio stations, searching for a signal, but all that came through was static. No radio. There was always radio. A sudden hard left brought them onto College Drive. The truck windows frosted over, and the light shifted. The infrared in sunlight made your skin feel warm, loose and soft, but this light was missing it; her skin pulled in, hairs on end.

A hedge beside the entrance had grown up and over one of the doors to the lab building, its branches stretching to form a cave. The other door had rusted on its hinges, and remnants dangled.

"It's time, Nedda," Betheen said.

Through the truck cab window, over the sequencer's shadow, she looked back at the woods, which seemed more alive and wilder than they'd ever been. Maybe the monkeys were running in there, looking for the monkey house or their little brother who was trapped in Mr. Pete's yard.

"I'm scared," she said.

"Be scared," Betheen said. "But don't let being scared keep you from doing something. Important things are always frightening. We can be scared, and we can work scared."

It was better than a kiss on the cheek or a hug. Nedda unbuckled.

They moved Mitzi from the truck and she slid the last few feet, landing on Mr. Pete's dolly with a crash so loud Nedda swore something must have broken. The echo of the wheels on the ramp into the building was loud enough to bounce off the sky.

As they pushed through, the last of the door crumbled, leaving them covered in rust that smelled like blood and old Band-Aids. Pete went back for the generators and the needle.

"It's going to take me a minute to get the wires attached right," he said.

"Do you want to see him?" Betheen asked. "You might want to know what we're working with."

He shook his head. "I've seen enough. Some things are just for family."

The narrow window in the lab door hummed with light. Her father was in there, him and not him. Terrifying. What did you do when you were afraid? You did the thing anyway, even if it might kill you. For the greater good. Judy Resnik knew. Gus Grissom knew. For the greater good. She opened the door and went to see her father.

When he stilled enough to really look at, he was older than he should be, his hair white, knotted around his shoulders like Spanish moss. His face had the same lines, but deeper, like he'd been folded too long and all the creases wouldn't come out. All his thinking faces had marked him. He'd bitten through his lip at some point, maybe while they'd been in the hallway. His skin knit itself together as she watched.

She wanted to be angry, or happy she was seeing him at all, but there was just sadness, dry like dead grass. He was right—Crucible could have fixed things, broken limbs, people. His hands. Maybe her brother.

He moved and it was painful-looking, jerking and heaving, like when someone got hit by a phaser on *Star Trek*. On TV it didn't look like it hurt, but this did. He was hurting and he was frightened. His glasses were gone, but his eyes found her, no matter where she moved in the room.

Betheen's drawing was still on the white board. His pens were still out, as though he might pick them up to make an important note, might start being himself at any second were it not for Crucible. Its legs spun, gliding, circling its core, and the room flickered and strobed with the movement, stuttering. Nedda climbed onto a table, setting her jacket beneath her to keep away the steel's cold bite.

His hair pulled back into his scalp. There was a baby doll that did that; the hair grew when you cranked its arm and receded when you wound it the other way. A doll, not a person. Not a dad.

"How much longer, Mom?"

Betheen pulled the kitchen timer from her coat. It was close to halfway through. "A few more minutes and we should be able to talk to him again."

The plaques on his arms moved up and down, and for a few seconds faded away. There, a week, maybe a few days, when it wasn't itching or bothering him, when his hands and feet might not have hurt.

"Soon now," Betheen said.

"How do you know?"

"It's the plaque on his back. It just showed up last week. See how it's shrinking? When it's small, almost like a quarter, he'll be close to us."

How did you know someone well enough that you could recognize the size of a spot on their back, know when it came and went?

"What do I say to him?"

"Whatever you want him to know," Betheen said.

"How do I know what that is?"

"It's the thing you're most afraid to say. Always."

There were too many words, so many that she knew there'd be none at all.

# Aboard *Chawla*

THERE'D BEEN A rainbow-colored assortment of mood stabilizers in the printer tray that morning, so Nedda assumed the call was from her mother. It was a shock when Denny's face took shape. The video screen lent him a flatness that was nothing like how she remembered him. Faces were mountain ranges no camera captured as well as the eye. Then, having one working eye leveled landscapes too. Though she'd had years to get used to it, the gray in his hair was still surprising. There was a lapse in the feed before he'd see her, before the signal cut through space, bounced off satellites, to find him at the other end. The him she viewed had already happened. Seeing him through the fog of her warping eye made it clear: They would never again occupy the same time.

His chin was square now, dark; he was terrible about shaving, which came as no surprise. He seemed nervous, lost and fidgeting. She hoped he would smile, that she might be able to make out his broken tooth. He had a grown man's face now. When you were away, alone, people reverted to how you best remembered them. To her, Denny would always be twelve.

"Hey."

The delay made his reactions slow, turning everything into a spit take. Twelve years old, but a grown-up.

"What happened to your eye?" His voice was digitized; there were corners to it she was unused to, but it was him, a dusky seaside sparrow out of time.

"Just space stuff," she said. "I doubt they've said anything on the news. We've tried to keep it quiet, but we're going blind. I let Louisa—that's Dr. Marcanta—do some spinal taps and take fluid out of my eye to see if it will help." The delay meant she saw the exact moment he heard *blind*. "It was always a risk. We understood that when we went up." It was a neat lie. Vision loss was a slow goodbye that was impossible to comprehend until you were in the middle of it.

"Blind? Jesus. How'd she get the fluid out of your eye?"

"With a vitrector. It's basically a big needle that's also a knife."

"*Jee*-sus."

There was a quiet between them while Denny contemplated that. Waiting was a risk; satellites moved.

"Betheen told me there's a problem with the module," he said. "There's nothing on the news. Not about your eyes or anything else."

"We're working on it. I'm going to fix it." Even before the lag caught up to his expression, she knew he didn't believe her. "I promise. We're fixing it." The last time she'd seen him her feet had been on the ground, actual Earth, a spit of Florida, and he'd been furious. Somewhere over the miles, she'd grown accustomed to the idea that she'd never see him again. That he couldn't forgive her for leaving. "I don't want to talk about that, okay? Just tell me how you are. I miss you."

"I sold the grove," he said, and then came the tooth, the jagged grin he'd never gotten fixed. Its appearance brought a deep ache in her chest. Hearts didn't pop out of ribs; they ran too fast, stopped, died. And yet.

"Betheen said your father died. She said she thought you might sell. Dates are hard to keep track of up here. How long ago was that?"

"Two years," he said. "I was going to run it. I tried for a little while." Seconds expanded as he searched for words. She wanted to touch the screen, but knew it would feel like all the glass on *Chawla*, cold, hard. It was a shame she couldn't touch his hair, feel the wiriness of the white and gray in the black.

"What happened?"

"Turns out I don't like oranges all that much. I guess I should have taken pictures or something to show you what it looks like now, but I didn't think about it. I'm sorry," he said. "Pop was there forever. His whole life was the grove. And I never had to make any choices about what to do with my life. The grove was there, waiting for me to run it. I didn't understand that until after he was gone. Maybe I couldn't understand it with him there. But then he went and died, and the grove and everybody kept going without him. The guys knew what to do for the oranges better than I did. They didn't need me. And then, my mom, you know? I didn't know how things were between her and my dad until I saw Mom without him. She's happier. It's kind of like she woke up.

I mean, he was nice to me after everything, so I didn't know any better, but after he died Mom finally told me what happened, what he did to me and why I was on the pruner in the first place. I got to thinking about you. I'm pissed off. You both lied to me about him and you did it for so long. My mom says she lied to herself a lot too. That she had to overlook a lot of things to stay with Pop. I understand that some. But I didn't understand why you did it. Then Betheen told me you'd thought you were doing me a favor, and that if I ever wanted to talk to you again I should probably do it now. That's fucked up, Nedda."

"I'm sorry," she said, though it wasn't enough. "I needed something good to come from it, you know?"

"It did, though, didn't it? Eventually."

"Yeah." The words were building up. "You look good," she said. Awkward and required, but also true.

"I miss you," he said. "I used to think you'd stay in Easter. I'd take over the grove, we'd get married and have kids. I didn't get why you wanted to leave. I was so fucking mad at you when you left for school."

"You're not mad anymore?"

"How am I gonna be mad at you with your eye like that? Come on." He fidgeted in his chair. "I should have called sooner."

Something in her let go. She could have tried to stay. It wouldn't have taken much bending to live with Denny, to fall into that kind of ease she'd thought married couples were supposed to have. The easiest hardest thing.

"You were always too nice for me," she said. "What happened to your dad?"

"What do you think? He stroked out yelling at a Department of Agriculture guy right in the middle of his office." His laugh cracked with static. It wasn't surprising at all; Marcanta would have tagged Pop Prater as a stroke risk on sight without ever hearing him yell or seeing his skin purple and blotch.

"If the grove runs itself, why didn't you keep it?" Her good eye started hurting. Marcanta said the headaches were her body trying to navigate the pressure imbalance. Denny asked if she was all right. "Keep talking," she said. "It's good to hear your voice. I miss you."

"Okay," he said. With her eyes closed, they could be lying on the floor of her bedroom again, talking up at the sticker stars. "I didn't want to stay. Not wanting to and not being able to are kind of the same thing."

"Exactly," she said. "So who has Prater now?"

"Some agricultural science conglomerate. They focus on reviving legacy crops and revegetating old farm areas. It turns out that Prater oranges are immune to Powder Spot, that super fungus thing that killed everything off. It looks like it started with fertilizers and cultivars in the late nineties. We missed it. Prater is one of three groves in the world without it. It's like a citrus museum. This think tank figures they can bring back oranges from our trees. They paid me a shitload for it."

"So what are you going to do now?"

"I bought Mom a house near where Port St. Lucie was before the flooding. She likes it there. She's got friends, does painting and stuff. I never even knew she liked painting, but she's not half bad. She does a lot of sunsets, but I guess that's a requirement. Nobody there knows she's a Gapper. She likes that."

No one had ever asked the Praters what they wanted. Denny was supposed to run the grove. Annie was supposed to be a wife, a mother. But Nedda remembered her soft hands, and all the times she'd tried to help, even when Denny was trapped. Annie Prater had held on to the sequencer. She'd helped lift the needle. Annie had made sure Denny saw her before she left for the space station. "I'm glad you did that for her. So she's okay?"

"Probably better than she's ever been."

"That's good. Tell her I say hi. Hug her for me, will you?" It was a hard thing to admit that you might be better off for someone having died.

"I bought a car shop," he said. "I specialize in the ones that run on gas, fix them up, convert them. Everything we grew up with is a classic now, and not many people know how to work on them. It's good money."

She laughed. "We're old as hell."

"Fucking ancient, but the baby face fools everyone. I got a boat too. It's not real big, just enough to take a few people out, that's all."

"What'd you name it?"

"*Flux Capacitor.*"

"*Doc Brown*'s a better name."

"Yeah, but boats are women."

"Everything's a woman. Cars, boats, houses. Anywhere that's safe or takes you somewhere better is a woman," she said.

"So, *Chawla* is a woman?"

"Obviously." She opened her eye to find him staring.

"Life was better for you after the gap, wasn't it?" he asked.

"I think so, but it's hard to see something when you're in the middle of it. I don't know what we missed, because we missed it." Had it not happened, it would have been a different life entirely. The time jump had offered her opportunities that wouldn't have existed otherwise, but nothing was without cost.

"But you miss him every day."

"Yeah. I still do."

"I miss Pop, even though I know he was an asshole. It's messed up." He stretched his arms above his head, and it hurt Nedda a little, knowing they'd never lie out on a dock again, that they weren't on the floor of her bedroom.

"You're always going to miss him, that's just how it works. And you're always going to see him everywhere too. That never changes." Every now and again, Evgeni's back looked like her father's, and it gave her a start.

"They're renaming Red Bug Road after you." What a gift to have a smile like that, one that looked better for being broken.

"When I die, they'll probably rename the school after me too."

"Shut up, jerk. Don't say stuff like that," he said. "I'm still mad at you for lying to me, you know. You went somewhere where I can't punch your arm for doing something stupid."

"Well, I can't punch you either. And you were supposed to keep the grove so I'd always know where you'd be. So even when you weren't talking to me I'd know where you were, what you were up to. That helped."

"I'm sorry," he said, when the pause grew too long.

"It's okay. How's Kate?"

"She's good. She still thinks I'm in love with you."

"She'll get over it when you have a kid." Kate. Perfectly lovely, cute in a way that made you want to smile. She fit Denny well, and she wasn't bending to do it.

"I don't know if we'll do the kid thing. It's not a great time to be a kid. I don't know if I could handle one." He leaned back in his chair, his shadow harsh on the wall behind him. The call rooms were tiny gray cubicles, little more than boxes with screens. "She wants one, but . . . I don't know how to explain to her that I'm not quite right. She doesn't understand our friendship either, but what am I supposed to say?"

"What do you mean?"

"She really does think that I love you. I watched you for years. I know it was only seconds to you, I get that. You told me and I knew it too, sort of. But years, you know? I was twelve, thirteen, fourteen, fifteen—I don't know when you left, but when you did leave I wasn't there anymore. I wasn't me. It took you probably a week to leave the shed. I knew you were running, but I fell asleep and woke up and you were still leaving. Then it was nothing for a long time, just me and that stupid pruner. I can close my eyes now and still see you in dark blue corduroy stirrup pants. You had a white T-shirt on that said 'Georgia Peach,' and a light blue shiny jacket with pink piping. Your hair was in one braid. You had bangs then and they were crooked. I still don't know how your mom cut them crooked when I know she used a ruler. There was dirt by your left eye and you tried to wipe it but it stayed there. If you were any closer I bet I could tell you what your fingerprint looked like. I thought about every conversation we ever had. For so long it was only you. We were the only people in the world. I did love you. You were everything. And then I was too old, and I wasn't me anymore, and you were gone. Kate's wrong, but not entirely. She just doesn't understand and it's hard to explain. She's a worrier."

"I didn't know you remembered that much." It was the only safe thing to say.

"Every year I remember a little more. It's like I'm catching up. That worries Kate too."

"Singh says that worrying about other people feels like you're doing something, but worrying about yourself just feels like worrying."

"Maybe," he said. He cracked his neck, revealing the bald patch behind his ear where he'd tugged his hair out. Maybe his body was catching up too. "Do you like this Singh guy? Everything I've seen about him makes him seem irritating as hell. He's got what, three degrees? Rescued sea turtles or something? He's too smart. I don't like it. He's too perfect."

God, but it was good to laugh. "Nobody up here is perfect. We're in a tin can, living in each other's farts, praying the plants filter them out before the stench kills us. Singh is a moody jerk, but I'm worse. And yes, I like him, but no, not like that. It's different here." They were all part of *Chawla*. Loving them was essential, but they'd never be Denny. She'd never be for them what Denny had described. "You'd get along with Evgeni," she said. "He's one of those lucky, happy people. It would drive me crazy, but it's hard to hate anyone you rely on this much. You'd probably hit on Marcanta, but she'd slap you."

She tried to imagine where he'd fit on *Chawla*, but couldn't. Denny was built for sun, for ground, and for Kate who worried. Kate who didn't understand that Denny was part of Nedda too—a bone in her leg that held her up. That was all and everything.

"I never told you, but I think I'm a better person because of what happened to me. I want you to know that," Denny said.

"You've always been a good person."

"I wasn't really good at being patient, or listening to people, really. I think having all that time with myself fixed some of that. Made me think about how much I need people."

"But right after you didn't want to talk to me."

"I was scared. I knew something had happened but not what. Things got jumbled. It's still hard to remember when anything was, or the order stuff happened in, or if I made it up. We tried catfish tickling once, right?"

"Yeah." She'd been nine or so. Pop Prater brought them to a lake away from the coast. The fish were sly, made of teeth and lake bottom.

"For a while, remembering anything from the equipment shed was like that. Like when your hand is down in the mud and you're sure you've got a fish, but it scoots away. I'd think I'd latched on to something, a solid memory, and then it was gone. Slippery, I guess. The only things I was sure of were the morning *Challenger* blew up, and when my mom grabbed me out of the pruner chair."

As much as she still saw him as twelve, she thought of him as everything he was and would be—fifteen, twenty-five, forty, sixty, eighty-eight. All of the lean, fast years he'd lived while the world sat still around him. "I should have stopped you from going that morning," she said.

"Ever try to stop a train?"

The treadmill was running, and the sounds of food prep came down the corridor. Louisa jogging. Amit with a knife. They should say their goodbyes. Instead she told him about Evgeni's horrible taste in music and penchant for sardines, Amit's pink hair ties, and what having a needle in your eye was like. They talked about movies they remembered that the rest of the world had forgotten. He told her about trying to catch bluefish off his boat. It was the comfort of shared history.

"If I don't get to speak to you . . ." she said.

"You'll call me."

"There's a chance I won't be able to fix it."

"You'll call me." The squareness in his voice melted away, taking with it some of the years and space.

"I will. I'll fix it."

They lied to each other, but they were good lies, meant to be true.

"Is it morning or night up there?"

"Hard to tell. It's morning, I guess."

"Then have a good day, Nedda. I'm lucky to know you. Tell Judy Resnik I say hi."

The feed cut, and Denny's face was replaced by Mission Control jockeys, sliding their hands arounds screens.

Nedda left the room, unable to speak.


There were five sights Nedda would forever remember: the smoke plumes from *Challenger* bleeding across the sky, Denny's bones stretching while she watched, her father the last time she saw him, Earthrise from the moon, and Evgeni's goggled face when the tape was peeled from her bad eye.

He was tender, separating each hair without pulling. All done by feel.

"You'd hate me if you lost an eyebrow. Everyone is vain when it comes to having half an eyebrow."

"Just rip it off, please."

"You'll want to scratch it and rub it. You're a picker. Don't think I haven't noticed. I hear you picking at your skin. Always picking, twitching like a bird."

The first light to her eye was textured, nap-in-a-sunbeam light, like nothing on *Chawla*. It bent around shapes, darkness, the side of a neck, then, the glinting edge of pressure goggles. Evgeni's eyes were large and blue, too big for him, fragile. Blown glass. She saw clear striations in his irises, minute veins in the sclera. There was a sheen to his skin. He'd had a shave that morning, an actual shave. She ran her hand against his cheek to be sure it wasn't glare or a halo. He was smooth, a little slick.

"I see you," she said.

"And I'm still handsome."

"No less than you ever were."

"Years into space, and you still think you've got to be a diplomat."

"You're wearing the goggles."

"Yes, look at how hopeful I am being and admire me." He grinned. "You let Louisa remove part of your eye. The very least I can do is wear goggles."

She closed her good eye—what had been her good eye. Evgeni was soft and sharp at the same time. His hair grew only in cowlicks. She wanted to press the center of one with her thumb, right by his temple, just above the goggle straps. Pale. If he'd grown up in Florida, he'd have flecked skin and a permanent brown burned into him.

"Do you ever think about how none of us are the colors we think we are? We're just reflecting different wavelengths." Nothing looked exactly the same for any two beings. Mice saw things in gray, yellow, and blue. Trichromatic vision was common between old-world primates and humans, but not with new-world primates. Not with marmosets. Not all humans had it either. Color blindness was particularly common in men, and most people couldn't see the full color spectrum humans were supposed to. Insect eyes processed colors she could never imagine. All those colors, all that light. Evgeni nearly glowed with it. "You're highly reflective," she said.

She could see. She could see to do the build.

Marcanta appeared with a cloth and shoved it under Nedda's eye. "Dab both eyes, but don't wipe. No pressure yet, okay? And no picking." She asked if there was stinging, pain of any variety, uncomfortable pressure.

There was no pain, just wonder. Earthrise from the moon had been blue and cold, starting in her toes rather than her eyes. She'd cried. Dr. Stein said that Earthrise made everyone do that. Evgeni-rise had been warm, bright. His face, his eyes, the glow of him had been a welcoming moon.

Louisa swatted Evgeni lightly on the shoulder. "Give me some room. We need to do tests."

"Abuse! I cry abuse," he said.

Louisa ignored him and pulled up a Snellen chart on the lab screen. "Top to bottom. Do it first with the eye I poked, then again with the other eye. No guessing. No cheating."

She'd been raised to perform on tests, to figure out answers even when missing information. It went against her nature not to try to answer correctly. The letters held their basic shapes; she knew them. "Fuzzy on the bottom."

"Give it time, but don't guess," Louisa said.

She didn't guess.

"Louisa, we're going to fix it."


At night, Marcanta hung from a rung in Nedda's cabin. "Me, then Singh, then Evgeni. We need to do me before we make any attempt at the drive."

"Makes sense. That way Singh will have a shot at Amadeus if I get fried." A flask floated to her. Nedda unscrewed the cap and took a small sip of rum, which Marcanta loved, but to her tasted burned and sour.

"I shouldn't dignify that with a response, but yeah. You're going to have to do mine. I'll lay everything out for you as much as I can. If we talk to each other, keep the video going, it should be fine."

"That's brave of you."

"No, it's just smart to not let Singh near me with the vitrector. Plus, you're you. You learn. If you mess it up once, you'll get it right the next time, but Singh wouldn't pick up the vitrector again. He's too afraid of breaking eggs. I can forgive human error. He can't."

"Did you know he tried to talk to his pet tortoise telepathically?"

Marcanta grinned and swallowed more rum. "Figures." She squeezed herself beside Nedda's sleep sack. "If we make planet—"

"When we make planet."

"If we make planet, your vision's most likely going to flip, so we'll do one eye each for now. On planet, the bad eye should clear up some, and the one I fixed, who knows? I'll put saline or an oil bead in to balance the pressure."

"We'll be fine," Nedda said.

They passed the flask in a careful dance of capping and recapping, covering with thumbs, and stretching to catch errant droplets. It burned, but it eased the loneliness.

Louisa had calls with her sister sometimes, and during them her laugh was broad and catching, but there was always sadness to it. Nedda stayed in Hydroponics, pruning and grafting, to hide from it. She'd never met Michael to know that kind of missing. Denny was it, but that was different too.

Louisa rested her head on Nedda's shoulder. Her face was flushed, a bright spot of warmth through Nedda's shirt. The back of her head was round against Nedda's palm, her hair soft, sleek, and black. She smelled like rum and rubbing alcohol, aloe, and the inside of her sleep sack, as complex and comforting a scent as a baby blanket.

Louisa had an ex who was a dentist. Singh found the idea repugnant and said so once while they were drinking. He'd latched a boot into one of the handles on the common room wall, and was rolling back and forth in midair, the closest he could get to the satisfaction of tapping his foot. "How did you deal with the dentist smell? The glove stink and drilled tooth. It's like burning hair. It gets in their clothes and it never leaves."

"Who fucks somebody with their clothes on?" Louisa had replied.

Nedda didn't remember a dentist's smell precisely, and things had changed from when she was little and in the chair at Dr. Lowell's office. She'd never had a tooth drilled. But she remembered how citrus oil could smell beautiful, and how it could turn your stomach. How two people could make the same thing smell entirely different.

Gloves and burned teeth. Butter and lemon. Solder and ozone. Rum, aloe, rubbing alcohol, and sleep sack. Louisa had loved the smell of dentist. Nedda loved the smell of the ship, of them. To others, they'd smell like burning tooth.

"Louisa, what if I blind you?"

"You won't."

Louisa held on until her arms tired, the rum making her loose. Nedda had expected loneliness and knew how to survive it: with books, with work, with curiosity, with learning. She'd not expected the rest.

They would never have children. It had seemed like so little to give up at the time. See an entirely new world, or have a child on a dying one? They'd never have wives or husbands, which hadn't seemed like a sacrifice either. They were driven people. But they knew one another as no other people ever could. They were wives and husbands and children together.

They were what light reflected.

# The Break

S HE'D SEEN HER father as a little boy, as an old man, and all the people in between, but none of those fathers were him. When sine crossed $X$, she knew him like she knew home, the cracks in the front porch steps she walked over every day, the creaky spot in the kitchen floor, how the living room smelled like all of them together. She knew him the way you know the smell of chocolate chip cookies in the oven, or the nap of a favorite blanket snuggled against your bare feet.

"It's okay if you want to talk to him," Betheen said.

A smooth wall was between them, the same slickness that was around the monkey, around Denny, a layer of time stretched thin. Through it she saw his crumbly fingernails, their rough tips.

"I didn't see Halley's Comet. I lied." She waited for him to say something.

"Why?" He was supposed to know everything, to always have an answer. For why he'd done it. For why she'd lied to him.

"I don't know." She wished she could grab his hand and wrench it. "Why don't you want me to grow up?"

"You should have all the time to do everything you ever want. Time is a good thing, the best thing."

Everything she ever wanted. Nedda wanted to go to the moon, walk on its craters. She wanted her own space shuttle and to feel what weightlessness was like. She wanted to name new things, and walk somewhere no one else ever had and maybe never would again. She wanted to fall asleep on a lab table while he told her about stars. She wanted to lie on a dock in the sun, catching fish with Denny. She wanted to smell Betheen's pistachio shortbread in the oven and help make cakes that looked like raindrops of champagne. She wanted to know her brother. Some of those things had happened, some could never happen, some wouldn't ever happen again. Because of him.

Betheen tugged her back. "Not too close."

Just because she couldn't squeeze his hand didn't mean she couldn't hurt him. "I want to grow up."

"I'm sorry," he said. It wasn't enough. It didn't matter now.

"I think we can stop it," her mother said. "We've rigged an electromagnet. If we time it right, it should be able to disrupt the field."

His smile was quick. "Good girl, Beth."

*Girl.* Like a little thing, a secondary thought. Nedda was a secondary thought to her brother. Crucible was meant to keep her from growing up, but he'd built it because of Michael.

"Theo, it's the whole town."

"I know. The whole place is floating, isn't it? The town is floating. The anomaly is in the water and the wires. Once it got in— I didn't think. You'd have spotted it earlier, wouldn't you? You always found and fixed all my mistakes."

"There weren't many," Betheen said. "The magnet is going to pull the machine apart."

"I know," he said.

Crucible spit frigid light, making Nedda and Betheen jump back.

"Little Twitch, I need you to listen. You have to be far away when it goes," he said. "There will be gasses and radiation and I don't want you and your mom here."

Part of her had known when she'd first seen him this way, trapped. Part of her had known the moment he'd first said *poisonous.* She suspected the answer but forced herself to ask, to confirm the hypothesis. "What about you?"

"Don't you worry about me."

Betheen interrupted. "The electromagnet is supposed to run in opposition to you, the time you're in. There should be a pulse, a big one, when you're ... when you're like you are now. Pete McIntyre has a launch sequencer. We're using it to run a cycle and start the magnet remotely," Betheen said.

"The power?"

"Two generators," she said.

He was going to die. He'd shift again soon and die. But he'd really die too. No return. The room grew colder and Nedda's toes went numb. They'd pull the magnet into the lab, start the generators, and run the sequencer from the hallway. Then Crucible would break. He would breathe in gas and radiation. Her parents spoke sweetly, looking each other in the eyes.

"Dad?" She wanted to hug him, feel the skips of electrical impulses, light.

"It's going to be fine, Nedda." He reached as though feeling for the edges of when he was, where he was. "Denny will be fine. I'm sorry this happened. But I'm not frightened and you shouldn't be either."

"But I'll never see you again."

"Please don't worry. It's already happened, and it's okay. I promise. Little Twitch, you're going to be fine and so will I. What did I say we all become? Gas and carbon. Heat and light. I'll be in the air, I'll be in the ground. I'll always be with you."

"That's stupid," she shouted, then wished she hadn't. Those might be the last words he'd hear her say. But it *was* stupid.

"It's not," he said. "You were with me even before you were born. Everything that would make you was already here, waiting to be you. It'll be like that, I promise. It'll be like I'm waiting for you."

"Will it hurt?"

"No," he said.

She wanted to believe him.

"Beth, if you can, after . . ." Clanging drowned his words; Mr. Pete had dropped one of the generators.

"I will," Betheen said.

"Can you stay for a little while," he asked, "but leave when I don't know what's happening?"

"Of course," Betheen said.

His face slid away, becoming someone else, some*when* else, a film rewinding. Nedda leaned into Betheen, and was grateful for her sharp hipbones, her wiry arms, her body that had no give.

"Nedda, you ought to wait outside." Mr. Pete stood in the doorway, the head of the electromagnet on the dolly. He'd turned a funny color. "That— You shouldn't see this."

She'd had enough of people saying what she should and should not do. She turned from him, back to Crucible's spinning, the cold that emanated from it, and her father's writhing body. "I need to watch."

"You're sure?" Betheen asked.

"I have to."

"She's fine, Pete."

They stayed with him through a cycle. His body shrank in on itself, his arms and legs retracting, growing thinner. He grew shorter, younger, fat blossomed on his face. The psoriasis crept up and down his body, and when his face was too difficult to look at, she watched his skin, how it moved, silver and red dancing all over him. His skin had nebulas.

"Mom. He's going to die."

Betheen scratched her neck gently, just below her braid. "We'll be fine, Nedda. It's not okay right now, but we'll be fine."

When he was a baby, he was round and screaming, like a doll, like someone else's person and not hers.

By her ear, breath tickling the fine hairs, Betheen said, "Here's a secret. You'll be stronger. Not at first. You'll miss him terribly. At first, you'll walk around and wonder where a piece of your heart went. You'll think maybe you died. But you didn't, and you won't. You'll learn how to live when you're hurt, how to work when you feel broken, and how to do better than everyone else even though you're suffering. All those other girls and boys who have easy lives, who don't know how to hurt— when they grow up and lose someone, it will stop them. But it won't stop you, because you'll know better. And I will be here, and I won't ever let you go. Not ever. Even when you grow up and don't need me anymore, I'll be here, just in case. This is it." She kissed Nedda's temple. "Nothing will hurt more than you hurt right now."

"It isn't fair."

"No, it isn't. But we'll be okay anyway."

Okay wasn't enough. Okay was going to school and having spitballs hit your cheek. Okay was your friend sleeping on your floor because he couldn't go home. Okay was living your entire life without knowing you had a brother who died before you met him. Okay was always reaching for something you could never touch. A shuttle. The moon. Him. Okay was walking around with your heart in a fist, breathing like you were running out of air. She dug the heels of her palms into her eyes, waiting for the pressure to make colors bloom, waiting for pain.

There was a change in the light, a pop of warmth, a bright burst skittering. The chill in the room receded, their breath no longer fogging.

"Betheen?" His voice was smooth, high.

He was young. Somewhere between Nedda's age and the age he was supposed to be. He was frightened; his mouth did the same thing hers did when she was scared.

"Betheen, you look—"

"Old," her mother said. "I know."

"What happened?"

"You were in an accident."

It was more than that, but it wasn't. Nedda tried to look away when he saw her, but couldn't. The confusion hurt.

"Beth, who is that?"

"This is Nedda Susanne. She's eleven, and she's brilliant."

He didn't know her. That hurt worse than anything, worse than Betheen said. But he looked at her the way she looked at the moon. Like he was lying on his back and looking at the stars.

"Are you . . ." he said.

"She's the smartest girl in her class. She's skipped a grade already. She's perfect and she loves you like you made the whole universe."

"I married you? We have a daughter." He tried to stand, but fell like a broken branch.

"Yes," Betheen said.

He laughed, the hard kind of laugh that cramped your belly. "Lucky bastard."

"Let him see you, Nedda."

Her father wiped his eyes, searched the floor for his glasses, but gave up. He pulled the skin around one eye, narrowing it to better see. Without his glasses, without his lines, Nedda saw his cheeks looked like hers, and so did his narrow-bridged nose, his thin top lip.

"Am I a good dad?"

"Yes," she said. Inside her pocket she found the scrap of her mission patch, and kneaded the last bit of the red apple into her thumb. There were other words, but they stuck to the roof of her mouth. She couldn't hear the room, Crucible, or the sweep of her mother's hands at her collar; she heard a memory: his voice opening the sky. Pointing to a spot in the black saying, *See? Pluto is our far star sailor.*

"We need to go soon, Theo."

He pulled his legs tight to his chest, wrapped his arms around them. One of Nedda's favorite ways to sit. A stone settled in her gut.

He rubbed near his temple, revealing a reddened plaque where hair didn't grow, a spot he'd worried at. "Nedda Susanne?"

"Dad?" He wasn't her father yet, but he would be someday. He would be in an hour, or a minute, sometime after they'd gone.

"This must be strange for you. I don't know you yet, but you know me."

"A little."

"Theo, you don't stay this way for long, and what comes soon isn't pretty."

"You're perfect," he said to Nedda, just for her. "If you don't see me again, if I'm not around, I want you to know that you are perfect. That was the first thing I thought when I saw you."

Crucible's legs inched forward, a spinning spider, and her father began to change. Nedda couldn't watch.

Betheen grabbed her arm, hard enough to bruise, and pulled Nedda from the lab. She was crying, so she closed her eyes and pictured the moon. She pictured seven plumes of smoke in the sky, gas, carbon, light, and heat. Combustion that moved too quickly to hurt.

The hall lights were out, making the sequencer a harsh block of shadow, the cables waiting snakes. Light flowed from the lab—Crucible was leaking time.

The walls shook as Mr. Pete switched on the first generator. He looked out from behind Mitzi's shadow and shouted, "The other generator is up and running good. All you need to do is let me know when."

The first generator hooked into the sequencer, providing power. The sequencer hooked into the second generator, which fed the electromagnet. In the end, her mother's equation was beautiful. A single line in graceful handwriting, the same slanting loops she used to write recipes. Betheen could write *Fold egg whites gently* and an equation that would tear Crucible apart and kill her father.

"How much time?" Nedda asked.

Betheen took the kitchen timer from her pocket. "Twenty minutes, then we turn it on. We really shouldn't wait longer." They could spend it with him, inside. But it would hurt more, wouldn't it? Would he even know? She leaned against the sequencer, her coat buttons clicking against Mitzi's metal case. Nedda sat beside her, touching but not.

"I could do it for you," Mr. Pete said.

"No, you can't," Betheen said. "Would you mind waiting in the truck for us?"

He said something about being just outside, and then his footsteps were stones skipping down the hall. If you died in the sky, if you were incinerated, your ashes spread on the wind and you covered the land and the ocean like fog, like the crop dusters that used to fly over Prater. You blew across the sky and for a while, maybe always, you were flying. Maybe you were light.

Betheen hugged Nedda to her. When the time came, she said, "It's now."

Her mother loved him. It was in the words.

"I'll do it," Nedda said.

She'd flipped the switch before, when the sequencer had stood in Mr. Pete's yard. Exposure had nearly worn Mitzi's lettering away, sun bleaching the type. SEQU NC ON was up. It was silver, the kind of switch her dad used when he showed her how to build a circuit, the same kind of switch that ran Crucible.

"You don't have to," Betheen said.

"Yes, I do." Switches were logical: on/off, if/then. If Betheen flipped the switch, then Nedda would blame her. If Betheen flipped the switch, then there would come a time when Nedda had to make a decision and would look to someone else to do it for her. If Nedda flipped the switch, then she would know she could do the hardest possible thing.

He was in pain.

*Things that are important are always frightening.*

*I want you to know that you are perfect.*

*For the greater good.*

The *click* was quiet, more sensation than sound. Fans whirred inside the sequencer. Red numbers ticked away fractions of seconds, counting down time until the generator ramped and sent a jolt of electricity into the electromagnet—the needle—aimed at Crucible's heart. If it was big enough, strong enough, it would tear the machine apart. The electromagnet would turn on when the bubble was at its thinnest. There would be a surge, and surges brought sparks, and sparks in rooms full of gasses were bad. Combustion was the boldest chemical reaction. Gas. Carbon. Light.

The sequencer's metal case was cool against her ear. The inside sounded like lines of dominos clacking against each other, toppling, Connect Four chips dropped into a frame.

Light pulsed from the lab door.

Arms were around her waist, dragging her down the hallway, down the stairs, away from the heat and rolling light. She was shoved through the brush and branches that covered the door. Whisking, stirring, folding, kneading—little movements done with great repetition across time made strength. A second pair of hands dug under her arms; they smelled like rust and motor oil. Then she was in the middle of the truck's bench seat, sandwiched between Mr. Pete and her mother.

Someone flipped switches for shuttles; there was always a person to do those things. Someone had flipped a switch for *Challenger.* Was it worse if you flipped a switch and didn't know it would kill somebody? Her dad would know the answer. She would be lying on the car hood, peering through a telescope and looking for comets, and he would say that no work that matters was ever without consequence. He would mean it. She wouldn't lie to make him happy.

She imagined his face—not the little boy, the old man, or the young one who'd said she was perfect. Him.

"Mom, am I going to forget what he looks like?"

"Yes and no," Betheen said. "Pictures will help."

Mr. Pete rolled the window down and lit a cigarette. The smoke trailed in ribbons. Streamers. Combustion and oxidation. Ash.

"Where are we headed, Mrs. Papas?"

"I want to see Denny," Nedda said.

"His mom is with him," Betheen said. "She needs time alone with Denny, okay?"

She needed time too. Just in case, so the last he saw of her wouldn't be her running away. "What if she didn't bring him the coffee berries? What if he doesn't know?"

"She needs time, Nedda."

At that moment, her dad was alive in the lab. Denny was stuck in the grove. She was in a truck with her mom and Mr. Pete and she'd done something hard, which was something to be proud of even if she would never be able to tell anyone about it. Nothing had changed yet. When her dad died, when he was gone and she felt it, she wouldn't really see it either. It would already be done. The light from the explosion would travel from the lab, through the air and into the truck window and then her eyes. It would take time. That distance might as well be a million light years.

Mr. Pete was talking. "If you're sure. Annie made it sound like when she left there, the whole town was getting ready to tar and feather him."

Her mother looked out the window. "But it's high ground, a good distance away, and people will go there. After." The sick sky had turned orange, lighting her mother up like a fire. "It's best to face things head on."

They were headed for the school.

Overgrowth cut off the end of College Drive and forced them to backtrack. Roads seemed to shift as they drove on them, and everything smelled like sawdust and melting rubber. Island Paradise Park was visible just above the trees. Kudzu had crawled up the side and bottom of the concrete head, bearding it. The gaslights still burned in its eyes.

Acacia Lane was the only route with a clear path to the school. They passed by Nedda's house, the eave that marked her bedroom window, and the trellis that Denny climbed. There were no lights. There should be light in the basement, a flash every now and again, a spark. They passed the Prater house. Denny's things were inside, his clothes and baseball cards, and his fishing rod, like an outline of him.

The kitchen timer beeped.

The hair on Nedda's arms stood up, and she craned her neck to look.

"Don't," Betheen said. "He wouldn't want you to see."

He would. She knew that.

An explosion was many things; this one was photons moving in waves, currents drifting into the universe, rushing like a flood. It wasn't so different from watching one on TV. There was a flash, but no screaming, no running, and no one telling her to pray. Her dad was in it. "We're not there," she said. "Light we see is from what's already happened."

Her mother looked forward, her back straight, her hand gripping the door handle. "It's a good thought, but not exactly true. You're always there, Nedda. It's always happening."

What do people become? What they always were: carbon, heat, and light, smashed together until they became something else for a little while. A star, a monkey, a boy. An old man. A baby.

"I can't get any closer. We'll have to walk the rest," Mr. Pete said.

Cars jammed the school lot, closing off the entrance. When her mother didn't move, Mr. Pete reached across to pop the door open. The air that came in smelled like school lunch—like onions, sweet, dirty, and sour—awful in its ordinariness.

They didn't bother closing the car doors. They ran through the cars that were parked on the grass, leaning drunkenly into the road. She recognized some. Ellery Rees's Gremlin, the weird truck car that Krissie's father drove. The mail truck. Heat was at their backs, growing. She looked for Denny's mom's car and Denny's bike, knowing they wouldn't be there.

The door opened.

Hands on her back—her mother, Mr. Pete—shoved her inside, into a crowd of arms, bodies, people.

When her eyes adjusted to the black, there were faces—Mrs. Wheeler, Joan from the Bird's Eye, kids from school. Vicki and Madeline. Jimmy La Morte and his mom.

Pop Prater. He moved people out of his way to get to the door, to get to them. She could see it, his fist hitting Denny's eye. For all the things her father had ever done, for not wanting her to grow up, for everything that had gone wrong, he never would have hit her. He would tear himself apart if he'd ever hurt a kid on purpose.

"Desmond," her mother said.

There was a flash.

Light ate the sky. Heat blasted through the doors, scorching, dry, like Easter never was. Whatever Pop Prater had been about to say died before it left his mouth. All that remained was heat and the crush of people. Her mother's hip, Mrs. Wheeler's back. Mr. Pete's heavy boots by her foot. Someone's dress, scratchy. The wetness of breath, moving in and out.

Then there was nothing but light. Burning yellow-green.

She felt them, everyone in Easter, bleeding together like water droplets, separate things fusing, all of one skin. A ripple of time moving through them. They were the same.

The bodies of the town clung together, a single roiling mass—grove pickers and hotel bums, children and parents, fading old money, the dog track men with their rattails and creased skin from late-night liquor, people who'd tumbled east and settled where the land ended. Crucible's trail cut the air, the sky, and the thin walls that made them separate people. Without those lines they were a single thought. Longing.

Yearning for a lover, yearning for a houseboat—a solid vessel to live long and lazy days on; to hold Mama's hand again and let her know she was loved; for money and ease; for a baby, to finally be a mother; for fame; for sleep without nightmares; for one day without aching joints; for a job; for Missy to come back; for someone to actually listen, just once, Jesus Christ; for a son, a goddamn son; for the sweet orange soda that they stopped making; for just one more hour and it would be enough; for a husband to take it all back and start again; for a truck; for a treehouse with three stories and a trapdoor rope swing; for galaxy cake; for a night in a kitchen with salt and steam in the air; for a space shuttle; for a father.

The sky cracked gold, then faded. They fell away from one another, skin and thoughts buzzing.

A small snap of a frayed thread.

Her father was gone. There was a hole where he had been. Nedda could trace it inside—not in her heart, but next to it, around it, a layer of skin gone missing.


Nedda buried her face against Betheen, cheek to collarbone, as lights came on in the lobby. She breathed her mother in and began to count. Seconds on the left hand, tens on the right. Two minutes. The rules said everything would be fine after two minutes. She wouldn't lose count.

"I think it's done," Betheen said.

"I want to go home," Nedda said.

When they opened the school doors, they blinked up into the brightness of an afternoon that was hot like early summer. A blue sky with clouds moving like they hadn't in days.

People pushed by, wandering to their cars, looking up at the sky and rubbing their necks, stunned.

Pop Prater called her mother's name, but they kept walking.

They walked through the woods, the trail she and Denny used. Her mother must have felt it too, the thread snapping. When they passed the coffee bushes, Nedda looked up and saw Betheen crying. Her hair had fallen from its French twist. There was grease and rust on her coat sleeves, wide brownish smears on the pink wool.

They walked through Mr. Pete's yard. There was a paler spot of paint on the back of his house, like a scar, where the sequencer, Mitzi, had been. Everything left outlines.

"Mom?"

"Yes?"

"Dad said when we die, we go back to what we were, and that everything comes from carbon. We just become carbon, gas, and heat too. I wanted to know what thoughts were, what happened to the other stuff after—everything you think and who you are, what you feel and everything that ever happened to you, your memories. He said it's all electrical impulses, that it's light and shocks and stuff. And when you think about how electricity travels, there's all this light to it, and it never stops. Right? It just keeps going. He said that maybe it keeps traveling forever. That all the light from the beginning of the universe is still traveling."

"It was kind of him to say that."

It made it hurt worse too, to know that he was traveling to places she would never see, that he was still in the universe but she was without him.

Nedda shrugged out of her jacket, afraid to wonder at the heat. Afraid to wonder what happened beyond the lab, beyond the grove.

"Mom."

"*Mm.*"

"I felt him die."

Betheen made a sound like a mouse choking. "Me too. We'll figure it out," she said, once she caught her breath. "We'll figure out what to do."

If all the light in the universe kept moving and never died, if all the light in the universe was still there, her father—like Judy, like the seven—was still traveling. Her brother was too. She wanted, more than anything in the world—more than to have her own lab, more than to stand on the moon, more than she wanted space and an Agena rocket— she wanted to touch that light again.

"I love you," Betheen said.

Had they been back on the kitchen floor, staring at the ceiling, with her father in the basement, Nedda would have said it back and not bothered to think whether she meant it. It was different now. There were things about her father she'd never know, an entire other person she'd never meet or understand. When the mixer had broken, her mother had said something to her about baby shoes that Nedda couldn't remember. Those words had meant something else too. She grabbed her mother's littlest finger. Any more would hurt too much.

Molecules, particles—everyone was made from the smallest things, and if she grabbed hold of them tightly, she might as well be grabbing the whole of something too.

They passed Haverstone House and stopped where Denny would have turned to go to his driveway.

Annie Prater's car was in front of the house. The lights were on.

She knew it like she knew the constellations: Denny was home.

# Revelation

RANDALL HOLT WAS asleep in his truck, and had been since crossing through Okefenokee. He wasn't supposed to rely on the driverless feature, but tell that to anyone driving thirty-six hours straight. The company didn't check logs, not until there was an accident, and he could drive the Atlantic route in his sleep. It's what kept his wife from pitching a fit anytime he left the house. He was dreaming about Marla and her beautiful feet, that her toenails were live butterflies. She was scared she'd kick them when she walked so he had to carry her everywhere—over his shoulder in a fireman's hold, or in both arms, like they'd just gotten married. Now, in his dream, her feet were resting on the dash beside him, those butterflies' wings flapping in the sun.

He was still asleep when the light on his dash blinked on. The onboard computer searched the GPS and located a fueling station. It signaled, more often and more accurately than Randall ever did, and pulled over to the left on the highway. At five in the morning the road was nearly empty.

Randall rolled over as the computer took an exit. Now Marla was on a television show, and everyone was saying her butterfly toes meant she was queen of something. He was getting tired of carrying her places. His arms had stretched out like spaghetti and dragged on the ground.

The truck's computer could do many things—course correct, prevent accidents, choose accident paths that would assume the least amount of financial loss—but it couldn't fuel itself, which was why Randall was a driver, and why, when he eventually woke up, Randall found himself looking directly at the sign for the Easter Gas n' Go.

Gas. Who used gas anymore? He hadn't seen a gas station since he was a kid.

A few hundred miles of road left your knees stiff and your bladder screaming to piss like a racehorse. He hopped out of the cab, palm-locked the door, and hunted around for a john and the charging station. Damned AI could plot a route around storms a hundred miles off, and navigate so you wouldn't hit a flea, but it couldn't find a plug any more than it could find its own ass.

Easter. Weird name for a town. He eyeballed the bays. No charger. There were cars in the back. Old, boxy looking things with long hoods, sharp corners. He'd wound up at a classic car shop. That explained the gas. Still, no charging station? Seemed like a shit business move. He walked up to the office, knocked on the door, but no one answered.

"Hey. I got a semi out here I need to juice up. Can you tell me where the nearest charger is?"

Peering through the window showed a refrigerator case filled with plastic bottles of ancient Coca-Cola, and something on the desk that looked like a rotary telephone.

Purists. Probably some kids in their twenties with wide pants and fingernail tattoos.

"Hello?"

*Well, fuck.*

In the end, he pissed off the side of the road, into a canal. He kept an eye out. If you weren't mindful you could wind up taking a leak on a gator, which never ended well. He stood in the shade of a billboard, and squinted up to take a look. Prater Citrus. Sounded familiar.

He was back in the cab, buckling in, when he remembered. His grandmother had a poster from Prater hanging on her living room wall. A girl in a bikini made of oranges riding sidesaddle on top of a heron with two giant grapefruits in its claws. His grandmother had baked grapefruits, broiling them with brown sugar on top until they tasted like cotton candy and summer. She said Prater grapefruits were the sweetest—something called a flame varietal. But then you couldn't get them anymore. They'd gone under or stopped shipping up to Georgia. God, it was more than thirty years since she'd died. The billboard was shining and new, like it had been put up the week before. He had a hankering for grapefruit, but it was almost impossible to get now. Still, he could use a meal and little exit towns usually had good diners.

Randall shouted at his phone to point him to the next charging station, and it came up with something in Titusville. Sounded right. He let the computer do its thing. The semi rumbled out of the station, with him leaning out the window to watch the sunrise, praying the battery had enough juice to get him to a charge.

The truck went into a town that could have been a movie set, with cars from what looked like the late 1970s and early '80s. A theater marquee advertised something called *Iron Eagle.*

The AI took him through little turns, down Red Bug Road. The streets were empty, but there was a man sweeping off a bit of sidewalk in front of what looked like a diner. With chrome. A throwback in a throwback town. Randall pulled over.

"Hey, you open?"

The man eyed Randall's truck strangely. "Yeah, just now. You gonna park that thing there?"

Randall Holt was the first man to enter Easter in fifty years.


Ellery Rees baked a grapefruit for the guy in the weird tractor trailer. What kind of truck had no exhaust on it? The guy also ate a grapefruit like he hadn't seen one in his whole life. It was a slow morning, and Ellery was still feeling sideways. He'd thought about not opening up. It'd been winter yesterday, but it was summer today, and the change left him feeling like jelly and fighting the start of a head cold, among other things. But lying in bed, staring up at the ceiling, he hadn't known what to do with himself except open. So he'd swilled coffee, doctored with the Cuban stuff, and served almost four whole grapefruits to a guy with the wildest truck he'd ever seen. How did it not have a grille on it somewhere? Where was the hood? He pretended not to stare, flipping through the paper.

"You got another copy of that?" the trucker asked.

"Nah, but I'm about done. Take mine. It's a couple days old anyway. Delivery guy decided not to show up," Ellery said, and tossed the paper to the trucker.

The man picked it up from the table like he hadn't seen a newspaper before. "That right?"

"What?"

"The date."

"Like I said, it's a couple days old."

"Holy fuck," the man said. "You're not screwing with me, are you?"

Ellery didn't charge the trucker for the grapefruit or the coffee. He was too happy to see him gone.

Not long after, a detail from Titusville Police Department showed up. Then the first reporter.


The state responded with disaster management. The power company and water authority had to restore service to pipes and lines that hadn't run in decades. Counselors were brought in. The television news called it *future shock*. Psychiatrists had a difficult time finding a diagnosis for the specific temporal dissociation the townspeople suffered from. Residents of Easter often refused to acknowledge the existence of technology at all. Mobile phones were confounding, as were computers, electric cars, cameras without film, tablets, televisions, the internet, the obvious signs of a digital age. The only other people to experience anything similar were prisoners paroled after long sentences. But the shock was different from how it was with prisoners. The town had no knowledge that time had been passing, that they'd all been trapped in the days after the *Challenger* disaster.

Tabloids dubbed them *Gappers*, for the chunk of time they missed.

Scientists arrived, testing the ground, the plants and trees, the blood of the residents. They pulled samples from a lab at the college that had exploded: Small particles of gold and glass, bits of charred wiring.

During the second week, investigators interviewed a woman whose husband had died in the explosion. She stated he'd been working on a treatment for degenerative joint diseases using localized doses of radiation.

The lab and surrounding building were leveled and filled with concrete.

# 299,792,458 m/s

H E'D SPENT HIS entire life in Florida, moving only once, from Tarpon Springs to the Atlantic coast. The more his body constrained him, the deeper the travels in his mind became. In death, all things expanded. From a single point bound by flesh, his very self protracted. At first, his light was caught in his laboratory, bouncing off Crucible's remains, a leg of which pierced what had been his chest. His light bled through the door, down the corridor and out, spreading into the sky, stabbing the pellucid skin of time he'd been instrumental in creating. Each facet of his life distilled to a wish or impulse, riding photons into the night and beyond.

As time broke over Easter, Theo traveled, flying through decades of day and night as a flickering aura, liquid and sheer. He moved with it, his thoughts glancing along the tops of waves. Everything traveled.

The moment of awe when he first saw Betheen in his class, a mint green pencil tucked behind her ear, reached the moon to slide along the Montes Taurus, brushing each jut and crevasse as he had the supple skin below her ear. The moment he'd touched Michael's thumb washed deep into space, riding a slow current, striving for the universe's end. His father's death wended to the center of the Horsehead Nebula, where it met other lights, others who had been but were no more. Their lights mixed, waves amplifying, surging together.

The light that was Theo Papas rippled across the universe.

Parts of him sloughed away, absorbed by blackness, caught against other thoughts, until he was a lone brilliant wave. The last of Theo traveled as light, a single memory of a sound—the first time he'd pulled a quarter from behind his daughter's ear and heard her laugh. She was five, perfect, owl-eyed, and her laugh was like clinking glass. It made him hurt with happiness. That final piece of him was a joy so full it was painful, stripped of the fear that came from losing Michael, from Betheen leaning away, the fear that came with Nedda growing up, worrying she would be hurt, that she would be alone, that she would leave him. That brilliant happiness—his best self, the one who loved her beyond all things—crossed the solar system, sluicing through an empty patch of sky they'd often looked at, sailing to far stars.

This thought touched a small planet in a near system, pinkening as it grazed the surface. Terraformers and bots began to move with ease, and fine blush dust fell from their joints as if swept away on a soft breeze. Atmosphere generators hummed, touched by the passing essence of one who loved and understood machines. The diggers and tillers, machines like ones from an orange grove, all welcomed this light, the wave of laughter.

He circled the bots, the leveled ground, and the mountains, blanketing the planet's surface, a wave reaching ever onward. In his wake, the air carried something of oranges, a touch of solder, and the subtle salt that makes a human. That best light mingled with the light of another sun, the star his daughter would spend the rest of her days beneath. To welcome her home.

# And After

COME ON. WE'RE going to the Bird's Eye. We have to eat, even if we're sad." Her mother reached under the covers to shake Nedda's ankle.

They hadn't eaten the night before. They'd slept in the parlor, falling asleep to radio static. They hadn't showered, hadn't changed clothing. Betheen was rumpled, dirty, and close, so close that Nedda had thought about slipping off the couch to sleep on the floor with her.

She'd asked about Michael. She'd learned about grief.

"If I could have been any other way, I would have," Betheen had said. "If we had a choice about how much we hurt, everyone would choose to hurt less. When you think about your dad, when you can, remember that. If we could have been better, we would have been."

Nedda had woken up, crying, hot all over, with Betheen shaking her. She still felt unsteady.

They walked.

"We'll get the car from Mr. McIntyre later," Betheen said.

It was stupid that she still wouldn't call him Mr. Pete. Or just Pete.

The roads had cleared, and things were different. Reporters had arrived. There were weird round-fronted vans with satellite dishes on top, and police cars in funny shapes, like they were made from balloons. She wanted to pop them. An ambulance was parked in front of Ginty's Bait & Tackle, and next to it were two enormous things that looked like camper trailers. MEDICAL RELIEF was plastered on their sides in large letters and lines snaked from them.

"Mom? What's happening?"

"I don't know." Betheen recognized a woman whose skin reminded Nedda of a crumpled tissue and walked over.

"Claire, what is all this?"

"Oh, everyone has to get flu shots," the woman said. "It's mandatory. The CDC sent folks all the way down here, can you imagine?

Apparently, there's some kind of national outbreak, and it's bad. I'd talk to a reporter and find out more, but I look a mess." She patted hair that looked like it had once held an aggressive permanent wave, and smiled at Nedda. "Is this your lovely daughter?"

"Yes, this is Nedda. Nedda, this is Mrs. Fergusson from the Rotary."

"They sent the CDC all the way to our little town to protect us. Doesn't that just make you feel special?" Mrs. Fergusson spoke in that sappy voice people used when they thought everyone younger than them was a baby.

"No," Nedda said. Mrs. Wheeler stepped out of one of the vans. There was cotton on her arm, held in place by a Band-Aid. "They're taking blood, too?"

"Well, I don't know anything about that. I was just told that it was mandatory." She turned her attention back to Betheen. "Didn't someone come get you? The mayor's got his staff going door to door and some of the CDC people are even doing it themselves. Zinnia came and got me, but Darlene said someone knocked on her door wearing a hazmat suit. She thought he was some kind of alien."

"I can imagine that would be shocking if you're not expecting it."

"Oh, and did Desmond Prater manage to find your husband? Everything got confused after the . . . well."

Nedda's stomach clenched. A person wearing a surgical mask and gown ushered someone up the steps into the van.

Betheen's hand tightened around hers. "You know, I'm not sure? It was good to see you, Claire, but I do need to get food into Nedda."

The streets were crowded, buzzing, and it was warm. January wasn't supposed to be this warm.

In front of the post office, someone held a microphone to Jimmy La Morte's mother.

Then they were seen. Some of the ladies Betheen baked for at the Historical Society. The one with the white hair who washed it with shampoo that turned it lavender crossed the street to avoid them. Mr. Mitchell from the grocery store looked down in that way people did when they were pretending not to see you. Like the sidewalk was really interesting. Jimmy La Morte outright stared.

"Head up, eyes front. You did nothing wrong," Betheen said, pulling her along.

Nedda didn't believe her.

Her dad was dead.

Their booth in the Bird's Eye boiled under the sun, and her hands stuck to the shiny green vinyl. When Ellery came by to take their order, he was pale and sweaty.

"Did the mayor come by your place?"

"No, not yet. Unless we missed him."

"You talk to any of the reporters yet?"

"I don't see a reason to," Betheen said.

"You don't know then, do you?" Bits of powdered sugar and sweat clumped on the ends of his dark mustache. "They're saying something like fifty years passed. They're saying it's 2036. May thirty-first, 2036."

Betheen twitched, small enough that Ellery wouldn't notice, but Nedda saw the tiny jump below her left eye. It was the sort of thing you noticed only when you knew someone's rhythms day in and out. Betheen was scared, but her smile was still pretty like that of an Orange Blossom Parade Queen.

"Well. We'd like two slices of vintage galaxy cake."

Nedda couldn't eat hers. Three bites in, Betheen stopped eating.

They sat for hours, and Ellery let them. More trucks rolled in, soundlessly. None of their engines made noise. Large glossy black panels unfolded from the top of a tractor trailor, and men and women hooked cables up to the truck and began unspooling them down the street, toward the fire department, toward the police department. Soon, lights were set up from them.

For a while, Ellery watched with them. "Any idea what on earth all that is?"

"Photovoltaic panels, I'd imagine," Betheen said.

"Solar power," Nedda said, when Ellery looked confused.

"Those things Carter put on the White House? Huh." He took a long drink from his coffee mug before walking away.

Betheen's fork rang too loud against the plate. "Twenty thirty-six. He's been gone so long."

A man whizzed by the window on a two-wheeled skateboard. No handles. No kicking. Her stomach lurched. A woman shouted at a piece of clear plastic that glowed neon around the edges.

She shut her eyes.

Years expanded and folded. Nedda had seen her father hours ago, his young self, and said goodbye. The world had been moving while Easter was trapped like the monkey in Mr. Pete's truck. Had anyone tried to find them? Had the monkey survived? Had it found its family? Were they dead now? Her father was gone, had been gone for a very long time. Fifty years. She was both eleven and sixty-one. Did that time still count? She picked at a flake of coconut. Were there moon bases now or colonists? Was there an elevator that could lift you through the atmosphere? There could be people on Mars; there could be anything. But her dad was gone.

Nothing fit inside her, and her orange juice fought to come back up. Being sad, angry, hopeful, ashamed, and scared at the same time was like having a stomach bug. Too much thought.

"Mom? I've been eleven for fifty years and seven months."

Underneath the table Betheen's knee pressed against hers. "It doesn't feel real, does it? We can try to go to the lab if you want to. Just to see what's left, if there is anything. That might help it settle in. But only if you want to."

They should go. Part of her wanted to see if there were any pieces of Crucible, and a part of her like an itch wanted to believe her father was alive, maybe a little younger, maybe a little older, but there. But he was gone and had been since that snapping thread. She wedged her fist into her stomach, into her diaphragm, to keep it from jumping and keep her from crying onto her plate.

"No," she said. Then, "Fuck."

"Fuck," Betheen agreed.

The blood draw was normal, even though the woman taking her blood was wearing a full surgical gown and mask. It was a needle like she was used to, and the head rush was just from watching what was part of her leave her body. Nedda bit her lip. Hard.

"Are you all right? You can breathe," the woman said. A calm voice, a good voice.

"I'm fine. You're really from the CDC?"

"Yes. It probably doesn't feel like it—I know I don't like people poking at me—but we're just here to keep you safe."

The vaccination was different. The woman held something the size and shape of one of Nedda's shooter marbles. It was clear and blue, with some kind of liquid in it. And when the doctor pressed it to her arm, she felt a bunch of needles pinch all at once, then a small hiss. A fist-size patch of her arm went numb.

"What is that?"

"It helps protect against Pan-Euro flu. It doesn't always prevent it entirely, but it shortens the length and duration. That's what the mask is for, it's protecting you from me. Not the other way around."

She wanted to say it was a shitty vaccine. But it was hard to say anything to someone who was wearing a mask, whose expressions you couldn't see. Medically appropriate distance gave them anonymity. It made it hard to say anything at all.

Outside the van, she rubbed her arm. Betheen was doing the same.

"Well, at least it's better than the smallpox vaccine," Betheen said.

"Don't forget to pick up your water," someone called. As they walked back home, they passed newly arrived trucks, and gloved people handing out bottles.

Betheen must have decided she was done waiting on lines for the day, because she kept walking.

"Mom?"

"I just can't now, Nedda."

Nedda peered around stacks of bottled water to look through the window in the door. The woman on their porch was a reporter. A van, a sloped white thing that looked more like a marshmallow than a car, blocked the driveway and a cameraman stood nearby. "Mom? She's back again."

"We'll wait her out," Betheen said. "We don't have to say anything, and if anybody asks something that you don't want to answer, you don't have to. Ever."

They deadbolted the door and hid in the kitchen, letting the reporter pound on the door. It was easy to do what her mother said, easy to take her directions. She watched as Betheen drank a full bottle of water. Disaster management said their pipes had to be tested for lead before they could drink their own water again. That their infrastructure had expired, whatever that meant. It meant a lot of bottles, but if you put a little salt in them after the water was gone, the plastic melted away and ran down the drain in a blob of gelatinous goo.

The knocking continued.

"Betheen Papas? Angela Valentini from News 6. Authorities are saying your husband was involved in the explosion. Do you have any comment?"

Nedda grabbed cookies from the jar by the sink, lemon. Fifty-year-old cookies that were four days old too. Through the thin yellow curtain, she saw movement at Denny's house. Pop Prater opening the door to his truck. He was big as ever, red from the sun, and he still made her skin jump. He climbed inside.

The porch door opened.

Denny. Skinny, messy-haired. He walked the same, moved the same, like he had before that morning on the pruner. He was the way he was supposed to be: twelve years old.

She tapped on the glass. Waved.

Denny looked at her, stared for a second. He didn't look angry, or frightened, but something else, something she couldn't quite read. He wasn't like him, not the way he'd been on Wednesday, or even Tuesday, and every day before. He ran to his dad's truck. She watched as Pop ruffled his hair.

Betheen handed her a slice of toast, soft from a river of melted butter. "He'll come around," she said. "But for now, just eat and rest."

In her room, she laid out mission patches. There was a coffee berry on the floor that must have fallen from Denny's backpack. Mrs. Prater probably hadn't shown them to him at all.

His eye hadn't been bruised.

*

The reporter knocked again in the evening. Nedda couldn't tell if she'd gone home and come back, or just decided that this time knocking was going to work. Betheen still didn't want to answer, but the knocking made Nedda want to throw things.

She opened the door to a woman with short, slick black hair. Her lips were a strange color that looked like khaki and skin.

"Hi, you're the daughter, aren't you? Nedda? I'm Angela."

"You want to ask questions."

"Only if your mom will let you talk to me."

"Why are people always yelling at those things?"

The reporter held up the plastic-looking square. "This? It's a telephone."

"How's it work?"

"I . . . I don't know."

"That's stupid. You should know that." The reporter's eyes widened. For the first time since it happened, Nedda was in control. "What year is it?"

"Twenty thirty-six."

"It's May?"

"The thirty-first, yes. What's the last day you remember?"

Betheen walked up behind her, floorboards squeaking. Nedda scooted onto the porch and closed the door before her mother could step out, leaning on it to keep it shut. "*Challenger* exploded Wednesday morning. Everybody on it died. Do you remember that?"

"Not personally, but I know about it," the woman said.

"Well, it's important," Nedda said. "I want to know if they stopped shuttles. I want to know when they started again. Is there a colony on the moon? Do we have a space station there?" The questions started in her chest, from the empty space where her father had been. She needed to know about the shuttles, about space. If the Russians sent people back to the moon. If people were going now. Where they were going. Where she could go.

"I shouldn't talk to you without your mother," the woman said.

"She doesn't want to talk to you. Come back when you can tell me something important."

Schools were closed until power and water were sorted out. The immediate surge from a long-dead town had shocked the power grid, sending much of the town into darkness almost as soon as it had come back. Newspapers trickled in slowly. On a Saturday night, Nedda saw a picture of herself in a paper, on the way to the grocery store. *Scientist's daughter, age 11*. She touched it and her fingers came away with black ink. She cut the picture out and tucked it in her drawer, next to Judy's.

She pulled out her notebook.

*Dear Judy,*

*I was thinking about time, where you are and where I am. You've probably traveled the entire solar system by now. I stayed in the same place. I didn't move at all, but I moved forward. I read about electrons once, how they jump like a skipping record. You traveled like a record playing straight through. I skipped the whole middle part of the song.*

The trellis rattled with shoes jostling bougainvillea. A week. Denny hadn't talked to her in a week. A week and fifty years. She listened for the tap on the windowsill.

"Can I come in?"

"I guess."

He climbed in like he always had, as though she hadn't seen him go crazy and pull his hair out, as though the town hadn't gotten stuck, as though her father wasn't dead. He sat on the floor cross-legged. He wore the Reeboks he'd wanted for weeks. They'd been brand-new in 1986 but were now so dated the store was giving them away. She looked for where he was different.

"Are you okay?" he asked.

"I don't know." She wasn't, but you were never supposed to say you weren't, not even to people who knew. "Are you okay? Do you remember anything?"

"Stuff's kind of fuzzy. Mom thinks I might have hit my head on the pruner. Pop is being extra nice too, so maybe. I know *Challenger* blew up. My mom said your dad died. I'm really sorry."

"It's fine," she said. It was worse hearing someone else say it. Nobody understood, not even Denny. Maybe especially not Denny. Her dad was light and heat and energy, like Judy and the other astronauts, like her little brother, like the Big Bang. Denny chewed on the side of his thumb. She'd never seen him do that before. "Is your eye okay?"

"Huh?"

"What's the last thing you remember?"

"You called Jimmy La Morte a cunt and you didn't even get in trouble for it."

Downstairs, Betheen was stacking notebooks, returning them to her father's shelves, or throwing them out. The thumping of books on the table was regular, like a heartbeat.

"Are you crying?"

"Yeah," Nedda said. Her dad had done one good thing, a really good thing. Time had rewound for Denny, just a little, skipping over a bad part, the part where Pop had hurt him.

"You miss him, I bet."

"No," she said. You couldn't miss someone who was everywhere. He said he would be, and she believed him. You couldn't miss someone you were angry with. You couldn't miss someone you killed.

Except she did.

"I can't even remember going into the shed. I wish I knew why I was on the pruner."

There were very few things Nedda could fix. This was one. He didn't know what his dad had done, or that his dad could do a bad thing, could hurt him. A lie greased with good intention, the words came easily.

"I wanted you to teach me how to drive it," she said. "I made you sneak out. You were about to show me when it looked like you got struck by lightning. I got scared and I ran. I'm sorry."

Denny chewed his thumb more, nipping a long piece of skin between his teeth. "That would have scared me too," he said. "Do you still want me to show you how to drive the pruner?"

"Okay."

The good of a lie was eleven years of having been the only star in her parents' sky. She couldn't have her dad anymore; she'd maybe never had him at all, not in the way she thought she had. She'd been sharing him with Michael. The good of a lie was to protect someone. To give them their dad.

The good of a lie was for Denny.

# 1989: Amadeus

THE SHRILL HUM and clicks of Avi Liebowitz's printer drowned out the subtle guilt that ran underneath his excitement. It was good work. Solid work. The best he'd done in years, even if it wasn't his. Enough of it was his to get him out of Oak Ridge, and likely back at NASA, over at JPL. That most of it wasn't his—there was nothing to be done about it.

He'd tried.

He'd called Theo after his last note. The final diagrams were good, if scaled too large. The choice of materials was also questionable, but structure had always been Theo's weakest point. Frail frames. Still, it was brilliant. Avi had called to tell him so, to toss around ideas for other materials, but Theo's phone had been disconnected. Avi tried his office at the college, but the call didn't go through either. Theo might have been fired. Quite likely. Papas wasn't an extraordinarily tactful man; if he was he'd have had an easier time landing at a lab. It was odd that the office line was gone, but who understood the ins and outs of small college telephone systems.

Theo might have disconnected it himself, if he were in a focused phase. His last notes had included something about his wife's gastronomy experiments driving him out of the house. That had made Avi smile. He'd met Betheen only a few times, but liked her. Once, at a department party, he'd made a comment that most of the interns were about one drink away from an orgy, then blushed when he realized he'd spoken too loudly and Betheen was standing next to him.

"Apologies, Mrs. Papas."

"Good thing it's not a chem lab party or they'd be on home-cooked amphetamines and screwing like rabbits," Betheen said.

"And she'd have been the one who cooked them," Theo said, grinning.

"Purely out of curiosity," she replied.

Liebowitz had tried calling again a week later, but the line was still down. He called information to get the main number for the school, but Haverstone College's directory line rang and rang until it disconnected. It was a small school, which meant funding was likely unstable, but Theo had mentioned nothing about it closing.

Frustrated, he wrote a letter.

Two months later it was returned as undeliverable, address unknown.

For a year and a half, Avi tried to find Theo. Missing persons reports were almost impossible to file when the police department you needed to file them with had itself gone missing.

How did an entire town vanish?

He continued work on Theo's notes, neatening, changing the materials just so, homing in on acceleration. So much of Theo's work focused on slowing decay, but the potential lay in speeding up half-life. The possibilities were endless. Compact fuel for long journeys, contained radiation effects. Had something like it been employed at Chernobyl, the catastrophic damage might have been stopped. He wrote, and continued to write, and slowly developed a generator.

Compact, lightweight, high-powered, and perfect for a space probe.

When he was near the end, he spent long hours in a cafeteria at Oak Ridge National Laboratory, drinking coffee and writing like a madman, snapping pencil leads, swirling the bubbles in his coffee cup. Watching them spin in place and cling to the edges.

One of the summer interns slid a tray next to Liebowitz. The kid still looked like a teenager, zits loosely strung together by what few scraggly beard hairs he could grow. Avi had looked like that himself once, only with unfortunate red hair that wouldn't quite curl or lay straight. Then he'd learned to nearly shave his head and occasionally wash his face. He clinked his spoon against the lip of his mug.

"Hey, have you ever heard of an entire town disappearing?"

The intern looked startled. Sure, it was a crazy question, but it was a crazy situation. Theo had vanished, as had everything around him.

"What do you mean?"

"Just what I said. An entire town, gone. *Poof.* All the people in it. Ever heard of anything like that happening?"

The kid shook his head. "Nope. I saw a car fall into a sinkhole once, and I guess a sandstorm could cover stuff up. I mean, that's what archaeology is about. I guess."

"You guess. What department are you working in?"

"Materials."

"Who're you working for?"

"Dr. Stanger."

"Do yourself a favor. At least one time, tell Stanger to go fuck himself. He likes interns who push back."

The idea of a sinkhole stuck with him. It was perfectly Floridian, fitting for that weird little town Theo lived in.

Liebowitz peeled the perforated edges from the final printed page, separating it from the one before it. It was good work, pioneering work. He'd love to claim it as his own, but it was Theo's too. He credited him where he could, how he could, in a way that wouldn't raise questions about his missing collaborator. If Theo ever resurfaced, they could work it out then.

Theo's given name was an ungainly mess. Avi had seen it on papers only once or twice. Even his identification badge had only listed *T.* Theo said it was a name his parents hung on to because it had appeased their church and his grandfather in one blow. *Theophilos.*

Liebowitz named the generator Amadeus. For Theophilos, whose name, like that of the musical genius, meant "friend of God."

Pasadena agreed with Avi better than any other place in the world. He tanned for the first time in his life. He could sweat and not have it stick to his body, and he'd managed to find a pair of sunglasses that balanced out his face. He wore them to read in the mornings, before heading to JPL. NASA wanted the drive he'd designed, and Jet Propulsion Lab was the best place to work on it, which meant moving to Pasadena and discovering the kind of weather he didn't know he'd been born for. Theo's letters were spread across a glass table—an indulgence he'd thought particularly Californian at the time, though it looked out of place in his bachelor apartment. All was not perfect. Almost, but not quite. Guilt chewed at him. He'd profited from work that wasn't entirely his, and he missed his friend. He found himself digging through what notes Theo had sent and noticing the size of the shaky scrawl. Why had the diagrams gotten large? The drawings themselves, yes, larger might have been easier on days when he could barely grasp a pen. But the measurements? Then he realized: Theo couldn't build small for the same reason Theo couldn't write small.

Theo hadn't been hypothesizing. He'd built that machine. And he'd used it.

What would a sinkhole be if it wasn't in the earth? What would it be if it was in time?

# Chawla

NEDDA WAS TETHERED to *Chawla* like a child to its mother. She'd walked on the moon, ground the chalky soil beneath her boots, leapt as if to fly. She'd worked on the Mars station after they'd done their first long-haul training mission as a crew. The surface of Mars was grittier than the moon's silky dust. She was lighter there than on Earth, though without the moon's free flight. On Earth, they'd trained to navigate micro gravity by spending long hours in swimming pools, learning to perform mechanical operations underwater. Eventually her body began to feel that air was too light. Through all that, she had never walked in space. Amit and Evgeni had. Louisa would never have the need; her entire function was indoors, as was Nedda's.

The blackness she'd looked into for years wasn't black; it was faintly light, fragile like the rays at the bottom of a swimming pool. *Chawla*'s lights cast her hull in bright blues, and Nedda's shadow stretched across it, long and lean, despite the bulk of her thermal suit and the sweater underneath it.

When the bay doors closed, the thump ran through her.

"Doors closed and sealed." Amit was tinny in her ear. "Papas?"

"Closed and sealed. Starting walk."

It was harder to move than she expected, harder to resist the urge to let her grip boots go, to fly into that thin, clean light.

"Sixty yards down, toward the engine. The panel you're looking for is numbered—"

"CAN1283. I've got it."

"Right. There are twelve tiles holding it in, plus the pressure latch. When you pop it, nothing should come out, but hang on just in case. There could be air from when we moved water over to Amadeus. There shouldn't be, but if it's there, it could blow you from the module."

"That's what the tether's for." Nedda hefted the tile puller over one arm. The other held the syncer they'd named Baby, due to its size. Both tools were tied to her as she was to *Chawla*. Years of running hadn't combatted muscle atrophy as much as she'd hoped; lifting her feet from *Chawla*'s surface left her thighs burning within a few steps.

"So ladder down. The water storage unit is going to be dark, but that's your safe room." The water unit was shielded with a heavy protective material. Weight mattered less when launching from the moon. "Evgeni's got a monitor light on, but it won't do much. Keep your headlamp on."

"Amit?"

"Yes?"

"Shut up. You're ruining space for me."

She was alone in the universe with Singh's laugh. For thirty seconds Nedda stood still, reveling in there being nothing above her head. Four solar years ago, there'd been an accident on a Mars orbiter. An astronaut on a routine walk took off his visor in the middle of space and froze to death. The event caused international mourning, and a new set of psychological evaluations for everyone in the program. New latches meant visors couldn't be opened without a specific stream of lucid commands. The man had given in to the wildest urge—to be in space, part of it, to touch it, skin to skin. For a moment, she understood. It was where all light traveled, and she was in it. There was no bigger sky.

"Walking," she said.

Near Amit's com, Louisa whispered, "Thank God."

*Chawla*'s hull was bulbous, marred by scratches from moon rocks. It was a lattice network of doors and tight hinges, all of which were meant to be reconfigured on planet to make a living space. Each door was marked by its manufacturer to indicate point of origin and function. CAN1283. CAN: Canadian territories. 1283: water storage access point.

The casing was a slide puzzle, not intended to be removed except under specific circumstances. The twelve tiles clicked and slid around the access point, until she was able to pull the sheet of them away, exposing the hatch beneath. Nedda folded the tile sheet into a smaller square, which tucked into a pack she locked to the hatch hook. Quiet. Without *Chawla*'s engines churning, there was deep quiet. Silence was all there had been before the universe began. She popped the latch, and waited for air to blow her off into space, for her tether to snap, to drift away into nothing.

Heartbeats.

"Tell Evgeni he moves good air."

"I'm not telling him that. We all share a cabin," Amit said.

"Free walking." Nedda hooked her tether to the side of the hatch. The ladder inside dropped to the cavernous room where the landing-cushion water normally would be. It was lit by a single light, dim enough to show the silver chamber shielding. Once inside, she closed the hatch.

"Papas."

"I'm good." She runged herself across the chamber, clipping her boots where she could. There was a wheel-handled hatch at the far end. Beyond it, Amadeus.

She reached the hatch. "Amit, I'm here. Flood it."

Instinct told her a flood was a wave, a canal overflowing and gators in the street, rats swimming in a basement, a car sinking. But the water didn't move that way. It was a great viscous bubble that splintered as it encountered other objects, as it encountered her. It was the closest she'd seen to a shower in space. As more water came, the fractured droplets rejoined, gelling together.

"Water storage is filling up."

"I'll give you the go once levels are equal."

"Okay." Pieces of the water—and it did feel like pieces—clung to her. What would become their radioactive landing cushion. If there was a hole in her suit, she'd die from the radiation. If there was a hole in her suit, she'd die from air loss. If there was a hole in her suit, she'd die from cold.

"Amit, I want to talk to Evgeni."

"Hello, Nedda. I've been listening in."

"Genya, tell me something bad. Really bad. Worse than this, okay?"

"My wake-up music is the next rotation and I've discovered a new band. You'll love them. They use found instruments and do no repairs. The sounds you can get from a broken saxophone? Better than a fixed one." She could hear him smiling.

"No, catastrophically bad. Chernobyl bad."

"As you're about to open our little reactor? No."

"Please."

"How about Fukushima? Nuclear catastrophe and a tsunami."

"I don't know much about it. I wasn't around then, I guess."

"Neither was I, but I still had to learn it. Are all Gappers lazy?"

"No, only me." A wobbling ball of water split around her waist.

"Just as I thought. What do you want to know?"

"After. Tell me about what happens to everyone after."

"The quick death? Not many people get that. The sickness? Yes. It is bad. Worse than you think. An entire generation gets that, plus the one after. After Chernobyl, the genome for much of Eurasia changed. Children born with holes in their hearts, blood disorders, bone disorders. Even I am different because of it."

They were the entire genome for the species, the four of them.

"But," he said, "something wonderful happened too. All the people went away. I don't mean the ones who died—death is terrible, obviously." The word *obviously* cartwheeled on his tongue. "The people who would have stayed in the area had to leave. It stayed untouched and became a land where no man went, and the grass and plants grew. It reverted to wild, how it was before people built things. An uncolonized, uninhabited place, as it was meant to be. It was beautiful. I've seen pictures. It was the last oasis in Russia. From death comes beauty."

The water grew around her, slowing her. So much like a time bubble. Like one of her mother's champagne water cakes, and she was the fizz trapped inside it.

Louisa turned on her com. "Papas? Your heart rate picked up. Slow your breathing,"

"I'm fine."

"Genya, stop telling radiation stories."

"You expect her to wait in a flooding room with no one to talk to? Cruel woman."

Their nattering calmed her, as did the thought of an irradiated pastoral world. Earth would be that, once they were all gone. Maybe that was how things were supposed to work.

"You're at even water level," Amit said.

"Okay. Going in."

She undid the hatch and runged into a room filled with familiar yellow-green light. She remembered the smell of solder, alcohol, all tinged with citrus, as though it were inside her helmet. She recognized the shape, but was startled by its size.

Amadeus was small, barely larger than the printer in her cabin. Water floated around the room in beautiful bubbles.

"The port you want is on the 'S' wall." She'd come in and locked onto the wall at an angle, and the *S* was on its side.

"EUR2020," Evgeni chimed in.

The light from Amadeus was bright enough that it blotted out her headlamp. She should rung over to the panel and hook up the syncer, but she was shocked to stillness.

It was familiar: the spinning, the blades. Vent hoses had been replaced by conduit, but it was similar enough that she imagined a miniature version of her father ducking beneath the wires, leaning to tweak a bolt, shaking out his hand. She inched closer. Gold, the center of it should be gold so it looked like a spinning sun, a capsule just for her.

It was Crucible.

*Oh, you little light that caused such trouble. Oh, you little light.* This was what her father longed to make, but couldn't. He'd followed her here. She reached out, the tips of her gloves brushing the yellow-green light, that familiar feeling from decades before, slick, like glass.

Were worlds perfect, his hand would be on the other side.

Gas, carbon, heat, light. That's what we all become.

And time. He hadn't said time.

"Nedda? Talk to me." Louisa this time. "Your blood pressure spiked."

"Ever have déjà vu?"

"Yeah, sure. We can talk about it when you're not about to be irradiated, okay? Plug Baby in and get out."

"Okay. On it, I'm on it."

She navigated to the panel. EUR2020 in bold black letters. With a little pulling it opened to reveal a network of wiring. She unraveled Baby's cord.

She'd fought the temptation to call the syncer a needle, though they were using it to pop a bubble. She'd even thought to call it the

"Space Needle," but that had been imploded a decade before, after a tidal wave's irreparable damage.

They'd built Baby, a magnet, with loops of wire harvested from *Chawla*'s docking rig. At the moon, on Mars, it had been essential, but now there would be no more docking, no other ships to meet. The rest came from Louisa's portable MRI, which she'd happily given up.

Nedda patted what had once been the MRI's casing. She'd seen Louisa slide frogs into it, Amit's leg, Evgeni's arm. She clamped Baby to a rung, and went about porting it in. Evgeni directed Amit on the wiring. Nedda had provided the equations. An electromagnetic burst would counteract the effect of centrifugal force, keeping the problematic rod from bending, hugging it tight to Amadeus's core. It would pulse in sync with the power spikes, stopping them before they began.

*Baby.*

Amadeus existed because her father hadn't wanted anyone else to lose a child the way he and Betheen had. It existed because he'd wanted her to have time her brother hadn't. She'd thought of him often, looking out the window for his light and wondering if she'd know it when it touched her. She knew now why she'd lied when she told him she saw Halley's Comet. She hadn't wanted him to think he'd wasted their time. She'd wanted him to see the stars.

A lifetime later and he was.

"Nedda? You are taking too long. I hope I didn't make radiation poisoning sound too good," Evgeni said.

"I'm almost done."

"Good. Get the hell out of there," Louisa said.

There was warmth on her back, through the layers of suit. Were she to try to touch Amadeus barehanded, the barrier around it would feel hot as it had with Denny, as it had when her father sped through himself.

She spliced, twisted, and locked Baby into place.

"Leaving," she said, then pulled herself back into water storage, locking the hatch behind her.

She didn't look back at the impossible thing that shouldn't be here, at Amadeus's light, at Crucible's light. Her father's light, warmer than the sun.

She waited for that same pressure to once more empty the room of water. Decades ago, a lifetime ago, he'd told her about a dish of marbles, half red, half white, and how if you shook them up, they'd mix together. When she opened the panel above, the droplets that escaped the vacuum became instant ice beads. But oh, how they caught the light.

Nedda retethered. Then looked up.

There was no up or down. East and west were nothing. Directions were meaningless in the map of the universe; relative distance was all that mattered, and it was ever shifting. From a distant world, were a little girl to look up with a powerful enough telescope, that girl would see *Chawla*. She'd see them thousands of years after they'd lived and died. Nedda's life did not tend toward chaos. If she could remove that divider between before and after, her life would still be orderly. Her father with her, her mother at home, Denny under the sun, and her in the stars. As it should be. Crucible worked. Chaos existed only in that they had not predicted the variety of outcomes.

She ever so nearly lifted her mask.

"Papas," Evgeni said. "What is that awful bird you listen to every morning?"

"Hush. I'm fine. I'm coming in." She grabbed the tether and crawled back to the bay doors, smiling into her mask.


They spent an hour as a twist of bodies, Nedda at their center. Amit had run their program. She asked him to. She'd flipped enough switches for a lifetime. The lights shuddered as the life support system power switched back over to Amadeus. All there was to do was wait.

They waited in Amit's room, pressed against the walls to keep from floating around, from floating loose. Louisa nestled her face in Nedda's hair. Evgeni held her waist, and Amit wrapped himself around her and Evgeni. Warm. After months and years, she was finally warm.

# Fall and Rise

ROVERS AND TERRAFORMERS chirped through *Chawla's* computers, feeding coordinates and trajectories. Progress. There was dust on the landing platform, buildup left by a passing windstorm. A string of data indicated that Trio was clearing the area, reusing particulates to level and fill the pad. Nedda saw the progress through Trio's cameras, a long pink-gray expanse of something that looked like concrete but wasn't. She could look through Trio's eye, but rarely saw the bot, unless Dué or Un happened to cross paths with it. It would be odd when she finally met them face-to-face, the patient little builders on which they relied. She switched cameras, hoping to glimpse Trio, but Un was percolating oxygen in a cell tent, and Dué was tunneling. Tessera and Fiver were mapping, collecting data.

Evgeni pulled himself in from the corridor. The skin around his eye was still raw from the tape removal, a black eye made of scabs. "We'll see planetrise tonight. It should be a good one."

She let go of the console. "Are you scared?"

Evgeni sighed, one of the rare few she'd heard across the years. "What's the good in being frightened? We're alive now. We've got work. We're doing extraordinary things. I can name a mountain after my mother should I choose." He said something in Russian. She'd picked up a good bit of it during their time together, but hadn't heard the words before. It was easy to forget sometimes how much he'd given up—people who understood him as only a native speaker could. Idiom. The tyranny of English now extended well beyond its home solar system.

"It's like running," he said. "Fear is a pain in my side. It's there, it hurts, I know it's a part of me, but do I stop? No. Not when I know why I run."

"And why is that?"

He rubbed at the skin below his eye. "Oh, because Earth is dying and to continue human life we must leave. And why should my life not be sacrificed for better? It's a good thing. For the science of it, and hope." He spoke with a politician's bravado, a certain charm she lacked, but the slant to his mouth gave away other thoughts. "The wonder," he said at last. "Any pain in my side, any blindness, even dying—they're nothing when it comes to the wonder."

The bots chirped, sending out a new set of data as Un switched from percolating oxygen to drilling post holes for what would be the hydroponic garden. Dué whistled happily as it mined new materials. They'd been speaking to one another for years, repairing themselves as needed. They were a small family, tending to one another.

She had the perverse urge to leave them that way. What if she, Amit, Louisa, and Evgeni never descended, and lived their last days aboard *Chawla*? The bots would continue building, mapping, fixing one another and cheeping songs across their world.

She thought she'd had fear burned out of her in 1986, that particular emotion replaced by grit. "I didn't think I would be, but I'm scared," she said.

"So was the first person who ate a lobster. But he was also hungry."

The laugh was better than anything in a long time.

"Want to watch planetrise?"

"But of course," he said.

Louisa and Amit were at the large window in the common area, hands pressed to the glass. Nedda and Evgeni stayed in the doorway, he on one side, she on the other, bodies touching in the narrow portal.

The light through the window was welcoming, almost familiar. They were still too far back to make out specific features; their new home was more a moon in the distance than a planet—a thought, days away from being reality. Home. It would be their home.

Amit and Louisa were silhouettes against the glass, small, but also everything.

She was meant to watch planetrise, to be the first to see a new world with naked eyes. Within a year, one or more of them would be dead. From radiation, from exposure, from a sickness Louisa couldn't cure, from starvation, if Nedda couldn't make things grow. They would be incinerated or buried in alien ground. There was a chapter in the mission book about the disposal of human remains, the recycling of themselves. She'd refused to read it until necessary. It wouldn't be necessary if she went first. Eventually there would be just one, and no one wanted to be the last. They avoided talking or thinking about how things that were noble at the outset were frightening the closer you came to their end. The printer generated a constant stream of pills: things to dull panic, raise or lower blood pressure, increase bone density. Days were numbered.

And yet.

It was what she'd meant to ask Denny, how it had been to be alone for so long.

Fingers knotted around hers. Evgeni bumped her hip. "Come on," he said.

"Show me where you're going to put your ski mountain."

His broad hand shoved her gently into Louisa's and Amit's backs. They clicked together like a puzzle, practiced. Light brushed her face, and it was Amit's hair, Louisa's fingers, Evgeni's laugh. For a single pure second, *Chawla* was the heart she was supposed to be.

"We're going to die there," Amit said.

"Not tomorrow," Evgeni replied. "Tomorrow we start to build, and then we begin dying. Right now, we watch. We're the only people alive who get to do this." There was eagerness in his voice, the lightness of a tongue expecting something sweet. This, Nedda realized, was the thing that made her love him.

Louisa's hand turned in Nedda's grasp. Nedda traced her knuckles, the bends and lines that made Louisa. Touch was a beautiful brushing of electrons, of atoms and molecules. Every touch left them a little less themselves, a little more each other. Had she brought a piece of Denny with her, a hitchhiker on her skin that moved with her across the universe? A piece of Betheen? A piece of her father, perhaps, though the likelihood of that was well below the measure of any significant figures.

This foreign planet with its pink dust would be their home until they were spread apart to nothing in its dry soil. They'd had many homes: an apartment in the middle floors of a tower overlooking green water and a sinking city; a tiny room of books in a Tudor house held together by centuries of shoddy patching; a seedy flat split between three students that reeked of liquor, sex, and life; a twisty house with a trellis up the side and the breeze of citrus and salt running through it. Home had been a blue planet. Home had been a ship, three other bodies, and the forgiving thrumming of machines. Home would be what they could build.

They were no longer themselves. They became everyone.

One carried a continent within him, funerals given for the living, a family of a thousand, thousand hands raised to the sky.

One carried in her all the medicine humans had ever made, tucked away in a single mind, fragile cells locking up and dying every day. In her lived the empathy that was humankind's best grace.

One carried a spirit that ice was unable to freeze from bones, that laughed in the face of fire, and flood, and starvation. The lightness of the suffering soul.

One carried within her women, all of them, and by nature the men who had destroyed them, those who had lifted them, and women who had tried and failed.

The sky would be purple, which she hadn't expected, but the surface of the world and the atmosphere made it so. Colors were what light reflected. Light had carried her here, brought her decades from where she'd begun. In the planet's purple glow, she found her father, the brother she never knew and his single painful hour. She saw them, the seven who woke her understanding that life had a terminus, and that an ending imbued meaning. They'd brought her to traveling to the sky's end. They'd woken her to life. She saw her mother.

Nedda took her hand from Louisa's and reached in her pocket. Inside was a scrap so worn it was little more than an idea. She pressed her thumb to it, to feel what ink was left. Her good eye watered, but it wasn't crying. It was washing away. The mass of words she'd held inside her for a lifetime dissolved.

She saw.

She touched the face of God.

# ACKNOWLEDGMENTS

I T WOULD BE criminal to write a book involving space without noting the extraordinary openness, accessibility, and generosity of NASA. Any errors and politicking portrayed in this book are the faults of its author, and not of this incredible organization. I view NASA and the people within it as our best hope, and our best teachers of hope.

The North Brevard Historical Museum in Titusville, Florida, offered key insights to the history of citrus and people along the Indian River. The American Space Museum & Space Walk of Fame was instrumental to my understanding of the culture of space, and the people who love it. Without them, there would be no Mitzi.

This book is the result of hope and powerful belief. I am grateful beyond measure to Michelle Brower, who remains a champion of my writing and bolsters me when my faith wanes. Her guidance and encouragement are unparalleled. Lea Beresford believed in Nedda and her families as much as I did. She viewed them and me with the kind of generous and insightful eye that makes us our best selves.

The team at Bloomsbury has been enthusiastic and supportive in the way all writers dream of.

Jeff Heckelman, Elizabeth Kazanjian, and Kris Waldherr were generous with their time, eyes, minds, and friendship. This book is better for their thoughts. My compatriots in this time-traveling circus are Jennifer Ambrose, Karissa Chen, and Juliet Grames. The books they have in them are as important and beautiful as the people they are. Adrienne Celt, Jason Gurley, Louise Miller, Aline Ohanesian, and J. Ryan Stradal write excellent words and have made this journey less lonely. They make writing novels seem like a noble pursuit. Lydia Chiu, Rune Conti-Reilly, Caterina D'Alessio, Vanessa Hambidge, Samara King, and Fran Stephens: You keep me sane and honest. Thank you for the group chat of a lifetime.

Everything I do owes an enormous debt to my parents and my somewhat odd upbringing. Their sacrifices afforded me a life in which I can write. I miss them daily, and hope I've done them proud.

I am grateful to Karen Swyler for knowing what is true and what I mean. Nedda's blue satin jacket was hers. I still covet it.

I am grateful to Robert for bearing with me, for making a phone call I could not, and for a desk that allowed me to run. I would pick you again and again.

# A NOTE ON THE AUTHOR

ERIKA SWYLER'S first novel, *The Book of Speculation*, was one of *Buzz-Feed*'s 24 Best Fiction Books of the Year, and a Barnes & Noble Discover Great New Writers selection. Her writing has appeared in *Catapult Story*, *Vida*, the *New York Times*, and elsewhere. She lives on Long Island, New York, with her husband and a mischievous rabbit.